THE DEFECTOR

By Evelyn Anthony

VALENTINA
THE FRENCH BRIDE
CLANDARA
CHARLES THE KING
ALL THE QUEEN'S MEN
VICTORIA AND ALBERT
ANNE BOLEYN
FAR FLIES THE EAGLE
ROYAL INTRIGUE
REBEL PRINCESS
THE RENDEZVOUS
THE CARDINAL AND THE QUEEN
THE LEGEND
THE ASSASSIN
THE TAMARIND SEED
THE POELLENBERG INHERITANCE
STRANGER AT THE GATES
MISSION TO MALASPIGA
THE PERSIAN PRICE
THE SILVER FALCON
THE RETURN
THE JANUS IMPERATIVE
THE DEFECTOR

Evelyn Anthony

The
Defector

COWARD, McCANN & GEOGHEGAN: New York

First American edition 1981

Library of Congress Cataloging in Publication Data

Anthony, Evelyn.
  The defector.

  I. Title.
PR6069.T428D4 1981   823'.914   80-25732
ISBN 0-698-11064-1

Printed in the United States of America

To my dear friends
Isidore and Blanche
with love

1

The man sitting opposite Davina Graham lit a cigarette. He smoked Sub Rosa, the fattest and most expensive Turkish cigarette, made by Sullivans in Burlington Arcade. The nàme amused him and it had become his trademark. A capacity to deliver bad news with an ingratiating smile was another characteristic; crisis never disturbed that avuncular calm, and he had never been seen to frown or glare like other people when he was angry. In fact, Davina thought, looking at him, he showed no genuine human feeling at all. The *bonhomie* was as false as the friendly concern he showed his people when they had gone wrong. A cold-hearted, calculating bastard. Which was exactly what his job required. Unlike the fictional heads of the Secret Intelligence Service, he had a name which was known to everyone. He despised the schoolboy approach to espionage, with its penchant for initials and silly code words for obvious things.

He was Brigadier James White, and though she had worked for him for five years, and he knew her father well, he had never called her anything but Miss Graham. She looked at him steadily as he talked; he didn't frighten her because he had never fooled her, either. She was used to men of his type; she neither admired nor disliked them. Like her, they had a certain job to do. Theirs was not a profession suitable for weaklings.

She had made her weekly report, and the Brigadier was considering,

9

making comments, listening to her replies. He sat back in his chair, drew on the cigarette and exhaled the sickly smoke.

"So in your view, he's not too happy," he said.

Davina nodded. "That's natural enough; he's still disorientated by what he's done. I expected depression at this stage, but not restlessness."

"And he's restless," the Brigadier said.

"Yes. He tries to hide it from me, but I know the symptoms."

"Not from personal experience, I hope?" he asked pleasantly.

"I'm not a restless type," she said. "I've proved that, I think."

"Of course." The smile widened and then was gone. "If he's restless, that's a bad sign," he said. "We'll have to think of something to make him happy. You'll have to think of something." He paused for a moment, and then said casually, "He's never asked for a woman. Could that be the trouble?"

"He's had every opportunity," Davina said. "He talks a lot about his wife and daughter."

"Eight months is a long time for some men," the Brigadier remarked.

"I'll see what I can do," she promised.

"Use your own judgment, Miss Graham. Don't worry about expense or anything like that. If he's dissatisfied, he won't give us what we want. Thank you very much." He bestowed his meaningless smile upon her and bent over the papers on his desk.

She went out. As she walked down the corridor she looked at her watch. It was 5:48. It would take two hours to get down to Sussex at this time. Right in the middle of the rush hour. Damn him, she said to herself. Why couldn't he see me earlier—

"Hello, Davina."

She had almost passed the man approaching her without noticing him. She looked up and stopped.

"Hello, Peter. What are you doing here? I thought you were living it up in New York."

He was a tall, dark-haired man in his late forties; he wore glasses and dressed untidily. He could have been a schoolmaster.

"So I was. But I'm back for what's laughingly called a spell of home duty. In other words, they felt the job should go to a younger man."

"And did it?" she asked.

"Come and have a drink; I'm on my way home," he said. "I need a shoulder to cry on. I'll tell you all about it."

She hesitated for a moment, calculating the difference it would make to the drive down to Sussex if she spent an hour with Peter Harrington. Then she saw the look in his eyes. It was lonely and expectant. He'd been very good to her when she first joined. Things had changed now. She was on her way up, and he was on the way down. A spell of home duty. She knew what that meant without seeing the need in his eyes. She had a shoulder, and he was more entitled to cry on it than anyone else she could think of at that moment.

"I'd love a drink," she said. "Where shall we go?"

"There's that pub in Queen Anne's Gate," he said. "It should be open by now. Should be pretty quiet too. We can talk."

Davina slipped her hand inside his arm. "Yes," she said. "We can."

"Vodka and tonic?" he queried when she ordered. "You never touched the hard stuff. It was always wine or sherry. What's got you into bad habits?"

"People change." She smiled. "I've learned to like it."

"*You* haven't changed," he said, leaning toward her. They had found a table by a corner; the pub regulars were beginning to come in and cluster round the bar. Most of them were businessmen and secretaries stopping for a drink on their way to the commuter stations or the long crawl home by car.

"In fact," he said cheerfully, "you've got better-looking."

Davina laughed. "Don't be bloody silly," she said. "All I've got is older. But you're looking well. Tell me about the States. From what I heard you were doing very well out there."

"So I was," Peter Harrington said. "I'd made a lot of contacts in the UN, including a really top-grade one, Rumanian, and another likely one in East Germany." He broke off and discarded the false cheerfulness. "I was doing damned well, Davy, and all of a sudden I start getting sharp messages from London and then without a word of explanation I am recalled. I have to give my two contacts to my replacement. That really hurts; I take months of work and patience to get near them, and then this new man will come sailing in and take over."

"Who is he?" she asked. He looked so downcast she repressed her irritation at being called Davy. Her parents had intended calling their eldest child David. It was just their bad luck she turned out to be a girl. All they could do was feminize the name.

"A fellow called Spencer-Barr—Jeremy Spencer-Barr. It sounded so bloody pouffy I thought here we go back to the old fairy days of Burgess and Maclean. But I was wrong. Have you met him?"

"Yes," she said. "As a matter of fact I have. It was nearly five months ago. He was trying to get my job. They thought a woman would do it better. So he got yours instead."

"What did you think of him?" he asked. "Honestly, I'd like your view. Naturally I'm prejudiced. And not just because he replaced me. It was the way he did it."

"I can imagine," she said quietly. "I thought he was a conceited little pusher. Sharp as a needle. Unfortunately I also thought he was probably as clever as he said he was. I didn't like him, anyway. He won't do as well as you."

"Thanks," he said. He reached across and patted her hand.

She had the reputation in the department of being as tough as nails. "Brilliant" was the other word used to describe her. He had rather liked her when she first joined. She seemed a quiet girl, not very self-confident. He had always maintained that with makeup and a different way of doing her hair she would be rather pretty. But nobody had taken her on. There were too many attractive girls available for men to bother with one who was discouraging to say the least. But she had nice eyes; they were big and green, and there was such an expression of sympathy in them that he had to swallow hard.

"Thanks," he said again. "I'll get you another drink." He pushed back his chair and hurried to the bar. Davina didn't want the drink, but she understood that he needed time to collect himself. He pulled his chair a little closer to hers when he came back.

"What are you going to do now?" she asked him.

He grimaced. "I'm assigned to the Personnel Section," he said. "In other words, White has sent me to the bloody Battersea Dogs' Home. Personnel—" He added a mild obscenity under his breath.

"You'll get out of it," Davina said. "You're too good to be wasted, Peter. Just hang on and keep your eyes open for a chance."

"Tell me about you," he said. "I've followed your meteoric rise from afar. You've got Sasanov, haven't you?"

"Yes," she said. "I've got him. That was the job your friend Spencer-Barr was after."

"Not surprising," he said. "It was a number-one duty. I always said you were a clever girl, Davy. Congratulations. Am I allowed to ask how it's going?"

She shook her head. "No," she said. "And don't call me Davy. I promise not to call you Pete in exchange."

He grinned. "Sorry. I forgot you didn't like it. Can I ask you what he's like, or is that contravening the Official Secrets Act?"

"I don't think so," she said. "Give me a cigarette, would you—I'll get some in a minute. Thanks. What's he like? I've asked myself that nearly every day for almost five months. And I'm not near an answer. He's a puzzling man, Peter. He doesn't fit into any category. Sometimes I don't know whether he's playing a game with me, or whether I'm playing one with him. Only time will tell. . . ."

"You'll win," he said. "No man in his right mind could resist you." He grinned at her, and she laughed and shook her head.

"You'd be surprised how many have," she said. "God, look at the time. I've got to go." She stood up and held out her hand.

He took it and drew her toward him. He kissed her on the cheek. "Thanks for the shoulder," he said. "Let me know when you're coming up and I'll give you lunch."

"I will," she promised. "And don't worry—I'll take you up on that lunch! Goodbye."

He watched her till she pushed through the door and vanished into the street. She hadn't finished the second vodka, so he drank it down. Ivan Sasanov . . . She had come a very long way indeed in five years.

Poor Peter. She said it under her breath and swung the Ford Cortina out to overtake a truck ambling in the middle lane of the expressway. There wasn't much straight driving down to her part of Sussex, and she made up what speed she could. But she never exceeded the limit. People like her were not allowed to appear in court or attract publicity in any way. Poor Peter, she said to herself again, what a rotten way to treat him. . . .

After fifteen years of excellent service, the Brigadier had tossed him into the department contemptuously known as the Battersea Dogs' Home. His career was finished; in due time he would tactfully be retired, or persuaded by the indignity of his position to resign. It was heartless and typical of the Brigadier. People simply didn't matter to him. Only results. She frowned, thinking about the two important contacts Peter Harrington had made in the UN. One Rumanian and an East German. Months of patient work had begun to show promise, and he had suddenly been replaced. By Jeremy Spencer-Barr.

". . . not just because he was replacing me. It was the way he did it." She could imagine how a man like Spencer-Barr had trampled Peter underfoot. When they had lunch she would ask him for more details.

Spencer-Barr was a ministerial protégé, everyone knew that. He had arrived to work in the lower echelons of the department, flourishing a first-class honors degree in economics and modern languages; he spoke French, German, Russian, Hungarian and Swedish with fluency and had a strong working knowledge of Arabic and Parsi. His reputation as an academic was brilliant; he had backed up his university career with a course in the Harvard Business School, where he had graduated top of his class, and served a four-year apprenticeship with one of the best known merchant banks in the City. His uncle was an undersecretary in the Treasury, and the Minister who had personally recommended him to Brigadier White was his godfather and a close family friend. It was only natural that everyone who had come into the department without such an august introduction, and with a less dazzling previous record, waited for the superman with suspicion and hostility.

She remembered him sitting in the Brigadier's office during the meeting to decide who should take over Ivan Sasanov. He was a rather small man, slightly built, with a smooth face and smooth fair hair that was a shade below his collar. He had excellent manners, but there was an arrogance about him which made him appear rude even when he was opening a door or offering her a chair. He had put his case for taking on Sasanov, and it sounded very difficult to fault. He had perfect Russian; he could insinuate himself into his confidence; he knew Russia, having traveled on a visa through Intourist with two separate parties in two years. He could play chess, which was Sasanov's hobby, and he was young enough not to be alarming.

Brigadier White had listened with his patient half-smile, nodded and said, "Thank you, Spencer-Barr," and then turned to Davina. "Well, Miss Graham, what qualifications would you have that are better than Mr. Spencer-Barr's impressive list? Do you speak Russian?"

"No," she had answered. "You know I don't. But Sasanov speaks English. I can play backgammon, but my chess is so bad that he can't help beating me. These are superfluous details, if you don't mind my saying so." She had seen Spencer-Barr stiffen, but she went on without pausing. "Three experts have been debriefing Sasanov since he arrived at the end of August, more than three months ago. In that time he hasn't given anything of real importance. Shutting him up with another man is just continuing the pattern on a more intimate scale. Which hasn't worked so far. I think a woman might catch him off guard."

The Brigadier had said nothing for a moment; his two immediate subordinates were present at the interview.

It was Spencer-Barr who spoke first. "If I may suggest, sir, Sasanov isn't the type of man to take a woman seriously. He would only think she'd been sent for a quite different purpose."

"He might indeed," the Brigadier said, and the two heads of department nodded and said "Yes" together. Davina saw the young man's hand come up and smooth his glossy yellow hair. He thought he had won, and the gesture was irritatingly smug.

"Which strengthens Miss Graham's case," the Brigadier said. "She could well gain his confidence where even someone as talented as you, Mr. Spencer-Barr, would fail. One question, however. If this extra dimension to your duties should be required, would you object, Miss Graham?"

"I wouldn't welcome it," she said. "But I would bear it in mind."

They had all looked at her then, seeing her objectively as a woman who might tempt the most valuable Russian defector since Perekov. Her mind, trained in the tortuous reasoning of men like James White and his colleagues, followed the same route. If a beautiful or desirable woman had been introduced to Sasanov he would instantly suspect that her purpose was to seduce him; he would avail himself and tell her nothing. But Davina Graham didn't suffer from being either beautiful or desirable. If he did sleep with her in the end, it would be because she had involved him, and emotion, not sex, was the key that unlocked the door to secrets. The Brigadier could imagine a strangely tantalizing situation developing between the clever, intellectual woman and Colonel Ivan Sasanov of Russian Security.

She and Spencer-Barr had been dismissed and thanked, and the next morning she was given the job. The Brigadier's advice was simple.

"Get close to him, Miss Graham. By whatever means you can. But remember; you must never get involved with him yourself. I don't favor too close a relationship beyond the meeting of your mind with his. But if it should develop, which personally I think unlikely, I know you can cope with it efficiently. Good luck."

"Thank you," Davina had said, and shaken hands. She couldn't decide whether he'd said he thought a sexual relationship unlikely in order to reassure her or to spur her on. The word that really stung was "efficiently." He obviously thought her as inhuman as he was himself.

But that was nearly five months ago, and the dull cold winter months spent in the house in Sussex had gone by at the pace of a cripple climbing stairs.

It was April now, unusually mild and warm for the beginning of an

English spring. The daffodils were out, waving their yellow heads in defiance of a late frost, and the countryside was burgeoning with fresh growth and buds eager to flower. She had left the short stretch of expressway behind and was nearing the turnoff toward Haywards Heath. The house was a mere twenty minutes away. She glanced at her watch and saw that it was nearly ten to eight. She had altered the times of meals, delaying everything by half an hour. Dinner was moved from seven-thirty to eight; it gave them time apart after the long walks in the afternoon and the ritual tea which Sasanov appreciated, with a samovar and little Russian wheat cakes. She always wore something different in the evening, if only a long tartan skirt and a sweater, or a pair of dark slacks. It was a lifetime's habit for her, and he seemed to adjust to it quite easily. They had a drink before dinner, and she made sure the wines were good and the food excellent. And then after dinner they played backgammon, since he was too good at chess to enjoy a game with a bad player, or they watched television. And they talked. Millions of words over the last four months and two weeks, all of them recorded and sent away to be analyzed. Experts examined their conversations like miners searching pans of grit for diamonds.

She saw the red-brick wall on the left of the road and slowed down before the gates. A sign said "Halldale Manor Nursing Home." There was a man on the gates and, when she honked, he came out and opened them. She called out, "Good evening," and drove on. Halldale Manor was a sprawling late-Victorian mansion, its ugliness compensated for by magnificent formal gardens. It had been requisitioned by the War Office during the war, when it was used as headquarters for Southern Command; its clandestine role was to accommodate agents leaving for missions in France from Bolney airport. The Home Office had later bought the house and its twenty acres of grounds; it had been used as a rehabilitation center for men whose nerves had been wrecked on active service, for the pathetic brain-damaged victims of high explosives. When it became a nursing home for the elderly in the late sixties, it was still the property of the Home Office. The separate wing occupied by Ivan Sasanov had housed other important refugees from Eastern Europe for periods of months while they were being debriefed. The wing was staffed by security personnel, and the genuine geriatric patients in the main building provided excellent cover for people coming and going. The nursing home was run by a Department of Health doctor, with a former army matron in charge. The wing where Davina Graham lived with Sasanov was accepted by the outside nursing staff as reserved for the treatment of violent patients.

She drove around the sweep in the drive, and on to the back entrance, marked "Ambulance." There were four garages reserved under the sign "Doctor"; she parked the Cortina in one of them, locked it, and walked across the yard to a gate set in the wall. Her key unlocked it, and it secured automatically when she pushed it shut. The private garden was surrounded by a red-brick wall; two lights set above the entrance to the wing illuminated every step in the spring darkness. She rang the bell, and a security man opened the door for her.

"Good evening, Miss Graham."

"Good evening, Jim. Everything all right?"

"Fine. Gets chilly at night, though."

"Yes, it does. Let's hope summer comes early."

He watched her cross the hall and go up the stairs. Nice legs, good figure. Always polite. About as approachable as the austere stone statues dotted round the gardens. He wondered how the "guest" upstairs got on with her—or didn't. He let his mind dwell on erotic possibilities, grinned to himself and then forgot about it. He had been working at Halldale Manor for ten years; his perquisites included a nice little house in the village for his wife and younger child and the use of a car. The pay was generous, too. He had long abandoned curiosity.

The wing consisted of a living room, a small dining room, five bedrooms and three bathrooms. It was comfortably furnished in the style of a country hotel; it had its own kitchen and domestic offices. Every room was electronically monitored for conversation, and there were two-way mirrors in the bedroom and bathroom assigned to "guests." The telephones passed through a private switchboard, and all calls were recorded.

Davina went to her own bedroom first and rang through to the kitchen.

"He complained about the tea," she was told. "I sent up vodka and lemon at six, as usual. He asked for more, and the decanter came down empty."

"Did he go out this afternoon?" Davina asked.

"No. Roberts went upstairs to check and he was just sitting, looking out of the window. Not in a good mood, Roberts said."

"Thank you." Davina hung up. Everything Sasanov drank was monitored like his appetite for food, the amount of exercise he took, the change in his moods when he was left alone. It had been a bad day.

She looked at herself briefly in the mirror, combed her hair so that it swept back from her forehead; it was long and she hated it to be untidy. There wasn't time to change out of her London coat and skirt. He'd had a bad day. She thought quickly and phoned down to the kitchen again. "Keep dinner till I ring." Then she hurried out of the room and down the hall to the living room. She opened the door and saw him leaning forward in a chair, his back toward her. The outline was tense.

"Hello," she said. "I'm sorry I'm late. The traffic was terrible." He turned around to look at her as she came in; he didn't speak. "I'd like a drink," she said. "Let's have one together."

She came and stood opposite him. There was a fire burning in the grate; the room was warm, and brightened by vases of daffodils she had arranged.

She poured vodka into a glass for him and squeezed the little piece of cut lemon peel into it. He didn't like ice. She filled her own glass with cubes to disguise the small amount of vodka. She handed him his drink.

"I'm sorry if you've been bored," she said. "I did try to get back early."

He had strong, large hands, and the little glass disappeared as he held it between them. The piercing blue eyes made her think of snow and bitter winds; he had a bleak, hard face to match his eyes.

"My daughter keeps a canary," he said. Drink had made his accent thicker; his speech was a little too deliberate. "She keeps it in a cage in our kitchen. I want you to get a message to her. Tell her to let it out. . . . Free. I know how that canary feels."

"We can't communicate with your family," Davina said quietly. "You know that. Besides, you're not really like that canary, are you? You wanted to come here. Nobody kidnapped you."

Ivan Sasanov leaned back in his chair and swallowed the glass of vodka. "What did they say in London? When am I going to get news—"

"I told you," she said. "Your family are perfectly well and safe. No action has been taken against them. You've no need to worry. You do trust me, don't you? I wouldn't lie to you about that."

He laughed. "You'd lie about anything if you were told to," he said. "They could be in prison or dead, and you'd go on lying. You are a bloody woman."

Davina smiled. "If you say so and you're drunk."

"No." He laughed again and shook his head. He had fair hair which was graying and he wore it cut close. "No, I'm not. When I'm drunk I sleep. Like that!" He snapped his fingers. "I have a little vodka inside. It speaks to me."

"How poetic," she said. She had experienced his moods and coped with them. She knew them all, from depression to truculence, to his normal swift intelligence parrying her own. There were times when he was relaxed, and she discovered that he had a keen sense of the ridiculous.

His mood was now wavering between truculence and something more disturbing; she responded lightly, hoping to divert the bad temper aggravated by drink.

"What does it speak about?"

He looked at her, and she saw suddenly that he was very sober.

"Home," he said.

She didn't register surprise, much less the dismay she felt. "Are you so unhappy here? If you are, it must be my fault."

He got up; he was tall for a Russian. He began to walk about, kicking the coals in the fireplace, inspecting the decanter of vodka with disgust. It was nearly empty.

"It's not your fault," he said. "You've done your best to make my time here pleasant. You have a job to do. I'm a professional, too, Vina. I understand." Unlike Brigadier White he used her Christian name; he couldn't pronounce it properly and shortened it. He had pointed out to her once, when they were out walking, that it was an anagram of his own name.

"I'll try again," she said. "I promise. I'll see if we can get some kind of message about them that you *will* believe. . . . Now, won't you have some dinner?"

She had become so sensitive to him that she knew what he was doing without watching. He didn't eat well; he crumbled bread and drank wine, and when he looked at her, he wasn't seeing her at all. Restless—that was how she had described him to the Brigadier. It was an understatement. She felt that for the first time since he defected to the West some kind of breaking point was near. But which direction it took was her responsibility. If he turned sour, then his information would be suspect, and he himself an expensive mistake. Their relationship with the Soviet Union was already cool because Colonel Ivan Sasanov had apparently vanished off the surface of the British Isles while on an official visit to the Foreign Office. Nobody was fooled, but it suited both sides to keep up the fiction that everyone was looking for him for the first few weeks. The British explanation that he must have killed himself, and that no doubt his corpse would be found in due time, saved his own government the political embarrassment of admitting they'd lost one of their top men.

In the meantime, in exchange for the asylum he'd arranged when still in Moscow, Sasanov had given the department details of the Soviet intelligence network operating in the Low Countries and a list of sympathizers in NATO, some of whom were already being watched. Three months with his male interrogators had disclosed only what he was prepared to give them; it was accepted by the Brigadier that Sasanov was bargaining, and that the final deal had not been made. So Davina Graham, who didn't play good chess, had spent the last five months shut up with him to draw from him scraps of information which could be assembled. The picture the experts put together could indicate much more than he meant to disclose at this stage.

They drank coffee at the table. He asked for brandy; she had reached a level of intimacy with him where she could say, "Don't drink too much. Let's have a serious talk tonight."

"Another one? What is the subject this time—how did I manage to get an agent into the Dutch Security Service? We talked about that yesterday, Vina. I'm sick of saying the same things. Again and again."

"I'm sick of hearing them," she said. "I don't suppose you've thought of that. So let's leave business till tomorrow, shall we?"

He peered into the brandy, holding the glass up to the light.

"Whatever you say to me is business. Everything is business, pretending to be talk. We are playing a game. Tonight I'm tired. I want to drink this and then sleep." He challenged her with a look. "Not talk."

"Not even about your family?" she asked quietly. "About your daughter and the canary—and your wife, Fedya? You spent today on your own, with no one to play the game with you, as you call it, and you've been thinking about them and worrying. Haven't you?"

"I've been asking for news for weeks now," he said angrily. "Nothing, nothing since the New Year—one photograph taken in the street to prove they're not arrested. And you sit there so calm and English and hold out hope of news one day—and then, so sorry, nothing. A bargaining counter, aren't they, my wife and child? I'll think of another agent name to give you, two or three names, then perhaps I'll see another photograph, eh?"

"That's not true," Davina said. "Your family are watched day and night. One contact from outside and they'd be taken in. You know that, Ivan. You know how Internal Security works. Watching the dissidents and the Jews the way your family's being watched now."

The art of debriefing wasn't all sweetness and light. She had needled him before, and with some success. Now he swore at her in Russian. She had a sudden thought of Jeremy Spencer-Barr, who would have understood.

"All right," she said. "You miss them. But you reckoned on that when you came over; you told me you were disillusioned, that you'd lost faith in the Soviet system, that you saw no point in your work, no point in going on. . . ." She paused, and then said more quietly, "Have you forgotten all that? Have you forgotten Jacob Belezky?"

"No," he said. "That's why I'm here; because of Jacob."

"And Scherensky and Bodin and Yemetova?"

"Yes!" he shouted at her. "Yes, because of them and what we were doing to them. You think you have the monopoly of conscience in the West? You think that Russians aren't capable of moral courage or a love of justice?"

Davina looked at him. "You've proved they are," she said. "What you did is just as brave as Scherensky and the others."

He gestured contemptuously at the room. "This isn't Camp Ten in the Archipelago," he said. "I'm in a cage, but a comfortable cage; I'm not getting drugs and shock treatment to send me mad! No, no, Vina—you can't catch me that way. Jacob didn't run away to the West."

"Jacob is dead," she reminded him gently. "There's nothing he can do to help anyone. But you can help the others."

"Perhaps I could help them more by going back," he said.

Davina got up from the table; she stepped on the bell hidden under the carpet for Roberts to come and clear away. She didn't want Sasanov to see her face. She was right, the breaking point was very near. And it wasn't going to be in the department's favor.

She shut the living-room door. He stood with his back to her, looking at the dying fire.

"Put on another log," she said. "It's cold in here."

The fire blazed up; he lit a cigarette, and they sat without speaking. He was leaning back, and the light of a floor lamp placed near for reading shone on his face. His eyes were closed and he looked tired and grim.

She couldn't back away. That would show weakness; the remark was either genuine or a new move in the game. A buildup to the final bargain with the Brigadier and the Foreign Office.

"Do you really want to go back?"

He opened his eyes and raised himself till he sat leaning forward. "I see that worries you."

"Not in the least," she said. "It's always been a possibility."

"A possibility that your people could *send* me back—not that I went of my own free will. I could refuse to tell you anything more, and what I have told you isn't important. Not what you were hoping for, all the big stuff—that's still in here." He touched his forehead. "I know when you're worried, because you have a little frown that comes, and you don't know it. I see it there now."

"What's made you think like this?" she asked him. "What's made you change your mind? I leave you alone for an afternoon and when I come back you're sulking and making stupid threats." She shrugged. "You can go if you like. You're no damned use to us as things are. Anyway, you think it over. I'm tired and I'm going to bed."

"Oh," Sasanov said, "it's a big frown now. Would you ever believe me if I told you the truth?"

She was on her feet. "I could try," she said. "If you'd ever really trust me."

Sasanov got up, threw his cigarette into the grate. She was a tidy person, and the habit irritated her.

"We can't trust each other," he said flatly. "But I can tell you, there are times when I could go mad in this place. Today was a bad day. I thought of Fedya and my daughter and the canary. And I missed you."

She felt the color rising in her face. He was forcing her to look at him; forcing her to acknowledge the gap he had made in her defenses. "I missed you." There was no mistaking the way he had said it. Not "I was bored, or worried, or had nothing to do," but "I missed *you*." The emphasis was on the last word.

"I'm sorry," she said. "I'm sorry I was away so long." It sounded very lame.

"It's not your fault," the Russian said. "Are we still quarreling?"

"No," she said.

"Then come and sit down. Don't go to bed yet."

She didn't want to sit close to him, but he held out his hand and, rather than take it, she slipped into the seat beside him. "He's never asked for a woman. Could that be the trouble?" The Brigadier's question nagged at her. She knew the answer; she had sensed it for some time. She felt it again as their bodies touched for a moment and then drew away. He was too male; it frightened her. In her imagination his sexuality held a tinge of menace. She didn't dare think what he would be like as a lover. She had known only one man, and he was nothing like Ivan Sasanov. If the occasion arises, they had said at the interview, you'll know how to cope with it. They had been wrong. The occasion hadn't merely arisen; in the last months it had lurked like an actor awaiting his cue in the wings. She had seen it from the corner of her eye and had resolutely turned away. Sitting beside him in front of the fire, she felt the brooding restlessness in him, and the unspoken question. He did want a woman; he wanted to forget himself, he wanted flesh and blood instead of cool companionship. She should have offered herself. She should have given him sex the way she provided toothpaste and cigarettes. But it was impossible. She had gone to bed with a man she loved and had suffered the ultimate humiliation—rejection, a very special rejection. She couldn't propose herself to Sasanov and know that he took her only because there wasn't anyone else. She didn't want to think of him as a man, naked, making love.

She said very calmly, "Would you like someone to spend the night with you? You must feel very lonely."

She knew at once she had made a terrible mistake. The look of surprise on his face changed to anger, and then contempt. He sprang up from the sofa.

"When I want one of your department whores, I'll let you know!" He turned his back on her before she could answer, and slammed the door after him.

"Oh, you fool," she said out loud. "You tactless, stupid fool. . . ." Five months had established between them a relationship which had taken root. He had become dependent upon her; the trust he denied had begun to exist between them. Even their few quarrels were a kind of intimacy. All that was missing was the intimacy of the night. And she had panicked when she imagined what was coming next, had ruined everything by offering him a paid whore, as if he was suffering from toothache and needed a dentist. She had never seen him look so angry; his contempt was bitter, and it stung her.

But no less than her contempt for herself. She had been in his life for nearly five months, had seen him go through the stages of homesickness, anxiety for his family, uncertainty about the rightness of what he had done, and had guided him gently to the point where the end was very near. Near to breaking, or near to committing himself wholly to the West. And he wanted more from her now than mere company. She hadn't been able to cope with that need without losing her head. To provide him with a woman would destroy their delicately balanced relationship; it would put her back on the Brigadier's side.

She got up, set the screen in front of the fire, and went down the hall to his room. She knocked on the door. He called out and she came in. He was in his robe and it made him look younger.

"I came to say I was sorry," she said. "I shouldn't have said such a thing to you. It was very crude of me."

His expression was still set and angry. "Why not? You're supposed to keep me happy, aren't you?"

"That's not the point. I don't know why I did it."

He came toward her; she was standing in the doorway, holding on to the handle. "They suggested it in London, didn't they?" He was close enough to touch her.

"Yes. Try to forget it, will you please?"

"I don't want someone like that," Sasanov said. "And if I did, I don't want it arranged by you." He leaned his hand on the door as if to shut it. "Do you understand that? There are some men who don't like making love to just any woman."

She held the door open against him. "I do understand. I'd better go to bed myself." She heard the nervousness in her own voice. "I'm tired, it's been a long day." The pressure on the door ceased. He stepped away from her. "Good night," she said.

"Good night."

Sasanov heard her steps fading down the corridor and the little click of her bedroom door closing. He lit a cigarette and sat on the edge of the bed. He wasn't angry any longer. He had never seen her cool professionalism ruffled like that before. Embarrassment suited her; she had blushed when he said he missed her, turned really red when she came to his room. He had stopped being angry because he believed her. London had suggested she get him a paid woman. She hadn't been told to offer herself. He was glad about that. He smoked quietly, thinking about her. For a long time she had puzzled him. He knew exactly what her official purpose was, but Davina Graham was a human puzzle. She was exceptionally clever, with an incisive, intuitive mind, a woman who could hold her place in any intellectual contest with a man. A challenge to someone like himself; they had been very clever to send a human puzzle to a man who played chess. Yet she was sensitive and feminine in a shy way. The shyness appealed to him, and her sexual remoteness intrigued him. Over the last five months he had grown very close to her. And very aware of her as a woman, instead of an opponent trying to win him over to the West. Thinking about her diverted his mind; he dreaded the night hours when the issues of his life confronted him and he was defenseless against his own doubts.

When he left Russia it had seemed so clear in his mind. He had left his homeland and his family because the death of his friend Jacob Belezky had broken his heart and the ties of loyalty to his own political system. As Davina had reminded him, he had lost faith in the Soviet system and his part in maintaining it. Jacob's death was a culmination of doubt and revulsion which had been eroding his ambitions and poisoning his life for the last four years. He had used his power to arrange his own escape; the months preceding his trip to London had been endurable because he saw an end in sight.

But he had been one of the best intelligence officers in the complex hierarchy of the KGB. He wasn't going to give his old enemies what they wanted until he had time to plan ahead for himself and his family. His family was the bargaining counter that he intended to exchange for the information Brigadier White was waiting for. Not a second-rate network in Norway or a few spies scattered in the outer circles of NATO; they had merely bought him time to think. But the detailed plans for Soviet operations against the oil kingdoms of the Middle East. The longer he kept the Brigadier and his people waiting, the stronger his position became. Yet now he wondered whether it was a position that he really wanted. Life in the capitalist West: plastic surgery, an assured income for life, a manufactured identity among strangers, a home in a country so different from his own. He could still go back. The propaganda value of his return in disillusionment from the West would balance out the trivial information he had given away. The British wouldn't murder him or keep him if he declared his intention to return. They didn't operate like that. They even allowed their own traitors to escape. Unless he was a willing collaborator, he was useless to White's Intelligence Service.

He finished the cigarette, got into bed and switched off the light. He lay in the darkness, thinking. He was no longer sure of his own motives. Longing for Russia plagued him, uncertainty about his wife and daughter gave rise to paranoid suspicions that they were dead or arrested and the news was being kept from him. If it hadn't been for the challenge of Davina Graham he might already have decided to go back long before the spring came. He settled down to sleep, but his mind roamed restlessly.

He hadn't slept well for some weeks. The luminous dial on his watch showed a few minutes before three when he drifted into an uneasy doze, and he woke just after dawn. He drew back the curtains to watch the sun rise, and opened his window to the joyously singing birds. The sound made him heavy and sad. Another day walking with her through the grounds. Eating lunch, talking, reading the English newspapers. The evening creeping over him like a shroud. . . .

He was dressed and pacing the garden in the dew when Davina looked out her bedroom window and saw him. She put a call through to the Brigadier at his private number and woke him an hour before his breakfast. He was irritable and uncooperative.

"You told me this yesterday—if you're worried I'll send someone down."

"I am worried," she said. "I want to try an experiment. He needs to get away from here: he's going crazy shut up with me all the time. As I told you, last night he was talking about going home. And I don't think it was a bluff. Will you give me permission to take him home for the weekend?"

"What? Good God, Miss Graham, what an extraordinary idea! Why should that amuse him?"

"Because he needs freedom," she said. "He knows nothing about life in England. He feels lonely and cut off. I think it might work. He'd trust me more if the visit was a success. Let me try it. He won't go off; he has nowhere to go to. You can have a man down there if you want him watched."

There was a pause. "How will you explain him to your family?"

"Leave that to me," she said. "Can I go ahead?"

"Yes." He sounded more reasonable. "Yes, if you think it's the right thing. Give my regards to your father."

"Thank you, sir, I will."

She hurried down to breakfast. Sasanov was sitting at the table drinking coffee and smoking.

"Good morning," he said. She saw the puffy skin under his eyes and the look of fatigue.

"Did you sleep well?"

"No."

"I saw you out in the garden very early this morning."

"I needed fresh air."

"You need more than that," she said. "You need to get away from here. I'm going to arrange it after breakfast."

"Harry, Davina's coming down this evening. She's bringing some man with her."

Harold Graham looked like a retired naval officer; he had the bright-blue eyes and weathered skin of men who have spent years at sea. The sea had left its imprint upon him as clearly as the sky subtly changes the men who fly. Harry Graham was a naval "type," and old gardening clothes didn't alter the aura of the quarterdeck he carried with him. He was a handsome man, not very tall, but very upright. He had a keen, humorous face, and a marvelous simplicity which ignored changing values in a changing world.

He had been married for thirty-seven years, and had enjoyed a satisfying, happy marriage, which had never been threatened by the occasional love affair when he was away during the war. He lived an active life in retirement, devoted to charitable work and the running of the village where they lived. He was on the Parish Council, read the lesson in the Anglican church, was president of the local British Legion, and spent two days a week in London working for the Ex-Services Mental Health Association, Naval Section. He had some private money apart from his pension, and was proud of the fact that they were able to keep their house and garden properly.

His wife was standing on the terrace outside the drawing room, shading her eyes from the bright sunlight with one hand. She was taller than he was, and very thin; she showed traces of great prettiness, with fine gray eyes and clear features. Her face was webbed with tiny lines, and her fair hair was nearly white. She was still so surprised by her daughter's telephone call that she repeated the message. "Davina's coming down—with a man."

"Is she really?" Captain Graham said. "It's rather last-minute, isn't it?"

"No, darling—no more than Charley. *She* rang last night."

"Yes, all right, so she did." He came to her and put his arm around her for a moment. "I'm really looking forward to seeing her, aren't you? She's such fun. I wonder what she's been up to, naughty girl."

"Goodness only knows," his wife said. "Who do you suppose this man is that Davina's bringing down? She said he was a Pole."

"A Pole—what on earth is she doing with a Pole? And why does she have to bring him here? What time did Charley say she was arriving?"

"In time for drinks," Betty Graham said. They walked into the house together.

"It was very hot out there," he said. "We're going to have a good summer. Everything's coming out ahead of itself. We'll have to watch out there isn't a sharp frost. We'd lose a lot of bedding plants if we got a frost now. I feel like a gin and tonic. We've got time before lunch, haven't we?"

His wife smiled at him. "Since I'm doing the cooking, of course we have. I'll get some ice."

Later, while they were finishing their drinks, Betty Graham said gently, "Harry darling, promise me you'll be nice to Davina."

His eyebrows rose, and he registered a pained surprise. "I'm always nice to her. Why shouldn't I be?"

"Because you much prefer Charley," his wife said.

"But I don't show it," he maintained. "I just find Davina rather difficult."

"She was never any trouble," his wife reminded him. "It can't have been easy being Charley's sister."

"Well, yes, but she never made an effort, did she? And look at the fuss she kicked up when Richard broke it off. Didn't come near us for over a year. Who is this fellow she's bringing along—don't tell me she's going to take up with a Pole."

"We've got to be very nice to him too," Betty said firmly. "It would be marvelous if she got married and settled down. I wish she wasn't so tied up in that dreary Ministry job. These career girls never seem to get married."

He gave a mischievous laugh. "I should think you'd had enough weddings with Charley," he said.

"You're hopeless," his wife said. "You'd forgive Charley anything."

"I think it's time Davina forgave her, too," he said. "After all, Richard was no damned good. Perhaps it's a good thing they're coming both together. Did you tell her Charley would be here?"

"Yes, I did," Betty Graham said. "She said she didn't mind; she said she'd be glad to see her, actually."

"Then let's hope it all goes off well. I don't want the weekend spoiled. They don't come down that often."

"No," she said. "I'm sure it will be all right. Now finish that drink and we'll have our lunch. I arranged for Mrs. Dixon to come in and cook over the weekend. I don't want to spend my time in the kitchen."

After lunch, she went into the garden with the wicker basket over her arm, and cut flowers to put in the girls' bedrooms. Long sprays of forsythia arched among the daffodils; she was clever with flowers and had always arranged them. Even when she was alone in the house and Harry was at sea during the war, Betty Graham kept the vases filled, as if she were preparing for him to walk through the door. Their only son had been killed in the Fleet Air Arm, long after the war had ended. He was only twenty; that was when she began to look old. They had grieved, she and Harry. Arranging a big bowl of forsythia in Davina's bedroom, Betty Graham remembered how differently her two daughters had shown their feelings at their brother's death. Davina was twenty-four and Charley seventeen. The love child of the immediate postwar, when she and Harry took up their life again, not expecting that she would have a pregnancy at forty-two, Charley had wept and clung to each of them in turn; they had been a trinity of sorrow, she and Harry and their younger daughter. Davina had looked gray for weeks, but they never saw her cry. She had never shown her feelings; that was the reason she and Harry found it difficult to love her as much as Charlotte. She smiled quietly, thinking how Charlotte had been impossible for the little girl to say; she had shortened her name, and she was Charley to everyone who knew her. What a pity that Davina was so different. And then when Richard asked her to marry him, and she seemed so happy and outgoing at last—that had been terribly difficult for them all. She put the memory aside and carried a vase of flowers into her younger daughter's room.

It would be lovely having them together for the weekend. She did hope the Pole would fit in. . . .

2

Brigadier White didn't like going to see the Home Secretary. He avoided it whenever possible, sending a deputy to make the routine report. He considered the incumbent of the principal post at the Home Office to be a liberal intellectual who disapproved of him and his department and frustrated him when he most needed support. In White's opinion he was soft. He opposed the death penalty, which the Brigadier thought ridiculous, with the crime rate, and especially violent crime, murder, armed robbery and terrorism, on the increase every year. White believed in death as a deterrent. It was also much cheaper to hang a man than to keep him for twenty years at the taxpayers' expense. His department would have welcomed a tenth of the subsidy spent on locking up bombers and child murderers in top-security jails.

This time he decided to see the Home Secretary himself because there had been a sudden stream of irritating notes from the Foreign Office about Russian protests at Britain's failure to find Sasanov, or a body, since it was asserted he must have killed himself. Nobody was serious, of course; the KGB knew perfectly well that Sasanov was under his protection. They were just trying to be awkward and stir up trouble for White. The Home Secretary was not sympathetic to White's clandestine operations. He objected to laws being broken in the name of security, and he carried his obsession about personal freedom so far that White had to mount some of his less savory operations very carefully. There was a lot the Home Secretary didn't know, but there was no way White could have

concealed Sasanov. The defection of someone so important was of interest
to the Prime Minister, who asked the Home Secretary for information on
what was happening, so that he in turn asked White. Now that the Foreign Office was meddling, because of the Russians, White felt that positive action was needed. Unfortunately he couldn't implement it without
the Home Secretary's agreement.

He drove along Whitehall in his blue Fiat, with a Special Branch man
at the wheel; he used different cars during the day and never traveled to
his office or his home by a regular route. He was a prime target for
terrorists. Although he took precautions, he wasn't frightened. He had
never been afraid of anything in his life and didn't understand or sympa-
thize with anyone who was.

He hastened into the Home Office and sped up in the lift to the first
floor and the Home Secretary's office. He was shown into the room,
which was empty. He strolled over to the windows and looked out onto
Horse Guards Parade, flanked by the elegance of the old Palace of
Whitehall. As a serving officer, James White had trooped the color of his
regiment on the sovereign's official birthday. It was an occasion that
moved and thrilled him, with its pageantry, color and superb precision.
All the more dramatic now, since the monarch was a queen. He was a
man for whom his country meant the traditions implicit in his regiment,
the Coldstream Guards, regarded as the oldest-established regiment of
the Line and founded by General Monck, who had helped bring Charles
the Second back to his murdered father's throne. James White had been a
dedicated soldier, who retired early because his skills were needed in the
Intelligence Service, at that time demoralized by lack of funds, the shat-
tering scandal of Philby's treachery, and the prevailing political climate
that considered spies and the secret service as outmoded and rather
immoral. White had changed the image. He didn't try to court the poli-
ticians, but he kept on the best of terms with the Treasury. The Foreign
Office had been hypersensitive to investigation on even the most harmless
level after Burgess and Maclean. He had proceeded with tact outside his
department, and with total ruthlessness inside it. He knew how to get the
best out of people by being courteous and unruffled, and pitiless if they
failed. White had known Davina Graham's father because they were
members of the same club and their family backgrounds had merged at
one point through cousins marrying. He had employed Davina as his
secretary because he knew that there was no question of a security risk
there. And he had seen her true potential. She was far too clever to waste
her time being a good secretary.

Taking Sasanov to Marchwood for the weekend showed imagination and courage. He admired her for the idea, but he hoped for her sake that it didn't go wrong. He heard a distant flushing sound, and smiled. Home Secretaries went to the lavatory like lesser men; there was a separate bathroom and lavatory adjoining the office. White was sitting in an armchair, looking relaxed, when the Home Secretary came in.

They shook hands and exchanged banalities about the weather. Neither man was at ease with the other; a truce existed, but the threat of open war was always there. The Minister was an academic who had come late into politics. He was a gentle man, steeped in the humanities, trusted completely by the Prime Minister, who valued his loyalty and integrity in public life. These virtues were said to offset his dislike of authoritarian methods, and a penchant toward mercy. He offered the Brigadier a cigarette and took his place behind the desk. The Brigadier was a type of man he abhorred. Hard, ambitious, lacking in scruple, capable of anything. The Minister had once heard James White described as a man of honor and had almost lost his temper with the speaker. There was an imperialist attitude in the Brigadier's approach to problems that the Home Secretary found not only offensive but positively dangerous. He settled into his leather chair and took up a defensive position.

"Could we come to the point of your visit, Brigadier? I don't want to seem discourteous, but I have a hellish morning, and a dozen people to see."

"I appreciate your giving me the time, Home Secretary," James White responded. "Actually it's concerned with the Soviet defector, Ivan Sasanov."

"Oh? What's happened to him?"

"Happened? Why, nothing. He's in excellent health and enjoying a stay in our place in the country. I assure you, he's our guest, not a prisoner." He allowed himself a slight sneer. "He did come to us of his own accord."

"So you informed me." The answer was brisk. "Which was about eight months ago, as I recall. I've had interim reports since then to pass on to the PM. But so far he seems to be marking time. You led me to believe that he was the most important Soviet official since Perekov to come over to the West. Otherwise it hardly seems worthwhile to have antagonized the Russians to the extent that we did. Isn't it time we had some results?"

The Brigadier kept the half-smile on his face; his eyes gleamed with dislike for a second or two, long enough to convey it to the man opposite to

him. He called him a contemptuous obscenity in his mind, and answered
with infuriating patience, as if he were explaining something simple to
someone unusually stupid.

"Sasanov is even more important than Perekov. He was the coordinat-
ing officer in charge of that section of the Soviet Ministry of External
Affairs that deals with the Middle East. His section is, of course, the
KGB. Soviet activity in that part of the world has increased in terms of
expenditure and agents in operation by fifty percent since last year, since
the overthrow of the Shah. They are aiming at the oil sheikdoms, Home
Secretary. And Sasanov knows the details of the operation being mounted
against Kuwait and Saudi Arabia and the United Arab Emirates."

"Then why hasn't he told us?" the Minister demanded.

"Because he wants to be in the best possible bargaining position before
he plays a hand of such importance. Defection is not an easy thing to
adjust to; it entails a great deal more than catching a taxi and presenting
yourself at Scotland Yard asking for asylum. The psychological upheaval
is acute; it takes months before a man like Sasanov can orient himself to
betraying his own country. Properly betraying, anyway. He's given us a
few snippets of information; enough to whet the appetite, so to speak. He
has been acclimatizing, as we call it. Settling in, coming to terms with
himself and the decision he's made. You can't hurry this process; I'm sure
you'd be the last person to authorize forceful methods to get the information." White gave his opponent a cool stare.

The Home Secretary said freezingly, "No such permission would ever
be given. In any circumstances. I hope that's understood."

"Of course, of course, it is," White protested. "Apart from which it
would be criminally stupid. The kind of information we will get from
Sasanov in due course—and we will get it, I am quite confident—needs to
be interpreted by him over a period. That, my dear Home Secretary, is
where his real worth lies. He knows the *minds* of our opponents, he can
gauge their feel for a situation as it changes hourly. That was Philby's
value to the Russians. He knew the people at home because he'd been one
of them for years. He's still interpreting Western intelligence for them."

"Yes. I know this, of course; but at least I can say to the Prime Minister that you are confident of enlisting Sasanov as an active adviser to our
own Service. No indication of time, I suppose? It would help to have some
guide."

"Weeks," the Brigadier said affably. "Not months. I have a very talented operative with him at the moment. I'm delighted with her progress."

"Her? Do you mean you've used a woman to debrief him?"

"I have indeed," White said. "Women have proved very able in my service. And now, after all, we have a lady in Downing Street." He gave the Minister a sly look, daring him to disparage the female sex. He shifted in his seat and said briskly, "But I'm wandering from the purpose of my call. Briefly, the Russians have been making a fuss through their embassy. It's just tiresomeness on their part, because they know perfectly well Sasanov is with us. But they're complaining because while our people insist he killed himself, we haven't produced a body. I would like your authority to take the necessary steps to satisfy them."

"You're going to find a body? How can you?"

The Brigadier gave his little bark of a laugh. He was thoroughly enjoying himself.

"Oh, we're not going to kill anybody! Oh, Lord no. I just want to be able to show them a dead man and keep them quiet. All I need is authorization to satisfy the local health authority if we hear of someone suitable. That's all."

"I'll send you the necessary memo," the Home Secretary said. He pushed back his chair. "Now I'm afraid I have someone waiting." His expression indicated chill distaste.

The Brigadier thanked him for his time and help, and walked out of the office with a springy step. He would get the memo, and it would be safely filed away. No politician would ever be able to accuse him of acting without authorization. Not on a trivial thing like substituting a corpse for a living man.

Another make of car was waiting at the entrance; he jumped in and told the driver to take him to his office. There he telephoned an old friend at the Special Branch of Scotland Yard. He invited him to lunch.

Later that afternoon, sniffing a good Armagnac, the SB man asked the Brigadier what he meant by a favor. White was rubbing a cigar close to his ear, judging the tobacco by the crackle that it made. The old myth about the best Havanas being those rolled by the Cuban girls between their thighs still died a slow death among the older generation.

"I need a corpse," he said. "Damn good, these. Try one."

"Too strong for me," the policeman said. "I'll stick to my cheap cigarettes."

They both chuckled. Long association and many off-color deals had brought them to a curious condition of trust and friendship.

"Cheap? There's nothing cheap about you, Tim. You've cost me enough at times!" James White bit off the end of his cigar and lit it. He

despised the fiddling tool for cutting them. Better men than he would ever
be had used their teeth.

"How much am I going to cost you this time, then?" The man puffing
on his cigarette was a professional policeman, risen through ability from
the ranks, then on to the branch of the CID that coped with terrorism,
treason and subversion. He was a pleasant man, with a bluff sense of
humor and a comfortable middle-class background. He could have been a
businessman, a broker, a solid citizen with a solid career. But, like James
White, he was above all a true professional. Some men, he had said once
when they were lunching together and working out a particularly difficult security operation where his branch's help was needed, some men
were hunters by nature. He and the Brigadier belonged in that category.
They couldn't help themselves. It was in the blood. He was also a patriot,
and he used the word without embarrassment. To his colleagues in the
Yard, criminals were the enemy. Or the quarry. He was honest enough to
admit the ambivalence. To him, the enemy was the subversive, the ter-
rorist, the traitor. There was no compromise, no excuse. "Seek and
destroy." That was his own directive to his highly trained men. He
admired and liked James White. They were akin.

The Brigadier shook his head. "Nothing, I hope, Tim. I need a corpse,
that's all. Shouldn't be too difficult. People are always dying."

"What kind of corpse?" the policeman asked. The Armagnac was very
good indeed. There was a bite to it he appreciated. "Natural causes, I
suppose?"

"No," the Brigadier said, pleased to have forestalled him. "Drowning.
Been in the sea for some time."

"Ah," the policeman said. "Difficult to recognize, eh? I see."

"No fingerprints," James White said. "That's essential. No hands.
The rest doesn't matter. We can fudge that. But fingerprints we don't
want. Give it a thought, will you, Tim? I'd be most grateful. I've got our
friend at the Home Office breathing down my neck." He finished the
brandy.

His companion scowled. "Oh, that bugger! Do you know, he's the most
hostile Home Secretary we've had in twenty years! One thing we'll never
bloody well forgive was quashing the conviction on that little rat Jim
French."

"The man who kicked a PC to death in the Walthamstow riots?" the
Brigadier said. "I remember that very well."

"We knew he was guilty. We bloody well knew it. He was seen laying
into our man when he was on the ground. Three separate witnesses saw

him do it. But they wouldn't identify him. Too scared. Two were women, living in council flats. The other witness was a policeman. And *he* quashed the conviction on a technicality. Don't worry, James, this won't cost you anything. I'll get some inquiries going when I get back to the office. Drowning victim. Give me the details."

"Male," the Brigadier said. "About forty-five. Five feet ten inches tall.

"Don't worry," the policeman said again. "We'll find you something."

"Salisbury Plain—I love this part of England," Davina said. She glanced sideways at Sasanov. He was looking out the car window; she was relieved to see signs of interest.

"It's rather beautiful," he said. "So much space. I've always thought of England as a little, cramped place."

"Some of it is," she said. "That's part of its charm. And it changes so rapidly; you go from one county to the next and everything's different— the countryside, the villages, the architecture. Red brick in the south, lath and plaster and black beams in the Midlands, yellow stone in the Cotswolds, gray stone in Oxfordshire. Pebble and flint farther north, thatch in the southeast. You get rolling hills and dead-flat country, and even mountains, a few hundred miles from each other. I never get tired of England," she said.

"You sound like a Russian talking about Russia," Sasanov said. "Except that to us it's thousands of miles. A whole continent; so many races, colors, cultures, all in the borders of Mother Russia. Your little country is like a doll's village compared to mine."

She smiled and said, "But the weather's better. You must give us that."

"You've never spent a summer on the Black Sea," he answered.

"Nor a winter in Siberia," she countered. "There's Stonehenge up on the right. Would you like to stop and look at it?"

"And what is Stonehenge?"

"An ancient ruin," she said, slowing down. "I used to come here as a child. There's always a wind blowing."

They parked behind a row of cars and brightly painted buses catering to tours. There was a garish souvenir shop selling postcards, colored slides and plastic models of the circle of great stones. They joined a group of people filing around the rope barrier which separated them from the inner ring.

"It looks much bigger; from the road it was small. You're right," Sasanov said, buttoning his jacket. "There is a wind."

"The Druids worshiped here," Davina said. Her hair was breaking free of its pins and beginning to fly in wisps around her face. "But the people who erected the stones were much, much earlier. It was two circles originally, but the inner one is all that's left. You see that big stone in the center there?"

He followed her pointing finger. He nodded. "Yes. I see it."

"That's the altar stone," Davina said. "The rays of the rising sun touch the exact center of it. That's when the Druids offered human sacrifice to the sun. They killed the victims on the stone."

"There's a reconstruction of it over there," Sasanov said. "And a view from the air. It's very symmetrical for something so primitive."

"Yes, it is," Davina answered. "It's supposed to be the exact center of England; all lines north, south, east and west converge on this spot. Some people believe it is evidence of spacemen landing—like those places in Central America. Photographed from the air there are definite lines and patterns that aren't accidental."

"Don't tell me," Sasanov said, "that you believe that."

"I don't know," she said. "But I feel something here—some kind of energy."

"It's the wind, and the space all around you," he said. "It's an illusion. There is no significance to this, it's just a primitive temple. But it's unusual. I'm glad I saw it."

"It's such a pity you can't go any closer." Davina steered him back to the car park. "When I used to come here there weren't any barriers. You could walk all round it; I even sat on the altar stone. People came up here to watch the sun rise and see the first rays lighting on the stone. Now the great British public just wants to carve their initials all over it."

Sasanov stopped. "I would like a postcard," he said suddenly.

Davina stared at him. "Would you? Really?"

"Yes, I would. But I have no money."

"I've got plenty," she said. "Come on, then, you choose what you want." She watched him deciding on which view to take; he seemed more relaxed than she had known him to be in five whole months.

"This one," he said. "It will remind me of you."

It was a photograph of the sunrise, with a brilliant shaft of light touching the center of the altar stone.

"You must have been a bloodthirsty child," he said. "What did you imagine when you sat there?"

"Oh, I don't know. I suppose I tried to imagine what it had been like with some terrifying Druid standing over you with a knife. I believe they sacrificed virgins, male and female. It's horrible, if you think about it."

"Yes, but it's very common. It answers a human need, to satisfy an angry god. . . . And, after all, if the sacrifice has any value, it must be pure."

She didn't answer, but the adjective struck her as odd. So he regarded virginity as a virtue. "Pure"—it was a strangely old-fashioned word, seldom heard applied to anything but consumer goods. Pure wool, pure silk, pure skin, food. . . . She hadn't thought of a pure person since she grew up and the Christian ethic joined the fairy stories. It was a pointer to remember. Sasanov was a prude. Insights like that brought his personality more into focus; when you could see the personality in three dimensions, the task of winning him over became easier.

She hummed a little tune to herself as they drove. It was a beautiful spring afternoon; she felt confident and cheerful. It was a feeling she associated with going to Marchwood, the house where she had been born and grown up. Like coming back at the end of the school term, there was a flutter of excitement as they reached the turn-off that had since become the expressway, and Marchwood village was signposted as three miles away. She had never told anyone how she felt about the house; it seemed pointless, because it was going to be left to her brother, and then when he was killed she was sure her father had left the house to Charley. Because of course her sister didn't make a secret of her love for the house. *She'd* never touched the walls and talked to it as if it were a living entity. Everything Charley felt was very public. Not that she minded now, Davina thought, and didn't realize that she had stopped humming the little song. What would a single woman do, rattling about on her own in a house that size? Charley was certain to marry again. Davina could regard her family with affection, understanding and objectivity. She had her own life, and she didn't need them anymore. And because she didn't need them, she would be glad to see them, and make the best use possible of the weekend. She wanted the man beside her to relax, to drop his guard. Not to think of her as an opponent.

"We're nearly there," she said. "I think you'll like my mother and father. My sister's going to be there, too."

"I must remember to behave like a Pole," he said.

"Don't worry about that," she said. "Just be yourself. I told them you were a trade secretary at the embassy. We met at a party in January— remember that. They won't ask questions; they're not that sort of people."

"Don't they mind Communists?" he asked.

"They don't look on the Poles as Communists." She smiled a little. "Not since the Polish Pope; that's made them quite respectable."

"And what is your sister like? You've never talked about her before."

"My sister—well, you'll see for yourself. . . . It's just up here; there's the lane."

She didn't realize how much her expectancy showed on her face as they turned up the county road. There was a clear, fresh scent of leaves and wildflowers, a quiver in the air that she had always associated with spring and nature's cycle of rebirth.

They drove through a small gateway set in a wall; on either side of the narrow drive, the grass verges were a rippling wave of yellow daffodils. Sasanov was reminded suddenly of the Crimea, where the spring flowers were a carpet of color. They rounded a slight bend and came to the front of the house. It was a beautiful Queen Anne house; its brickwork glowed rose pink in the sunshine. A deep-green magnolia climbed up one wall, its leaves like shining spears, with the pregnant buds of blossom hiding among them. A weathervane on top of the eighteenth-century stable block stirred in the breeze.

Davina glanced into the rearview mirror and exclaimed, "My God, look at my hair! It's all over the place." She found a comb in her bag and began dragging her hair back from her forehead, pinning it into place.

Sasanov was going to say it suited her better loose. It was a dark red that was almost brown, and the severe upswept line from the forehead made her look older.

"There," she said. "That's better."

He didn't say anything.

"They must be round the back of the house—my mother's dog usually bounds out when he hears a car."

He took their two suitcases out of the trunk while Davina went and opened the front door.

"Leave them in the hall," she said. "We'll go through to the garden."

"I feel strange," he said suddenly.

She stopped and turned to him. "Why? Why strange?"

"Because I haven't left my cage for so long. I haven't talked to people."

She had avoided physical contact with him before. On the few occasions when they touched, it made her nervous. Now she put her hand on his arm.

"You're out of the cage," she said. "And talking to other people is just what you need. Come on."

He could see the little group out on the terrace, through the windows at the far end of the hall; and then Davina had opened a door and was walking out into the garden.

"Darling—we didn't hear you arrive." He saw the tall white-haired woman kiss her, and the smaller figure of a man get out of his garden chair and give her a quick peck on the cheek.

"This is Pavel—I won't try and pronounce the rest of it. My father, Captain Graham; my mother." He shook hands with them, and then he heard Davina say behind him, "Hello, Charley. How nice to see you. . . . Pavel, my sister, Charlotte Ransom."

He turned around; hearing the man's name, he had expected to see a man.

She was beautiful. There was no other word to describe her. Pretty, attractive, glamorous—these were commonplace adjectives, applicable to many women. But she was beautiful.

He shook hands with her. She smiled, and the effect was warm as sunlight. Hair like Davina's and yet not like, because it was the vibrant color of Spanish mahogany, heavy and shining, falling naturally to her shoulders. Enormous gray eyes, framed in eyelashes that should have been false but were her own. A face that at first sight was classical, every feature in harmony, and that changed when she smiled, becoming sensuous and challenging. She wore slacks and a shirt, with a sweater knotted around her waist by the sleeves. He noticed gold chains around her neck, and a wide gold ring on her left hand.

"Hello," she said. "Isn't it a lovely evening? Let's sit down, shall we?"

He hesitated, and Davina said, "Shall we take our cases up first?"

"No, dear," Mrs. Graham said. "You can do that later. We're having a drink out here, before it gets too chilly. Do sit down, Pavel. What would you like?"

"I'll get it," Captain Graham said. "Davina?"

"Vodka and tonic, please."

He leaned toward Sasanov. "I'm sorry I don't know your proper name. But if my daughter says she can't pronounce it, then I'm damned sure I wouldn't be able to! So we'll all call you Pavel. What would you like to drink?"

"Vodka," Sasanov said. "No tonic, thank you."

He found himself sitting beside the sister. Even in the garden he could smell the scent she wore; it was heavy and provocative. She leaned back, her hands clasped behind her head. The attitude showed off small, perfect breasts.

"What are you doing in England?"

"I'm at the embassy," he answered. "I am a trade secretary."

"Isn't that supposed to mean you're a spy? I thought all trade secretaries were really spies." She laughed, and it covered an embarrassed silence.

"Really, Charley—" Mrs. Graham protested.

"No," Sasanov responded. "The commercial attachés are the spies. Not the trade secretaries. I'm very harmless."

There was a general laugh; he didn't look at Davina.

"How long have you been in England?" Charley Ransom asked him.

"A year," he said. "I like England very much."

"And are you and Davina old friends?" The beautiful gray eyes were twinkling, as if there were something risqué about being a friend of her sister's. The charm was coming at him in waves, like the scent.

"Not very long," he said. He wished that Davina would interrupt the flow of questions. But she was talking to her mother.

"Do you live near here?" He took the initiative away from her.

"I live in London," she said. "I've got a flat in Portman Place. You must come round and have a drink."

"That's very kind," Sasanov said.

She had begun to play with one of the gold chains around her neck; a large medallion hung on it, engraved with the Aries sign of the zodiac. She had beautiful hands, with long, painted nails. The wedding ring was a broad band set with a small diamond.

"Charley," Captain Graham said. "You haven't got a drink."

Sasanov glimpsed the look of excessive fondness that he exchanged with his daughter. He was glad of the interruption; it relieved him from Charley Ransom's questions. He looked across at Davina, finished his drink quickly and stood up.

"I will take the cases upstairs," he said.

"I'll show you your room." Davina's mother walked in front of them.

He heard the father and the younger daughter laughing at some private joke as they went inside the house.

The stairs were narrow; he followed Davina, carrying the two suitcases. Mrs. Graham opened a door on the landing.

"This is your room," she said to him. "The bathroom is across the passage there. Davina darling, you're in your old room, of course."

Davina came up to Sasanov. "I'll take my case," she said.

He held on to it. "No. It's heavy. I'll carry it for you."

He was surprised by her bedroom. It was a pretty room, with fresh flowers and a narrow bed; there were books and wooly toys, and a collection of small china animals arranged on a shelf. It was a child's room. It showed no sign that its occupant had ever grown up.

"Thanks," Davina said. "Just leave it on the bed. We'll be down later," she said to her mother.

"Don't hurry, darling. Dinner's not till eight-fifteen. I'm sure Pavel might like a bath. I'd hurry up before Charley takes all the hot water."

"Yes," Davina said. "She always did, I remember. I'll knock on your door in about half an hour," she said to Sasanov.

She turned to the bed and opened her suitcase. She dressed very simply; years ago she had recognized that she wasn't the type who could carry off elaborate clothes or wear a lot of makeup. "You look much better without all that stuff on your face," her father had said when she began trying to improve her looks. "Just be natural—that's what suits you." She had given up without resistance; it was a waste of time trying to compete with a sister who was so beautiful that conversation stopped when she walked into a room.

She unpacked her clothes and hung up the long wool skirt she intended wearing that night. The dear, familiar room—the haven of her childhood. She picked up the shabby tiger, minus an eye, that had been a Christmas present twenty years ago, touched the glass animals one by one, remembering the birthdays and when each one was added. As a child she had loved animals; her ambition as a teenager had been to become a vet. Running away, of course. She understood the motivation now. Seeking a substitute for the dangerous love of human beings. Animals were faithful, and uncritical. There was no risk of rejection in loving horses and dogs and rabbits when her sister was claiming everyone's attention. She opened the window and looked out over the garden. Charley and her father had gone inside; the little group of chairs stood empty on the terrace below. They'd left the tray of drinks behind.

Sasanov had been fascinated by her sister. She'd seen it happen so many times. She hardly needed to watch them to know that Charley was exerting her lethal brand of sex appeal and charm, and, like every other man who met her, the Russian was responding. She left the window open and began to put out her brushes and the few articles of makeup. She let her hair hang loose and brushed it; the wind on Salisbury Plain had tangled it; brushing hurt. She saw her face in the mirror, and the reflection stared back at her with a set mouth and eyes stinging with tears. Tears from smoothing the tangles in her hair. The other kind of tears had been cried out, a long time ago. This time it didn't hurt her to lose a man to Charley; she could sit back with grim detachment and watch her sister seduce Sasanov, because this time it would work in her favor. Charley could soften him up, unravel the tension which was making him so restless and uneasy. Charley, the irresistible, who didn't know how to stop taking other women's men, would be used in her turn. The face in the mirror was hard and plain, the mouth turned down. It would be ironic if the sister who had wrecked her private life should help her with Sasanov. It was a touch the Brigadier would have found amusing.

She changed out of her skirt and blouse, slipped into the hall in her dressing gown, and found the bathroom locked. Charley was inside. Taking all the hot water, as usual. She washed in the basin in her room, changed into the dark-blue skirt and sweater. And with cynical bravado she made up her face and arranged her hair in a high, smooth sweep. Charley would appear, so skillfully disheveled that it took hours, to give the impression she'd run a comb through her hair and tossed on some clothes. And Sasanov would be the object of her attention, a victim selected and pursued, with the indulgent approval of their father. He had always delighted in his beautiful daughter's conquests; sometimes their mother showed embarrassment, but she too had accepted Charley's effect upon men as inevitable and not her fault. She was just too beautiful and attractive. Davina glanced at herself once more in the mirror. Too tall, too thin, too neat. And too clever. Charley's got the beauty and Davina's got the brains.

She went down and knocked on Sasanov's door. There was no reply and she opened it. The room was empty; he'd already gone downstairs. There was a tight little smile on her face when she went into the drawing room and found him playing chess with her sister.

3

The senior police officer who had lunched with the Brigadier at his club set about supplying his friend with a dead body before he went off for the weekend. He lived just outside Dartford in Kent, with wife and two sons in the final stages of advanced education. He liked to spend Saturday mornings playing golf. It relaxed him. He left instructions with his office to make inquiries around the coast, and to put a security cover on anyone recently drowned in the Thames area. His immediate subordinate did not go home on the weekends, or have time to play golf. So by Friday evening, while the Brigadier and his wife were driving to a neighbor's house for dinner, while his superior was settled in front of the television for the evening, and the Grahams with their two daughters and their guest were sitting down to dinner, four dead men of approximately correct requirements had been reported to the Special Branch. Two were identifiable and had been reported missing; both were suicides with mental histories. The third was little more than a male torso, caught in the net of a trawler fishing off Skegness, and, from the brief report upon it, appeared to be a murder victim. The fourth was a body that had spent some time in the sea; it was badly decomposed but carried a tattoo on one forearm which suggested that the man had been a seaman. A quick examination had showed gold dental work which was not typical of English dentistry. This dead body seemed the most likely to fit the requirements.

The body was removed from the south-coast mortuary under a special

45

authority signed by the Special Branch chief before he left on Friday afternoon, and placed in a small private mortuary under official seal. After the weekend a surgeon would amputate what remained of the left hand at the wrist, and sever the other at the elbow, removing the tattoo as well as any chance of fingerprints. In due course a dentist would perform a passable job on the teeth, duplicating as far as possible the dental work already documented on Sasanov's teeth. The body had no other distinguishing marks; the age was approximately right, and the dead man had been of similar build and height. The cause of death could definitely be stated as drowning. The length of time the body had been in the water did not approximate to the date of Sasanov's disappearance, but then you couldn't have everything.

It was most inadvisable to disturb the Chief at home during weekends, so the young officer made out a report for him and left it ready for Monday morning. The dead man, a metal identity disc tagged to his left foot, stayed in the chilly darkness of his refrigerated berth over the weekend; the relatives of Per Svenson from the tiny village of Staghan on the north coast of Norway would never know more than the sad fact that he had fallen overboard during a storm.

Ivan Sasanov looked around the dinner table at Marchwood. Mrs. Graham was beside him; the candlelight flattered her, as it did Davina. It gave a marvelous softness to the beautiful girl sitting on his other side; the light made her throat and the one shoulder exposed by her dress a pearly color that reminded him of the voluptuous Rubens seminudes in the Hermitage. For a very slim woman she was fleshy, her skin smooth, her arms rounded, the lovely face framed by an erotic abundance of red hair.

He had let her win at chess; as soon as they began to play he realized she was hopelessly limited. And yet there were flashes of cunning that surprised him, and at the end of their first game she had looked at him and said accusingly, "You let me win—you're far too good not to have foreseen that last move."

"I did see it," he said. "I just wanted to find out how you play. You must know your opponent's mind if you want to beat him."

She had laughed and set the pieces in place. She had a laugh he found difficult to describe. There was an old-fashioned word for it. Merry. Carefree and full of enjoyment. They played a second time, and they were in the middle of the game when Davina came in. She poured herself a drink and stood watching them for a few minutes. She looked rather pale and stiff; Sasanov felt emotion play like lightning between the two sisters, and then it was hidden by a veneer of friendliness which didn't deceive him. Davina hated her; he hadn't gauged how Charley reciprocated. She showed less of her feelings because they appeared to be so obvious. She laughed and joked, and teased him, glittering like a star in the family circle, while Davina's hatred glowed around her like a nimbus. He beat Charley the second time, and brought them to checkmate just as dinner was ready.

He didn't like English food; he found it too bland. His tastes were catered to by the private cook at Halldale Manor. He viewed the chicken dish in a wine sauce, and the inevitable dull vegetables, without much appetite. He ate more than he wanted, to be polite, and allowed Captain Graham to keep his glass filled with wine. He was surrounded by a high degree of comfort and good taste; the dining room, its table bright with family silver, the pictures and the furniture were uniquely English. Nothing ostentatious or new; slight shabbiness was in order. Nothing offended the Grahams and their kind more than vulgarity and display. Mrs. Graham had asked him a few polite questions and then launched into a long discourse about gardening. He wasn't bored, because no effort was required of him. He merely smiled and nodded, not quite listening.

He heard Davina's father say, "This is quite a treat, my dear. We haven't had a visit from you for a long time. How is Jim White?"

"Very well," Davina answered him. There was a slight formality between the father and the elder daughter, embedded in their tones of voice like a tiny splinter of glass. Sasanov concentrated, smiling at Mrs. Graham's description of layering carnations.

"Does he bully you? Or have you got him under your thumb like a good secretary should?"

"Nobody bullies me, Father," she said. "And I can assure you, the Brigadier is not under my thumb or anybody else's."

It shouldn't have sounded sharp, but it did. So that was what she was supposed to be—White's secretary. And that was how her family thought of her. The spinster secretary, efficient, brisk and sexless. He was beginning to understand the puzzle better, just by sitting within her family. He finished his wine, and found that Charley's hand lay like a dove on his sleeve. She leaned across him, and the voluptuous scent was strong.

"Mummy darling, you mustn't monopolize Pavel—let me get a word in."

"I'm sorry," Mrs. Graham apologized to him, "I love my garden and I do get carried away when anyone lets me; I'll take you round tomorrow if it's a nice morning."

"I would like that very much," Sasanov said.

He had a small dacha outside Moscow at a place called Zhukova. It was one of the privileges that went with his rank and importance. Fedya and his daughter, Irina, loved spending weekends there; they used to go for long walks together, his daughter's dog bounding beside them, barking and dashing to and fro with excitement. But they didn't have a garden. Not a cultivated work of art like the gardens he had seen from the terrace at Marchwood. The memory of the dacha blotted out his surroundings for a few seconds; he could smell the pine trees and the crisp fresh air. The pain was sharp, like a stab wound.

He looked across and saw Davina Graham watching him. Her sister's hand still lay on his sleeve as she was talking to him. He smiled and didn't listen. Instead he watched Davina gauging his reactions. She had a calm detachment that sometimes goaded him and sometimes soothed his nerves. Her eyes were not normally expressive; she showed only those feelings he was meant to see. But now her face was a sad mask, and the polite little smile was full of hurt. He moved his arm, and the sister's white hand fell away. He turned to Harry Graham and lifted his wine-glass.

"To your wife's beautiful garden. And her charming daughters."

Charley answered the compliment in a low murmur. "I hope you'll see more of both," she said.

"Mother," Davina said. "Don't you think we should leave Pavel and Father for a few minutes?"

"Yes, of course."

Both men stood up as the three women left the room.

Captain Graham carried a decanter of port and two glasses to the table and sat beside Sasanov. "I've got brandy if you prefer it, but this is rather a good Cockburn's 'sixty-two." He looked gratified when his guest accepted the port.

"Would it be indiscreet if I asked you what you thought of our present government? I don't suppose you approve of it, but I'd like to hear a view from outside. And one does have the feeling that Poland is friendly to Britain deep down—we fought a damned good war together."

"Indeed yes," Sasanov agreed. Captain Graham settled down to enjoy himself.

Davina went to her own room; she was putting a little powder on her face, thinking that she was already too pale, when she saw her sister reflected in the mirror. She turned around.

"Davy," her sister said. "Can I come in?" That was why she hated the masculine abbreviation of her name. Charley always kept it up.

"Of course," she said. "I won't be a minute here."

"That's all right," her sister said. "I don't want to do anything to my face. I just wanted to talk while we have a chance."

She took a cigarette out of her bag and lit it. "How are you?" she said. "I mean, how are you *really*?"

"I'm fine," Davina answered. "Very busy. I gather you and Brian are splitting up."

"Yes, we are; it's unfortunate, but we weren't good marriage material." She smiled her beautiful smile. "Too selfish, I suppose. He likes his way and I like mine. We're better apart, but the details are always a bore."

"They must be," Davina said. "Why do you keep marrying? Wouldn't it save a lot of trouble and expense if you just lived together till you got fed up?"

"I'm not the one who insists on marriage," Charley answered. "It was never my idea to marry Richard. I tried to tell you that at the time. I wish I felt you'd forgiven me."

"I might have been able to, if you'd loved him," Davina said. "But you took him away from me for fun. Dull old Davy had a fiancé—and you didn't fancy being out of the limelight, did you? So you threw yourself at him."

"I didn't," her sister said. "I told you, but you wouldn't listen to me. He never left me alone. I never wanted to marry him; I didn't know how to get out of it after he broke off with you. Davy, for God's sake can't we bury the past? After all, you didn't miss much. You saw how he turned out."

"I saw what you made of him." Davina said.

There was silence then. She expected her sister to get up and go out, but she didn't. She sat on the bed and smoked.

"Your Pole seems nice," she said at last. "Just so I don't put my foot in it, is he a boy friend?"

"No," Davina said. "Just a friend."

"I think he likes you," Charley remarked. "He keeps looking at you. That's a sure sign."

Davina got up. "There's nothing in it; he's just a friend."

"Mother thinks he's most attractive," Charley said. "Why don't you encourage him a bit, Davy? You're so remote with men; they get frightened off."

"You live your life, Charley, and I'll live mine," Davina said flatly. "I'm going downstairs. Are you coming? And try not to drop that filthy cigarette ash all over the floor."

Her sister shrugged. "If you don't relax," she said, "you'll never get a man. You're turning into a real spinster, Davy. And I'm not being a bitch. I'm just telling you the truth."

"One day," Davina said quietly, "you're going to face the truth about yourself. I'd rather be a spinster than a tramp."

She hurried out and down the stairs. Her father and Sasanov had come into the drawing room and were standing by the fire, talking. Her mother was sitting in her armchair beside a lamp, wearing glasses and sewing; she looked serene and she gave her elder daughter a tender smile as she came toward her.

"Come and sit down near me," she said. "Tell me what you think of this pattern."

Mrs. Graham was an accomplished needlewoman; cushion covers and chairseats were examples of her work. Davina sat beside her.

"It's lovely," she said, looking at the embroidery frame. "That's the Bargello pattern, isn't it?"

"Yes, darling. I'm covering the two hall-chair seats—they've got rather tatty. You ought to do this, you know. It's so soothing."

"I don't have the time," Davina answered. "Or the patience. I never could sew anything properly."

"No, you couldn't." Her mother smiled. "That's quite right. You look a little tired—are you working very hard?"

"Quite hard," she admitted. Day and night, in fact, locked in combat with another human being. The hardest work of all.

"I wish you'd come down and see us more," her mother murmured. It wasn't a reproach. "Your father was so delighted when I told him you and Charley were coming this weekend."

"I'm sure he was," Davina said; her mother didn't notice the gentle sarcasm, or, if she did, she ignored it and went on.

"He likes your friend Pavel. I think he's charming. I remember some of the Polish army officers in the war—they were such dashing young men. We all fell in love with them." She didn't look up or interrupt her sewing. "Is there anything between you—anything serious?"

"No, Mother," Davina said. "Charley asked me the same thing. We're just friends, that's all. He's rather lonely in London and I thought he'd like to meet you and spend a weekend in a family. Don't start marrying me off to Pavel, for heaven's sake."

"Of course not," Mrs. Graham said. She put the embroidery frame aside. "Davina darling, having a career isn't everything, you know. You ought to think about getting married. There must be some nice men around in London—you can bring anyone down here you like, you know that."

Davina put a hand on her mother's arm. "I know," she said. "Don't worry about me, I'm perfectly happy. I've got a very full life."

"It's not still Richard, is it?" The faded blue eyes were anxious.

"No," Davina shook her head. "I got over that a long time ago."

"Are you still angry with Charley? I feel there's an atmosphere between you. I wish you could forget it and be your old happy selves again. Blood's thicker than water, and you *are* sisters."

"We're all right, Mother," she said. "He was no damned good or he wouldn't have run off with her in the first place. I never gave it a thought."

"I'm so glad," her mother said. "I do, wish she'd meet someone and settle down for good. I thought Brian would be the answer—but all he thinks about is his career, apparently. He's made Charley really miserable."

"That's a shame," Davina said.

Her sister was talking to Sasanov; he and her father laughed at something she said. She had never heard him laugh aloud before. She felt a little color burning on both cheeks. ". . . he likes you. He keeps looking at you." Charley's words floated into her mind. Mocking, patronizing— she didn't know which. He wasn't looking at anyone but her sister, and besides his laughter there was an air of excitement about him. A full-blooded man responding to the challenge of a desirable woman.

The room seemed suffocatingly hot. Surely they didn't need a fire at this time of year. She had offered him a woman; why should she mind so much that he had found one for himself? Jealousy, she chided herself angrily. You're jealous because it's your sister. And you offered him a professional whore sent by the department. Because you didn't have the courage to go to him yourself. Remember how angry he was, how you nearly unbalanced the whole carefully constructed pas-de-deux you've shadow-danced with him for the past five months. He didn't want clinical sex. He wanted you, and you backed off. Now you've lost him—to Charley. Like Richard, who left you to marry her; like all the men who ever met her.

She got up and went over to the group by the fireplace. She slipped her arm through Sasanov's, and saw the look of surprise on her father's face. She smiled at him and at her sister.

"I'm going to take Pavel for a walk in the moonlight," she announced. "It's got so stuffy in here."

Charley and her father were so unprepared that for a moment they just stared at her. Davina had never been intimate with any man in public. She had never claimed Richard, even when they were engaged, the way she was now claiming the Pole. Davina did not take men for walks in the moonlight.

"How romantic," her sister said.

"Don't stay out too long," her father said. He looked embarrassed. "It's getting late and I want to lock up the house."

She steered Sasanov out of the room. At the door to the terrace she dropped his arm.

"I hope you didn't mind," she said. "I thought you might need a break from them. Father and Charley together can be quite overpowering."

"I like your father," he said. "We talked politics after you left the dining room. He is an amazing reactionary; I was most interested."

"He's the only grass-roots Tory you'll ever meet," Davina said. "There aren't that many of them left. And I'm afraid Charley is rather a flirt." She couldn't stop herself from saying it.

They were standing in the hall; she hadn't opened the terrace door. Sasanov reached and turned the handle.

"You said we would walk," he reminded her.

"That was just an excuse," she protested. "You don't have to go outside."

"I would like to," he said. "Fresh air helps me to sleep."

There was a full moon, and the garden was silver and black in the translucent light. He walked beside her along the brick paths around the flower beds. It was a still, soundless night. They didn't touch each other; there were no steps and they could see the garden quite clearly.

"I hope this was a good idea," Davina said at last. "If you want to go early tomorrow I can make an excuse . . ."

"I'm enjoying myself," Sasanov answered. "It's a new world to me. I find it interesting. Everything about the way you live is different: the way your family thinks and talks, the customs here. It's like another planet to a Russian."

"I wanted you to see a little of what life in England could be like," she said quietly. "You and your wife and daughter could have a place in the country. Or in a town, if you prefer. You could all be happy here. They could be free, too."

He stopped and looked down at her. "I wouldn't know what to do with your freedom. Nor would my wife and child. Russians have never been free. We need a strong hand over us if we're going to be happy. You wouldn't understand that. You wouldn't understand that in Russia men like your father don't talk about their government. They never have done. Not in Tsarist times and not now."

"You're closing your mind," she said. "You're prejudiced because my father talked politics to you after dinner."

Sasanov protested. "That's not true; I was expecting it. I like political discussions; but there was no challenge, no risk."

"Now, that *I* don't understand," Davina said. "I don't see any fun in being frightened to speak your mind, and I don't think you do, either. You're just being bloody-minded!" They faced each other in the middle of the path.

"And you are trying to pick a quarrel," Sasanov said. "Why?"

Because it's not working out, she wanted to say; because I've made a mistake bringing you down here. You can't see yourself or your family fitting into English life. And I know you'll go to bed with my sister before the weekend is over, unless I can get you away. And that I cannot bear. . . . A bank of cloud covered the moon. Suddenly they were in darkness.

"I'm going in," she said. "I hope you sleep. Maybe you'll be in a better mood tomorrow."

She began to walk away, and promptly tripped over the edge of the path. She heard him laugh behind her. He caught her by the elbow.

"Don't be stupid," he said. "You can't see."

"Nor can you!"

"I didn't fall over," he remarked. She tried to pull away, but he wouldn't let go. They proceeded slowly and carefully back toward the lighted windows of the house. Then the moon slipped free and she broke away from him. He barred the way to the house. She couldn't see his face.

"Wait, Vina. Don't go in. I miss my wife," he said slowly. "More than ever. I don't want to be alone tonight."

She answered before she could stop herself. She felt frozen and empty. "You won't be, if I know my sister."

He put both hands on her shoulders.

"I don't want your sister," Sasanov said.

There was a little clock on her dressing table; the dial was luminous, and the hands showed five minutes to three. It was impossible to sleep in her narrow bed, although they had both dozed for a time and then awakened.

She had never felt so exhausted in her life. She had slept with her fiancé, Richard, and found sex tender and fulfilling. There had been a lot of love in their lovemaking. At least on her part. But it was a poor preparation for going to bed with Sasanov. She didn't want to remember Richard, but he came into her thoughts, and with the Russian's heavy arms around her the memory was of a feeble, ineffectual lover. It was a strange revelation, and the implications were disturbing. She would consider them tomorrow, she decided, and then realized that tomorrow had become today, and the man beside her was stirring and active again.

Sasanov leaned over her and kissed her afterward. "Are you all right?"

"I feel I've been run over by a bus." And she laughed softly.

"I'm sorry. Am I such a bad lover?"

"No, no, no—don't apologize. It's just I've never had a man who was so impatient. It's very flattering." She twisted her arms around his neck; she couldn't see him in the darkness. She kissed him. "I feel ridiculously happy," she said. "Every woman should have someone like you for Christmas."

Oh, Brigadier White, she thought suddenly, if you could see me now— and my lovely sister who hops in and out of bed like a chestnut on a hot griddle.

"You can't sleep in here," she said. "Do you want to go back to your own bed?"

"No," Sasanov said. "I want to talk; I like to talk afterward. Do you mind?"

"Of course not." Davina reached out and switched on the bedside lamp. He blinked and, stretching over her, turned it out.

"That's horrible," he said. "I'll pull the curtains back if you want light."

The sky was cloudless and the bright moon shone into the room. His naked body turned to silver. She made what room for him she could, and he slid into the bed again.

"What do you want to talk about?" Davina asked him. Her own body had a complacent, lazy life of its own, enjoying its exhaustion. Now her mind snapped to attention. . . . "I want to talk."

"Do you want a cigarette?" she asked him.

"No. Next time, we will have some vodka in the room. Then we can drink together. That's very good; you'll like it."

"I'll get some," she promised. She waited, not taking the initiative.

"Jacob Belezky Memenev was my friend since we were children," Sasanov said suddenly. "We went to the same village school, and I wanted to marry his sister when I was fourteen. Did you know that, Vina?"

"No," she said. "You actually grew up together?"

"He was very clever, clever as a Jew, we say in Russia. He went on to the Science College in Moscow, while I took a course of political studies in Leningrad. His sister became a doctor, with a practice in Moscow. I used to take her out, before I met my wife." His face was turned away from her, looking at the window.

"I didn't know you were that close," she said. "I don't think anyone did."

"He became a physicist," Sasanov went on. "He had a brilliant brain, a great future. He was moved to Moscow, where I was assigned to the Ministry for External Affairs. We took up our old friendship. Our wives were friends, too. He would come to our apartment on Nevsky Street and we'd all sit round and eat and drink and talk all night. I thought of it this evening, sitting with your family. It was so different, so calm and formal, like a play in the theater. I tried to explain to you in the garden, how different it was. In my apartment we have a big table in the kitchen. The family lives there; our samovar is in the middle of it, like a god; there's always food and tea and vodka, or wine. When our friends come, we all sit together, around the table and the samovar. I have a very good apartment, with three bedrooms, and a dacha out at Zhukova. But we live and eat and enjoy ourselves in the room with the samovar. It is the heart of the Russian home. You would find it very noisy; everybody shouts. And it's the place where people speak their thoughts out loud. You can't do it in restaurants or public places. You have to be careful."

I've done it, she was thinking, I've broken through. He's really talking to me now. "But Belezky felt safe with you," she murmured.

"Yes, he trusted me. He wanted to change me, so he took the risk."

"How change you?"

"Make me see our way of life through his eyes. We used to sit up all night, arguing about so many things. The rights of the individual; he was always saying how important they were—the freedoms, he called them. Freedom to worship a god, if you believed in one; freedom to speak, to read and write, to travel. Freedom to take work or change your job without permission."

"And what did you say?" she asked. "How did you answer him?"

"I told him the truth," Sasanov said. "Those freedoms were impossible for Russians. The Soviet system can't operate without controls. I made a good case; it seemed good at the time. Freedom to work where you want means unemployment for another man. Religion perverts the minds of the young and teaches them superstition. To write and read and speak freely means that our people are exposed to propaganda from outside, that error and subversion can undermine the state. Besides, as I said in the garden, we have never been free in the way you mean." He raised his arms above his head and stretched; he brought the right one around her shoulders.

"We need a tyrant," he said slowly. "A tsar, a Stalin. We need the protection of a strong man. Then we can find our own way to get round the laws when it's needed. Jacob couldn't accept that."

"I find it difficult, too," Davina said. "Difficult to believe you accept it, either."

"I did," he countered. "I was part of the tyranny; I helped to keep it in power. Jacob made me see it in terms of people. Of himself and his wife and the friends they were making who thought the same."

"According to what you say," she pointed out, "you should have denounced him."

He said something in Russian which sounded like a curse.

"I kept trying to persuade him to keep his mouth shut! He had everything he wanted—a top post in the space-research program, a wife he loved, a good salary; he'd have a dacha soon, I told him. What did the rest matter? Why not enjoy life? He wouldn't listen. He had that Jewish soul which isn't satisfied unless it suffers. And then he asked to go to Israel. Of course he was refused. He must have known he was too valuable to be allowed to leave the country. He was provoking the authorities. Demonstrating that he wasn't a free man. And he started to say these things openly. He was dismissed from his post; they were turned out of the apartment. Jacob couldn't get a job except as a low-paid manual worker. Everybody shunned him."

"You too?" Davina asked him quietly. The pattern he described was so familiar.

"He was my friend," Sasanov said angrily. "It was safe for me to see him, because I said I was watching him. Then he signed the declaration monitoring the abuse of human rights in Russia. He and Scherensky and Botkin. You know what happened to them. He doomed himself. When he was arrested I tried to help. I went to see him, I tried to persuade him to plead guilty, to ask for mercy. All they needed was a public confession that he had been wrong." He paused, and Davina noted his use of the word "they" when he was talking about Belezky's persecutors. That was when he had really severed the link with his colleagues in the KGB.

"He didn't do it," she said. "He committed suicide."

She felt Sasanov stiffen. "He was sent to a mental hospital, two months before the trial—they diagnosed a personality disorder." She felt the rigid muscles in his arm, the tension in his whole body.

"He didn't kill himself," he said flatly. "They killed him. So many shock treatments he had a heart attack and died."

"My God," she whispered. "What a dreadful thing."

"Jacob was lucky," Sasanov said. "Scherensky and Botkin are still in the place. They'll never come out. The others are being arrested one by one. Jacob's wife was charged with malpractice and sent to prison for twelve years. I remember looking around our kitchen, and thinking we'd never see them again. No more arguments, no more evenings together. That was when Jacob won. He had to die to make me see that he was right."

"I'm sorry." She reached up and touched his face. His cheek was wet. "I'm so sorry. I didn't know it was as bad as this."

"You'll have a lot to tell your Chief," he said.

"Don't say that—please."

"I don't mind," he said. "I understand. I knew what I was doing when I asked you to take me into your bed. I had come to the end. I needed you, Vina."

"I'm glad," Davina said. "I'm really glad. And I'll do everything I can to help."

"I can't see what to do," he said. "To stay, to make a new life here . . . I think of Russia and my family, and this place seems like the moon."

"Wait till the morning," she whispered to him. "Don't try and think about it now."

"It is the morning," he answered. "Look, there's a gray light in the sky. It's five o'clock. You will be tired today. I must go and let you sleep."

She moved herself upright against him; the covers had fallen away from them, and he looked at her; he traced the outline of her breast.

"You have a beautiful body," he said.

She laid her hand on his chest; he had a lot of fair, wiry hair that came
to a point at the base of his throat. She pulled at a strand of it.

"I thought you had fallen for my sister," she said. "Don't you think
she's beautiful?"

"Very beautiful," he agreed quietly. "But all she would do with a man
is take. I needed a woman who could give."

She looked up at him. "Don't go back just yet," she said. "Stay with
me."

Jeremy Spencer-Barr looked at his reflection in the bathroom mirror. He
was pleased with what he saw. A clean-shaven, regular-featured face,
with wavy fair hair, fashionably cut a little long, brown eyes that were
bright with health. A good-looking man in his early thirties, possessing a
fit, lean body and a mind that matched it. He smiled slightly at himself.
There was a blister on his lower lip, where the girl still asleep in his
bedroom had bitten him. They had been living together for the past eight-
een months and she had begun showing signs of wanting to get married.
It was a pity, because she was very attractive and he was fond of her. But
marriage was not among his plans. It was lucky from that point of view
that he was going to the States. But it wasn't the job he really wanted.
Taking over from a has-been like Peter Harrington in New York wasn't
the same as being minder to Ivan Sasanov. The sharp-faced Graham girl
had landed that fish. He could only speculate on how she was progress-
ing; it was impossible to find out anything positive about Sasanov. He
was looking forward to New York; he liked the pace of life in the States; it
stimulated him, and he had made friends while he was at Harvard.
Ambition ran in the family. His father was the head of a prestigious
stockbroking firm in the City, his uncle's Civil Service career had been
just as brilliant; and he, Jeremy, with a younger brother and sister at
Cambridge, was the most promising of them all. He had never spared
himself. The young man in the bathroom mirror, putting toothpaste on a
brush, was the result of remorseless self-discipline and demonic drive. He
concealed the less attractive side of his personality beneath impeccable
manners and a sort of boyish charm which older women found appealing.
But he was driven by fiends; fiends of ambition and love of achievement.
As a child, he had enjoyed something only if no one else could do it. He
had nearly killed himself rock-climbing in the Pennines. The rope held
and the Spencer-Barr luck with it. The next time he attempted that particular climb, he reached the top in record time. He said of himself that he
had no nerves; this wasn't accurate. He had a finely tuned and ultra-

sensitive nervous system, which supplied his intellect with the imaginative fuel it needed, but he was always master of himself.

That was why Brigadier White's department was his chosen venue; it required exceptional skills to be a successful intelligence operative. He scorned the word "counterspy" as overdramatic. Intelligence was now a science, an exercise in technology allied to human intellect. The world and the forces directing the destiny of its peoples seemed like a gigantic jigsaw of interlocking parts, each part an independent puzzle where the shape of every piece could alter just as it began to fit. He finished brushing his teeth, took a mouthful of water and spat out the froth.

Mary Walker was a director of a fine art gallery in London; they had met at an exhibition and she seemed to fall in love with him almost at once. He was very fond of her indeed; she was a clever girl, with a head for business, and she constantly told him how wonderful he was. And she had improved his sex life. Jeremy was good at everything, except making love. His temperament was too intense, his energies diverted into too many channels, to leave him much sexual drive. He was a bad lover who couldn't relax, and until he met Mary he'd avoided relationships with women. They damaged his ego and made him aware of a deficiency in himself that he couldn't put right. She was three years younger than he, divorced while in her early twenties, and she had the skill and patience to nurse them through to a satisfying love life. He really might have married her, he thought suddenly, if he hadn't been told that at this stage in his career a wife would be a hindrance. So he had told her he was going to New York and expected to be out of England for two years.

He was touched and flattered when she cried. He made up his mind to buy her a nice present, something to remind her of him when she wore it. He went back into the bedroom, and she woke up, throwing the bedclothes aside, one arm across her eyes against the daylight. There was only a fortnight left before he took up the American post. He wanted to make the best of it.

"It's ten o'clock," he said. "I'll bring you some coffee."

"Thank you, darling."

She watched him, smiling, as he left the room. She could hear the dash of water in the kettle, because the kitchen was very close. He showed her little considerations like bringing her coffee in bed over the weekends. He loved her in his own way, and she didn't ask for more than he could give. She was going to miss him very much. And anyway, New York wasn't all that far. She could make trips to see him. He wouldn't find another girl who understood him as well as she did. Two years wasn't all that long.

Jeremy didn't know it, but she was a very determined person, and she wanted to get married. The worst way to go about it was to fuss him with too much sex. She used to show-jump as a teenager, and she remembered the adage, always end on a good note. Last night had been particularly successful. She would leave it there. She got out of bed, put on her silk pajamas, brushed her hair, and was sitting up wearing her glasses and reading the *Telegraph* when he came back.

They drank their coffee and discussed the news in perfect amity. He had planned a drive into the country and lunch at a well-known riverside hotel. They both liked to do something on weekends. He couldn't have endured a day spent in idleness. That evening she was taking him to a friend's Chelsea house for drinks.

They were both looking forward to their day together.

"Charley, darling," Mrs. Graham said anxiously, "have you seen Davina this morning—she looks like death!"

"She looks very tired," her daughter said. "Maybe she didn't sleep."

"I think she overworks," Mrs. Graham said. Charley had slept late; she had been coming down the stairs as Davina was going out. She spread a slice of toast with butter and marmalade. She'd noticed the dark shadows under the eyes; if it hadn't been Davina a ribald explanation would have come to mind. The Pole had followed her. Charley had given him her most brilliant smile. She had almost expected him to come to her bedroom door last night. When he didn't she went to sleep instead.

"I saw her going out with Pavel," she said to her mother. "Where were they going?"

"She said they were going to walk through the woods," Mrs. Graham answered.

"You know, Mother—I don't believe her about Pavel. I think there's something brewing there. Who on earth goes for a walk at this time in the morning? I think she wants to take him off alone."

"Oh, darling, don't be silly. Davina's never been like that. You were the one who went off hand in hand to our woods—and came back with the poor man looking like a dog following a bone!"

Charley burst out laughing. "It doesn't sound very romantic, does it? You are beastly, Mother, putting it like that. Besides, I always went for walks at a civilized time, not at a horrible hour like half past nine! Do you remember that nice Tony French? The one who was Brian's best man?"

"I do," her mother said. "Give me some tea, will you?"

"He asked me to marry him." Charley giggled. "After he'd got his divorce, of course." She went on laughing and spilled tea into the saucer. "Aren't they funny, men? And there was Brian snarling and snapping with jealousy. Why did he have to change after we got married? Such a pity. We really could have had fun. But it was nothing but his bloody business after the first year. Oh, dear, never mind. . . . I wonder what they're doing out there."

"Davina and Pavel? I don't know; walking, I imagine."

"Through the dew and the nettles," Charley said. "I wonder what they talk about? World affairs—or trade behind the Iron Curtain. I'd love to be a bird in a tree in those woods!"

"Finish your breakfast, darling, and get dressed," her mother said. "And you're not to be mischievous when they come back. Davina won't like being teased."

"No, she never did like it," Charley said. "She's never forgiven me for Richard. You know that, don't you?"

"She will," Mrs. Graham said soothingly. "Just as soon as she's found somebody of her own and she's happy, you'll be friends again."

Charley got up and slipped an arm around her mother's shoulders. She kissed her lightly on the cheek. "You're such a sweet optimist. Let's hope you're right." She went upstairs to dress.

"I thought of staying," Sasanov said. "Of making contact with the West and working with them like Penkovsky. But in Russia the life of a traitor is short. I wouldn't have lasted long enough. So I made plans to come over. I gave a long report on Jacob and his wife; whatever I said couldn't harm him—but I tried to clear her of political activity. It didn't make any difference. She will be an old woman when she comes back from twelve years' hard labor. Probably she'll die too. She wasn't a strong girl."

"How long did you take to make up your mind?"

Davina walked beside him. The grass was very wet, but a bright sunshine filtered through the trees, and there was a smell of green things growing, mixed with the pungent earth. It was a clear, glorious morning.

"I can remember the day. Really it was the middle of the night. August twentieth. We were in the country for the weekend. My wife was asleep beside me. I hadn't made love to her for months. Not since Jacob's death. She didn't ask me why; she knew how disturbed I was, how unhappy. She was asleep and I was awake. I knew I couldn't go on living as I'd done before. I couldn't go on with the KGB. This job was to track down people like the Belezkys and bring them to the authorities to punish. To put in asylums and destroy them with drugs and torture. Or to send them to the Gulag, like Jacob's wife, who'd never done anything but love him.

"I made my choice then. I would defect. I slept afterwards, for the first time in many, many weeks."

"You had to leave your family," she said. "How could you justify that?"

"Because I couldn't take them," he answered. "I knew I had to go alone. Nobody could blame them if they were left behind. So long as they knew nothing, they would be safe. That's what I thought then. Now I'm not sure anymore. I have that one photograph of them walking in the street. And your promise that they are free and well." He stopped and looked at her.

"Have you lied to me? Tell me. I must have the truth now."

"I haven't lied," Davina answered. "They're perfectly all right."

He turned away and began walking. "I have something your Brigadier wants," he said. "More than just information. I can tell him how to make use of it. I can put a weapon in his hands that will save the Middle East and the oil."

"If you tell me," she said, and she managed to keep the excitement out of her voice, "I'll put it to him. And we can work out a deal together."

"I don't want to live the rest of my life in this little country," he said. "It suffocates me. I want my wife and daughter with me. I'll work with your people for two years. After that, I'll choose where we want to go."

"That's very reasonable," she said. "I'm sure he'll agree to that."

Sasanov quickened his pace. "He'll agree to anything I ask," he said. "But I don't want words from him. I want Fedya and my daughter— here, beside me. Then I will talk to him and his people. They come over first."

They had reached the end of the little wood; they came out into the sunshine, at the top of a rolling field. The views across the hills were so spectacular that Davina caught hold of his sleeve and made him stop. The village church probed a gray stone finger of steeple into the sky, and the majestic undulations of Salisbury Plain stretched out on either side of them like a colored quilt.

"Look at that," she challenged. "How can you say you'd suffocate here!"

He saw her smile at him, and slowly he smiled back. "You would understand only if I could show you Russia," he said. "One day maybe you will go there. Then you'll think of me."

They began to walk across the brow of the field. The constant wind that swept across the plain whipped at Davina's hair and stung their faces.

"Supposing your family won't come over," she said. "Then what happens?"

"You must get a message to them—from me. I know they will come."

"But you've got to face the alternative," she persisted. "What will you do if they refuse? Or we fail—"

"If they refuse," he said, "I will go back."

"You can't!" Davina swung around on him, both hands holding her flying hair off her face. The wind rose suddenly and buffeted them.

She said again, "You can't—you'll be killed! If they did that to Belezky, what do you think will happen to you?"

He took her hand and turned her around. With their backs to the wind they broke into a stumbling run down the hill to the shelter of the wood. He shouted his answer.

"I can make a deal; there was no deal for Jacob and the others. For a man who goes to the West and then comes home, there is always forgiveness."

"I can't hear you properly," she said. "Oh, this damned wind."

They were in shelter as quickly as the wind had caught them. The sky was serenely blue, and the sun shone. A flock of little clouds flew past them to the west.

"I can protect myself," he said. "I can be publicly rehabilitated. And perhaps I can work against them from inside."

"Then you won't stay without your family?"

"No."

"All right." She nodded. "Then we'll just have to get them for you. Do you want to walk down to the village? It's very pretty. You've never been into a pub, have you?"

"Are you sure your Brigadier would allow it?" he asked her. "I don't believe he's let you take me off without some security arrangements."

"I'm quite sure he hasn't," she said. "But we won't see them. Not unless you go off on your own."

"Take me to your pub, then," Sasanov said. "But, please, not to drink your beer!"

She laughed and said, "I promise."

There was a fine color in her face; the shadows of their sleepless night no longer showed; the severe hairstyle was in total disarray, and she looked younger, more buoyant. As they walked down the road toward the little village pub she took his arm possessively.

Sasanov knew how she was feeling. The long months of patience had ended in success. Professionally, she was elated, and excited. And she had stepped across the barrier that was her best protection. He was a man and not a challenge anymore. A man who had chosen her bed in preference to the sister who had undermined her confidence and somehow earned her hatred. He amused himself wondering which of the parked cars in the village street belonged to the Brigadier's surveillance men, and whether some of them were crowded around the bar inside the pub.

He remembered the postcard she had bought him at Stonehenge. He had no money.

"Lend me something," he murmured to her. "I want to pay for what we drink."

"Most men don't mind these days if a woman treats them," Davina said.

"I mind," Sasanov retorted. "Lend me the money."

"I'm surprised Russians are so old-fashioned," she whispered. "Here's five pounds. I'll have a glass of white wine."

He took the money from her and shouldered his way to the bar.

Davina saw a man reading the *Mirror* in a corner seat lower the paper just enough to take a look at him. Special Branch, she said to herself. Or the department's own surveillance team. He talks so confidently of going back to Russia if things don't work out. . . . She folded her hands and studied her nails; if she painted them they would look quite nice. . . . He must know what he was talking about. It was just that she couldn't imagine the Brigadier letting him go.

They stayed in the bar till half past twelve. When they left to go back up the drive to the house, the man reading the newspaper put it on the table beside him and stood in the window for a minute. The driver of a parked Ford Cortina on the other side of the road started the engine and began to cruise in the same direction till he saw the man and woman turn in at the gates and disappear. He made a note that they were arm in arm and seemed to be on very close terms. He spoke quietly into a radiotelephone and went on past Marchwood House. Someone else would take over from him for the afternoon.

4

"Do you have to go so early?" Captain Graham couldn't hide his disappointment.

Charley leaned toward him; she was balanced on the arm of his big chair, with one arm resting on the back. They made a charming picture; age and beauty smiling at each other. Her announcement that she was leaving after tea had changed her father's smile to a reproachful frown.

"You haven't been for such a long time, and you're dashing off so quickly. Why don't you at least stay for dinner?"

"I would, darling," she said, "but I promised this girl friend of mine I'd go to a party she's giving. She'd be so upset if I didn't go. Don't be cross with me." She murmured quietly, "I'll come down next weekend—I promise. If Davy isn't here."

"Let's go outside," her father said. "A quick stroll in the garden."

Davina saw them leave together; she was reading the newspaper, and Sasanov was dozing in an armchair. His face looked tired and gaunt in repose. She noted her father and her sister walking past the window a minute later, arm in arm and talking earnestly. He had never been intimate with her, or taken her arm. She didn't care, she thought; she wasn't jealous anymore or hurt because he made such a display of favoritism. She had her own life, her own world. She could shut *him* out now.

She was glad Sasanov had relaxed enough to fall asleep. She kept her sense of triumph and excitement to herself, confident that nothing showed. And it was more than just professional satisfaction. She had proved something to herself, or rather the Russian had proved it to her. She had something to offer a man. His dismissal of her sister was devastating in its perception. He hadn't been fooled by the beauty and charm and sexual magnetism that had made idiots of clever men before. ". . . all she would do with a man is take." And with that assessment, Sasanov had discarded Charley. "I needed a woman who could give."

She had given gladly, and she would go on, if he wanted it. She could help him get the best possible terms from the Brigadier, insist on his wife and daughter being smuggled out of Russia. And feel no jealousy that he wanted them. She knelt by the fire and lit it, watching the little flames flickering among the wood and catching hold.

The room was still and peaceful, and the fire warmed her as she sat on the floor, still holding the matches. She wanted Sasanov to be happy. They were allies now, instead of adversaries, and she felt a tremendous relief. There was a movement behind her and she turned. He was awake, watching her.

"You look like a little girl, sitting on the floor," he said.

"You slept for a bit," she said. "Do you want some tea?"

"I hate English tea."

"Don't be bad-tempered. I'll put lemon in it."

"Where has everyone gone?"

"My mother's in the garden I think, and my father and Charley are out walking."

"You have an obsession in this country," he remarked. "Every minute you go for a walk."

Davina saw the provocative look in his eye and stood up. "I'll get some tea for you," she said blandly. "Don't let the fire go down."

In the garden, Charley was explaining her reason for going back to London.

"It's not just my girl friend, darling," she said. "I don't like to say it to you, but it's difficult for me with Davina here. It's nearly two years since I've seen her, and she's just as angry over Richard. You'd think after five years she'd have stopped hating me for it."

"I was afraid this might happen," her father said grimly. "I warned your mother she'd be awkward. The trouble is, she's never found anyone else. He was her one chance, I suppose." He sighed. "You can't help it if Richard fell in love with you. The pity is, you married him. She can't get over that—anyway that's what your mother says, and she's probably right. But it's a damned nuisance. I'd been looking forward to you coming down and spending a nice weekend at home. After all, it's her own fault if she wants to be an old maid! She's never made an effort with anyone else. But she won't come down again, not for a time, anyway. So you come next weekend, Charley darling, and we'll have you to ourselves."

She squeezed his arm affectionately. "I will; I promise. And don't say anything to Mother about this, will you? I don't want to upset her."

"I won't," her father said. "Let's go in, shall we? It's turning cold. Have some tea before you go?"

She saw the pleading in his face, and said, "Of course I will. We'll have some together in the kitchen. Then I'll pack and be on my way."

They had always been intimates; even as a tiny child, she had felt a sympathy with her father that was closer than with anyone else. He gave her a feeling of comfort and reassurance; when she was naughty as a little girl she never doubted his forgiveness, and she had the same certainty in adult life. He hadn't reproached her for taking Davina's fiancé and marrying him, even against her family's advice. When that marriage ended in under two years, with her husband drinking and near-bankrupt, Captain Graham had welcomed her home and set his solicitors on the unfortunate Richard. Her second attempt had seemed more promising; this time the man was not an infatuated young architect, but a very rich man some ten years older, with a property and investment company. When that marriage too fell to pieces, Charley sped home to be comforted and reassured that for the second time she was in the right.

Yet she believed it only when she was with her parents. Or when she was at the beginning of a new love affair, and it seemed that she was going to find the same unequivocal adoration she associated with her father. Then her self-assurance and optimism overcame her common sense, and the new adventure was begun without a thought for the outcome. Love for Charley was a constant search that always promised perfect happiness and ultimately always disappointed.

She was devoted to her parents, but she couldn't stay with them too long, unless she was hurt or unhappy and needed to be set right. She had never understood the need to run away from them after a time; she merely followed her impulse, and felt vaguely guilty. She made tea now for her father in the kitchen, and they shared it like conspirators. Then she said she must pack and start the drive back. At the kitchen door, Charley slipped an arm around her father's neck and, reaching up, kissed him.

"I'm sorry the weekend's been so short," she said "And don't forget— you're my best beau!" It was her way of saying good night to him when she was very young and going to a party or a dance, with some admirer fidgeting by the front door. She didn't recognize that, unfortunately for her, it was the truth.

She said a brief and casual goodbye to Davina. She and the Pole were crouching over the fire with teacups in their hands, and for a moment Charley had a feeling she was intruding. She didn't approach Davina; she stood in the doorway, displaying another facet of her amazing good looks. The beautiful traveler about to embark, suitcase in one hand, the other raised in a graceful wave. She saw them turn from each other and look at her, and there was something close, almost intimate, about them, although they were not sitting together, not touching in any way. The Pole stood up, but didn't move toward her as most men did, looking for an excuse to hold her hand while they said goodbye. He loomed with his back to the fire and the lamplight behind him. He seemed solid, menacing, not the easy captive she had first judged him. And her sister's face held something secret and yet triumphant.

"Goodbye," they said, one after the other. She echoed it with a gaiety she didn't feel, and quickly shut the door on them.

"Well," Davina said loudly. "That was a short visit. She must have some poor devil in tow in London. Let's have a drink."

Sasanov pressed heavily on her shoulder with his hand. The fingers hurt.

"Let's go upstairs," he said.

Normally, Jeremy Spencer-Barr avoided beautiful girls. They made him uncomfortable, with their expectation that he was going to be attracted to them. He spent the first half hour at the cocktail party that evening talking to a man who was in a City merchant bank and getting Mary to introduce him to a playboy financier much mentioned in *Private Eye*. He sought contacts and information wherever he went, storing up the most trivial information in case it should link up with something else. His appetite for conspiracy was whetted by the merchant banker's remarks about the financier, and by rumors that he was involved in arms deals from America en route to the IRA.

"Oh, there's Charley Ransom," Mary said, tugging at his arm. "I don't think I'll introduce you, darling. She's a real man-eater."

Jeremy looked across at the girl who had just come in. He didn't like red hair, but she was startlingly beautiful. The description of a man-eater didn't recommend her.

"You don't have to worry about me," he said.

"Her sister works in the Ministry, too," Mary said. "There was quite a scandal in the Graham family when Charley walked off with the sister's fiancé."

"Did you say Graham?" he asked her.

"Yes, she was Charlotte Graham before she got married. I've never met the sister; she's some kind of high-powered secretary. Come on, darling, of course I'll introduce you—I was only joking."

"All right," Jeremy said casually.

He followed Mary and found himself standing next to the beautiful girl with the hair he didn't like. There were several men circling around her. He saw Mary kiss her; it was a habit that mystified him. He disliked the social kiss between men and women; when two females did it, it was either hypocritical or pointless.

"Jeremy Spencer-Barr, this is Charlotte Ransom."

"Charley, please," the girl said. "Charlotte's such a mouthful." She gave him a dazzling, friendly smile.

Graham, a high-powered secretary in the Ministry of Defence. He just wanted to make sure. He was mentally recalling Davina Graham on the one occasion they had met, and he couldn't see any family likeness to Charlotte Ransom. Except, of course, the hair. Not as red or as abundant, but similar in color. Darker, more auburn.

"I hear you have a sister who works in the Defence Ministry," he said. "I work there, too. I wonder if we've met."

"I don't know—have you? Davina never talks about her work. Funnily enough, I've seen her this weekend at home."

"Really. It's a big place and there must be a lot of Grahams working there. Who's her boss?"

"An old family friend. Brigadier James White. Have you been away or do you spend the weekends in London?" she asked. Men didn't usually talk about a third person when they met her. She thought him quite good-looking, but rather cool.

"Yes, unfortunately. I don't go away all that often. I think I have met your sister—what a coincidence. She isn't like you, if I may say so."

Charley accepted the compliment and decided not to move away just yet. "We're not really alike," she said, and laughed. "She's the serious one. I'm the one who gets into mischief."

"Lucky mischief," Jeremy responded quickly. He saw the gratification in her smile and called her a silly cow in private. He hated women who demanded flattery.

"Where have you been, then?" he said. "Where's home?"

"My parents live near Salisbury," Charley answered. "We've got a darling old house there, where Davy and I were brought up. I adore going back whenever I can tear myself away. I'm just in the middle of a divorce, and it's too depressing and dreary. You're Mary's friend, aren't you? I've heard a lot about you."

"I hope it's good," he said.

"Oh, yes—apparently you're quite something, Mr. Spencer-Barr. Lucky Mary."

"Yes, aren't I?" Mary Walker said. She slipped her arm through Jeremy's and gave Charley a sweet smile.

"I'm trying to think when or where I met your sister," Jeremy said. What the hell was she doing away for the weekend? Did that mean she'd been taken off Sasanov, and if so, who had replaced her? "She's not married, is she? Some people go on using their maiden names when they're working."

"No," Charley said. "She's not married."

She was becoming bored again with the return to Davina as a subject, and poor Mary Walker standing guard over her property in case he was lured away. The remark that followed was defensive, because Mary Walker knew what had happened with Richard; also there was a pause, and Charley liked to keep a conversation going.

"She had a rather peculiar Pole staying the weekend, too," she said gaily. "I just had a feeling romance was in the air. Not that she'd admit anything, of course. Next thing we know, she'll be whizzed behind the Iron Curtain."

There was a general laugh in which Jeremy joined. A Pole . . . Good God above—could it be? He needed a moment to think and recover himself. He offered to get them drinks and slipped away. A Pole—it must be Sasanov; there was no other explanation. A weekend away from supervision, introduction to a family. Romance in the air. He must have broken and committed himself to cooperating with the West. And if that supremely vain and superficial girl was right, the minder had become the mistress. He went back with three glasses and a bright smile. The rest of the platitudes and party conversation floated over him. He let Mary steer him away and then pretended to be going to the lavatory to get away from her. He came back into the room and passed Charlotte Ransom, who was holding court over a group of grinning men. He touched her lightly on the arm.

"We're leaving in a minute," he said. "Could I phone you sometime?"

It was such a normal occurrence for other women's men to make approaches to her that Charley didn't even hesitate.

"I'd love that," she said. "I'm in the book. Portman Place."

"I'll be in touch," Jeremy murmured, and passed on. A few minutes later he left the party. He took Mary out to dinner and was especially nice to her. Compared to women like Davina Graham's sister, she was pure gold. If it hadn't been for his career, he really would have married her. As it was, he was going to telephone Charlotte Ransom and take her out to dinner. He was going to New York in a fortnight and he hadn't any time to waste. . . .

Davina took Sasanov back early on Monday morning. Both parents stood outside the front door, waving politely as they drove away. Her father had been noticeably cool to her, and her mother fussed to make up for it. The last part of the visit had been less successful than the beginning, and she connected the change in atmosphere with her sister's early departure. If Sasanov was aware of a strain between them, he didn't comment. He had accompanied Mrs. Graham on a long tour of her garden, and she whispered to Davina later that she found him really charming and most interested in plants. He rumpled his bed in the morning to pretend that he had slept in it, having spent Sunday night with Davina.

She glanced in the rearview mirror as they swung out onto the main road, and noticed a gray Audi following them. It had picked them up as soon as they drove out of Marchwood; it would remain with them until they were safely behind the gates of Halldale Manor.

Sasanov had seen her look in the mirror and he had noticed the escorting car. "Back to the cage," he remarked.

"Not for long," Davina said quickly. "As soon as you've reached an agreement with the Brigadier, you can choose where to stay. I think I'll go up this afternoon and see him."

"You should be promoted for this," Sasanov said.

"I don't mind about that," she answered. "I just want everything to work out well. I want you to have your family with you, and to give us your full cooperation. That'll be my reward."

"You like a happy ending," he said. "Like the fairy stories? Russian stories don't have happy endings. The witch turns into a wolf and eats the children."

She glanced at him, and then concentrated on the road.

"You're the most morbid person I've ever met," she said. "You love looking on the black side. I think you do it just to annoy me."

"Perhaps I do," Sasanov admitted. "Perhaps I am just superstitious, and afraid of tempting the fates."

"There's no such thing as fate," she said firmly. "People make their own destinies. Fate didn't bring you to England, you decided to come. And it certainly won't be fate that gets your wife and daughter out of Russia!"

"What will it be if you fail?"

"We won't fail," she said. "I promise you."

She didn't know what made her think of Peter Harrington on her way up to London. Perhaps it was her own success contrasting with his failure and depression; on impulse she rang through to his section in Personnel while she was waiting to see the Brigadier, and suggested they meet for a drink afterward.

As soon as she walked into his office, James White knew that she had come to report success. There was an air of confidence about her, of buoyancy, that was unusual. He gained his impressions in a few seconds, while he got up and shook hands and she settled into the chair in front of his desk.

He smiled at her, and before she could begin he said, "You've made progress, Miss Graham. I can see that you're pleased about something. The weekend went off well?"

"It was the catalyst we needed," she said. "He's ready to make a deal with you."

"Congratulations," he said gently. "How did you do it?"

"He did it himself," she said. "He reached his crisis point and I happened to be there. He wants his wife and daughter brought over here. Then he'll cooperate fully with us, for the next two years. He doesn't want to settle in England after that; he doesn't like it here. My guess is somewhere like Canada."

The Brigadier didn't answer at once.

"The wife and daughter . . ." he said slowly. "That's a pity."

Davina looked at him. "Why? Nothing's happened to them, has it? My God, I promised him they were all right!"

"And so they are, as far as we know," James White answered. "Did you guarantee we'd be able to smuggle them out?"

"I had to," she said flatly. "Otherwise he wants to go home. And he means it. I don't know if you can prevent him."

"Not with our present Home Secretary," the Brigadier said sourly. "And unless he's willing, he's useless to us. But you've done very well; I do congratulate you. Taking him home was your idea, and I must confess I thought it rather an odd thing to do. But obviously you judged the situation absolutely right. When had I better see him? Is he ready now?"

"Not ready to do more than whet your appetite," Davina said firmly. "He's made his terms quite clear. I think it would be a good thing to keep the momentum going; he just might slip back and get depressed if nothing happens quickly. He'd like to meet you and start preliminary talks."

"We can arrange it now," the Brigadier said. He looked at his desk diary, and frowned. "This week, you think . . . hmmm. Thursday seems possible, with a little juggling." He switched on his desk intercom. His secretary answered.

"Change my late-afternoon appointments for Thursday, will you? No, never mind, put them off till the next week. Yes. Thank you."

"Will you come down?" Davina asked him.

"No." He considered for a moment. "No, I think it would be less conspicuous if we met in London. At my club. I go there once or twice a week anyway, and nobody is going to suspect anything unusual. They certainly won't expect to see Sasanov walking into the Garrick at five o'clock on a Thursday." He gave a little chuckle. "Put a hat and some spectacles on him and deliver him there on Thursday. I'll arrange for a security cover for both of you. You wait in the car and I'll be in the hall to meet him at five o'clock."

He got up to end the interview; his eyes were bright and friendly.

"You're a clever girl," he said gently. "I knew I was right in giving him to you."

There was a few seconds' pause while he looked at her and didn't put out his hand to shake hers. She felt suddenly that he was going to ask the one question she didn't want to answer. Which was irrelevant anyway. But the Brigadier said nothing. He shook hands with her and walked with her to the door.

"Keep him happy till Thursday," he said.

She went out of the room wondering exactly what that last remark had meant. He couldn't know; there was no way he could find out that Sasanov had made up his mind after making love to her. In the best tradition of female spies, she thought, and smiled to herself as she went down in the lift to Personnel to pick up Peter Harrington.

Peter rejected the local pub as a suitable place to talk over a drink.

"To hell with the expense," he said, grinning at her. "We're going to get pissed in style this time—I'm taking you to a dark romantic little bar in wicked Jermyn Street."

"Jules's," she said. "I know, it's your second home when you're in London. It's a pound every time you eat an olive. I suppose I'm put down to expenses?"

"You are," he agreed. He watched her as she drove up Pall Mall. She seemed relaxed, less shut into herself. Quite an attractive woman, he decided, and was surprised at the way his imagination was working. He had never thought of Davina Graham in the nude before.

They settled into a corner in the little bar, and he ordered a vodka martini for her and whiskey for himself. The waiter brought a dish of olives, and she took one and laughed.

"How's life in the country?" he said.

"Very good," she answered.

"It seems to suit you," he remarked. "I know you can't talk about what you're doing, so I'll tell you all the deepest secrets of Personnel."

"Tell me about New York instead," she said. "Has Spencer-Barr gone out yet?"

"No, he hasn't. Due in a fortnight or ten days. He called in and asked me out to lunch. To brief him on *my* contacts."

"Did you go?" She sipped the martini.

"Yes, I went. I chose the most expensive things on the menu, drank myself stupid, and gave the sod the bare minimum. He knew it, too, but he couldn't say anything. He just paid the bill and walked off. I wove my way back to the office and fell asleep over the Bs in the card index."

"Why the Bs?"

"I don't know," he said. "I must have been trying to look him up—hoping his name was Barikov, or something. Anyway, he'll have no joy at all with my Rumanian. He'll turn on that upper-class public-school charm, and Gregory Vitescu will run a mile. Three years' ground work chucked away. . . . The East German may take to him; he wants money and he'd trust the type. Personally I hope he makes a real cock-up of both of them." He swallowed a lot of his drink. "I've never hated anyone before. But I hate him; I wonder why."

"Because he's a conceited, ruthless little climber," Davina said. "And you told me, he walked all over you when he got the posting. That's reason enough."

"Yes, I suppose it is," he muttered. "And yet it isn't, quite. I've met shits like him before; they're in the Service like everywhere else. Run you down without a backward look. All right, I was furious at the way I was recalled; I hated having some bloody jumped-up new boy put in so he can get the credit for the hard work I did. But apart from all that, I just get a gut feeling when I'm with him that he's nastier and more unscrupulous than anyone I've met in a long time. And he's young, Davina—fifteen years younger than I am. I ought to be able to wipe the floor with him."

"I wonder how he feels about you," she said. "Don't underestimate yourself, Peter; you can be quite a hard-nose, too."

"He despises me," Harrington answered. "He despised me for getting drunk and showing I minded when we had lunch. He despised me for trying to hold back anything he'd find helpful. He knew exactly what I was doing. I told you, outside the bloody restaurant he just turned his back on me and walked away."

"You mustn't let it get to you like this," she said slowly. "He's going out there, and if he makes a mess of your two contacts the Brigadier won't find any excuses. Forget about him, Peter. Why don't you enjoy yourself, now you've got a bit of time? I remember you moaning about missing test matches, and longing to get married, but who would put up with the life—all that sort of thing. Kicking isn't going to do you any good. Work away at Personnel; grin and bear it and wait for the little beast to fall on his face. Then you can go to the Chief and gently remind him about your old job."

He smiled and reached out, squeezing her hand. He held on to it, until she pulled it away.

"You're a wonderful girl, Davy. And you're dead right, of course. I'm in the doghouse and the more I grumble, the longer I'll stay there. What I really need is a new assignment, something I can get hold of and prove I'm not finished. Do you know that's one of the things White said to me? 'You're not a young man anymore, my dear chap. Spencer-Barr has youth on his side.' As if experience didn't count. . . . Waiter? Two more, please."

Davina leaned back and said casually, "How much did you drink in the States, Peter?"

He jerked round to look at her. "What the hell do you mean, how much did I drink? Who's been talking to you behind my back?"

"You have," she said. "Listen, Peter, I'm fond of you, and we've known each other for a long time. But I'm not going to sit here listening to you moaning and groaning unless you tell me the truth. Was your drinking a factor or not?"

"Oh, well, hell—yes, I suppose it was," he said sulkily. "I got a bit of a reputation, and the word got back. It never made any difference to my work—everyone in New York and Washington gets pissed out of their minds now and then. It had nothing to do with it."

"They don't get pissed when they're trying to recruit two double agents in high-sensitivity areas," she said. "Why don't you face that, to start with? Stop drinking. Be seen to stop drinking. Never mind what's wrong with Spencer-Barr. Take a good look at yourself, Peter, and for God's sake either put the cork in the bottle or resign from the Service and do something else!"

"My God!" He stared at her aggressively. "My God, I'm glad I asked you out for a drink! Any more lectures before I pay the bill?"

"I asked to see *you,* as it happens," she said calmly. "And I've had an idea, but there's no point discussing it with you if you're going to be adolescent. Spencer-Barr may be fifteen years younger than you, but he struck me as fully grown up. Get me some cigarettes, will you?"

The waiter had brought their second drinks, and she waited for Harrington's reaction.

"What do you like?" he said sullenly.

"Twenty Benson and Hedges," she told him.

"I'd just like to know," he said when he returned, "why you've suddenly decided to kick me where it hurts."

She gave him a cigarette and lit it for him. "I'm not trying to hurt you, you idiot. I'm giving you very good advice. You're a Service man; you wouldn't know what to do outside it. I wouldn't, either, and I haven't been in it half as long. You've let yourself slip, Peter. That's why you were recalled. You're far too young and too valuable to be retired, and that's what will happen. Don't think Spencer-Barr won't have dropped hints about the lunch—he's just the type. Go on the wagon and make sure everyone knows it. And keep yourself fit. You've got flabby."

"Oh, Christ," Harrington moaned. "What are you suggesting—a run round the park every morning?"

Davina sipped her drink and smiled. "It's an idea," she said. "You might need to run for it one day."

"What on earth are you talking about?" he said. He had stopped being angry.

"I told you, I've got an idea. Nothing may come of it; but nothing will, unless you pull yourself together. You want to get back to active work, don't you?"

"Yes," he said. "I'd give anything. And you're right, I've let myself slip. You can't tell me any more?"

"No, not till I've thought it out properly. And I'm afraid I can't say anything till I've sold it to the Chief."

"You won't find it very easy to sell me," he said. He picked up the whiskey and looked at it. "I don't want to waste it," he said. "Especially as it seems likely to be my last."

He drank it, and pushed the empty glass away across the table. "I'm sorry if I was rude to you, Davy. I just wasn't expecting to be told I'd turned into a boozy slob." He grinned at her, half defensively. "Even though it's true. Do you have to get back or will you stay and let me buy you a nice dinner? I'd really like to—to say thanks, for helping me. And just incidentally because I'm bloody lonely and I think you're looking particularly good tonight. Stay, won't you?"

She hesitated. He looked even more bedraggled and tired, and the hand holding his cigarette was shaking slightly. She knew it would annoy Sasanov if she came home late. The empty glass stared at her like an eye.

"I'll make a call to see if everything's all right," she said.

"There's a booth at the back there," he said. "Nice and private for making lovers' trysts and phoning up a tart for the evening. Here's some change."

She dialed the private number at Halldale, and immediately Roberts answered.

"It's me," she said. "Put him on, will you, please?"

There was a pause, and then Sasanov's voice came through. She didn't let him talk.

"I won't be back till late," she said. "I'm having dinner here."

"Why? I am expecting you." She heard the irritation and allowed herself a little smile.

"I'm trying to make arrangements," she said. "Travel arrangements. I'll be back about twelve. I'll look in to see if you're awake."

"I'll wait for you," Sasanov said. "In your room."

"No," Davina said hurriedly. "No, don't do that. I'll explain later. I'll come to you."

She hung up. Explain—about the bugs and the two-way mirror, monitored by Roberts and his assistant. She thought of the word Sasanov used. A cage. Now it was a cage for them both.

She went back and sat down with Peter Harrington. She managed a cheerful smile. "That's fixed," she said.

"Good." He looked pleased. "Tell me one thing—don't you get sick of having to hold his hand?"

Davina shook her head. "No comment; that's classified information. Where are we going to eat? I feel like spaghetti and red wine."

"And that is what you'll have," he said. "Let's go, shall we? I know a nice little place in Lower Belgrave Street."

Outside in the street he took her arm. "But I'm right about one thing," he said, guiding her across the road. "There's something wrong with Spencer-Barr!"

Elizabeth Cole had worked as a filing clerk in the Moscow embassy for three years. She was a plump, friendly girl with a regular boy friend on the security staff; she blended well into her background and was regarded as efficient but not too intelligent. She had worked for SIS since she was twenty-two, and had been recruited into White's organization by an uncle. Her uncle had parachuted into France with the Special Operations Group, and he remained in close contact with his colleagues. Like all her paternal family, Elizabeth Cole was bilingual in French; her grandmother came from La Boule, and her children and grandchildren maintained their French language and affiliations. Outwardly there was nothing Gallic about Elizabeth; she was as typically English as cheese and pickles—it was a description she published about herself. She worked in the filing section of the embassy, and her true function was to maintain contacts with the Russian dissidents in the capital.

She was given her instructions by the chief intelligence officer in the embassy, and at three o'clock on Tuesday afternoon she set off. She shopped at Gum first, spending a long time on buying a poor-quality sweater which she didn't want. Then she took a bus and went into a little café. She chose an empty table, ordered tea and sweet cakes, and opened her Russian newspaper while she waited. Fifteen minutes later, a young woman joined her. She too ordered tea. The café was filling up with casual customers, tired and thirsty. The volume of noise increased as the two women talked.

Elizabeth knew that the girl was a former lecturer in economics at Moscow University. She had been suspended for signing a petitition for the release of the imprisoned poet Vladimir Bokov. She was in disfavor but not yet deeply suspect. It was hoped to rehabilitate her at the university.

"What news of Sasanov's family?" Elizabeth asked her in French. The other girl didn't speak good English.

"They haven't been harmed. They're still living in their apartment. The daughter is still allowed to go to her classes."

"Can you get a message to them?"

"I don't know. It would be very difficult. I can't approach them myself."

"Could you find somebody else?" Elizabeth asked. "We don't want to risk one of our people."

"Nobody goes near them but police spies."

"What is the daughter's attitude? Can you find that out?"

"I have friends in the university," the girl said. "They are trying to get me reinstated. I have to publish a retraction and an apology." Her eyes filled with tears. "If I'm going to fight them, it has to be done from inside. I will do what they want. I can make inquiries about Sasanov's daughter. If she's safe to contact, I can maybe get a message to her in the university. Otherwise, it can't be done. They are being watched at home, and Sasanov's wife hardly ever goes out."

"If you can find someone we can trust, someone in the university," Elizabeth Cole murmured. "This is very important."

"I know it is," the Russian girl answered. "We know that Sasanov tried to help poor Jacob Belezky. Wherever he is or whatever has happened to him, it's our duty to help his family if we can. I'll meet you here next week and tell you what progress I've made."

"Thank you," Elizabeth said. "And take care."

The girl smiled sadly. "I'll do my best. It's the hypocrisy, the lies, thinking what Bokov will feel when he hears I've abandoned him."

"He'll understand," Elizabeth said. "I'll go now. I'll be here at the same time next Tuesday. Good luck."

She paid for her tea, gathered her shopping bag and newspaper and went out into the sunny Moscow streets. The Security Police has stopped following her a long time ago. She had established a routine of buying something at Gum on her day off and relaxing in the same café over a cup of Russian tea. She had never met anyone there or varied her routine for the first year of her posting. By which time she was classified as filing clerk, and of no political importance. The word that she was clear took a little time and a very circuitous route to reach London. When it did, the café was chosen as her rendezvous with fellow agents.

The Soviet dissidents were part of a closed circle of Russian society, where the different grades tended to mix exclusively with their own kind.

The dissidents came from the upper intelligentsia, from those artists and scientists whose privileged position in the Soviet hierarchy encouraged them to challenge authority. What the humble people thought of liberty and human rights had no chance of being heard. Jacob Belezky became the friend and confident of Bokov the poet and Scherensky the physicist. The dissidents had become a group, and they were making their opinions public to the West. Arrests, imprisonment, false accusations of treason, and heavy punishments failed to silence their protests. The infamy of psychiatric punishment had replaced the traditional agony of Siberia as the worst fate for a Russian.

But a few brave voices cried for justice; as one was silenced, so another spoke up. The young lecturer was a rarity. She was going to renounce her dissident views and become an agent for the West. When she was fully recruited Elizabeth Cole would pass her on to another controller.

Elizabeth signed herself into the embassy, humming cheerfully, and later she added the sweater to a trunkful of shoddy clothes that she would never wear.

5

Sasanov was bored by television. He had eaten alone, complaining to Roberts about the food and demanding more drink to be sent up. He read the newspapers again and threw them aside. The television news was full of gloomy economic predictions and followed by a turgid drama with four-letter words instead of dialogue. He was irritable and uneasy because Davina hadn't come back. She was talking about travel arrangements. The meaning was obvious and he suspected it was not true. The delay was part of a campaign to undermine him; she was waiting for the Brigadier's answer, and either he hadn't given the assurance Sasanov wanted or he was preparing a counterproposal, which Sasanov decided to reject on principle.

Pessimism had been gaining on him throughout the day. It had begun on the drive back from Wiltshire, when the frustrations of life at Halldale were already closing in on him. He felt unsettled and suspicious, and the longer he waited for her the more uncompromising his attitude became. He knew he had deliberately chosen to defect to England rather than the States; it had seemed marginally less treacherous to ally himself with a country that was only a secondary enemy of his own. He had fled when the opportunity arose; what he now had to give the head of SIS, in exchange for his resettlement with his family, was the key to Western recovery, if not to its survival. He could make his gesture in memory of Jacob Belezky, and all the other victims of totalitarian tyranny. He could

81

rank in his own eyes with the Russian patriots who had defied the Tsarist autocracy only to be betrayed by the beneficiaries of their struggle. He could live at peace with himself if he could strike that vital blow at his country's political system.

But he wasn't going to give it for nothing. He got up and began to pace around the room. Where was she? And why had she warned him not to go to her room? Was even that comfort to be denied him, just because they thought he had weakened and pledged himself too quickly? He poured a vodka and drank it down; on an impulse of bad temper, he tossed the glass into the grate. He looked at his watch; it didn't seem to be late, but it felt as if he had been waiting for hours. He was damned if he was going to bed and let Roberts and his cronies tuck themselves away for the night.

He rang the bell, and Roberts appeared in the doorway.

"I want vodka, pickles, black bread and sausage," Sasanov said. "I'm hungry."

"I'll bring it up," Roberts said woodenly. Sasanov snarled at him under his breath and turned away. How well he knew that type: the concrete face, the toneless voice, the overdeveloped muscles under the jacket.

When the tray was put in front of him, he didn't look up or speak. Very clever of them to send a woman to soften him. She had a way of meeting his moods and providing the right stimulus. He ate some of the food and drank the vodka. When he came home in the evening, his wife always had tea, black bread and vodka ready for him. She used to pour out the drink and cut the bread and dip it into the salt for him. He had always found her loving and protective; there were times when he liked to be a child and let her pet him. His daughter spoiled him, too. His home was a bastion against doubt and self-disgust; his wife understood, without needing to be told, how he was ripping himself to pieces because of Belezky. She would come to the West. He was certain she would come.

He pretended not to hear the door opening; he let Davina reach the sofa before he looked up.

"You shouldn't have waited," she said. "I drove back as quickly as I could."

"You seem pleased," he said. "You're smiling. I hope you can make me smile, too."

"I think I can," she said. "Why are you eating at this hour? Didn't you have any dinner?"

Her concern mollified him. He held out his hand to her, and when she took it he pulled her down to the sofa beside him.

"I missed your company," he said. "You are prettier than Roberts."

"Thank you." Davina bowed her head. "I can see you've been in a perfectly bloody mood. Never mind. Give me a drink and I'll tell you what happened."

Sasanov listened without interrupting.

"So we meet next Thursday. Is this club a safe place? Will you be there?"

"No, I'm the driver, that's all. The club is a marvelous rendezvous. No one is going to expect you to walk in, I can promise you. And he's very receptive; I made it clear that you wanted your family, and that unless they came, you would prefer to go back and take your chance. He knows exactly what the position is, and he didn't quibble at all."

"What does 'quibble' mean?" he asked. "I don't know that word."

"I'm sorry; it means hesitate, argue. Your English is so good I take it for granted."

"Five months of talking with you has helped," he said. "We find English very difficult."

"Well, you can see things are moving," she said. "You won't be in this cage for long. Aren't you happy about it?"

"Yes," he answered slowly, "yes, I think I am happy. Now we can go to bed."

She put a finger to her lips and shook her head. She found paper and a ballpoint pen in her bag and wrote on it: "We must be discreet. The rooms are bugged. I didn't say anything about that." He read it and wrote underneath: "I'll come to you later. Why didn't you tell him?" She scribbled a sentence in reply: "Because it's none of his business." He looked up at her and then screwed the paper into a long twill. She thrust it into the fire. He came behind her and kissed the back of her neck.

"Good night," he said.

"Good night," she answered. "Sleep well."

They went to their separate rooms, and the security staff allowed a decent interval and then retired to bed. While Davina waited for him, she justified to herself her reasons for not telling White that she was sleeping with Sasanov. It was not relevant; it was incidental, and she was therefore entitled to withhold it. The fact that they were lovers had nothing to do with Sasanov's decision, or the terms on which he would cooperate fully with the SIS. Quite the reverse, if you considered his insistence on his wife and daughter joining him. What happened between him and Davina was an interlude before that reunion. Professionally she was just as detached as she had ever been. The fact that they were lovers need not affect or concern anyone but themselves.

She didn't switch on the light or speak when he opened the door. He climbed into bed beside her and she put her arms around him.

The porter at the Garrick Club was a jovial bearded man with a sense of humor and an individual style of dealing with the members. He approached the big foreign-looking man standing in the outer hallway. Hearing the Brigadier's name, he nodded and led the guest up the short flight of steps to the main hall.

"He's in the members' room upstairs, sir. Up the main staircase; it's the door on your right."

"Thank you," Sasanov said. He didn't hurry; he appraised his surroundings with interest.

There was no comparable institution in Russia, no relic of the Tsarist past that compared with the supremely English institution of a gentleman's club. The Garrick itself was a magnificent building, the interior of the main hall decorated with busts in bronze and marble with inscriptions underneath that made no sense to Sasanov as he paused to read them. The main staircase was majestic, and hung with portraits and scenes from famous plays of the past. He paused on the top landing beside a display case glittering with paste jewelry and objects of extraordinary variety, from a lady's fan to a lock of graying hair. There was nothing of great value in the glass cases, but references to Shakespeare enlightened him a little: the Brigadier's club had connections with the theater. Sasanov couldn't imagine anything less appropriate to the head of Britain's Intelligence Service than a setting of eighteenth-century flamboyance.

He went into the room the hall porter had described, and found it enormous, with a high gilded ceiling, walls covered in pictures, and a few ugly mahogany tables and red leather chairs and settees. A central table displayed the latest newspapers. He saw a man rise from the far end of the room and recognized Brigadier James White. They had met briefly on his arrival in England. Little had been said on that occasion; they had circled each other mentally, in readiness for the encounter that had now come. There were only two other people in the room besides themselves: an old gray-haired man talking earnestly to a younger one. The acoustics of the room made it impossible to distinguish a word of their conversation. James White held out his hand, and Sasanov shook it.

"Sit down," the Brigadier said. "Can I offer you some coffee, and a brandy perhaps?"

"Coffee, thank you," Sasanov said. He could have the brandy later.

James White leaned back in his chair and looked at the Russian with an expresssion of calm satisfaction.

"I'm very pleased to hear you have reached a decision, Colonel," he said. "Miss Graham gave me a most encouraging report."

"Miss Graham is always optimistic," Sasanov said. "She has a cheerful nature."

"I'm glad you found it so." The Brigadier smiled. "She's a very intelligent and dedicated person. I felt sure you and she would reach an understanding. She tells me you have decided to cooperate with us and remain in the West. I hope that wasn't the optimism you mean?"

"No," Sasanov said. "She hasn't exaggerated, Brigadier. That is my decision; depending upon one thing, of course." He lit a cigarette, offering the packet to White, who refused.

"Your wife and daughter's safe arrival in the West," James White said. "And a choice of final home and identity for all of you after two years."

Sasanov blew smoke and watched it rise and disappear. "Are these conditions acceptable?"

"Acceptable, certainly," James White answered. "But possible is another matter. We're both professionals, Colonel, and you know even better than I do how difficult it is to extract Soviet citizens from Russia."

"It is not impossible," Sasanov said flatly. "You've done it before."

"With people like yourself," White reminded him. "Not a woman and a girl."

"I know it's difficult," Sasanov answered, "but it's your business to overcome the difficulties if you want the information I can give you."

"Oh, we want it," White said quietly. "We want it very badly, Colonel. But before I commit my Service to such a dangerous enterprise inside the Soviet Union, I would like more details of this information."

Sasanov leaned back in his chair and puffed the last of his cigarette.

"In the last seven years the West's sphere of influence in the Middle East has been steadily declining. Zionist sympathies in America were resented by the Arab world; Soviet hostility to Israel opened doors to us which had been closed before. We made very good use of the opportunities given to us by the Yom Kippur War; our military advisers were followed by technicians, and they joined the political experts who were already in Egypt, Syria, Libya and Iraq. War against Israel had nearly been won; the Arab world intended to win the next time, and we were going to help them. British influence was low, America was suspect; the training of the Palestinians had resulted in a powerful terror weapon which was used to harass Israel and its friends in the West. We were coming nearer and nearer to your oil supplies, Brigadier, and if it hadn't been for Sadat and Egypt, we would have got them.

"You know all this; you know how America succeeded in dividing Egypt from the rest of the Arab world, except for the Saudis and Iran, so Sadat made peace with Israel and threw our people out. He went to the West, and our work was destroyed. Our sympathizers and undercover agents were arrested and imprisoned. Egypt was lost to us. So a very important decision was made in Russia, at the highest level. A new campaign to disrupt Western economy was mapped out and the details were finalized. Libya we had, Iraq and Syria were still ours. The appeal of Arab nationalism had been weakened, because of Sadat. Another cause had to be found, Brigadier, and we found it—Islam."

James White was watching Sasanov as he talked; his expression was calm and interested, as if they were discussing matters of no importance—the price of cigars or the merits of the club clarets.

"Iran," he said. "That was a blow to us, certainly. But I can't accept that it was achieved in Moscow and not in Paris and New York, Colonel."

Sasanov smiled. "The mistakes of our enemies are our good fortune, Brigadier. That's an old Russian proverb. Khrushchev used to quote it to annoy your people. But it was true. France sheltered Khomeini because she wanted to embarrass the Americans, and then when it seemed the Shah was going to fall and the Ayatollah would come back in triumph France supported him, to safeguard her own oil supplies. America allowed the Shah to fall; not because they didn't know the revolution was gathering, but because they thought it would succeed, and they too wanted to be in favor with the winning side. We had a lot of luck, Brigadier, but it was our plan and you know very well how successful it has been. It was the first move in a whole series."

"And what is the second move?" White asked him.

"That is what I have to offer," Sasanov said. "I will give you the details of Soviet intentions in the Middle East for the next two years, and I will interpret events as they take place and explain to you the sequences which will follow. This much I'll give as a proof of goodwill: The next target is the Saudi royal family."

"I see," White said. "A complete encirclement of the Middle East oil

supply, one source after another, with a strike at NATO in the heart of
it? Colonel, I think we will be able to reunite you with your wife and
daughter, if I have to go to Moscow myself. Shall we shake hands on
it?"

Sasanov reached out and they shook hands. Both had a hard dry
grip.

"One more thing, Brigadier."

"Yes?"

"I would like to move from my lunatic asylum."

"Oh dear," the Brigadier said, "I'm sorry you feel like that about it. I
thought you were quite comfortable. Miss Graham should have told
me."

"I am comfortable," Sasanov said. "But I am sick of the same little
cage, day after day for eight months. And I have no privacy."

"Well, of course, if Miss Graham is getting on your nerves—"

"Not Miss Graham. Roberts and the others. I want a safe house, not a
cage. No bugs, no trick mirrors. I have to trust you, so you must trust
me."

"That's only reasonable," the Brigadier said. "We have a place which
I think would suit you while we get this business organized. A change all
round would be a good thing for you. I have an excellent colleague, a
first-class chess player, as it happens—"

He saw the quick scowl on Sasanov's face. "I don't want a chess player.
Miss Graham suits me very well. I don't want anyone else."

"Very well." James White smiled. "Just as you wish, Colonel. We'll
walk down together and you leave first. She's parked outside waiting for
you, I believe."

He saw Sasanov pass through the outer door while he took his time
putting on a light overcoat and a bowler hat. Davina Graham had done a
very good job indeed, if the Russian's reaction was any guide. A better
job, perhaps, than she'd admitted to him. He went down the steps and
through the little hall out into the street. There were no cars outside the
entrance, only a warden advancing ominously toward a van parked on the
opposite side of the road. Sasanov had gone.

The Brigadier liked walking, and he walked through the garish no-
man's-land of Piccadilly and down toward St. James's Park. He had a
number of discreet little houses and flats at his disposal. He had decided
on one which would suit Sasanov. A little love nest for him and the austere Miss Graham? The idea amused him and he smiled as he strode
along. But she should have told him how much Sasanov depended upon

her. Her reticence was a mistake. The little smile lingered on his lips; it was not reflected in his eyes.

Jeremy Spencer-Barr booked a table in the restaurant of the Connaught Hotel. It was one of the most expensive places to eat in London, but undeniably one of the very best. Its food and service justified the cost, and, besides, this would go down as expenses. He collected Charley Ransom at seven-thirty, had a drink in her flat, which interested him, because he liked to see a person against their own background. Charley's background surprised him; she had discreet good taste, and the furniture and modern pictures were exceptionally good. He had to admit that she looked beautiful; instinctively he resisted her attempts to charm him. A woman with her sex appeal would certainly expect from him more than he could possibly give. But if he dismissed the laughing mouth and the huge, seductive gray eyes, he allowed himself to admire the simple, elegant black silk dress, the mass of gleaming hair that looked less red in the artificial light. They talked about trivialities, and discussed her pictures.

"Presents from my last mistake," she said gaily. "I chose them, he paid for them. He loathed modern art; I had a lot of trouble getting rid of his Neapolitan flower girls and those ghastly cardinals merrymaking!" They both laughed. By the time they were settled at their table in the Connaught, he decided that she was very amusing.

"I love this place," she said, looking around her. The way the head-waiter had greeted her showed that she was a constant client. "It's got such a restful atmosphere, and, my goodness, they do spoil you! I adore being spoiled."

Jeremy was sure she did, but he only smiled and said, "I'm sure people adore spoiling you," which she rewarded with a sweet smile.

They were drinking coffee, and she was deciding to have Cointreau instead of brandy, when he brought the conversation around to her sister and the Pole who had stayed the weekend.

"It's extraordinary," he said, "how different you and your sister Davina are—not just to look at, that's obvious, but as people."

"Is that in my favor or not?" she asked. "I hope it's not an odious comparison!"

"Quite the reverse," he said. "She's rather a forbidding type—very cool, I thought. They think a lot of her, you know. She's terribly efficient. I don't think she'd refer to her ex-husband as a 'mistake.'" They both laughed.

"No, poor lamb, she wouldn't," Charley agreed. "But then she hasn't had a husband; I'm afraid that was rather my fault."

"Oh? Why?" She made a little grimace; he thought for a moment she was genuinely embarrassed.

"Her fiancé fell in love with me," she said at last. "I honestly didn't encourage it, but he just wouldn't leave me alone. I never wanted to marry him, either, but he talked me into it. Davina's never forgiven me. I suppose I can't blame her."

"Oh, I suppose not," Jeremy conceded. He hoped he had kept his amazement properly concealed. "But you've been married twice?"

"Richard—that was Davina's boy friend—Richard and I got divorced after a couple of years. He started drinking, and his business went to pieces; we quarreled all the time. It was too awful. I think he knew he'd made a mistake in choosing me and leaving her. I rather hoped he'd go back to her, but he didn't. This Cointreau is good. She never made an effort after that. My father says she turned her back on men deliberately and set out to make a success of her job. I must say being a secretary can't be very exciting, even if your boss *is* James White. Anyway, that was years ago and we've kept out of each other's way since. She didn't come to my second wedding. Then there she was at home that weekend, and with this rather attractive man."

"Tell me about him," Jeremy said. "Didn't he fall for you, too?"

The big eyes opened wide in innocence, but the giggle redeemed her.

"No, damn it, he didn't! I quite liked him, too. He was so different from the people I normally meet. Terribly square and rather overpoweringly male. You know what I mean—the Slav type."

"Yes," he said. "I think I can picture him. Fair hair and blue eyes; gold teeth?"

"No, not at all. Grayish hair, actually, and funny-colored eyes, certainly not blue. And his teeth were perfect."

Jeremy grinned at her, as if he were teasing. "Short and squat, then?"

"Taller than you," she answered. "But much bigger."

"He sounds like one of those Russian villains in long overcoats and felt hats in a TV thriller."

He dismissed the Pole, offered her a cigarette and ordered himself a second brandy. She drank very sparingly, and he approved of that. He hated women who tried to keep pace with men, or even to outpace them. He was, and he admitted it, rather a prude at heart.

"And do you think your sister is mixed up with the Pole, then?"

Charley frowned slightly. She felt less awkward talking about Davina than she had done for a long time. It helped to confess to strangers. And this smooth-talking man would never be anything else.

"I think so, yes," she said. "My parents didn't. I think my mother was hoping so; she's terrified Davina won't get married. It's rather sweet and old-fashioned, really. You'd think she'd had enough marriages with me making a mess of it twice. But anyway, she didn't think there was anything there but friendship. I thought there was. And I'm not a bad judge when it comes to lovers."

"Meaning you've had quite a few?" he challenged.

She nodded, and smiled straight into his face. "I've had a lot," she said. "I love men, and I like them to love me. I always hope I'm going to find the one-and-only, every time. So far I haven't. But it's been great fun and I don't regret a thing."

There was nothing he could say to that. The epithet "tart" floated to the surface of his mind and just as quickly disappeared.

"Getting back to your sister," he said. "Do you think they were living together?"

"You're terribly interested in her, aren't you?" Charley said lightly. "You've talked about her most of the evening."

"I know," he said. "You see, I remembered all about meeting her after I met you at that party. I knew the name rang a bell, and of course I'd done more than just bump into her. In fact, she and I were interviewed for the same job. We spent some time together waiting for the interview. I thought she was a confirmed bachelor girl, and pretty tough, if you don't mind my saying so. She told me she lived in a service flat off the Fulham Road. I can't marry this Pole up with the woman I met. That's what's so fascinating. Especially as she got the job instead of me." He finished his brandy. "She wouldn't have been chosen if they'd known she was having it off with a man," he said.

"What was the job?" Charley asked. "I didn't know she'd been promoted."

"She's White's assistant," he said. "That's what I was after."

"Oh." Charley shrugged. "I didn't know anything about that. But you're not going to go and make trouble for her, are you? I mean, it was just my opinion—I've no proof of anything."

"Don't worry, it's far too late to make any difference now," he said. "She'll be found out anyway. White keeps a very tight check on anyone who works for him."

"But is a secretary, or an assistant, so terribly important? Surely they're like a civil servant? You're not in a confidential post, are you? I'm sure Davina isn't."

"Neither of us is," he said firmly. "We're both what you call civil servants. But that job is big promotion and I was very keen to get it. So that's why I'm interested in your sister. And now I'd much rather pay attention to you. I won't suggest a drink at Annabel's because I've got a nine-o'clock appointment tomorrow and I've got to keep a clear head."

"I never go to Annabel's," she said gently. "I hate it. I much prefer Tramps. Or Regine's. Have you been there?" Jeremy had to admit he hadn't. "Well next time I'll take you. It's wildly expensive but very smart. Let's get the bill, shall we? I don't want you to be tired tomorrow. It must be terribly important if you need ten hours' sleep."

"It is," he said. "I'm taking a post with the UN in New York in a fortnight. I start being briefed tomorrow." He signaled the waiter and paid the bill.

They drove back to her flat in silence. Charley looked out the window and hummed. She felt extremely depressed. Rejection was so rare that she seldom suffered the pangs of self-doubt and inordinate humiliation which produced the nervous little tune under her breath. He was a smug, smooth bore, totally immersed in himself, and it was ridiculous to mind because she hadn't made a success with him. Ridiculous and childish. She couldn't think of one man among the last twenty who'd taken her out who had preferred a good night's sleep to an evening dancing with her and perhaps coming in for a drink. He shook hands with her in the street, promised to telephone before he went away, and went off in his car without noticing that there were tears in her eyes.

As soon as he had engaged the clutch, Charley was out of his mind. . . . Tall, big build, grayish hair. A typical Slav. There was no such thing, in fact, but she had given him a very good description of Sasanov. And where Davina Graham was, there would the missing defector be.

At home in her apartment, Charley Ransom poured herself a cup of hot milk and swallowed a sleeping pill. She allowed herself a little childish weep before she drifted off.

"Don't," Davina protested, "do that when I'm driving!"

She heard Sasanov laugh beside her. "Why not? You don't mind other times." He looked at her profile turned resolutely away from him, concentrating on the traffic ahead. But her lips were turned up in a smile. He took his hand off her knee.

"You're a bad driver," he said. "You can't keep your mind on the other cars."

"Much hope when you're getting in the way," she retorted. Her hand left the steering wheel and slapped his lightly. "I know you're in a good mood, because you're always impossible. Actually you're impossible when you're in a bad mood. I just can't win."

"You've won," he said. "You've turned me for the British. That's a big victory for you. But I'm happy today. I see the way ahead for me and my family. Do you know, the Brigadier was so anxious to get my information he offered to go to Moscow and get them himself?"

"Like hell he did," Davina said. "He won't put his neck in the noose. He'll find someone else for that little trip, don't worry."

"Why are you being so difficult?" Sasanov complained. "You should be glad it went well. Instead you behave like a cross little schoolteacher. I warn you, when we get back to that cage of yours I'm going to behave very badly!"

She glanced at him briefly. "There's nothing different about that," she said.

He settled back in his seat; he felt contented and excited at the same time. He understood her very well. Of course she was pleased at the success of the interview. It was part of the game they sometimes played, to pretend to be at odds with each other. Then he thought of Halldale Manor, of Roberts and the electronic invasion of their privacy, and he sighed.

She heard the sigh, and said quickly, "What's the matter—what's wrong?"

"I feel like celebrating," he said sullenly. "Instead we go back to the old lunatics and the cage. It depresses me."

She drove on for some minutes without answering. They were approaching the route out to the southeast; the traffic was already building up and they began crawling between traffic lights.

"I don't want you to be depressed," she said. "We've got to go back to Halldale, but we can stop on the way. Would you like that?"

"What do you mean, stop?" he asked her.

"I mean stop for dinner. Talk; celebrate. I can get clearance on the radio. Would you like that?"

He nodded at her reflection in the rearview mirror.

"Yes, Vina, I'd like that. I'd like it better if we could stop for the night. I hate making love in silence."

Again she drove for a time without answering. Then at another stop, caught in a crossfire of immobile traffic, she turned to him and said, "I'll ask for that too, if that's what you want."

"It's what I want," Sasanov said. He settled back into his seat and closed his eyes; she didn't know if he had really gone to sleep, but he didn't move or speak, even when she used the car telephone, connected to a special exchange.

Visiting hours at Halldale Manor nursing home were between two and four, and five-thirty to seven. In the chronic geriatric ward, a dozen old women in the final stages of senile dementia lay in their beds, mouthing vacantly or dozing in a drugged trance. Few ever had visitors; they passed through the final stages of their lives in a twilight through which the nurses moved like shadows. It was so rare for any relative to come before being called to the deathbed that the grandson of one of the patients aroused a friendly interest among the nursing staff.

He came in to see his grandmother Mrs. Burns quite unexpectedly one afternoon. The old lady hadn't had a visit for three years; she lay propped up on her pillows, mumbling in confusion to herself, and sleeping. She had to be fed like a child, and, like the others, she had no bodily control. There was always a faint stench in the ward, combined with disinfectant and the smell of bodies sweating their decay through the pores of their skins. He was a nice young man, who held his grandmother's hand and didn't seem to mind when she pulled it away and grumbled that she didn't know him. A lot of relatives were distressed by the aggression or the lack of recognition, and didn't come to the nursing home again. The ward sister remarked on the grandson's devotion to the patient, and he spent some of the time chatting to her and drinking coffee with her in her little cubicle at the end of the room. He came three times a week, bringing flowers which were arranged by the old woman's bed, and once he brought a box of chocolates for the nurses.

"You do such a wonderful job," he said. "What would become of these poor old people if it weren't for all of you?"

The ward sister began to look forward to his visits; one of the young nurses eyed him with longing.

"I think it's a shame the way families neglect their old relatives," he said. "I was really upset to hear Granny was in here and my mother hadn't been to see her for two years. We don't treat our old people like that in Ireland."

The ward sister, who came from Limerick, agreed with him. She felt so sorry for the poor things, left to rot and die; and then when they did die, the family came around wiping their eyes and pretending to care. Wouldn't he like a cup of coffee? He mustn't think Mrs. Burns didn't enjoy his visits because she was so confused and didn't know him. In fact, she seemed much brighter in herself since he'd been coming.

"That's all that matters," he said. "Just so she feels she's not forgotten."

At the end of the third week he asked the young nurse out for a drink when she came off duty. It took him nearly a month of seeing her before he learned that there was a section of the nursing home which was reserved for violent patients, and ordinary staff never went near it.

"Gives me the creeps sometimes," she confided to him over a beer in the Crown at Haywards Heath. "There's that big wall at the back, and the gate's always locked. They have specials looking after the patients in there; they don't mix with us."

Mrs. Burns's grandson expressed surprise. And how many people were locked away? he wondered. She didn't really know, but the rumor was not more than one or two. There was a woman who came in and out, but whether she was a private nurse or a relative, they didn't know.

"How awful," he said. "If I wasn't a Catholic, that kind of thing would make me believe in euthanasia." He ordered them both another beer.

She didn't mean to break any rules about showing him where the violent wing was; it just happened as they were strolling around the lovely grounds on a fine afternoon. Groups of patients were sitting in the garden; some wandered about; the sun was shining and the air was beautifully warm. The gardens were magnificent, carpeted with daffodils and grape hyacinths. Mrs. Burns's grandson smiled at anyone he passed, and gently hooked his arm through the nurse's elbow.

"Is that the place where the poor devils are kept locked up?" he asked. And she said no, that was the laboratory, where they did their own pathology. The other place was over there, behind that high brick wall. And look, there was the woman she'd mentioned, coming out the gate. What a funny coincidence. She didn't look like a nurse, though. Fancy having someone shut up in there and going to see them; of course, they were able to keep them under drugs now.

He got a good look at Davina Graham, and agreed silently with the chattering girl that she didn't look like a nurse, either. He walked on a little faster, and before she got into her car he lit a cigarette, shielding the lighter from the breeze which wasn't blowing. He came back to see his grandmother twice more, and dashed all the nurse's secret hopes by telling her he had been sent to Glasgow, but of course he'd write. The visits stopped and no letter with a Scottish postmark ever came for the nurse. Mrs. Burns mumbled and dozed, and the ward never saw an outsider again. But the photograph taken of Davina as she got into her car was studied and identified.

Mrs. Burns's grandson went on working as a kitchen hand in a South Kensington hotel until Tuesday, April 28, two days before Sasanov went to London to see Brigadier White. He didn't give notice, he just disappeared; his employer cursed the feckless Irish and hired someone else. He had called himself Murphy in London, but he checked in at a small hotel fifteen minutes from Haywards Heath under the name of Porter. This time he had no Irish brogue. He used a motorcycle, which made it easy for him to go through the familiar town without fear of the staff from Halldale recognizing him in crash helmet and goggles.

It took no more than half an hour of telephoning around the stores to find out which one delivered groceries to Halldale Manor. And that a van was calling later in the afternoon. They would be very pleased to include a present from him to one of the patients. He promised to come in and pay for his order, and hung up. There was only one van at the back of the shop, with its name painted on the side. He tinkered with his motorcycle until the driver came out carrying half a dozen cardboard boxes which he loaded into the back of the van. When the doors were closed and the driver went around to the front, the watcher jumped on his machine, kicked it into action and sped off in advance. He waited by the side of the road which led to Halldale; it was a minor road and there was no one about. He saw the van approaching, and advanced into the road, limping and waving it to stop. The driver didn't get time to speak to the injured motorcyclist; a blow to his head knocked him flat onto the roadway.

The cyclist pulled him to the side, stripped off his buff overall and cap. The body was tumbled into a ditch, out of sight. The motorcycle was hidden in a break in the hedgerow, and within five minutes the van was entering the back drive of Halldale Manor. The delivery to the nursing home was in two sections; four boxes and a small crate for the main house, and a single box of groceries marked "Halldale Manor Annex." He drove to the back entrance by the kitchens and, under the eyes of a woman he thought to be one of the cooks, loaded the boxes into the larder, gave her the bill to sign, and then drove around to the gate set in the high wall.

Inside the back of the van, he slipped a large can in among the groceries for the annex; the label said "Garden Peas, Extra Fine." Then he carried the box to the gate and rang the bell. A large man in blue overalls answered; he held out his arms for the box and took it inside. He shut the

gate without signing anything. The driver slammed the back doors of the
van, jumped inside and rattled out along the bumpy little road. He drove
slowly to the place where his motorcycle and the van man were hidden,
satisfying himself that there was nothing coming in front or behind him.
He dressed the unconscious man in his own overalls once more and
dragged him quickly into the front seat of his van. He started the engine
and sent the van crashing into the ditch. The horn mechanism jammed,
hooting continuously. The cyclist pulled his machine out of hiding,
mounted it and roared off toward the main London road.

Inside the kitchen that supplied food for Sasanov and the staff, the cook
checked on the items and picked up the can of peas. It was not on his list;
he hesitated, and then decided that it wasn't often you got something for
nothing. They spent enough with the grocer, anyway. He put the can on
the larder shelf with the other goods.

Davina stopped at a motel on the A415. Her instructions had been less
flexible than she had hoped, but there was a compromise. They could
spend as long or as short a time as they wished stopping en route to
Halldale, but they must radio in before midnight to say they had
returned. Sasanov was sulky at first; she ordered him a drink and fussed
over him with peanuts and chips until he seemed more cheerful. He
watched her and at last he smiled.

"I'm sorry," he said. "I'm disappointed we can't stay the night. I won't
spoil our dinner."

"Well, I was thinking," she said. "We are at a motel, after all. We
could take a room and leave when we felt like it. . . ."

His eyes gleamed and he touched his glass against hers.

"We could," he said. "I'd like that."

"So would I," Davina said. "I'll go and fix it."

She booked a room, facing down the receptionist who smirked as she
handed her the key, and as she walked back to join Sasanov, Davina
thought suddenly that she had no qualm of embarrassment in paying for
the use of a bed for a couple of hours. No embarrassment, no sense that
she was in any way diminished by taking sex at such a basic level. They
wanted each other and it was natural to make adjustments so they could
be together.

"That's all right," she said. "I paid for the night. I was just thinking
that if anyone had told me I'd book a room to sleep with a man in a place
like this, I'd have said they were raving mad. You've certainly changed
me."

"Are you sorry?" he asked her.

She shook her head and laughed.

"No. Not in the least. I wouldn't have missed you for anything."

"Then why don't we eat quickly?" he suggested. "The food will be filthy, and I'm not hungry. Not for food."

The look he gave her was so frankly sensual that she felt tempted to suggest they forget about dinner altogether. But she didn't and they spent an hour eating steak and drinking wine while he teased her by looking at his watch.

In the motel room, she began to get undressed; it was a drab little place with hideous furniture and a double bed of mean proportions. Sasanov stripped quicker than she did; he began to help her and then changed to making love to her before she was ready. She had no restraint with him, no pretensions to false modesty. He had never given her time. She twisted her arms tightly around his neck and lost herself in him. At one moment she thought how much this rough, masculine lovemaking aroused and satisfied her, and was overcome by tenderness for him, until the gentler emotion was swept away by mutual passion. He slept very briefly, and she lay awake, anchored to the bed by his weight, and felt again that blend of gratitude and joy which was perilously close to love.

But she mustn't love him. That would mean disaster for them both, when his wife and daughter were united with him and there was no place for her in his life. He had liberated her, and she had no right to try to chain him in return. She switched on the ugly little overhead light and he woke.

"It's time we started back," she said. "Let me get up." She looked at herself in the little mirror on the wall, and began to put her clothes on. "I must do something with my face," she said. "I look a terrible mess."

"You look like a woman who's been making love," Sasanov corrected her. "Will you do me a favor?"

"Another one?" She turned to him, fastening her dress. He was ready, sitting on the edge of the rumpled bed, smoking.

"A little one," he said. "Don't brush your hair back like that. It looks better down."

"It looks like a gypsy!" she retorted. "Untidy hair doesn't suit me."

They switched out the lights and left. She turned on the radio in the car; they were less than forty minutes away from Halldale Manor when the radiotelephone buzzed. She picked it up, steering with her right hand. The codesign for her call was repeated.

Sasanov heard her say, "What? Oh, my God! Yes, yes, all right. I've got that. Right away."

He saw her face in the semidarkness and said quickly, "What's happened—what's wrong?"

"There's been a fire," she said. "The whole annex was burned to the ground. Nobody got out. It's still blazing and we can't go near it. We've got to go back to London; they've given me an address."

"Fire?" Sasanov said slowly. "How could it burn so quickly—you say nobody was saved?"

"No," she said. "Think of Roberts and the others—how horrible!"

She swung the car around and sped back toward London. "There wasn't time to raise an alarm. Apparently the place went up like a torch. Do you realize—" she glanced hurriedly at him—"if we hadn't stopped at that motel we'd have been there, too?"

"Yes," he answered after a moment. "That's what they intended. Slow down or you'll get us killed anyway! There's only one thing that starts a fire like that. Not a fire, a firestorm. I'm afraid I've been discovered, Vina."

"Oh God," she muttered. "Don't say that. How could you be discovered, how could anyone know you were there?"

"I don't know, but they did," he said. "Somehow they got a firebomb into the annex. It was meant for me. Where are we going?"

"To a flat in Holland Park," she said. "A car's picking us up at the intersection between Putney Bridge and King's Road. They'll escort us there. I'll radio in just before we cross Putney Bridge. Don't worry." She laid her hand on his knee. "Don't worry, you'll be safe. If this is an attack on you, then we'll let them think they succeeded. Don't you see, you'll be really safe then?"

He didn't answer. He squeezed her hand and returned it to the wheel.

"You drive too fast," he said. "You need both hands."

They didn't talk again. At the intersection beyond the bridge, a car in a side road dipped its lights as they approached, and fell in behind them. Sasanov watched the lighted, empty London streets slip by. It was nearly 2 A.M.

The bodies in the burned-out annex would be identified; there would be an inquest, managed by White's department; everything would be covered up and officially registered as a gas leak or a major electrical fault. The KGB might think they'd killed him—until whoever had betrayed him told them he was still alive.

6

James White had the pathologist's report on the charred corpses at Halldale in front of him; he also had the findings of the team of experts on arson and explosives who had rooted among the smoldering ruins of the annex. Prompt action by the local fire brigade and the nursing staff had saved the main buildings and contained the fire. The story had made all the national newspapers, and both television channels carried stories and on-the-spot reports of what was described as "Fire Horror in Old People's Home." One of the best men in the department had been put in charge of investigations. He was a thin bespectacled figure who looked more like a teacher than a specialist in the art of sabotage. His name was Fisher, and he sprawled awkwardly in the chair by the Brigadier's desk, as if he couldn't compose his long legs and arms in harmony with the rest of him.

The Brigadier put the papers aside. "Trace of high octane fifteen. That rules out any possibility of accident," he said.

"Certainly does." Fisher took an unlit pipe out of his mouth. "That stuff is used in conjunction with tyron multiple two; the corrosive agent has a time-setter for eating through the separating compartments and allowing the two agents to mingle. The second they do—boom! You get a minor explosion that releases the activated agents, and on contact with ordinary oxygen you get a chain reaction that literally sets on fire the air and everything in it.

"I reckoned that if the device was in the kitchen—and it looks from what we found as if the fire started there—it was timed to activate at just before midnight, when everybody would be upstairs asleep. They wouldn't have had a chance of getting out, it spreads so quickly and the heat and smoke generated are so intense."

"Hmm . . ." the Brigadier said. "Nasty stuff."

"Very nasty," Fisher agreed. "Makes the old American napalm look like a box of safety matches. It's been used before in cases where they wanted a blanket operation—eliminate everybody at one crack. It's highly sophisticated stuff, and only available to the Center professionals."

"From the police reports," White said, "there might be a link-up with the van driver found in his van in the ditch. He'd apparently just made a delivery to the nursing home, and to the annex. What doesn't tie in is why he should have been going in the wrong direction when he went off the road. The other goods in the van were invoiced to a housing development leading *away* from Haywards Heath, not toward it.

"He's also suffered head injuries which don't appear to be related to his injuries when the van crashed. I think we'll find something there. If he recovers enough to tell us anything. The medical outlook isn't too good. He's been unconscious since they found him."

Fisher suggested, "Surely a Center man would have killed him."

"You'd think so—although they're not infallible," White remarked. "I'm sure there's a connection. Somebody got that bomb into the annex, and it must have been something the staff would have accepted without question. Like groceries. I'll get some of our chaps to join forces with the local police. They'll probably come up with something. But it doesn't answer the real question." He lit a cigarette, and Fisher felt encouraged to light his pipe.

"How did they know Sasanov was there?" the Brigadier muttered. "How the hell did anyone know exactly where he was—except for his minder, the staff at Halldale, and me."

"One of the staff, maybe," Fisher suggested. "They got killed for their pains at the same time. No chance to investigate the leak."

"We're looking into that," White said. "It seems the most likely. Serves whoever it was bloody well right. Anyway, thanks, Fisher. I'll take the matter in hand myself. Thank your assistants, will you? They did a splendid job."

When he was alone, the Brigadier flicked through the papers, glancing at items at random; he wasn't really concentrating. Someone had found out where Sasanov was hiding. Someone had alerted the KGB. It would be easy to imagine that the traitor was on the security staff and had died for his pains. But the Brigadier didn't believe it. They had a mole, and the mole had found Sasanov. If the Russians thought they had now silenced Sasanov, that was exactly what he wanted them to think. If they made no further inquiries about their missing delegate, it would connect their intelligence service with the Halldale fire. They wouldn't do that; the Soviet Embassy would make representations to the Home Office and continue to cause as much trouble as they could over the vanished Russian. Therefore the charade would have to be played out. Sasanov must be produced; his body had, after all, been waiting in cold storage after the beauty treatments given to it. White buzzed his secretary and asked for his friend the Police Superintendent's office number.

They exchanged a few words about their health and their mutual interest in cricket, and then White said, "By the way, I think we could pop our frozen fish back into the sea. Can you arrange that? And find it in a day or two, will you? Oh, thanks, that's fine. Yes, plenty of publicity—that's what we want. How about lunch next week?" He made a note in his diary and rang off.

The KGB were going to get themselves a body; if they chose to take it back to the Soviet Union to bury, or rather to play with to establish its identity, he had no objection. What he was really concerned about was keeping Sasanov in total isolation while he began investigations into whether the Russians' informer had indeed been burned at Halldale with the innocent, or was at liberty and watching.

"Irina, would you stay behind? I'd like to discuss this essay with you."

Irina Sasanova nodded. The rest of the class of students had put their books away; the lecture was over. Her teacher in sociology was a young man, less dictatorial than the senior lecturer in the subject; he enjoyed making his students laugh and encouraged a degree of open discussion which was rare in Moscow University. She came up to the rostrum; he had her latest essay on the table in front of him.

Seeing her expression, he said, "It's good, don't worry. I'm not going to give you a bad mark. It's just that I see certain lines of thought in your work recently. I wondered if you were aware of them, that's all."

"I don't know, Comrade Poliakov. I'm not conscious of anything. Please explain to me."

"Sit down." He offered her his chair and swung himself up on the edge of the table. She had turned rather pale and she looked anxious. She was pleasant-looking rather than pretty, but the fair hair and blue eyes were attractive. She very seldom smiled these days, and her contacts with her fellow students were perfunctory. For the past eight months she had been under an invisible cloud, as the daughter of a senior Soviet official who had gone to the West and disappeared.

"You have a definite trend toward individualism," Poliakov said gently. "Your work emphasizes more and more the role of the state in relation to the individual, instead of the other way round."

The color rushed into her face; the next moment he would tell her that she was showing signs of deviation in her political thinking. He saw the fear in her eyes.

"I'm not aware of it, Comrade. I promise you, if that's what you see in my essays, it's quite accidental. Just please point out to me where the errors are so I can put them right!"

"I don't think they are errors," he said. "I much prefer the view of sociology that you're expressing, however tentatively. I'm not criticizing you, I'm congratulating you. And I know how difficult things have been for you in the past months. Stop staring at me, Irina Ivanovna, as if I were trying to trap you and denounce you to the KGB."

The girl's eyes filled with tears. "I don't know what you mean," she mumbled. "I haven't done anything wrong. I didn't mean to write anything. . . ."

He shook his head. "There's no word of your father, is there?"

She glanced up at him in panic. "No. No, we don't talk about him."

"But losing him has affected you, hasn't it?" he asked gently. "Believe me, Irina, I'm taking as big a risk talking to you as you are in answering. Will you trust me?"

He didn't know it, but she had been weaving romantic fantasies about him ever since he became her lecturer. Daydreaming about him had kept her mind occupied. This time she blushed for a different reason.

"Trust me," he said again. "Please."

She nodded, afraid of breaking into tears.

"You miss your father, don't you?"

"Yes. . . ." It was a whisper.

"And do you think he's dead, or gone over to the West?"

"I don't know," she said. She hesitated and then said in a rush, "My mother thinks he's gone over. She told me he was upset because a friend had been arrested. She doesn't say too much. We try not to think about it."

Poliakov took a packet of cigarettes from his pocket. His hand trembled slightly as he lit one. He had gone far enough, and common prudence advised him to leave the conversation there. But there was misery and fear in the girl's face that angered him beyond caution. He felt overcome by pity and indignation.

"If your father has gone over to the West, what would you feel toward him? Don't be afraid to answer; don't you see my life is just as much in your hands now?"

She looked up at him. "Why are you asking me these questions? How do I know you aren't working for the police?"

"You don't know," he said. "You'll have to take that chance. How would you feel about your father?"

"Ashamed. . . ." she said slowly. "But glad too. Because he was alive."

"Would you ever forgive him—see him again if he came home?"

"Of course," she murmured. "But it wouldn't be possible. It wouldn't be allowed."

"And would your mother say the same as you?"

"I don't know," Irina answered. "I can't speak for my mother. She cries every night, I know that."

"All right." Poliakov slipped off the table; he gathered her essay papers in a neat pile. "I want you to think about one thing. How would you feel if you could see your father again? And how would your mother feel? Think about it. I'll talk to you again at the end of next week. Go on now."

She got up and for a moment stood in front of him, not knowing how to leave. He placed his hand on her shoulder.

"Go on," he said gently. "I have to take another class. And don't betray me, will you, Irina Ivanovna?"

"Never," she said. "Never in my life." She turned and hurried away, her head bowed to hide the bright color and the unshed tears.

That evening, Poliakov went around to a colleague's apartment and, against a loud background of radio music, told her that he had made the first approach to Sasanov's daughter and the reaction seemed favorable. She could convey that message the next time she met Elizabeth Cole from the embassy.

But before she did so, there was an item published in *Pravda* and *Izvestia* reporting the discovery of Colonel Ivan Sasanov's body washed up on the beach in the south of England. It was stated that he had committed suicide by throwing himself off a nearby promontory called Beachy Head; the badly decomposed body had been trapped in rocks and only just released by heavy seas. The colonel had been suffering from depression and had received medical treatment before leaving the Soviet Union with the trade delegation.

The body was being flown back to Russia for burial.

"Well," Davina said. "That closes the file for you." She handed him the English newspaper, with its secondary headline—"Soviet Colonel's Body Found."

"So I'm officially dead," Sasanov said. "Suicide—I see. And I'm going home to be buried. What about my family? They'll believe this—they won't trust any approach to them that your people can make." He threw the paper aside. "Your intelligence have got together with ours," he said angrily. "They've agreed to save everyone's face by accepting a body and saying it's mine. Our service thinks I was burned at Halldale, and your Chief is pretending that they're right. This is not what was agreed."

"The fire hadn't happened," she pointed out. "We probably had to release the body prematurely. Don't worry about your family; they'll be contacted and told the truth. But they've got to be sounded out first— moving too quickly could wreck everything." She hesitated, and then decided that he had better face the possibility of failure.

"Supposing we get a negative response," she said. "Supposing your wife and your daughter don't want to come over. You mustn't take too much for granted. You've been away eight months. That can be a long time to be alone and under suspicion."

He looked up at her, frowning. "I know my family. My wife knew what I was planning, even though I never said it. She knew when I left for England that I wasn't coming back. She won't have turned against me. Neither will my daughter. They'll come."

He picked up the newspaper and began to read it. Davina didn't argue; she knew that on this one point he was beyond reason. His family would join him. That was the end of it. She went out and made a shopping list.

They were living in an apartment house in Shepherds Bush; the building was owned and staffed by the Brigadier's department. People came and went on short visits; no flats were available to anyone outside. They had provided her with a different car after the journey back from Halldale. To her surprise she and Sasanov had changed over to the escort car in central London. One of the security men had driven hers away. Precautions were very strict. Sasanov was not allowed to leave the flat in daylight. He had to take fresh air and exercise at night, and wherever he went with Davina they were shadowed by two armed men. The atmosphere became tense between them. They had far less freedom than at Halldale, and Sasanov was fretting at the restrictions.

He reread the story about the discovery of the body. Burial in Russia. . . . He imagined the anguish of his wife and daughter, and he burned with anger. What did Davina mean when she talked of moving too quickly? He had been stung by her remark that eight months was a long time. He trusted his wife, but no one knew better than he the pressures suffered by innocent relatives in cases of disloyalty to the state. Perhaps they had not been strong enough. Perhaps they would accept the substitute body and be glad to believe he was dead and they could start life again. Moving too quickly could ruin everything. So could delaying too long. He wasn't going to gamble everything on British caution. It looked more than possible that his wife would reject an approach for fear of a KGB trap. He got up and went into the bedroom. He found what he was looking for in a drawer.

When Davina came back he was in the kitchen, drinking tea and waiting for her.

"I want this given to my wife," he said. "And I want her answer. I'll be ready for debriefing when I get it. Tell the Brigadier that I don't want to wait, and I know he doesn't, either."

"You're sure," Davina said. "You're sure you want to risk this?"

"There's no risk," he said. "This will prove I'm alive. It can go in the diplomatic pouch to Moscow."

Davina turned over the postcard of Stonehenge at sunset and looked at the back. One side of it was covered with Cyrillic writing; the space for the name and address was left empty.

"Why this?" she asked him. "Why not a letter?"

"Because of what I've written on it," he said. "She will know it comes from me. Will you do this today?"

"I'll try," she said. She saw the look on his face, and said quickly, "All right, I'll get it sent off this afternoon."

She began to make lunch for them; he had gone back to the living room. She tried to ignore the inexcusable depression that had begun when he gave her the postcard. He wanted his wife and daughter. She had always known and accepted that. It was no time to be possessive, to spoil the relationship they had by resenting his need for his family. She felt so guilty she left the cooking and came into the room where he was sitting, and put her arms around his shoulders.

"Don't worry," she said. "I'll get everything moving, if that's the way you think is best. You don't need to snap at me."

He reached up and touched her face. "I'm sorry. But I want them to stand at the grave and know that I am still alive. I want Fedya's answer in my hands."

She left him, with a cheerful expression on her face, and the inevitable sinking in her heart. By five o'clock the postcard had been delivered to the appropriate authority and was sealed in an envelope for inclusion in the next diplomatic pouch for Moscow.

The Ilyushin jet landed at Moscow airport just after six in the morning. The coffin was taken off and loaded into a small van, which sped away toward the city center. By nine o'clock the body was lying under a bright light in the private mortuary owned by the KGB, and there were three men grouped around it. One was a police surgeon; the other two were high-ranking officers of the KGB dressed as civilians. The taller and older-looking of the two stared down at the discolored, mutilated corpse for some moments without speaking. Then he spoke to the surgeon.

"How much will an autopsy tell us?"

"Approximate date of death, General; length of time in the water; age; whether he died from drowning or was killed and put in the sea. Analysis of the organs depends upon the degree of decomposition."

"What you mean," the General said sarcastically, "is that you can't make a positive identification with Ivan Sasanov." He gave the surgeon a baleful look and was gratified to see him wince.

"The teeth, General . . ." the surgeon said hurriedly. "Dental records will prove whether it's Sasanov."

"Dental treatment can be faked," the General said abruptly. "But have it checked anyway. Tatischev." He glanced at the younger man beside him. "You've got all the records?"

"Here, Comrade General."

The file containing all Sasanov's medical data was passed to him. He read through it slowly, glancing at the grisly remains on the table as he did so.

"Yes," he said suddenly. "That's interesting." Both men looked at him expectantly. "Tatischev—put a call through to Dzerzinsky Street. Tell them to pick up Sasanov's wife and bring her here."

He turned away and said to the surgeon, "Tea while we wait; have that thing covered up." He walked out of the mortuary room, followed by Tatischev, who hurried to a telephone.

Fedya Sasanov knew whom she would find when she answered the persistent ring on her doorbell. They seemed to tower over her as she stared at them, though in fact neither of the men was tall. Fear invested them with height and bulk and gave them a menace which was quite imaginary. They asked her very politely to come with them, and waited in the narrow hall as she pulled on a coat. Her hands were trembling too much to fasten it properly, and the coat hung awkwardly from the wrong buttons. She sat in the back of the Zil, one man driving and the other beside her. Her companion offered her a cigarette, which she refused. They had been told not to frighten her.

Her fear reached a crescendo as the car swung into Dzerzinsky Street and she thought she was being taken to the KGB offices; her vision swam and she thought she was going to faint. But the car went past the dreaded building and turned left.

"Where are we going?" It was almost a whisper, and the man beside her leaned down as if he were deaf.

"To the city mortuary," he answered. "Your husband's body is there."

"Oh," she murmured, "oh, I didn't know it had come. Thank you, Comrade; thank you for fetching me . . . for a moment I was confused. . . ." She didn't go on and he looked out the window to let her collect herself before she said something stupid.

They brought her into the mortuary room and she hesitated, staring at the shape lying on a table, shrouded in a green plastic sheet with a brilliant light beamed down upon it. For a moment the men standing near were in deep shadow. When the General stepped forward, she recognized him immediately. He held out his hand and took hers; he noticed how cold it was, and the tiny nervous tremor.

"General Volkov . . ." They had known each other socially for nearly twenty years; he had a dacha in the same select area, but it was bigger than theirs, in keeping with his rank. He had been Ivan Sasanov's immediate superior when he first came to Moscow. He had been responsible for the arrest and punishments of the dissidents. Antonyii Volkov. He had sent Belezky to the psychiatric hospital.

"Your husband's body arrived from England this morning," he said. "I know this will be very distressing, Comrade Sasanov, but I am afraid we want you to make a positive identification. You must be brave; it will be difficult to recognize him. Tatischev will get you a brandy."

He took her by the arm and guided her to the table; the brilliant light almost blinded her when she tried to look up. She stood there waiting, staring at the green plastic, gripping both hands together in front of her ill-fitting coat, and tried to think clearly. If it was her husband under there . . . if he was really dead, and not in hiding . . . God forbid, she thought, using the word quite unconsciously. And yet, if he was dead—if it could be proved he hadn't defected—they'd be reinstated. Irina would have a future; *she* could sleep without nightmares and open the front door without fear. Her eyes filled with tears at the thought of her husband dead; they slipped down her cheek, and she brushed them away with the back of her hand. She wanted him to be alive; her reaction to the news that his body had been found, a suicide by drowning, had been desperate grief. And then the doubt came, growing stronger by the hour. He had not been suffering from any mental illness, or receiving any treatment. Those items printed in *Izvestia* were lies. And if they were lies, then so might the body be. She glanced timidly at Volkov. What did he expect her to say—what did he *want* her to say?

Tatischev was beside her with a glass of brandy. She took a sip.

"A little more," he suggested. "It will be a shock for you." She obeyed, and after a further moment's pause Volkov asked her, "Do you feel strong enough to look at the body, and take time? Time to examine it closely and make absolutely sure?"

She nodded. The brandy was burning its way down. The surgeon stepped forward and removed the green plastic.

She gave a gasp and turned away, shutting her eyes. Tatischev caught her elbow and gently turned her back.

"You must look," he said. "Not at the face, look at the body only."

She opened her eyes and kept them focused on the horrid corpse, avoiding the ghastly bloated, eyeless deformity that was the head. The brandy had helped her; slowly she steadied herself, and her memory supplied clues. There were no hands. It was impossible to tell whether the man she had loved was the pitiful horror below her. But she studied it, searching for recognition. If he was dead, she and Irina would be safe. She put a hand up to her mouth, and then searched in her bag for a handkerchief. She wiped her lips and then her eyes.

"It's Ivan," she said. "I identify it. It's my husband." She turned away and burst into tears.

"You are quite sure?" Volkov asked her.

She nodded, weeping without restraint.

"You can go home, then," he said kindly. "Don't speak of this to anyone."

"No, no, Comrade General."

"We will meet at the funeral," he said.

The security officers guided Fedya Sasanov to the door. Volkov turned and walked away, his junior officer at his heels like an attentive dog; the cover was flung over the dead body, and it was returned to refrigeration. The bright light went out. The door was locked.

Back in her apartment, Fedya Sasanov calmed her quivering nerves with a cup of hot tea laced with a little vodka. She sat by herself at the kitchen table and cried while she sipped the tea. Finally, exhausted by strain and emotion, and lulled by the vodka and the brandy, she fell asleep at the table.

Antonyii Volkov leaned across his desk. He thrust the open file toward his junior officer.

"Read that," he said. "Fifth line down. Then tell me how long the Sasanovs have been married."

Tatischev read the few lines and paused. "Twenty-three years," he said.

"Right. Though he wasn't a Jew, Sasanov had been circumcised. The genitals on that body were in bad condition, one testicle gone, the other partly gone. But even I could see the man hadn't been circumcised. Whatever mistake a woman might make over her husband's body, she wouldn't mistake that. She was lying."

"Yes," Tatischev said. "Of course. Why, General? Why would she identify a strange body?"

"Because she knows he didn't commit suicide," Volkov answered. "She knew he had defected. She identified him to put us off the trail; and to make life easier for herself."

"What should be done about it?"

"We'll arrest her," Volkov said. "After the funeral. You can see to that. Perhaps I hoped to find her genuinely innocent. . . ."

He shrugged. "If she'd rejected that body, I would have rehabilitated her and the daughter, cleared them of any responsibility for what that swine has done. But now . . ." He shrugged again. "So we have an interesting situation. The British say Sasanov is dead, and give us that lump of offal to prove it. His wife says the same, and our agent in England says he was burned to death in a fire." He paused, liking Tatischev as an audience. "Brigadier White has given us a body to bury, and we've accepted it, because we know in fact that Sasanov is really dead; it ties up the ends and leaves no propaganda for the West. It's all very neat and a good example of intelligence services working together unofficially. That is how it seems, eh?"

"I don't see why the British should save us embarrassment," Tatischev ventured.

"Nor do I," Volkov murmured. "The only reason they would give us an advantage is because they have gained one for themselves. Whatever happened in the fire, Sasanov is still alive. But for now we must play out the charade.

"We will go to the funeral and it will be widely reported. The grieving widow and daughter will be photographed. And we will wait for our agent's next report from England."

Charley had come back from the hairdresser when she found the message her daily help had scribbled on the telephone pad. "Mr. Spencer-Barr phoned. Please ring him at this number."

Charley read the message and frowned. He had not contacted her since their dinner at the Connaught. She had forgotten about him, and life was running at its usual pace of invitations and parties. There had been something that disturbed her momentarily, and she remembered it now, reminded of it by seeing his name. The political columns of the newspapers didn't interest her; she was bored by international affairs; they were always depressing and full of violence. She ignored them, concentrating on the pleasant items and the gossip columns, where she had often been featured herself. It was a photograph on the front page that had caught her attention. Then she read the story. "Missing Soviet Delegate's Body Found." She skipped through the details and looked again at the photograph of the man whose body had been washed up on the Sussex coast.

It was not a good photograph, obviously blown up from a group picture, but there was a familiarity about it that intrigued her. It had a vague resemblance to the Pole her sister had brought home for the weekend. Slavs did tend to look alike, after all; she turned the page and started reading something else. But the likeness worried her. She turned back and studied it again. Just something about the set of the eyes . . . She'd spent a lot of time that weekend looking at Davina's friend. More to observe her effect upon him than to memorize his face, but the impression had stayed. Missing Soviet delegate. Sitting under the hairdryer, she had felt a funny little cold chill. It was nonsense, of course. The man had been dead for months, according to the story. And Slavs would look even more alike in a bad photograph. She had put it out of her mind and lost herself in a long article on spring fashions in *Harper's* and *Queen*.

With Spencer-Barr's message in her hand, she thought of it again. He had taken her out and spent most of the evening talking about her sister and the Polish boy friend. Now, when she supposed he had gone to America, he had suddenly rung her up again. He had been very interested in their relationship. Charley remembered his saying Davina had got a job he wanted, and how an affair with a Pole would count against her.

She lifted the phone and pushed the buttons. An operator answered, "Ministry of Defence. Can I help you?"

Charley asked to speak to Mr. Spencer-Barr. His voice was curt, intimidating. "Spencer-Barr." When she gave her name, the tone changed. He sounded friendly and enthusiastic.

"Oh, how nice of you to ring back. I've tried to get you several times in the last week, but no success."

"You liar," Charley said to herself. "If the daily's not in I have an answering service."

"I got your message," she said. "I was surprised, I was sure you'd gone to the States."

"No, not yet," he said. "Is there any chance you'd be free to come to dinner tonight? I've got an old friend come in from Germany and I thought I'd get a party together for him. He's very nice, great fun."

"I'm not free, actually," Charley said. "I'm going to the theater."

He sounded disappointed. "What a shame. I'd told him all about you and he was getting very excited. Look, we're having dinner fairly late and then going on to the Regency Club. Why don't you join us there?"

"I could, I suppose." She hesitated. The idea of the nice German who was great fun tempted her. "Can I leave it open?"

"Yes, of course, but do try, won't you?"

"Yes," she said. "It rather depends on how late the theater party breaks up. If it's early, I'll come on to the Regency. Goodbye."

She went into her bedroom, looked at herself in the glass and was pleased with the way they had set her hair. It looked casual and abundant, its color gleaming like new-minted copper. The Regency Club was full of Arabs; she never went there. It was the kind of invitation she wouldn't have considered accepting, except that he had made the German sound intriguing. She shrugged. A particularly faithful admirer was taking her out that night, with another couple. She had rather lost interest in him; he was so abjectly in love with her that the affair had lost excitement. She might go to the Regency if there was nothing more amusing in prospect.

Elizabeth Cole sipped her hot tea and looked at her watch. Her contact was late; she had been waiting nearly twenty minutes and twice prevented a stranger from sitting at her table. When the young man came up, she shook her head and said in passable Russian, "I'm sorry, that is my friend's place. She's just coming."

The man said very quietly in French, "She is not coming. She sent me instead." He sat down in the empty chair and put his tea in front of him. Elizabeth Cole sat completely still and said nothing. Her plain, cheerful face became a sullen mask. Her nerves had given a frantic jump, as if an electric shock had passed through her. Then she froze. The young man gave the lecturer's name.

"She is back at the university," he said. "She can't meet you anymore. I have made contact with Irina Sasanov. My name is Alexei Poliakov."

For a moment Elizabeth stared at him; her expression was surprisingly grim for such a pleasant type of girl.

"All right," she said at last. "Tell me about it."

"You can trust me," he insisted. "I spoke to her after class. She believes her father is dead and that the body they flew home is his. I tried to convince her, but she won't believe me. How can I prove it to her?"

Elizabeth hesitated. She asked about the woman lecturer to gain time. "Has she been fully rehabilitated?"

"Yes." Poliakov nodded. "She has written a denunciation of Bokov. It will be published next week. It broke her heart," he added. "She spent a whole night crying, without sleep."

"How do you know so much? Personal details. Were you with her?"

He looked into the English girl's flinty gray eyes and said simply, "After Bokov's arrest, she stayed with me. But I'm not suspected. They believe I influenced her against the dissidents."

"I see," Elizabeth said. She couldn't fault him, and her instincts believed him genuine. She decided to take the chance.

"I have something which will convince Irina and her mother," she said. "But you are taking a very great risk. I have to warn you of that."

"I understand," he said quietly. "I am quite ready." He repeated the Russian girl's remark. "Sasanov tried to help Belezky; we must help his family. I know it's dangerous, and I'll be careful."

"It's dangerous because you have to trust the wife and the daughter," she said. "If either of them gives you away, it will be the end of every one of you." Including the foundation of my little network, she thought.

She drew a brown envelope from her bag and passed it to him under the table. "This is from Sasanov," she murmured. "It will prove that he's alive. Give it to Irina after the funeral. She must think he's dead until then. Can you keep it safe?"

The envelope went into his jacket pocket. "I can promise you, nobody will find it. I have a class with her student group on Wednesday, the twenty-sixth. That's a week after the funeral takes place."

"That will be time enough," Elizabeth said. "You're quite certain she's really sympathetic? For God's sake, make sure before you hand this over."

"I know she is," he said. "She is a New Russian at heart. I know it."

"Well," Elizabeth said, gathering her bag and the shopping from Gum, "I hope you're right. For all our sakes. Meet me here this time next week. I'll go first."

She walked out of the café without a glance at him. He finished his tea, lit a cigarette and read the newspaper for the next twenty minutes. A middle-aged woman shared his table, and they exchanged a few words before he too left the café.

"I am going mad shut up in this place!" Sasanov said it with his back turned to Davina. "And every day the same thing—no news!"

He turned and faced her; his look was sour and suspicious. She had come to know it well since they were shut up in that safe flat.

"I don't believe my wife has had any message from me," he said. "It is three weeks now, and nothing. What are you keeping back, Vina? Has something happened to them? Or didn't that postcard ever reach her?"

"I've told you," she said, "again and again, it's being delivered and we're waiting for news. And for God's sake stop accusing me of deceiving you! I'm not going to put up with it."

"Yes you are," he said. "You will nurse me along until the moment your Brigadier White says you can leave."

"And by nursing you along," she said angrily, "do you mean sleeping with you?"

His temper flared, glad of an excuse to release the tension pent up inside. He took a step toward her, white with anger.

"That too," he said. "That's part of the service!"

She had never struck a man in her life; she had never lost control of herself, even when Richard left her. She slapped Sasanov as hard as she could across the face. For a moment they stared at each other in furious confrontation. She saw his hand clench and then drop back to his side. She turned her back on him and went out of the room.

He didn't move; he heard the front door slam and slowly went to the curtained window and looked out. There was nothing to see but a blank wall. The apartment faced the inner well of the block. They couldn't see or be seen. He dropped the net and rubbed the side of his face. The blow had hurt him. He lit a cigarette and threw himself back into one of the common little armchairs with a force that broke a spring. He closed his eyes and gave himself up to anger and despair.

The abyss of melancholy beckoned him; sorrow and fatality were as much a part of Sasanov as of every Russian, heritage of a long history where life offered little beyond birth, suffering and then death. His spirit faltered, wavered at the edge, and then drew back. He had sunk to the depths after Belezky's death; he had climbed back to the living world because he had made up his mind to leave his country and to fight Belezky's cause. But he wasn't fighting anything. He opened his eyes sharply and sat up; the cigarette was crushed in his fingers and flung into a wastebasket. It had a garish red rose painted on it; Sasanov hated it as if it embodied the alien sentimentality of the alien British. Nobody else would paint a flower on something they used for rubbish. He stared at it with loathing. No, he wasn't fighting; he had played the bargaining game with all the skill of his professional training; he had made his demands and had them accepted. It had seemed to be going so smoothly; he should have been forewarned that life just did not treat people in that sunny way.

The fire at Halldale had been the awakening. The attempt to murder him had failed only because he had insisted on spending time in the motel. He owed his life to sleeping with Davina Graham.

But now the element of time was all-important. Important so that his wife and daughter shouldn't accept the bogus corpse as his and plan their lives without him. Important that he should get to work with the British Intelligence Service, and by so doing discover which among them was working for the Russians. He couldn't protect himself from attack while he remained entombed in the dingy flat, taking a little exercise in the darkness, shadowed by security men; waiting, waiting. . . . He cursed out loud in Russian, as if he were challenging the fates, the British and his own service all together. He was becoming paranoid, suspecting everyone, even the woman who was now in love with him. He wished he hadn't insulted her. He cursed himself for that. Behind the anger in her face he had seen pain, and he hated himself for hurting her.

But she couldn't give him what he needed, the sense of deep identification known only between Russians. If he loved her, it was a separate thing. His wife's face was what he wanted to see; to touch her cheeks with his finger, to bury his head in her breasts and hold her close to him. To see his daughter smile, to take her hand and walk out in the clean fresh air with her. He had lost his roots, and the sickness in him was growing stronger than his resolve to right the dreadful injustice done to his friend and others suffering in the name of human freedom.

There had been moments, and as he sat alone in the cramped living room this became another, when he almost welcomed the idea of going back, of being tried and punished and joining Belezky in that way, rather than struggle out his life among strangers. He got up, found another cigarette and lit it. His hand, normally steady, trembled like a drunkard's. He threw the shaking match away and lit another.

He couldn't get out now, even if he wanted to. He was hemmed in against the menace from his own side. He was helpless, defenseless against doubt and anguish, dependent upon the one woman for news, for comfort, for hope itself. When he heard her come in, he sprang up and burst into the hallway. He pulled her into his arms, and while he mumbled his apologies and tried to kiss her, she realized that he was crying.

James White's second-in-command had been a history instructor at the university where the Brigadier's son was an undergraduate. His name then was Grant Mitchell; his family were staunch Scots Presbyterians and he appeared to be a typically staid product of his background. His friendship with the Whites' son Philip had brought him into their family circle, and James White detected something unusual about the young man. Five years later he appeared unexpectedly at the Whites' house in Kent. James White had listened quietly to the anguished story of Grant's struggle against homosexuality and seduction by one of his own students. His lover had tried to blackmail him. White's attention riveted on him. What kind of blackmail? he inquired gently. There was a look of defiance on Mitchell's face.

"He threatened to expose me unless I agreed to pass information to the Russians. He knows I want to go into the Foreign Office." White had put an arm around his shoulders. "I can't help being what I am, but I'm not a bloody traitor."

White listened to the words and nodded. He sent Mitchell to bed with a stiff whiskey and soda and told him he had nothing to worry about. He had come to exactly the right person.

Grant Mitchell didn't go into the Foreign Office. He completed his term at the university, and then unaccountably failed the Foreign Office exam. By this time the Brigadier had been given a number of names and details of a literary group operating in south London which was another recruiting center for left-wing sympathizers. Grant Mitchell then went to

America, where all trace of him was lost. He returned under a false name, with a passport and documents prepared by the Brigadier's department, and went to work for him at St. James's Place. His name was no longer Grant Mitchell; he had been Humphrey Grant for many years. He was a cold, forbidding man, completely cerebral. Since his emotional life had jeopardized him, he had discarded it. He lived for his work, for the excitement and the challenge of intelligence at the top level. He was known in the department as the Sea-Green Incorruptible, and the nickname was apt. The Brigadier was aware of it, as he was aware of everything that happened among his subordinates, and thought the reference to Robespierre very acute.

For the past two months Grant had been in Saudi Arabia, negotiating secretly with representatives of the United Arab Emirates. The results had not been satisfactory. James White was glad to have him back—he was the man to head the team working with Sasanov. He had spent the best part of a week reading the file on Sasanov, going through Davina Graham's reports, studying the findings of the pathologists and arson experts on the Halldale Manor fire. By the weekend, he had prepared a summary for the Brigadier, and they studied it together in his office.

"In your opinion, then, the informer was not at Halldale?"

Grant shook his head. "No. The staff there were checked and counterchecked. They were all long-standing, reliable department men. None of them had money which couldn't be accounted for, or pressing family problems, or any evidence to suggest they could have been working for the Russians. And all were killed in the fire. We've got to look elsewhere."

"I was afraid of that," the Brigadier said. He sighed. "It looks as if we've got another one tucked in here somewhere. Christ, I wish we had the death penalty for this sort of thing!"

"Not with our present Home Secretary," Grant said dryly. "He'd send the bastard to a psychiatric clinic to find out just what pressures made him become a traitor and charge it to the taxpayer. We'll have to find this one and deal with him ourselves, this time."

"Oh, we'll find him," the Brigadier said.

"Or her," Grant amended.

White looked up quickly. "You're not suggesting Miss Graham?"

"No, I'm not suggesting anyone," he said. "But I'd like to look into her as closely as we've looked into those poor devils who got burned to death. What's the harm, if she's got nothing to hide?"

"No harm at all," the Brigadier said. "Do you propose to talk to her?"

"At some point, yes. I'll do a little preliminary digging first. And I ought to make contact with Sasanov. He seems very anxious to start serious work with us. We ought to take advantage as quickly as possible."

"He's reached the same conclusion as we have," James White said. "He knows we've got a mole, and he won't have a chance of fading out of sight himself until we've caught him. It'll be easier when we've had a reaction from his family. It's a month since we sent his message, and there's been no definite answer. Miss Graham says he's building up a considerable head of steam, being shut up in the flat and getting no news."

Grant pursed his lips, and tapped them with the end of his pencil. "I suggest we make immediate contact with Swallow and stress the urgency. People are apt to take their time over these things when they're in their own sphere of operations. Shall I organize that?"

"Yes," the Brigadier decided. "Send it through today. We must have an answer, otherwise we just might find Sasanov has decided to say nothing at all until we've discovered our double agent. And that could take even more time."

"And time," Grant said quietly, "is something we haven't got. I learned that from the Saudis, if nothing else."

He gathered his file and walked out of the office. By noon, a coded message was on its way to the embassy in Moscow, for the commercial attaché who was the head of intelligence. Elizabeth Cole, code-named "Swallow," received her instructions from him in a memo which she immediately put through the shredder.

She set out for the café at teatime. A message for Poliakov was phoned through to the university. Books he had ordered were waiting for him in Moscow's biggest bookshop on Red Square. If he collected them at four, they'd be packed up to take away. He said thank you, yes, he'd come at that time. He was already waiting for Elizabeth Cole in the café when she arrived.

Irina Sasanova watched her mother drinking tea. Since the funeral she had seemed less nervous, more calm in herself. The funeral had been an ugly occasion, a quick cremation with no relatives except themselves, and two officials flanking the somber figure of General Antonyii Volkov. The group was photographed, which surprised Irina and her mother; Fedya

Sasanova cried through the ceremony, while Irina stayed unmoved, supporting her mother. To the eyes of Volkov, there was more relief than sorrow in the widow's tears. The white-faced daughter showed real human agony. She at least believed that the dead man was her father. He shook hands with them afterward, and they were driven home in an official car. Inside the apartment, Irina broke down and wept bitterly until she went to bed and fell asleep. A week later, after the sociology class, her lecturer asked her to stay behind and go over her notes with him.

"I must talk to you," he said. "About your father."

She had looked down, tears filling her eyes. "Please don't. He was buried last week." She shrugged. "It's all over now."

Poliakov had laid a hand on her shoulder. She blushed at the contact.

He said quietly, "Your father is alive. I have something which proves that body belonged to someone else."

She stared at him, eyes wide with amazement.

"Take this and give it to your mother."

She put the envelope into her pocket. The risk he had taken appalled her. So did the extent of his involvement with what was certainly treason. It was one thing to theorize and talk about her views on sociology and whether she would forgive her father if by chance he ever came back. Dangerous enough to merit a harsh punishment. But delivering that envelope could mean his death. Receiving it and passing it to her mother carried the same penalty for her. Her color faded, leaving her very pale indeed. She closed her hand around the shape in her pocket.

"What is it?" she spoke in a whisper.

"I don't know," Poliakov said. "I only know it will prove your father is alive. Give it to your mother and if she has anything to say, write this in your next essay: 'Lenin was the high priest in the religion of the proletariat.' Can you remember that?" She repeated the phrase.

"It's meaningless enough to have me question you about it," he said. "If there is no message, then write: 'Lenin was the champion of the proletariat.' Do you understand?"

"I understand," she murmured. Poliakov had done something which sprang from two causes; one was sympathy for her dilemma and the other was because he had rightly interpreted her blushes. He kissed her lightly on the cheek. He saw by the look in her eyes that he had sealed the pact of mutual silence.

"Destroy it afterward, whatever it is. Leave no trace."

She nodded and hurried out of the lecture room.

A fellow student, one of the few girls who spoke kindly to her these days, smiled and said, "I think he's in love with you, Irina; he pays more attention to you than to anyone else." She laughed out loud at Irina's crimson cheeks, and went her way.

That had been three days ago, and still Irina had not given the envelope to her mother. She had opened it, and seen the incomprehensible picture of a sunrise and a circle of big stones, and had recognized instantly her father's writing on the back. And read the message: "The sun rose once for us, Fedya. Join me and it will rise for us again. Your husband, Ivan, who loves you." She hadn't done what Poliakov told her; she hadn't given it to her mother and she hadn't destroyed it. She kept it in its envelope, hidden in her brassiere, and it was instinct that made her delay until that afternoon when they were drinking tea. There was something unnatural about her mother, as if the funeral had pacified her fears. She slept better and seemed more cheerful in a guarded way. She made Irina uneasy.

"Mother?"

Fedya looked up at her. "Yes, dearest?"

"Are you still unhappy over what happened to Father?"

"But of course! Why do you ask such a strange question? Do you think I've stopped missing him when only a week ago we stood by his body?"

When Irina didn't answer, she added, "I can't weep forever. And you have your life to live. Maybe now the authorities will realize we did nothing wrong. He didn't defect, he had a breakdown and killed himself. We can't be blamed for that."

"Then in a way you're glad he's dead," her daughter said in a flat voice.

"No, no, how could I be glad!" Fedya protested. "I loved him dearly, you know that—you know how much he suffered after Belezky died." Instinctively she spoke very quietly. "But the way it has turned out is better for us. Better for you."

"You identified his body," Irina said. "Tell me the truth, Mother. Was it really he?"

Fedya hesitated; her daughter looked tense, odd. Why all the sudden questions, and that final, terribly dangerous question? A wild suspicion flashed into her mind. Children had been set to spy upon their parents before now. Then reason prevailed and she shuddered at what fear could do to the deepest relationship. God forgive her for thinking such a thing of her own child, even for a moment.

"No, darling," she said gently. "It wasn't your father. But Volkov thinks it is. The disappearance is explained—you saw the pictures in *Pravda* and the reports. We'll be safe now, just so long as we forget all about it. We must think of him as dead, too."

Slowly Irina took the envelope out of her dress and placed it on the table.

"I knew you were hiding something," she said. "You could have trusted me, Mother. Read what's inside that. Then tell me if we can think of him as dead."

Fedya covered her mouth with one hand as a cry of surprise escaped her. She had looked at the written side of the card first; she turned it over quickly and then back, reading the few words again.

"Oh, my God," she said. "My God—it's from him."

"How can you be sure?" Irina asked her. "It could be forged, it could be a trick. I don't think it is, but we dare not risk anything."

"It's from your father," Fedya Sasanova said. "No one could send that message except he. Nobody but I would understand it. 'The sun rose once for us.' He sent this."

"What does it mean?"

"When we were married," her mother said, "we went to the Crimea for a week. We had a room in a holiday chalet, deep in the country. It was spring and the flowers were like a carpet. He took me for a walk very early one morning before the sun rose. We made love among the flowers, and the rising sun touched us, as in that postcard." She put her head down and began to cry.

"What does he mean, join me? Oh, God, how I miss him!" She looked up suddenly, and fear distorted her face. "Where did you get this? Who gave it to you?"

"Someone I trust," her daughter said simply. "They will send a message back for us. He wants you to go to him. I want to go, too."

Her mother wiped the tears away. She picked up the postcard and then let it fall to the table.

"We can't," she said. "We could never get out of Russia. It's madness."

Irina leaned toward her. "But why? He must know of a way or he wouldn't suggest it. Mother, don't you want to go to him?"

"Of course I'd go," she mumbled. "I lie awake thinking of him, long-

ing to be with him. But I'd reconciled myself to life without him. I knew
when I saw that body that he was safe in the West. And I was glad
because I knew you'd have a chance again. Your career at the university,
graduating as teacher . . . We've been under a cloud for so long, and
the strain has been so awful! When they came to take me to the mortuary
to identify him, I thought I was going to be arrested—I nearly died of
fear. No, this isn't possible. If we get involved in anything and it fails,
we'll go to the Gulag, or the mental hospitals. I might risk it myself, but
never for you."

She poured a glass of steaming tea from the samovar and sipped it.
"My mind is made up," she said. "Put that card in the stove, Irina."

"No, Mother. Wait till the morning; think about it. I want to go; I
don't want to go on living here, frightened of every knock on the door.
Make up your mind tomorrow."

Her mother moved slowly, as if she were very tired. She took the card
from the table and kissed it. Then she lifted the lid of the stove and
dropped it inside.

"I have decided," she said. "Your father will understand. I have had a
good life; I want to see you settled and safe, with a man of your own and a
child. We won't talk about it anymore."

Irina didn't answer. For a few moments while she argued with her
mother, her courage had risen, minimizing the difficulties, ignoring the
penalty for failure. Escape to the West seemed to answer the problems of
loneliness and the drab fear that invested their lives. But when Fedya
Sasanova dropped the postcard into the stove, Irina faced reality again. It
was not possible. Nothing could be done. Her mother was right. She saw
the sorrow on her face, realizing suddenly how her mother had aged in
the last nine months. She sipped her tea and bowed her head like an old,
exhausted woman. Irina came and put her arms around her.

"Little mother," she whispered, using the old-fashioned endearment.
"I love you; we have each other. We'll be all right."

At five o'clock in the morning, in the dead hour before dawn, Fedya
Sasanova was wakened by the terrified caretaker of the apartment block.
Two men loomed in the bedroom door behind her. She got up and
dressed, and crammed a few clothes into a plastic bag. Irina woke as they
were leaving; still half asleep, she opened her door and saw the figures in
the tiny lighted hallway. She had one glimpse of her mother's white face
before Fedya Sasanova was hustled out and the entrance door was
slammed. The dividing walls between the little apartments were thin,
and their neighbors heard Irina screaming. Nobody came to comfort her.

7

Jeremy Spencer-Barr's suitcases were all packed and labeled; he had letters of introduction and his accredited papers for his new post at the UN. Everything was ready, and his girl friend Mary had arranged to drive him to the airport. He came up to Humphrey Grant's office, expecting a final briefing. He felt confident and eager, and he was determined to impress Grant. He considered him the most important member of the department after the Brigadier himself. Unlike his colleagues, he didn't call him SGI behind his back or indulge in infantile jokes, like drawing a guillotine in the margin of one of his memos—that was Peter Harrington's level.

Grant looked up when he came in, and gave his bleak smile for a moment. Spencer-Barr sat down and waited. Grant shuffled papers. Then he put them in a neat pile and said, "I expect you're all packed and ready for New York?"

"Yes," Jeremy said eagerly."I'm off next week."

"Well," Grant remarked, "I'm sorry about this, but we've decided not to send you." Spencer-Barr stared at him. He was so taken aback that he groped for words. "Not going? But why? Why not?"

"Because the Brigadier has another job for you," Grant said. "We're sending someone else out to New York."

"Harrington—is he going back?" There was an angry flush under the young man's eyes, like blotches.

"No," Grant said. "He's not going anywhere at the moment. Someone

123

from the Washington embassy is going to be transferred to the UN. We think you can be more useful here." He looked at the man on the other side of the desk and noted the signs of anger and bewilderment becoming charged with suspicion.

"One thing I must know, sir. Is this a demotion? Have I done anything wrong?"

"On the contrary," Grant said smoothly, "what we have in mind for you is much more important than playing along two Iron Curtain contacts. Harrington always thought they were more important than they really were. I can assure you, this change of plan is no reflection on you. Quite the contrary," he repeated.

"Thank God for that!" Spencer-Barr said. He had regained control. "When will I know what my new job will be?"

"In a week or two," Grant said. "When the details are worked out. In the meantime I suggest you spend the interim at the language center. Brush up your Russian."

He didn't give Spencer-Barr time to ask more questions. He stood up and said briefly, "That's it, then. If you've run into any expenses through this U.S. trip being canceled, list them and send them in. I'll see that you're reimbursed."

"Thank you," Spencer-Barr said.

He turned and went out of the office. He paused in the corridor for a moment. "Russian," he said under his breath. "This is something big." Then he walked on, his step quickening. He hurried down the stairs to his own section, and saw with a flash of irritation that the figure coming up was Peter Harrington. For a second or two they stared at each other, nakedly hostile; then Harrington grinned his impudent, infuriating grin and said, "Not gone yet, old man?"

"No," Spencer-Barr said. Harrington stopped and it was impossible to get past him without pushing him aside. He noticed that the older man looked less disheveled than usual and had lost weight.

"What's the delay?" Harrington asked. "I thought you'd gone already. Someone keeping the seat warm for you, are they?"

"I'm not going after all," Jeremy said. "The plan's been changed." He took a step downward, but Harrington didn't move.

"Who's the replacement, then? Don't tell me those stupid buggers upstairs are just leaving my contacts—"

"Not at all," Spencer-Barr snapped. "Someone from Washington is going to New York. I must go, I'm in a hurry."

Harrington stood aside. "And what are you going to do, join Personnel?" He laughed as Jeremy went past him without answering.

He watched Jeremy's retreating figure as he hurried down the stairs and out of sight. "You little turd," he muttered. Then he continued on his own way up.

He had been trying to contact Davina Graham, but without success; she hadn't been in to the office for weeks. Her regular reports to White were no longer made in person, and nobody knew where she was. A pall of uncertainty had settled over the existence of Sasanov and his "minder." Harrington got no response from colleagues who might have seen her or been in contact. She had vanished immediately after the fire at Halldale Manor. He sat by himself in the evenings, holding on to his resolve not to drink, and wondered whether the vacuum left behind meant that she was dead. But if an operative was dead, then Personnel was always notified. Nothing had come through to him.

He busied himself at his desk, writing up details on a list of files, his mind concentrating on other things. So Spencer-Barr was not going to New York. He hadn't appeared to mind, so he must have been assigned to something else. And at short notice too, because Peter Harrington knew exactly when his replacement was supposed to leave, and his remarks had been purely malicious, a feeble stab at a successful rival. And in spite of his string of languages and degrees Spencer-Barr was a bloody amateur at the game. Only a fool would have told him that a Washington diplomat was going to take the UN post. That was classified information; he wondered whether to make use of the information to damage Spencer-Barr, but he himself didn't stand high enough in anyone's opinion to warrant a hearing.

He had followed Davina's advice, denying himself the ease of a drink when he was tired and lonely, had cut out the carbohydrates and enrolled at a gymnasium, where he worked out twice a week. She had held out a hope of reinstatement that night when they talked in Jules's Bar. He had clung to the hope and done what she suggested. But nothing had happened; no call came to promote him out of the limbo of the Personnel Department. The ache for a big, warming Scotch was growing in him. At the end of the day he didn't go to the local pub; he went straight home to the dull little flatlet in Earls Court, switched on the television and settled down to watch until close-down. He made himself a sandwich and some coffee; when the telephone rang, he jumped, and swore because the hot coffee slopped over and spilled on his leg.

When he heard Davina's voice he laughed out loud with relief.

"Christ, I thought you'd dropped through a hole. How are you? Where have you been? Nobody knew where to contact you."

"I'm fine," her voice said. "I haven't been to the office, that's all. But I'm glad to think I've been missed. How are you, Peter?" He knew it was a genuine inquiry.

"I'm sober, and about six pounds lighter. I've been living a life of self-denial, and I'm not joking. No booze, no sex, and I go to a PT class twice a week. It's driven me up the bloody wall, but I've kept my promise. When are you going to keep yours? And where the hell are you?"

"What exactly did I promise?" she said.

"To help me get going again," he answered, and there was no levity this time. "To make a fresh start."

"I'm coming up to the office tomorrow," she said. "Let's have lunch at the pub. I can't wait to see the new Peter Harrington."

"He can't wait to see you," he said. "Come and rescue me from Personnel about twelve-thirty; okay?"

"Fine," Davina said. "Twelve-thirty."

She hung up, and he put the receiver down. Coming up to the office. That meant she was somewhere in the country. He didn't know who had started the rumors about Halldale Manor, but they crept from office to office and were murmured over drinks on the way home. And unlike most rumors, this one was spread by someone who hoped to pick up an answer to the question. He frowned, trying to remember where he had first heard it. The frown became deeper when he realized that it had originated from someone in Spencer-Barr's office: a junior officer, still changing the typewriter ribbons and checking the carbon paper. All agog about the fire, and was it true that the nursing home was part of the department's safe custody system. That was where Peter had first heard it, from a stooge in Spencer-Barr's little circle, a sidekick who wouldn't have known enough to put the question together. Harrington made himself more coffee and sponged the stain off his trousers. Twelve-thirty tomorrow, he would see Davina Graham.

The bright boys wouldn't have counted on that.

One of the students in the sociology class nudged her companion; they smirked as they saw Irina Sasanova stay behind with the young lecturer. The class emptied and the girl said to her friend, "There's something going on there. She can't stop gawking at him and going red. I wonder if she'll sleep with him."

"Maybe she has already," her companion giggled. "Her essays aren't *that* good." They followed the others away from the classroom, still giggling and speculating.

Poliakov waited for Irina to come up on the rostrum. Her appearance had shocked him. She looked gray-faced, gaunt; he thought immediately that she had been ill.

The essay was almost incomprehensible, as if she had filled up the pages without any thought of content. On the final page she had written in a strong hand, "Lenin was the high priest of the religion of the proletariat." It made more sense than the rest of what she had written.

"Irina," he said. "Irina, you look ill. Tell me, is anything the matter?"

Her eyes filled with tears and overflowed down her cheeks. She didn't wipe them away or try to stop them.

"My mother was arrested last week," she said in a low, trembling voice. "They took her in the middle of the night."

It was Poliakov's turn to freeze with horror. "The message I gave you—"

"She destroyed it," Irina said. "They found nothing. She won't tell them anything because of me."

"God help us," he muttered. "God help us all."

"You needn't be afraid," the girl said. "I found out why she was arrested. I went to Antonyii Volkov himself."

Poliakov stared at her. "Volkov—you went to ask him about her?"

"He came to the funeral. My father worked under him for years. I went to his office and I wouldn't go away. They threatened to arrest me, but I just sat outside the door, and in the end he let me come in. And he told me that my mother had been sent to a rehabilitation center. Not the Gulag, he assured me about that." She gave a grimace of a smile, full of hatred at the memory.

"He was kind, patient, explaining to me that my mother had told a damaging lie about my father, which could have saved his life if the authorities had been warned in time. She had been selfish and disloyal and my father's suicide was mostly her fault. She had to be reeducated to a sense of her duties as a Soviet citizen. Then of course she would be allowed home. I had nothing to fear, I was a good student, a faithful member of the Young Communists. My record was excellent. I must go on with my studies, and remember to call on him if I needed help in any way."

"And was this true?" Poliakov questioned her. He didn't believe that the unhappy Fedya Sasanova wouldn't be forced to betray them.

"Not as he told it," Irina answered. "My mother did lie. She told me she identified that body, knowing it wasn't my father. To protect us and make the authorities believe he was dead. They must have known she lied, and that's why she was arrested. So I thanked Antonyii Volkov and went home to the empty apartment. I stayed inside for three days; all the neighbors knew what had happened. Nobody dared to come near me. The caretaker came to tell me I must get out; I slammed the door in her face. And I wrote the essay for you, with the line you told me."

"I am sorry, Irina Ivanovna, so very sorry for you . . . and for your mother."

He put his arm around her and she crept closer, clinging to him. She hid her face against his chest and sobbed for a few minutes. He held her, soothing her with words and stroking her hair. Rage engulfed him, driving out the initial terror of betrayal.

"My poor child," he said, again and again, while he cursed the injustice, the iron-hearted tyranny of his country's political system and the monsters it spawned.

"We'll help you," he promised. "There are a number of us, we'll take care of you."

She raised her head and looked up at him.

"Send a message back to my father. Tell him I want to come to him. If I have to stay here, I shall kill myself. Can you do that, Alexei—can you promise me to send that message?"

He nodded, and said something that she had never heard before. "I swear by the Holy Saints and the Mother of God," Poliakov said. "The message will be delivered."

Elizabeth Cole knocked at the senior attaché's door and poked her head around when he called out.

"The head of chancery wants to see you, sir."

He got up and left the room immediately, following Elizabeth. They didn't speak till they got to the little room next door to the head of chancery's main office. This room was clear of all possible electronic listening devices. When the door was closed, Elizabeth wasted neither time nor words.

"I've just come back from seeing the daughter's contact," she said. "The very worst has happened in one way: the mother's been arrested."

"Christ." The attaché, a seasoned and highly skilled intelligence officer, interrupted her. "I'll say the very worst has happened! This'll blow everything to pieces. Where did you meet him?"

"In the Kremlin Museum; that's our emergency venue," she said. "Hold on, it may not be as bad as it looks. The daughter had been to see him; she told him the news about her mother, and if you can credit it, she had the guts to go and brazen it out with Volkov himself!"

"Guts is hardly the word for it," he said somberly. "He's one of the worst since Schelepin. Go on."

"Apparently he said her mother was being rehabilitated because of some lie she was supposed to have told; he played the kindly uncle to the girl and told her she was in good odor and didn't have to worry. The daughter told her contact that the real reason for the arrest was because her mother had lied about the body they buried and Volkov had caught her out. She'd given the mother the message, and by some really lucky chance she'd destroyed it the night before she was arrested. Daughter is certain mother won't say anything, and anyway she doesn't know who passed the message to daughter. The point is, daughter wants to go over and join father."

The man was puffing on a cigarette, concentrating. "We'll get that down on tape, and then think it through when we've rerun it. I'll set the machine. Start again and put in every detail you can think of."

Elizabeth told the story a second time, without his interruptions, and then they sat and listened to the playback. There was a coffee machine in the corner, a facility copied from the Americans, and they both drank a cup. Elizabeth watched him making squiggles on a pad; she had worked with him for a long time, and this apparent trifling meant that he was thinking very hard indeed. He looked up at her at last, and the pen was set aside.

"We've got to get the daughter out," he said. "And not just because the father wants her. If Volkov decides to do an in-depth investigation of that poor woman she'll implicate the daughter, and if they pick *her* up that's the end of your network, Lizzie; they'll smoke them out of the university like rats. It's just possible that going to see Volkov threw him off the scent; he may genuinely think the daughter's innocent. If that's the case, we'll have time to set it up for her. But we won't know that till we find out what they've done with the mother. There's no such thing as rehabilitation, that's balls. It's either the Gulag or the labor camps. When was she arrested?"

"Last Thursday morning," Elizabeth said.

"That's eight days ago," he said. "If she's still in the Lubyanka by the

end of the week, it means they're investigating her. And she won't hold
out for long. I'll try and get our contact inside to make inquiries. The first
thing to do is get this through to London. Lizzie, you make a full report
and I'll send you on the London flight with the courier tomorrow morning. You can brief the Brigadier on the situation at first hand."

"Thanks," she said. "I'd like a trip home."

"You can have forty-eight hours," he said. "I'll get the route organized
for the daughter this end. We've got to get her out as quickly as possible.
I'll have some papers to give you, too."

He left her alone in the room, where she ran the tape once again and
began to type out a special report for James White. After that she erased
the tape, gathered her papers and went off to pack for the flight back to
London.

Sasanov lay awake and watched the dawn break in the patch of sky
visible from the bedroom window. Like the other rooms, it looked out
onto a wall, but from his vantage point in the bed he could see the sky at
the top. He had slept early, Davina beside him, and awakened, as he did
every night, at the hour when man's life force is lowest. His watch
showed 4 A.M.; he hardly needed to look at it to know that it was the same
time as the other nights. He didn't try to sleep; he moved away from her
and stretched his arms above his head and stared into the darkness, waiting for the dawn. There was no answer from his wife; he didn't ask for
news, because he had come to the conclusion that there wasn't any. The
Brigadier couldn't withhold a refusal indefinitely, and he would know by
Davina if she was hiding anything from him. There just wasn't an
answer, and he knew what that meant.

They wouldn't come. He was dead and buried for them both, and they
wanted to be left in peace. He thought of his wife, Fedya, and the memory was so fresh she could have been beside him instead of the Englishwoman who loved him. He remembered that brief honeymoon spent in
the magic Crimean springtime. They were both very young, and in spite
of their enlightened upbringing there was an old-fashioned quality to
their courtship and the wedding in the Wedding Palace. They had slept
together before, but the real consummation of their love took place in the
sweet-scented grass under a glorious sunrise. He had realized afterward
that this subconscious memory had selected the postcard of the dramatic
sunrise over the pagan temple on Salisbury Plain. He had been in love
with her for a long time; his love for her remained when their passion had
lost its freshness. She had been his friend, his mother, the recipient of his

most secret thoughts. Living and working in a world of suspicion and deceit, his private life was a complete contrast. And from that contrast he derived an independence of mind which welcomed friends like Jacob Belezky; within his family circle, freedom of thought and expression was a cherished thing. Fedya had a simplicity which shamed him, if he brought his professional standards home. His daughter was his companion and his pride; clever, uncomplicated, a happy girl with a good future. He had lived within a charmed domestic circle, and his love for Jacob was as deep as the love for his wife and child.

Fedya's strength had helped him make the decision to defect. He turned and gazed at the sleeping woman by his side. They had little in common, except a basic integrity of spirit. Fedya had common sense and intelligence, but she was a mature woman who had never suffered inhibitions. Davina Graham's brilliant intuitive mind was part of a personality that had not fully developed.

In her midthirties she was still growing up. Her love for him was a mixture of submission and protectiveness, with outbursts of independence when she felt too exposed; and the child still lurked in the background, finger in mouth, uncertain of itself. He needed impetus to start on his new life, the quiet encouragement of his wife, with her understanding of him and his innermost feelings. Her silence gave him more comfort than the dialectical arguments of an intellectual like Davina. Davina could never convince him that he was right in working against his homeland, because she was not a part of it. She would never understand what he had given up, because she was not a Russian.

She had thrust off the bedclothes, and he covered her against the early-morning cold in the bedroom. For the past week they had gone to bed and slept. He hadn't felt like making love to her, and she had been sensitive enough not to approach him. She looked unhappy, when she thought herself unobserved. She did her best to interest him and to hold out hope of good news from his family. But her own confidence was sinking, and it was her suggestion, not his, that she should slip out of the flat and be driven by one of their security men to see the Brigadier.

She was going that morning; he regarded the loneliness ahead of him with dull despair. The abyss was at his feet again, and he felt tempted to give up and let himself fall into it.

She moved, and reached out a hand to touch him. At the same time she woke up.

"Ivan? Are you awake?"

"Yes, it's very early. Go to sleep."

"What's the matter?"

He could see her eyes wide and searching, the look of anxiety on her face.

"Nothing. I'll sleep in a minute."

"No, you won't," she said. "You've been doing this every night. Waking up at four and just lying there."

She reached up and switched on the garish bedside light. She looked pale and unrested.

"I'm going to make some coffee," she said. She got up, and shivered. "It's cold—they don't put the central heating on till six. I'll turn on the electric fire."

She went out to the tiny kitchen and began to make the strong French coffee that he liked. The room grew warmer and lighter; when he sat upright he lost the little square of rosy sky and closed his eyes against the drab brick wall. She came back and poured him a cup of coffee, climbed into bed in her robe and sat sipping her own. They didn't speak. She glanced at him quickly, not to be seen doing so, and noticed how heavy and lifeless his face seemed in repose.

Russian melancholy, she thought, suddenly furious with him; bloody Slav gloom and doom. It's so real I could almost pluck it out of the air. And then her anger melted, leaving the miserable ache of unhappiness that was becoming the predominant feeling in her life. He's wretched because he's losing hope, and it doesn't matter what I've done, I can't make up to him for *them*. And I don't want to make up for them, unless by some awful chance they can't or won't come to him. I don't want to possess this unhappy man. I want to make him happy; I want to give him back something because of all he's given me—probably without even knowing it, she thought. Just by wanting me and teaching me what loving a man really means.

"Ivan," she said. "Listen to me, please. I know you're depressed; I know you don't think anything is going to come of my seeing the Brigadier except a lot of promises to gain more time. Isn't that true?"

He turned and looked at her, and he nodded. She had this way of directness, of seeing into his thoughts and speaking them for him.

"Yes, that's very much what I feel. You are doing it to try and help, but there's nothing you can do. They are not coming to me . . . I know it."

"I don't believe that," she said. "I think they've had your message and by this time there must have been an answer. I'm going there today to find out what it is. And I'm going to tell you, even if it's bad news. I can't stand by and let this drag on and on. I promised you we'd bring them over if they were willing to come. You trusted me, and I'm not going to let you down."

He put his around her and pulled her close. "You're going to fight for me," he said. "Don't fight too hard, Vina, or they'll think you've got involved with me, and we'll be separated. I know how these things work."

"So do I," she said. "I won't play it like that, don't worry. But I'm going to make them tell me what's happened. Will you try and be a bit more cheerful—just till I get back?"

He kissed her instead of answering; he felt no desire, only tenderness because she was showing how much she was on his side. That was her way of loving him: to fight for him with her own people, to turn to him with such a hungry response that his dulled senses woke and, as the morning lightened into full day, once again they made love.

Humphrey Grant went to Heathrow to meet the BA flight in from Moscow. He met Elizabeth Cole and the courier, and escorted them to London. The report from the embassy was handed over in the car. They drove straight to the office, where the night security man let them in, and sped up in the lift to Grant's office. He sat down with Elizabeth and went through the report with her.

"We'd better run this through the copying machine," he said. "Make two copies. I'll have the original filed."

He didn't offer Elizabeth a drink, or apologize for keeping her in the office after the long Moscow flight. She knew Humphrey Grant from her early stint spent in the London office, and she wasn't at all surprised by his lack of consideration. She was too involved in the business to think about being tired or wanting dinner. She came back with the two copies.

"What do you think we should do?"

"I don't know yet," Grant said. "Certainly not make a decision in a hurry."

"We must get the girl out," Elizabeth said. He glanced up at her, disapproving of her vehemence. "That's up to the Chief. You'd better be here by nine in the morning. He'll want to see you."

"Right," she said. "I'll get back and sort myself out." She yawned, and Grant noticed how very tired she looked.

"I'll get a taxi and drop you off," he said.

She showed her surprise. "Oh, that's very nice of you. Thanks."

They sat in silence in the taxi that they picked up in Victoria Street, till it turned into the Cromwell Road, where she was booked into a tourist hotel.

"You've done a good job," he said suddenly. "We mustn't lose your network."

"No," she said. "Does that mean you'll back me up tomorrow?"

"I won't make any promises," he answered. She got out, pulled her small traveling bag with her, said, "Thanks for the lift," and shut the door. Grant gave the driver his private address in Chelsea, and the cab drove away.

His service flat was small and impersonal; there were no photographs, few personal belongings to give it identity with the man who had lived in it for nearly five years. He switched on the TV to the late news program and settled down with a glass of beer.

He didn't feel hungry, and he never ate unless he felt like it. There was an interview with a well-known left-wing MP who talked earnestly about the injustices of capitalist society. Grant knew the formula by heart; he had heard the same reasons put forward in his university days, the same appeal to idealism which had attracted so many men of real compassion into a political system of tyranny on a gigantic scale. He thought of the wife of Ivan Sasanov, dragged into the dark, her memory a diminishing cry like a light vanishing into a tunnel, until even the pin-point went out. There was no justice for her, or for the millions like her. Soviet power was built on the dead. Blood and tears were its lubricants.

He leaned forward and angrily switched off. Elizabeth Cole was a good operative. A steady type, not given to exaggeration. "We must get the girl out." But it wasn't so easy; it took time to make the careful arrangements that had been used before. And they might not have any time at all. Not if the mother was still in the Lubyanka being interrogated. "In-depth" was the departmental euphemism for horrid pain and mind-destroying drugs. They wouldn't know the answer to that question until their man in the embassy had his reply from their contact inside the prison itself. That couldn't be hurried, either.

Intelligence work had taught Humphrey Grant superhuman patience and a steely capacity for taking risks when necessary. He knew that the Russian defector's "minder" was coming to the office in the morning, requesting an urgent interview. He had been making his own inquiries about her since the slaughter at Halldale Manor. Some interesting facts had been turned up.

Tomorrow might be a good time to face her with them, if she attempted to be awkward. He washed up his glass and dried it; everything in the kitchen was tidy, and the tray was ready for his coffee and wholewheat crackers in the morning.

He went into his spartan room, undressed and settled into bed with a book. He read detective stories for relaxation.

Davina Graham traveled in a London taxi from Shepherds Bush to the office in St. James's Place, at the back of Queen Anne Street. It was a London taxi, except that it never drove around the streets or accepted an ordinary fare. Its driver dressed like a London cabbie, but he carried a gun. He was a crack shot with small arms and an expert in self-defense. He was one of a small fleet of a dozen special transports used for making pickups or taking high-security passengers for short distances.

In the back, Davina looked at herself in her compact mirror. Now she carried the tools of female vanity in what used to be a handbag filled with practical things like a notebook and spare pens. She had reverted to the severe hairstyle that Sasanov disliked; she was pale and tired, but the reflection was carefully made up, with dark mascara that flattered her large eyes. She didn't realize how different she looked until she walked into White's office and saw the quick appraisal that he gave her. Grant's look was longer; they had never liked each other. She was too aloof and competitive, and he was coldly sarcastic if they disagreed. None of this surface discord worried the Brigadier, who believed it was better to divide a little in order to rule over his divergent, clever pack of individualists. He shook hands with her warmly.

"You're looking very well," he said. "I expected to see signs of strain, being shut up in that dreary little place for so long. I expect it *has* been a strain."

"It has, but not for me," Davina said. "That's why I'm afraid I insisted upon breaking cover and seeing you. Sasanov can't take any more. There must be an answer from Moscow by now."

She stared hard at him, challenging. He thought to himself that Grant's information hadn't gone far enough in assessing the change in Davina Graham. The very position she took up, sitting forward, stiff-backed, with her hands gripped into fists, portrayed the antagonist instead of the colleague.

"Could you explain that more clearly?" Grant interposed. "What exactly does it mean?"

She turned to look at him, and the department's cruelly apt nickname flashed into her mind. The Sea-Green Incorruptible. He had the skull-like face of Robespierre, with that ghastly colorless skin. He wouldn't waste any pity on Sasanov; he'd never been known to see a human dilemma except in terms of advantage or otherwise. To him, Sasanov was like one of his own chess pieces to be used in the game of East–West political warfare.

"I mean that he is giving up hope," she said. "He's getting more and more apathetic, more unhappy. Before, he was restless and difficult. Now I feel he's dying inside."

There was a moment of silence, and the Brigadier coughed gently.

"Aren't you being a little dramatic?" Grant asked. "Ivan Sasanov's record in the KGB doesn't accord with the man you're describing. What did you say—dying inside? As far as he was concerned, other people did the dying."

Davina turned right around to face him and do battle.

"Yes," she said. "People like the dissident Jacob Belezky, who was his childhood friend. His death brought Sasanov over to the West. He could have asked any price he wanted for his cooperation with you. I can think of some of them who wanted a half million in a New York bank account just for a start. All he's demanded is his wife and daughter. I stand by what I said, and I ought to know, Humphrey; I've been with him day and night for so many months now."

"Yes," the Brigadier interposed quietly, "day—and night. Why didn't you report that you were sleeping with him? That was very irregular—and foolish."

She faced him coolly; she had expected an attack as soon as she came into the office and sensed the atmosphere.

"You were the person who first mentioned the possibility. Only you didn't think it very likely, did you, sir? I didn't put my personal sex life into the report because I didn't see it had any relevance. It didn't affect Sasanov's decision to cooperate; it was just something that happened between him and me. It certainly hasn't changed his feeling toward his own family. If I've broken the rules by not telling you, then I'm sorry. That's all there is to it. Except I'd like to know how you found out. You did promise there wouldn't be any surveillance, any bugging."

"I kept the promise," White said. "But inquiries were made into everybody after what happened at Halldale. Your intimacy with Sasanov came to light as a result."

"I see," she said. "What did you do, Humphrey, look at the sheets?"

"Miss Graham!" James White snapped the two words at her. "That's enough. You seem to have lost your sense of perspective over this man. That last remark was most unnecessary. Withdraw it at once."

"I withdraw it," she said. She turned so that her back was to Humphrey Grant.

"You will have to be taken off the assignment." Grant spoke coldly. "And before you leave here you'll sign an undertaking never to see him again."

Davina turned toward him; she had become very pale. "That isn't necessary," she said. "I don't have to sign anything; I'm not a criminal."

"I have to remind you," he said, "that, as a member of this department, you are bound by the Official Secrets Act. If you are required to sign this document, you will do so. And you will abide by it."

She swung away from Grant. "Brigadier, you gave me this assignment. You trusted me and believed I could manage Sasanov. Well, I have managed him. He's ready to give his full cooperation; all he needs is some news. I've told you, he's losing heart. I know the man; I've lived with him—in every sense of the word, if you want to consider it like that. If you take me away from him like this, he'll break. And you won't get him back."

James White leaned back and made an arch with his fingertips. "It so happens that we do have some news to give him," he said. "But I don't think he'll be very happy when he hears it. Humphrey, pass Miss Graham Swallow's report, will you?"

Neither spoke while she read it. She put it down on her knee and said slowly, "Oh my God."

"His wife has been arrested, and his daughter wants to come over to the West. As you know him so well, what will his reaction be?"

She got up and put the report back on the desk. "He'll go back to Moscow to get his wife released. And he won't do anything for you unless you agree to send him back. That's what will happen."

"He can't go back," the Brigadier said. "Not now. Other people's lives are at stake, and a network that's taken more than a year of patient work to build up. Sasanov is not going back to wreck everything for us. His daughter can't be left in Russia, because she knows one of the principal contacts. We'll have to bring her out. He stays here, willing or not. You'd better put the case to him, Miss Graham, and make it stick."

"You gave your promise to him," she said slowly. "Your solemn promise. He could go back if he wanted to. You never meant to keep it, did you?"

"My dear," the Brigadier said quietly, "my duty to my service and my country takes precedence over my personal word to any man, woman or child. He could have gone back before this happened. He can't leave now. It's up to you to persuade him to help us, even if it's just to avenge what's happened to his wife. You say you have a very deep relationship with him. You must make him listen."

She moved around the room and stood looking out his window, over the panorama of St. James's Park.

"He won't trust me after this," she said. "But I've got an idea. I've had it in the back of my mind for a long time, ever since he asked for his family."

Grant hadn't spoken for some minutes; he was watching her, assessing her.

"What idea is this?" James White asked.

"It was rather vague at first," she said. "I hadn't any details worked out, or any time in mind. But it's getting clearer now. You want Sasanov to work with you; you want him to commit himself totally to life in the West. Then let me tell him you'll try to get his wife exchanged. And to prove my good faith to him, let me go to Russia and help bring his daughter out."

"And that was your idea?" Grant asked her. "To take part in this rescue yourself? Good God, I've never heard such nonsense! You've no training or experience of anything like this. Absolutely impossible!"

"I know," she said. "I'd need backup. But I could pass for an East German; my German is good enough. And a woman can get in and out of places easier than a man. I'd even picked out someone to go with me from here."

"Oh?" the Brigadier said. "Really—who?"

"Peter Harrington." She saw the surprise on his face and heard Grant snort with contempt.

"You can't be serious, Miss Graham. Harrington made such a mess of his job in New York he had to be recalled. He's permanently on the shelf."

"I know about that," she said. "He got into heavy drinking in the States and generally let himself slide. I hinted I might get him a second chance. I had this thing in mind and I wanted to have him with me. I'm seeing him after I leave you."

She came around to the Brigadier's chair.

"I need to do this," she said. "Not just for Sasanov, but for myself too. I've *got* to get his daughter out."

"As Grant said, why you?" the Brigadier asked.

"Because I've allowed myself to get emotionally involved with him," Davina said slowly. "Not just sexually, that wouldn't matter. But emotionally. And the best way to get out of it is to reunite him with his family. Then I can step out of the picture." She hesitated. "I'll sign the undertaking before I leave the office, if only you'll let me go. I'll never see him again when this is over."

"Perhaps you'd be better just to resign your job with Sasanov," Grant suggested dryly, "instead of dashing off on some fool's errand to Russia."

"I'm not so sure," James White said. "I don't think we should dismiss the idea out of hand. Miss Graham has been very honest with us. And she might be useful in putting our original plan into operation." He looked back to Davina. "Go and keep your appointment with Harrington, but don't discuss this. Grant and I will talk it over. Come back to the office before you go home to Shepherds Bush."

"Thank you," she said. "I'll be back after lunch."

When she had gone Grant said, "Good heavens, Chief, why did you say we'd think about it? We've got our man lined up to go in for Sasanov's family. You're not really considering Davina Graham, are you?"

"As a matter of fact," James White said pleasantly, "I am. I think she might be a very good foil for Spencer-Barr in Russia. Look at the time; I'm going to be late for lunch. I'm seeing an old friend at the Garrick. Be here by three, will you, Humphrey? We'll need to go over the plan with Miss Graham before we say anything to Spencer-Barr. And get that official undertaking drawn up."

"Well," Peter Harrington said, "what do you think of the new me? Six pounds lighter and not a drop of juice since we last met!"

"It shows," Davina said. She smiled at him. "You're looking very trim, Peter. And about ten years younger."

His gratification was so obvious, she laughed. He had a relaxing effect on her, even when her nerves were strung like catgut after the morning's interview. He did look well: his clothes were brushed and clean, his skin had a healthy color; the loss of flabby weight had made him look his proper age.

"I can say the same to you, Davy—sorry, Davina. Country air seems to suit you."

The local pub was full; they had managed to get a table in the little snack bar upstairs. He ordered wine for her and drank water himself. She didn't feel hungry; when the steak came it looked coarse and unappetizing. She left most of it.

"What's the matter?" Harrington asked. "You're not eating anything. Something go wrong this morning? Don't tell me that old SGI has been on your back too."

"What do you mean, too? Has he been on yours?" She glanced quickly at him.

"Certainly has," he said cheerfully. "He had me into his office and wanted to know exactly when I'd seen you last. God knows how he knew I'd seen you at all, as it was out of school. Wanted to know where we went and what we talked about, and how friendly we were."

"And what did you tell him?" Davina asked.

"Oh, just that you were madly in love with me, and I didn't know how to fend you off," he said. "He didn't think it was funny."

"I'm sure he didn't. This was after the fire, I suppose."

"Yes; they ran quite a witch-hunt, including the families of the poor sods who got burned. You were there, weren't you, with Ivan the Terrible?"

Davina shook her head. "No comment, Peter. Can't you stop playing the idiot for a minute? I want to talk seriously to you."

"Not another lecture?" He raised his eyebrows and made a face.

"No, no lecture. You asked me about my promise, remember?"

"I know I did," he said. "Actually, I was very low that night. My iron will and mighty self-confidence were strangely wobbly. I wanted a drink. And then you rang, and I got all emotional about a second chance." He glanced quickly at her, apologetic and hopeful at the same time. "There isn't one, is there? Any chance of anything . . ."

"There could be," she said. "I can't talk about it in any detail yet. But if something did come up, involving both of us, something quite difficult, how would you feel?"

He leaned toward her. His expression was very serious. "I'd feel on top of the world," he said. "And whatever it was, I wouldn't let you down. What do you mean by difficult?"

"Not easy," she said gently. "That's all I can tell you for now. But I can definitely put your name forward for this business. Is that right?"

"Only if it's dangerous," he said lightly.

"It is," she said. "Make no mistake about that."

"Oh, Christ." He feigned alarm. "Can't stand the sight of blood, especially if it's my own. What are we going to do, Davina—kidnap the Politburo?"

"You've guessed it," she said. "I shouldn't have tried to fool you. Just to change the subject, tell me about Grant asking questions. Why should he ask you anything about me, and what exactly was the line he was taking?"

"He was looking for a lead on who tipped the opposition off about Halldale. I know you can't say anything, but it was known to be a top-security safe house. But known only to people like myself who'd been in the active field. They realized that the fire was no accident but an attempt to silence your friend. So they were worried about who might have connected you with him. They knew I knew you were his minder, so naturally they came to find out what, if anything, you'd told me and who else I'd talked to. I was able to tell old Robespierre you never gave a clue to anything. So he want away disconsolate. I think he was quite sorry it wasn't me. I'm not his favorite type of employee."

"I'm not, either."

"He doesn't like women," Peter Harrington said.

"He doesn't like anybody," she corrected him.

"When would you know about this job we might do together?" he asked her.

"In a day or two," she said. She looked at her watch. "It's nearly three—I've got to get back."

"You going to the country?"

"I'm going to the office," she said. "Can you give me a lift back?"

"Pleasure," he said.

He paid the bill and took her arm as they left the pub. He held it firmly until they reached his car. He opened the door for her, and as she looked up at him he bent down very quickly and pecked her on the mouth.

"That's just to say thanks," he said. "And I won't forget what you've done to help me. I won't let you down."

"I know that," she said as they drove away. "That's why I've asked for you."

He waited with her by the lift. His department was below ground in the building. She got in, and the doors shut. Harrington stayed, watching for the red eye on the indicator to light up. It stopped at the fifth floor. He turned and walked away. He knew she had gone to see the Chief.

8

The roster of prisoners in the Lubyanka was divided into three sections. Grade 1 included suspects being held for interrogation. Grade 2 were criminals awaiting trial. Grade 3 were the convicted on their way to the camps in the Gulag. A minor subsection noted a very few who were in fact released having been in in Grade 1. The name of Fedya Sasanova was in Grade 1. She was held in a cell one level down. Below that level were the interrogation rooms, soundproofed, air-conditioned, sealed off from the outside world. She had not been taken down there yet.

The cell was very small, walled and floored in concrete; set in the ceiling was a powerful electric light that was never turned off. There was no means of telling day from night or keeping any track of time; a shelf bed with two dirty blankets was bolted up against the wall, so that for the first two days Fedya Sasanova crouched on the floor when she couldn't stand any longer. A pail with a lid was the only means of relieving herself. For the first two days she was not allowed to empty it. She was given water and a vegetable soup once a day, and the effects of hunger were becoming part of the physical misery of her conditions. She was spied on at regular intervals through an eyehole let into the cell door. There was very little noise; the silence was occasionally broken by sharp sounds. By the end of the third day Fedya began to move around the walls, to stop herself from beating on the door and screaming.

Then she found the inscriptions deliberately left behind, to terrify each

143

new occupant. "God help me." "Stop tomorrow. Stop the pain." "Lost.
Darkness. I'm lost." Scrawls made with the tip of the tin spoon provided
for the soup. She knew it was the tool because she made a feeble scratch
with it herself. The inscriptions terrified her. So did the defaced names.
There were many names, but few of the pitiful phrases graven into the
concrete walls. Fedya wept and shivered, and curled up in the corner to
try to sleep. The guards watched her from the other side of the door. By
the end of the week she was tormented with stomach pains and a blinding
headache. They let down the shelf bed and she threw herself on it with a
cry and sank into a deep sleep. An hour later she was roused and shaken
to her feet. The bed was raised and padlocked. She wailed like a child.

At the end of ten days it was decided to question her. The guards were
men; they came into the cell with a bucket of hot water and a bar of
scrubbing soap. She was told to strip and wash. When she hesitated, the
younger guard ripped off her filthy stained dress and threw it in the
corner. She took off her own underclothes and washed naked in front of
them. She dried herself on a thin little towel and put on the clean prison
overall. She tried to ask them a question, but they didn't answer. The
man who had torn her dress off pushed her into the corridor. She took one
look at the long, bare, brightly lit tunnel, and her legs crumpled. She was
hauled up on her feet and supported on either side until they reached a
lift. Fear swept over her, assaulting her sanity and self-control. She was
going to the interrogation room. And then, just as suddenly, the fear
receded. They were going up, not down. The relief was so euphoric that
she visibly straightened herself and stood independently of the two
guards.

They came out into another corridor. This time there were windows,
but she saw they were covered with a fine steel mesh. No suicides, she
thought, no chance to escape through death. They had made death their
servant. When she was brought into Volkov's office she started to tremble
all over again. He was sitting in a chair, drinking tea. He got up when he
saw her, and said, "Bring Comrade Sasanova a chair. Would you like
some tea, Comrade?"

She lowered herself onto the chair seat, gripping the sides, her body
visibly shaking. Volkov looked at her as if everything were normal and
she were paying him a visit.

"Tea?" he offered again.

"No, thank you, Comrade Volkov," she said. "I would spill it."

"And why would you do that?" he asked gently. "Because your hands
are shaking?"

She nodded.

"Why are they shaking, Comrade? Are you afraid?"

She looked into the pale eyes; they were like metal, and she screamed inwardly at her jangling nerves to be still and let her concentrate. She had to answer, and the stake was her life. And not only her life; her mind held feverishly to the reality. But the life of her child, Irina. Irina who had brought the message from Sasanov, her daughter who was in contact with dissidents.

She said in a low voice, "Yes, I am afraid, Comrade Volkov. I don't know what I have done wrong."

"And you can't think of anything?" The question was asked in the same friendly tone.

"Please tell me," she begged. "Tell me, Comrade, so I can confess it and ask for mercy." Tears trickled down her face.

Volkov viewed her with distaste. At least she was clean; he couldn't bear bad smells. Before he questioned any suspect after ten days in the prison, they were always washed and given clean clothes. She was a stupid woman, he decided. Being from an intellectual family himself, he recognized the peasant in her, and despised her. The daughter Irina had her father's intelligence and something of his looks. Volkov knew Sasanov was fond of his wife. He only regretted he couldn't be there to see her.

"You mean you'll confess to whatever I tell you? Is that what you think of Soviet justice?"

"No, no, of course not. I never meant that—I'm just confused, I haven't slept or eaten—"

"Are you complaining about your treatment?"

She looked at him in agony; he compared her with a trapped animal, surrounded on all sides. It didn't amuse him to torment her. She was too stupid. He stopped wasting time.

"Why did you identify that body as your husband's when you knew it wasn't?"

She opened her mouth and stuttered. But deep in her mind the peasant mentality he dismissed with a sneer warned her not to deny it. Tell the truth . . . then perhaps he wouldn't ask any more questions.

"I thought it would be best," she said slowly. She raised her head and looked at him. "We've been hoping he was dead. Anything except he'd just disappeared. I wanted to please the authorities."

"By telling a lie?"

"I didn't think it would matter. I wanted to be back in favor, Comrade Volkov. I wanted to forget about my husband and start my life again." The sharp maternal instinct urged her on.

"Irina had suffered so much because of him," she muttered. "She was so ashamed when he vanished like that. She lost all her friends. She wanted him to be dead. We both wanted it. That's why I said it was he. She was so happy, like a different girl." She lowered her head. "It was wrong of me, Comrade Volkov. I deceived you. I deserve to be punished."

"Yes," he said reprovingly, "you do. Your daughter came asking for you." He saw the quick, frightened glance and misinterpreted it. "I reassured her," he said. "I told her you would go to a correctional camp."

"You didn't tell her what I'd done?" she begged. "She'd never forgive me. She's such a good Party member, if she thought I'd lied, she'd never have me back." She gave way to a real outburst of noisy crying.

He finished his tea and nodded at the guards. They came and pulled Fedya Sasanova to her feet.

"Thank you, Comrade Volkov," she whimpered, "thank you for not telling her."

He nodded again, more sharply, and she was hurried out of the room.

. . . Thank him for not telling her daughter that the body buried with so much publicity was that of an impostor. . . . He lit a cigarette and poured another cup of hot tea. There wouldn't be a trial for Fedya Sasanova, because there mustn't be a record of her offense. The KGB ran its own camps and she could be sent there under his personal authority. Her arrest must be kept a secret, if the lies told about her husband's mental breakdown and suicide were to be maintained. He thought about Irina Sasanova. He had impressed upon her that she must keep her mother's misdeameanor a secret if she hoped for a light sentence. She too could be picked up; he hesitated, considering the idea. But she was a university student and a promising one. It would cause too much comment if she vanished. He thought another interview would be the best. An invitation, perhaps. She was young, and quite pretty. There was a freshness that appealed to him. He wrote a personal note and sent it down for his driver to deliver to the Sasanovs' flat. It suggested that Irina might like to have dinner with him at the Bear Restaurant near Zhukova, twenty miles outside Moscow. It was an elite and secluded place; reserved for senior officials of the Party. It was within twenty minutes' drive of his country dacha.

"Believe me," Davina said again, "we'll get her exchanged and we're going to get your daughter out. It's all going ahead."

She sat on the arm of his chair and put her arms around him.

He had gone into the bedroom when she first told him of Fedya's arrest, and she had waited helplessly outside. She knew when he came back that he had been crying.

"I'll go back," he said. "I'll give myself up."

"That won't help her," she said. "Be sensible; you know the way Volkov works. If a defector had come back and tried to bargain, would you have let his wife go?"

"No," he said. "I'd have arrested him and used her to make him denounce others, confess—to whatever we needed at the time. And I'm humane by Volkov's standards."

He looked at her, and she saw that a burning anger had replaced despair.

"I was never cruel for its own sake. Volkov is cruel. The next will be my daughter."

"No, it won't," she said quickly. "From our information she's in favor with him. And she's been clever enough to play on it. Our people are going ahead to arrange her escape as quickly as possible. And don't lose hope for your wife. The Chief promised to make a deal. And he never breaks his word," she said. Except when it suits him, was her private aside. Thank God she had been able to argue Sasanov out of trying to go back. She felt a desperate tenderness for him; she had been close to breaking into tears herself when she told him what had happened to his wife.

"They won't bother to save Irina now," he said slowly. "Why should they? Fedya's in prison and I can't go back. I have a motive for working with them now—revenge for what's happened to my wife. Why should your Chief risk his agents going into Russia?" He pulled away from her and stood up. "They'll lie to you, so that you can lie to me. Irina will never come."

"Are you going to work fully with us?" she asked him.

"Yes," he said. "At the beginning it was for Jacob and his principles; now it's for Fedya. I'll work with your people; I'll give them everything I know." Suddenly he shouted. "I want to destroy Volkov, I want to smash them all to pieces!" He turned his back on her and covered his face with his hands.

"Ivan," she said after a pause, "Ivan, please don't. . . . I'm going out myself to get Irina. I'm going to Russia to bring her back."

He swiveled around to face her. "You? No, I don't believe it."

"It's true," she said. "It was all agreed this afternoon. Now you know we're not going to cheat you. You're going to another safe house, where

Grant and a team will start serious debriefing. You've got to work with them while the rescue operation goes ahead. That's the only condition."

"You go to Russia?" He repeated. "No, that's impossible. You can't. . . . It's ridiculous—you don't even speak Russian."

"I speak very good German," she answered. "And in any case there's no argument. I'm going."

He didn't move, he stared at her.

"This is madness. You will be caught. I forbid it; I won't work, I won't cooperate!"

"Yes, you will." She came to him and placed her hands on his shoulders. "Because I'm going anyway. I asked to do it, for a very special reason."

"You want to leave me," he said.

"I want to make you happy," she said quietly. "I know what's happened to me and it's been happening for some time. I'm on your side now; my people know it, too. I love you, Ivan, and that's why I've got to go and bring your daughter back. Then I can get out of your life and try to sort out my own."

His arms closed around her and she leaned against him.

"You've given me so much. I want to give you what we promised."

"If anything happens to you," he said slowly, "I have nothing left."

"Nothing will happen," she promised. "I want to see your face when I bring Irina home. . . . Now why don't we get ourselves a drink and I can tell you what has been arranged."

She felt his hand stroke the back of her hair; he was not normally tender in a physical way. He muttered something in Russian which she couldn't understand; and then he said, "I'll say that to you in English when you come back."

They came to take Sasanov to Grant's safe house in Hampshire at three-thirty the following afternoon. A message had warned Davina to pack for him and get ready to leave the flat herself. There were two security men, and a third man she didn't know who arrived at the flat, shook hands with her and introduced herself to Sasanov as John Kidson. One man took the bags down, while the other lingered by the front door in the little hallway.

John Kidson asked if Sasanov was ready. He had a pleasant anonymity; the kind of man whose eye color, height and type would be impossible to remember five minutes after he had gone.

Sasanov said he was ready to go, and there was a slight, awkward pause while Kidson opened the door into the hall for him. He went up to Davina; he held out his hand and she shook it.

"Goodbye," she said. "I hope everything goes well for you."

"I hope so," he said.

They looked at each other for a long private moment; Kidson had turned his back on them.

Sasanov took her in his arms. "Goodbye," he whispered. "Come back to me."

Then he walked away. The door closed and Davina was alone.

Her own bag was packed; the flat had a deserted air. There was an ashtray with stubs in it, and a glass with a film of vodka in the bottom where Sasanov had had a final drink. She walked into the bedroom; the bed was stripped, nothing had been left behind. The room held no imprint of them. It was empty and dead, like the rest of the place. She emptied the ashtray and washed the glass. Then she dialed a number on the phone. It connected with the security office on the ground floor.

"I'm ready to go," she said. "I'll be in the hall in a couple of minutes."

"Right," came the answer. "The cab'll be waiting outside."

She was driven to the office in St. James's Place. The first outline of what was code-named Operation Skylark was scheduled for discussion in the Brigadier's office at four-thirty that afternoon. Jeremy Spencer-Barr, Peter Harrington and Davina Graham met each other in the outer office at exactly four-fifteen.

"Hello," Jeremy said when he saw her.

He showed no surprise, yet she felt instinctively that her appearance was a shock.

But the real shock was Peter Harrington. Spencer-Barr didn't try to hide his surprise. He said, "Good Lord," just loud enough for them to hear, and turned to look out the window.

Behind his back, Harrington lifted two fingers, and Davina frowned at him. The Brigadier's secretary saw the gesture, and smiled. Harrington had been around for a long time, and Spencer-Barr was not well liked. At four-thirty exactly the buzzer sounded, and she told them they could go inside.

"Daddy? Hello, darling, it's me."

Captain Graham beamed with pleasure at his younger daughter's voice.

"Charley! What a nice surprise—your mother tried you a couple of times last week, and couldn't get an answer. She left messages on your answer-phone thing."

"I know, I meant to call back, but I've been so rushed. Listen, Daddy, could I come down this weekend? You're not full up, are you?"

"Of course not," he said eagerly. "We've got a couple coming to lunch on Sunday, but otherwise nothing. We'd love to see you, Charley. You're not bringing anyone, are you?"

"No," she said. "I've no one to bring at the moment, actually. Has Davina been down again?"

"No," her father said. "I'm afraid she doesn't bother to keep in touch. We'll see you Friday evening. Are you driving down or coming by train? I can meet you—"

"I'm driving," she said. "I'll be down in time for a nice drink. 'Bye, darling."

Captain Graham hurried into the garden. His wife was on her knees, weeding a bed where the roses were coming into flower. She was so absorbed she didn't hear him call from the house; she dug with the little trowel, carefully extracting the weeds down to the root, murmuring to her flowers as she worked.

"There, that's got that nasty thing out—heavens, what a long root! You need a little drink of Liquinure, don't you?"

She looked up as he called from close by.

"Darling, Charley's just rung. She's coming down on Friday."

"Oh, good. That'll be lovely," she called back. Her husband looked so animated that she smiled to herself. He did adore his younger daughter. It had never occurred to Mrs. Graham to be jealous. She was delighted to see her husband so happy, with a spring in his walk as he went back down the path to the house.

Davina hadn't been in contact with them since she came down with the Polish diplomat, oh, nearly three months ago. The daffodils had all been in flower at the time. Mrs. Graham had a habit of noting time by the flowering seasons in her garden. The roses were coming out, and that was June. The full glory of her herbaceous border was July into August. She was looking forward to seeing Charley; maybe one day she'd find the right man and really settle down. It was no good hoping for grandchildren from Davina. She settled down to the weeding again and carried on her gentle monologue to her flowers.

Charley Ransom put the telephone down with a pleased little sigh. It was so lovely to be able to ring and just fly home whenever she felt down.

They were darlings, the way they never said no when she wanted something. It was marvelous to be loved so much. She told herself that quite often, but especially if she was bored and lonely, which occasionally happened. It had happened lately, with the end of her long affair with the man who was dotty about the theater, and nothing to amuse her but last-minute invitations from Jeremy Spencer-Barr. Every time she went out with him, she made up her mind not to go again. He was charming and could be very interesting, but there was nothing personal in his attitude to her. He never told her she looked nice, or sent flowers or telephoned unless he wanted to take her out.

His effect on her was not a good one. He made her insecure, and there was no other man in her life to assure her that she was as beautiful and irresistible as ever. Besides which, her ex-husband was being very difficult about the ownership of her expensive flat. She needed to go down to Marchwood and nestle under the parental wings for a couple of days. . . . And there was something else that niggled at her. Jeremy Spencer-Barr again; not just his indifference to her, but his constant and inexplicable interest in her sister Davina. She had spent some time thinking about this, and wondering why it should make her uneasy. She had been merely irritated by it at first, and then worried that he was trying to find out about her sister from motives of professional jealousy. Charley didn't want to be the means of hurting Davina in her career, dreary though it sounded. After all, she had nothing else. That was the point where Charley stopped thinking about her. The broken engagement was such a long time ago. Any ordinary woman would have put it aside and got on with her life. As her father said, she was determined to be a spinster. But it would be nice to talk to her father and make sure that Jeremy wasn't trying to cause her any trouble.

The evening stretched ahead of her without engagement. She never understood some of her women friends when they claimed to like being alone. But then they had husbands who went on business trips; she supposed it was nice to be solitary if you lived with someone all the time. But she wasn't involved with a particular man and she hated the rare occasions when she was by herself. She didn't even enjoy having the chance to read or wash her hair, or go to bed early and watch TV. She started going through her address book to see whom she could ring up.

Brigadier White sat back and listened to Humphrey Grant. He admired his economy of words and the speed at which he came to the point. He also observed very carefully the faces of the three people sitting in the

room, listening. Davina Graham first. Very intense, concentrating totally. Pale and rather strung up. The interview with Sasanov must have
been painful. He was on his way to Hampshire and a new setup, where
the skilled interrogators headed by Grant would begin to unlock his
mind. The link with Davina had been broken now. Missing her might
make him malleable. There was a man on the team especially selected to
get onto a personal level with the Russian. Grant was too chill and
humorless to be any use for that. . . . Pity about Davina. The least
likely woman he could think of to throw everything away for a man. But
that *was* women, after all. Like all her sex, Davina Graham had her own
X factor. The vulnerable spot for the right man; or, as in this case, the
wrong one. He understood her anxiety to go on the mission to Russia
better than she did herself. Her eagerness was pathetic; she was hanging
on to every word Grant spoke. It just happened to fit into the Brigadier's
own plans to let her have her way. Then Peter Harrington. Tidy, sober,
only occasionally making one of his ill-timed jokes, listening attentively to
Grant, but not completely absorbed like Davina. Able to shoot a look at
Spencer-Barr to see how he reacted, and then to the Brigadier himself. A
man trying for a second chance. An operative who had once been very
good on active missions, who'd begun to slide in a desk job in New York
until he had lost credibility at home and had to be recalled. A man who'd
won the woman's sympathy and confidence.

And then the younger man, Jeremy Spencer-Barr. He had everything
right, including an uncle in the Treasury and a senior Minister to recommend him. A dazzling academic career, and a personality like a well-
cut diamond. Smooth, hard and brilliant. A hungry type, the Brigadier
thought. Hungry for success. He had few friends in the department. His
colleagues talked of him as bright and ambitious; he wasn't popular with
anyone. A cold type, with little or no feeling for others. He was concentrating on Grant's briefing, poised like an athlete at the tape. His tutor at
the language center described his Russian as remarkable. This mission
was his big chance, the opportunity that comes to men in his profession
once or twice in the course of their careers. It had come very early to
Spencer-Barr. He wasn't happy about his two colleagues. His expression
showed distaste whenever he glanced at Harrington; his manner with
Davina Graham was wary. He didn't like the prospect of working with
either of them. The Brigadier speculated why, as he leaned back, himself
part of Humphrey Grant's audience.

The plan so far worked out was comparatively simple. Davina and
Peter Harrington were to go into East Germany as West Germans.

When they arrived in East Berlin they were to disappear, being replaced by an East German couple. It was a convenient way of getting agents out, although Grant didn't specify this. In East Berlin, Davina and Harrington would be contacted and outfitted with new identities and passports, with visas for entry into Russia. They would travel as husband and wife with an Intourist booking to the Black Sea resort of Livadia in the Crimea. It was a very popular holiday spot for tourists as well as native Russians. One of its attractions was the old Tsarist palace where the Romanovs had spent their summers. Spencer-Barr was to travel alone, and his destination was Moscow. His cover was as a replacement for one of the trade secretaries in the Moscow embassy. He would go to Moscow ahead of Harrington and Davina and take charge of the arrangements being made with Irina Sasanova. Grant announced this and then paused.

"Any questions so far?"

"Isn't it a bit chancy, having a new man make contact with the Daughter?" Peter Harrington deliberately used the code name for Irina. "No reflection on Spencer-Barr," he said, "but aren't her present contacts enough? It seems to be adding to the risks to send another man in. Jeremy is certain to cause comment when he arrives; they usually put a top-priority security screen for at least six months on anyone who comes out."

Grant stared at him, his eyebrows slightly lifted.

"I didn't know you were a Moscow expert," he said.

"I'm not," Harrington answered. "But I've been around here long enough to know a number of people who were. After all, you did ask for questions, didn't you?"

"Yes," Grant snapped. "So long as they were relevant to your own part in the operation. I suggest Spencer-Barr is the person to concern himself with the Moscow end."

Harrington shrugged. "I suppose so. One point about Davina and me: if we're going into the Crimea, what backup will we have for getting out if something goes wrong in Moscow?"

"None at all," Grant said. "If Moscow goes wrong, you won't have an option except to swim for it. If you're lucky and it's the right date, you'll be picked up by the boat intended for the Daughter. Miss Graham? Any questions?"

"Has there been any further news of Fedya Sasanova?"

There was a little silence; everyone seemed to be looking at her.

"I don't see the relevance," Grant retorted.

"It could make a difference to the Daughter's attitude."

Peter came to the rescue. "If she'd been released, for instance. The girl mightn't want to come out."

The Brigadier interposed then. "I don't think there's any chance of that," he said gently. "The latest word from Moscow was that she was still in the Lubyanka. It's too soon to know whether she's been interrogated or just kept there till they decide where to send her. She won't be set free."

"These agents coming over from East Germany in our place," Davina said, "are they really refugees or Western agents? If they're refugees isn't it very risky to trust them?"

"Miss Graham." Grant's tone was acid. "It's well understood that this is your first active mission. But do try to ask questions that make some sense. You can safely leave the security aspect to us."

He turned away from her, and behind his back Harrington mouthed the word "bastard" at Davina and grinned encouragingly at her.

"Mr. Spencer-Barr?" It was obvious from Grant's changed tone that he was relieved to be dealing with someone capable.

"I fly to Moscow as a replacement," Jeremy said. "I shall be under surveillance as a newcomer. Any contacts I make will be noted, my movements will be monitored. Doesn't this inhibit me for some months, as Harrington said?"

"I don't believe so," Grant answered. "The way in which you take up the post will remove any suspicion that you are connected with us. Besides which, we intend to recall Swallow. Her connection with the Daughter and the dissident contacts has gone on long enough. The Russians will be busy watching her replacement to see if Swallow's pattern repeats itself. It won't, of course, because you will be acting instead. Anything else?"

"Who will my immediate superior be?" Spencer-Barr asked.

"The senior trade councilor, he's an old Moscow man. But he'll be instructed to give you a free hand. Your job is to position the Daughter so that she gets to the rendezvous point where Harrington and Miss Graham can pick her up. Your responsibility ends once she's made contact with them."

"Thank you, sir." Jeremy sat back.

Grant sat down, and the Brigadier gave a little cough to gain their attention.

"Grant has given you the bare outline," he said. "You will each receive your personal instructions with details like timetables, hotels, emergency contacts and your regular controller in each area, who'll pass you on. I needn't stress how important this mission is. If it fails we may find that Sasanov is useless to us because he believes we betrayed his trust. That is one reason why Miss Graham has very gallantly offered to go. He has a high regard for her and complete faith in her integrity. This is a good opportunity to contratulate her on a superb job; we owe Sasanov's cooperation entirely to her skill in managing him." He smiled at Davina, and Grant managed a wintry grimace.

"I needn't impress on any of you how dangerous it is to try to abstract a Russian national. And not only are your lives at stake, and the Daughter's, if anything goes wrong, but we shall almost certainly lose a number of agents and a network that has taken a long time to establish. Harrington, you're the experienced operator in the field. You'll have plenty of backup, which you'll be told about in due course. Spencer-Barr has an equally difficult task, but he will have the embassy to cover for him, and he can claim diplomatic immunity if he gets into trouble. You and Davina, Harrington, are out in the open. I have to say this when I send people out. If you get caught, we know nothing about you. And there won't be much we can do to help you for a very long time. If ever. Is that clear?"

"Quite clear," Davina said.

"Yes." Harrington and Spencer-Barr nodded together.

"Good," the Brigadier said. "I hand you over now to Grant's chaps. They'll start kitting you out with everything you'll need. You're due to leave at the end of the week. I shan't see you again till you come home. So I'll wish you luck now."

He shook hands with them in turn. He murmured to Davina, "Take care, my dear. Remember, you asked to do this."

"I know I did," she said. "Don't worry about me."

They went down in the lift together.

"A week," Spencer-Barr said. "That's rather quick, isn't it?"

"Time enough to stick on a false beard." Harrington grinned.

Spencer-Barr gave him a cold look. "You're the one who's going to need that," he said.

The lift doors opened and they came out. Davina nudged Harrington.

"He won that round," she said.

"For the first and last time," Peter Harrington said. "Come on, let's get a cup of coffee."

"I won't, thanks," she said. "I want to get on as quickly as possible. I'll clear up some stuff that needs filing. You can give me dinner tonight."

"Delighted." He looked pleased. "Where shall I pick you up?"

"At Burton Court, Flat Five. I supposed I'm allowed to go home—"

"I should expect so. The form is to gather us all under one roof forty-eight hours before we go. Or it used to be. Things may have changed."

She went on to the little office which had been closed up during her months away and spent the rest of the late afternoon filing copies of her last report on Sasanov and going through her desk, putting papers through the shredder. The calendar was unchanged at the date when she first went to Halldale Manor, November 7 of the previous year. Now it was June. Eight months. It felt like her whole life. She put a call through to Grant's office to check that she could be found at her own flat, and was told to go down to the language center the next morning for a quick briefing on the latest colloquialisms in Germany. The building also housed the forgeries and special-effects department. She would have a busy day.

Humphrey Grant spoke to the Brigadier on the telephone.

"I let them go home," he said. "She stayed in her office clearing up till nearly seven. No telephone calls. Arrived at her flat without any detours. Harrington arrived at eight and they left for a Chelsea restaurant by eight-forty-five. Harrington had gone back to his place by six-forty; he made three calls, they're all being checked. Then on to Burton Court and out to dinner. Spencer-Barr stayed in his office, clearing up, then drove to the International Sportsmen's Club and played squash. He went home, too, and hasn't been out. His calls are being checked out. The girl friend is staying with him."

"Well," James White said, "we'll just have to wait and see, won't we?" He was relaxing in a big armchair, with a glass of port beside him. His wife was reading on the other side of the fireplace; the room was warm and subtly lit with lamps and a picture light showing off a fine Raeburn portrait of an officer in scarlet and white. There was a long military tradition in the Brigadier's family.

"Yes," Grant agreed. "But if anything is going to bring our friend the Mole out into the open, it's this. Good night, Chief."

"Good night," the Brigadier said, and, putting the receiver down, he reached for his port.

"Is it true? Did you really volunteer for this just to convince Ivan the Terrible we were playing straight with him?"

Davina put her glass of wine down. Dinner was over and they were talking over coffee. Harrington hadn't drunk anything but water.

"Partly," she said. "And partly on my own account."

"I don't see it," he said. "It's a high-risk operation; you've no practical field experience. I can't think why the hell they ever let you in on it in the first place."

"Because I suggested it," she answered. "I asked to be allowed to go."

"You still haven't said why," he reminded her.

She hesitated. She had resolutely turned his questions about Sasanov whenever he asked them; now she was no longer in contact with him, and Harrington was in the same position of trust as herself. It would be a relief to talk to someone who might understand.

"I got myself into a mess," she said. "This seemed the best way out of it."

"No wonder you're in this bloody outfit," Peter exclaimed. "Can't you give a straight answer? What sort of a mess?"

"I got involved with him," she said. "Is that clear enough for you?"

"Oh, Christ," he groaned. "It's beginning to be. Bed and the rest of it. Doesn't sound like you."

"No, I'm sure it doesn't." Her tone was sharp. "Doesn't sound like good old frigid Davy, who wouldn't look at a man. And no man would look at her. But it happens he did."

She searched for a cigarette, and lit it before he could find his lighter.

"And that's what brought him round," he suggested. He didn't know whether she was angry or upset; her cheeks were very pink. "Well done. You're a very attractive woman."

"Then why were you so surprised?" she countered. "I'm *not* a very attractive woman, Peter, and you know it. But he liked me, and I suppose it was the first time anyone had ever wanted me. Not loved me, but wanted me. Must sound ridiculous to you, but there it is."

"So you fell in love with him," he said quietly. "I see."

"No, you don't." She stubbed out the half-smoked cigarette. "I didn't fall in love like some sickly old maid. I liked him first. I liked him in bed and I liked him as a person. And then, after a time I got fond of him. He used to get very depressed, worrying about his wife and daughter. They meant so much to him and he couldn't relate to Britain or the West at all. He had to have them with him before he could face the future as an exile. And I'd promised him they were safe and we'd get them out if they wanted to come. I had to keep his hope alive. You get very close to someone when you're doing that. I always had this idea at the back of my mind—that I should carry the promise through and go and get them. I don't know why, because at that time I wasn't nearly so mixed up with him. Maybe I was getting there and didn't know it."

"Funny," Harrington said. "If you were in love with him, you wouldn't have wanted his wife and daughter to come over would you? Not even a spot of jealousy?"

"No." She shook her head. "I just wanted him to be happy."

He gave her a quizzical look. "You really do care about him, don't you?"

"Yes," she said. "But that's the point of this. We've got no future; he has to have someone else. And I've got to get him out of my system. This is the way to do it."

"And do the Chief and old Sea-Green know any of this?" he asked her.

"They know some of it," she said. "I didn't say we were sleeping together, and when they were investigating the fire at Halldale they went snooping around everyone, including me. So they found out. The Chief wasn't very pleased, because I hadn't included it in my report."

"I can imagine." Harrington watched her take another cigarette out, and this time he was ready to light it for her. She was very strung up while she talked; he noticed the slight tremor in her hand, the nervous smoking.

"I stood up to him over Sasanov's daughter. I told him we'd promised to get his family out and if we didn't he would probably go back and give himself up." She smiled a sour little smile for a moment. "That's when he told me we couldn't let Sasanov go. So much for promises."

"It must have shaken you," he said. "Your first experience of perfidious Albion in St. James's Place?"

"I was disgusted," she said. "I let them see it."

"I'll bet you did," he said softly. "And then you volunteered to go into Russia like Joan of Arc and bring the daughter back? I wish I'd seen their faces."

"The only time they looked a bit odd was when I suggested taking you," she retorted.

Harrington grinned. *"Touché.* So you went back and gave Ivan the news. How did he react?"

She hesitated for a moment, turned the cigarette over in her fingers.

"He didn't want me to go," she said.

Harrington leaned forward and tipped more wine into her glass. "That sounds to me as if he was hooked on you, too," he said.

"Well, it doesn't matter now," Davina answered. "He's gone to Grant's people and I'll never see him again. Which is just as well. Let's get the bill, shall we? It's been a very long day."

He came out onto the pavement, and they waited for a taxi.

"What happened to your car?" he asked.

"Gone into the pool: I couldn't use one after Halldale."

"I thought that's where you were hiding Ivan," he said. "You and he were bloody lucky not to get fried to a crisp in that place."

"We certainly were." She tugged at his arm. "There's a cab!"

"How did you manage to escape?"

"We weren't there," she said.

The cab pulled in to the curb and he opened the door for her. "I'll drop you first, Davina. . . . Where were you, then?"

She didn't know how triumphant she sounded. "We stopped off at a motel. He wanted to go to bed with me."

Harrington glanced at her, and then the old casual grin appeared and he hooked his hand through her arm and squeezed it. "You must be quite something, darling. I'll have to see if I can live up to all this when we're in Russia."

The safe house in Hampshire had been bought by the Ministry of Defence as an officers' training college. It was an ugly mid-Victorian mansion, the monument to a successful City merchant whose descendants had been only too glad to get rid of it after the war. It had a great advantage in its dual role of putting likely young officers through assault courses and the rougher arts of war, and of accomodating a team of experts in complete seclusion. It was not, by any standards, warm. Its polished floors and bare staircase gave it a public-school atmosphere, which made some of its incumbents nostalgic for the discomforts of their youth. The quarters set aside for Sasanov and Grant's team were in the south wing; they were centrally heated, close-carpeted and served by a special staff and a separate kitchen.

Sasanov looked out the window onto the parkland. The window was open, and faint shouts of mock battle drifted across the warm summer air.

The man assigned to him in place of Davina was setting up a chessboard in the room; he was John Kidson, who had collected him from the flat. He glanced at the Russian's broad back from time to time. Sasanov stood like a tree, blocking out the light. Kidson spoke Russian, Polish and Hungarian, and he was ten years older than Sasanov. He had seen a long and arduous service in the Balkans during the war, and his gifts for insinuating himself into other men's confidence had been invaluable in dealing with the partisans.

He had been Sasanov's constant companion for the last three days. Grant had made a brief appearance, shaken hands with the Russian and told him that everything was being set up and would be ready for him before the end of the week. In the interim, he must try to relax and not attempt to discipline his memory. It would work better without pressure. He hoped that Kidson was looking after him.

Kidson proceeded very slowly. He didn't intrude on Sasanov.

"If you want to be alone," he said the first day, "for God's sake say so. I'll take myself off for a walk. If you want a game, or just to chat, I'm here. But I won't be a nuisance to you."

Sasanov had been dour, but he didn't ask Kidson to leave him. He didn't want to be left alone. He seemed content to read the papers or spend time staring out the window. On the second evening they had a game of chess and to Sasanov's amazement Kidson beat him. After that they played through until the small hours.

"It's set up," Kidson said. "Do you want a game?"

Sasanov turned around slowly. "What are all those shouts outside?"

"Officers' training course. They're quite tough, you know. These chaps are rather select material; I wouldn't like to go through their training here."

Sasanov's expression was cynical. "The next war won't be fought by armies. You're wasting your time teaching men how to be conventional soldiers. The war will be over in twelve hours."

"If it's nuclear, of course," Kidson agreed. "But there might be a quick land attack without the ultimate weapons. Otherwise what's the point of an army your size? And a navy and air force?"

"It supports our economy," Sasanov said. "And it frightens the world. When Russia fights, it will be to obliterate the enemy. Satellite-based missiles. A lightning strike so fast and instantaneous that there won't be time for full reprisals. We'll lose a city or two—Moscow, Leningrad. You will lose the war before you've had time to fight it. That's what will happen."

He closed the window.

"Do you want a game?" Kidson repeated.

Sasanov sat down heavily, dropping his weight into the chair.

"No. I'd like a drink."

"Of course." Kidson poured them a glass each of the Stolichnaya that the Russian liked.

"I've never quite believed in what you say," he said after a while. "If the Soviet Union is going to turn the Western world into a wasteland, what good will it be to her if she is the victor? At the present calculation, nuclear war would make the areas affected totally uninhabitable for a period of at least fifty years. Even then the mutations in plant life would make it impossible to cultivate the land; the seas would be empty, the whole balance of nature which makes life possible would have been irrevocably upset. You'd rule over a graveyard."

"An American graveyard," Sasanov said. "Not Europe, or the East. We'd have those fall into our hands as soon as America was destroyed. China could be subdued in a conventional war. We would have all the mastery we wanted, and across the Atlantic there would be this huge poisonous continent where there was no life of any kind. Teaching a lot of men to climb assault courses isn't going to stop that."

"I suppose not," Kidson agreed. "What's going to prevent it from happening?"

Sasanov frowned, swigged at his drink. "Encirclement of the Soviet Union," he said. "In the air, on the land and in the seas. Close to the heart of the country. That's what America and the West are trying to achieve, isn't it? But they're losing. They're losing the game."

Kidson said, "Political weakness, economic recession, oil, inflation— we know all the arguments, but we're not getting many answers at the moment. We need answers and very soon, if you're not going to be proved right. And I take it you don't want to be, or you wouldn't be here."

It was the first time Kidson had stepped into his real role.

"No," Sasanov said. "I don't want it to happen. I don't want our political system to win. And I don't want to see even one stray nuclear bomb fall on a Russian city."

"You can do a lot to avoid that possibility," Kidson said. "And you've had plenty of time to think about it. Even a little insight into living in the West. We're keeping our side of the bargain and you've said you were ready to keep yours. Are you?"

"Yes," Ivan Sasanov said. "I am ready now. I will start with your team as soon as they like. But one question: Where is Vina Graham?"

Kidson was prepared for this. "She leaves England this evening," he said.

It was a lie, because at the moment she was in the language center practicing her German. But Sasanov wouldn't want to hear the truth. He needed a catalyst to set the scene for his betrayal of his country and his past. His face changed for a second; the meaning was difficult to assess. It became a heavy mask again. He finished his vodka.

"When do we begin?" he said. "I want to begin today."

Kidson got up and rang through on the internal telephone. He muttered into it, and Sasanov didn't bother to listen. Kidson looked up at the Russian and nodded before he put the receiver down.

"Downstairs in the conference room at three o'clock," he said.

The Bear Restaurant is situated outside Moscow near Zhukova. It is built on the lines of a log cabin, and it lies in a wood away from the main roads. Security patrols operate in the woods and around the rough country roads leading in and out of the forest. The Bear is patronized only by privileged members of the Party hierarchy and the senior officers in the KGB. It is not frequented by artists or scientists, who have a special venue of their own, some thirty miles away in the heart of another forest. The dachas of the elite are within the same fifty-mile radius, divided into compounds. The members of the Politburo have luxurious country dachas all closed off into one select area; the Chairman of the Praesidium lives in a mansion in the woods, strongly guarded and secluded from public gaze. He can be approached by his intimates in the Politburo, but his privacy is as absolute as that of the tsars.

The invitation to Irina Sasanova was delivered to the university, and the messenger waited for her reply. It came during her break for lunch, when she was sitting on her own as usual, trying to eat the unappetizing food. When she was called out and given the envelope, she started to tremble and could hardly open it. The messenger, a KGB private in civilian clothes, stared woodenly ahead of him. He was accustomed to frightened people. The note inside was in Volkov's own hand: "I would like to talk to you about your mother. Come to dinner with me this evening. Tell my driver and he will collect you after classes. Volkov. P.S. Wear something pretty; we are going to a special place." She folded the note and took a deep breath to steady her nerves.

"Thank Comrade General Volkov," she said. "I'll be very happy to accept."

She hurried back to the apartment as soon as she was free. "Wear something pretty; we are going to a special place." For a moment she wondered if that last line was not a vicious joke and the special place might have a horrible significance. She had heard her father say that Antonyii Volkov had sadistic tastes. She felt faint with terror at the idea.

Then she calmed herself and reasoned that the note meant what it said. He had been very friendly to her when she came to his office. Irina was not a fool, although she was shy. She knew instinctively when a man was being more than friendly. She'd seen her father's dreaded chief smiling at her and glancing at her legs. She had thrust the unpleasant thought aside; now it returned and she considered it. She shuddered. Then she began to look through her wardrobe to find something suitable.

The same man came to the apartment at precisely seven in the evening. He wore the green and red insignia of the military arm of the KGB. She wondered whether Volkov would be in the car, but she was alone in the rear. The evening was delightfully warm and she gazed out the window at the countryside as they left Moscow behind. The summers were hot and dry, but the green forests stretched invitingly across the rosy skyline; there was a light peculiar to the Russian summer, soft-hued and misty, like a watercolor. She felt moved by her country's beauty. Her parents used to talk about it with their friend Jacob Belezky.

She recoiled from the thought of him, but his words came back to her, overheard one night when they were all arguing and drinking, and she was reading in her room: "Russia survived the tsars. She survived the German invasion. Brezhnev and Kosygin and the KGB may rape the Russian people, take away our human rights, persecute and punish us, but Russia will bury them as she's buried every tyranny in the end." And then her father, warning him, pleading with him to be careful. And not succeeding. She remembered feeling so frightened she put her hands over her ears and stared at her book so as not to hear any more. Belezky had died in the psychiatric hospital. The tragic sequence was her father's disappearance, the months of fear and isolation and then her mother's arrest. She began to cry when she thought of her mother, and wiped the tears away quickly, looking anxiously into her mirror to see if her eyes were red.

Volkov might be able to help her mother. Not might, could, if he could be persuaded. All she had to do was tell him about Poliakov and the message from her father. He would exchange one woman for a university tutor who was in contact with the defector in the West. And not just the tutor but all the others who formed links in the chain leading to her father. They turned off the main road into the minor road that ran through the forest; the car was checked by two guards who stepped out and then immediately waved it on. It came to a halt outside the one-story building built of logs; lights beamed through the windows, there was a tinkle of music in the air. She got out, straightened her skirt and tucked her bag under her arm. She walked up the short flight of steps and went inside. . . .

"Now," Volkov said, smiling, "what do you think of this place? Isn't it nice?"

Irina couldn't disagree. "It's wonderful," she said.

It was decorated in a rich style which was quite new to her. Red plush seats and gilded mirrors, colored-glass lamps on every table, and fresh flowers. A man dressed in old-fashioned peasant costume wandered through playing a balalaika. That was the music she had heard. The exterior had seemed simple, even rough. Inside, it was so luxurious that she couldn't help looking around at everything. The tables were full; men were dining with well-dressed women, their clothes bought from the special shops reserved for the KGB, where goods from the West were stocked exclusively for the elite. The food was excellent.

"It's so kind of you to bring me here, Comrade Volkov," she said.

He smiled again. He looked less daunting in casual clothes, a little younger.

"It's not kind at all," he said. "You're a charming girl, my dear. I'm pleasing myself as much as you. Besides . . ." He poured wine into her glass and filled his own. She had drunk very little in spite of his prompting. "Besides," he went on, "you've had a miserable time this last year, haven't you?"

She nodded, not knowing what to say.

"And all through no fault of yours, that's what is so unfair about these family situations. I haven't mentioned Fedya Pavlovna because I didn't want to spoil your evening."

She glanced up at him, nakedly afraid. "What's happened to her? Oh, please, Comrade, tell me."

"Now, my dear, calm yourself. Nothing has happened to your mother. Fortunately for her, she is under my protection. So she is quite unharmed."

"Oh, thank you, thank you," she whispered. She blinked away tears. "Where is she? Can you tell me?"

"Of course I can," he said gently. "She's still in the Lubyanka. Waiting for a decision to be made. My decision, as it happens."

He saw the anguish in the girl's face, and felt a tremor of excitement. She was very fresh and young.

"Please," she said, "don't punish her. Whatever she did, it wasn't meant. She's not a clever person, Comrade Volkov; she wouldn't mean to commit a crime. . . ."

He frowned, pretending to be stern.

"But she did commit one," he said. "She told a deliberate lie. She lied about your father's health. As a result he was allowed to go abroad, and we know the result. He killed himself. I find it very hard to forgive her. Your father was not just one of my colleagues, you know. He was my friend."

She gazed into his eyes, fixed by them as if she were a rabbit frozen by the stare of a stoat; she accepted the lies with her own eyes, blinking and submissive. Her father had never been a friend. Her mother hadn't lied about anything except a corpse which Volkov knew was a fake. If he got the slightest whiff of insincerity from her, her mother was lost. And her mother was being put forward as part of a bargain not yet explained. But a major part of it, she knew, consisted of herself. She lowered her head and fumbled in her bag for a handkerchief. Volkov watched her with satisfaction. The rabbit simile had occurred to him, and it suited her. Pink and white, with the pretty blue eyes and hair like ripe wheat. A soft, yielding little rabbit.

He reached over and laid his hand on her bare arm.

"Don't cry," he murmured. "I'm not a hard-hearted man. You'll find that out. I'll get you a little Polish brandy; that will make you feel better." A waiter appeared, and he gave the order. The glasses were brought immediately. There was no delay, no sullen service in the Bear. That was the lot of the tourists and the ordinary Russians who tried eating in Moscow restaurants or hotels.

Volkov let her sip the brandy. He lit a cigarette. "You want to help her, don't you?"

"Yes," she said slowly. "I'll do anything."

"She spoke very well of you," he said thoughtfully. "She was very anxious about your reaction to what she'd done. She said you were a devoted Party member. You are, aren't you, Irina?"

"Yes," she said again.

"Good. I didn't need to ask. We know these things." He touched her arm again, and this time he stroked it.

"When we've finished our brandy we'll go for a little drive. I'll show you my dacha. It's not far from here. You don't mind getting back a little late, do you?"

"No, not at all, Comrade Volkov." She gave him quite a bright smile.

"Not Comrade," he said. "Antonyii—when we're alone."

He didn't touch her in the car. The journey took just over twenty minutes. A security man was on duty outside the dacha. The moon was up and she could see it was a single-story white-painted bungalow, surrounded by bushes and screened by a belt of pine trees. It was much larger and its garden area much bigger than their old dacha. That had been taken away as soon as her father went missing. He led her inside, and the room was well lit and furnished with the latest Swedish sofas and chairs. A picture above the fireplace wouldn't have found favor with the Academy of Soviet Art. The signature below it was Chagall. Volkov had a taste for decadent art.

He came toward her and took her in his arms. "You're a very pretty girl," he murmured. "I like you, Irina. Do you like me?"

Rather to his disappointment there was no fear in her face when she answered, "Yes, I do like you, Antonyii."

He began to kiss her, and without even being asked she unhooked the back of her dress and pulled it off. Not quite such a rabbit after all, he thought as he put her on the sofa. Frightened at first, but quite steely when she'd made up her mind. A little more of a challenge than expected. She might last longer than they usually did. He was surprised to find that she was a virgin.

At four-fifteen on the Thursday afternoon, during office hours in the trade section of the British Embassy in Moscow, Michael Barker collapsed at his desk. He was a junior trade secretary who had been in his post just over a year. He complained of chest pains and pain down the left arm; the embassy doctor was called, and amid a lot of flurry and telephone calls to the head of chancery it was announced that Michael Barker had suffered a minor coronary. He was taken to his quarters, a nurse was installed, and arrangements were made for him to be flown home as soon as possible for rest and treatment. The ambassador dropped in to visit him in bed, and commiserated; the embassy doctor took a second EKG and pronounced him well enough to fly home. The Soviet authorities were notified, and after a lapse of forty-eight hours, during which time Barker was put on the BA flight to London with a nurse in attendance, the Soviet Foreign Ministry was informed that his place on the staff would be taken by a Mr. Jeremy Spencer-Barr. Mr. Spencer-Barr's credentials were duly checked and found to be impeccable. He was on the Foreign Office list and had been employed in trade for the past two years since leaving the United States after a course at the Harvard Business School. His background was copybook upper-class; relatives and sponsors in the Establishment. His name was put on file. The following day Elizabeth Cole was relieved of her post and sent back to London. An embassy leak let it be known that she was said to be in touch with dissidents. The political wing of the KGB, which was integrated with the military wing, raked back over their records of Elizabeth Cole, and discovered something sinister in her weekly trips to Gum and the same café. Angry directives were issued to watch every move made by whoever replaced her.

Jeremy Spencer-Barr stepped off the plane at Sheremetyevo airport just a week after Michael Barker began enjoying an unexpected holiday in Portugal, courtesy of the Foreign Office. He had never felt better in his life, and never connected the sudden attack of pain and dizziness in Moscow with the cup of tea he had been given by one of the girl secretaries. Spencer-Barr was met at the airport by an embassy car and a junior trade official. His arrival was noted by the Soviet authorities. Their interest in him was perfunctory because the replacement for Elizabeth Cole came on the same flight and shared his car. She was a particularly good-looking girl, and her photograph, along with Jeremy's, was taken under cover in the arrivals hall. As the car turned into the commercial section of the British Embassy on Kutuzovsky Prospekt, Davina Graham and Peter Harrington were registering in the middle-grade hotel on Wielandstrasse in West Berlin. Their Federal Republic passports named them as Dieter Jaeger and his wife, Helga, resident in Hamburg.

Humphrey Grant took off his jacket and lowered himself into an armchair. He stretched wearily, and sighed. It was a contented sound. He glanced across at John Kidson. Each man had a whiskey and soda beside him; there was an hour before dinner, and they had finished their session with Sasanov. It was the end of the first seven days, and already the results were startling.

"Well," said Grant, "I can do with a drink tonight. And I think we've earned one."

"We have indeed," Kidson said. "He seems to unroll it like a tape. I've never come across a more detailed memory."

"Photographic," Grant agreed. "The more we ask, the quicker he gives the answers and more besides. It's as if some kind of mental evacuation is taking place."

"Emotional too." Kidson drank some of his whiskey. "He's very wound up. He's made his decision and there's part of him that wants to get it over. And to make it final by holding nothing back. Once or twice I wondered whether it wasn't coming too easily."

Grant glanced up sharply. "What do you mean?"

"You remember how long it took to get real information out of Perekov? Apart from the preliminary softening up—that was months, even longer than Sasanov. And then when he came down here it was like pulling teeth for the first few weeks. Until he became acclimatized to saying things he'd been conditioned *never* to talk about. It's a painful process, undoing the psychological knots that have been tied up all your life. Treason isn't easy, and whatever these jokers tell you, to them it's still treason and the West is still the enemy. They have to turn themselves inside out before they cooperate properly."

"And you don't think Sasanov's done that?" Grant's voice was sharp. "You're not suggesting he's telling us a prepared scenario? For Christ's sake!" He sat bolt upright and put his drink down. He was seldom if ever heard to swear.

"I'm not suggesting anything," Kidson said. "I'm just speculating— clearing my own mind, that's all. I find him a puzzle. I find his attitude uncanny; that sounds a silly word to use, but it fits somehow. He's doing something he hates doing, and he seems to be taking a kind of perverse pleasure in it. I think he's under some very strong pressure."

"What kind of pressure?"

"I don't know," Kidson said. "Whatever it is, it's tearing him to pieces."

"Everything he's told us has been checked and so far it's right," Grant muttered. "I'm going to see the Chief tomorrow morning and I'd like a report from you, setting out what you've told me."

"Certainly," Kidson said. "I'll put it together this evening. Don't get alarmed, Humphrey; you know me, I'm always looking into corners. We've got someone so important in this chap that we can't afford to be complaisant. Personally I think he's straight, and that side worries me as much as the other possibility. We need to settle him down; we need to have him on our side and cooperating every step of the road after we've collated all the information."

"That's why we've sent a team into Russia," Grant argued. "He knows that. He knows we're going to try to get his daughter out and bring her to him. That ought to provide him with his anchor."

"It should do, yes. Funnily enough, the only outside question he's asked me since we came here was about Davina Graham. Anyway, I'll type up my opinion and you can discuss it with the Chief. Finish your drink, Humphrey, I could do with dinner; these long sessions make me hungry."

"Thanks to you," Grant said sourly, "I've lost my appetite."

James White had the map of the Middle East set up on the office wall, replacing the large-scale one of Europe which normally hung there. He and Grant stood in front of it. For nearly three days they had been studying the information supplied by Sasanov, going over it point by point, cross-checking as much as possible with their own sources of information. At one stage White had said, "Good God—*he* can't be working for them," and then gone on reading.

"So the picture is beginning to emerge," he said to Grant.

"Afghanistan is one vast military base, ICBM sites aimed at China; nuclear strike forces in easy reach of every major city in India and Pakistan. We've had enough information to suspect it was pretty bad, but not as bad as this. Iran is still anybody's guess. President Rezai is holding it together by the skin of his teeth: Communist-aligned Fedayeen and Muslim revolutionaries; Kurds, Baluchi, Bakhtiari, all trying to fly at each other's throats. Of course, the Russians won't need to do anything, it'll happen by itself. Chaos followed eventually by a socialist government with Moscow alignment. This is what worries me." He pointed with a ruler at the cluster of the United Arab Emirates, Oman, and Saudi Arabia.

"If Sasanov's right, they've made a massive penetration in the area. It's a time bomb, ready to blow the Western oil sky high. Which will mean American armed intervention. I think I shall have to go and see the Prime Minister and make a report on this. We shall have to bring in the Americans sooner rather than later." He turned away and went back to his desk. His expression was grim.

"Do you really believe that they've got these people in their pay?" He had a thick folder in front of him, containing a résumé of Sasanov's information. Kidson's report was beside it.

"The King's favorite son . . . and this man. Good God, he's been a friend to the West for twenty years! I can accept some of the others; if you look at Dubai it's not surprising. It's a pure power struggle between their man and the ruling family."

"All this presupposes that he's telling the truth," Grant said. "You've read Kidson's report—he's got some doubt nagging away at him. And he's not easy to fool."

James White said, "He's the best there is, at this stage. I think he's worried because the normal pattern is different in this case. Sasanov isn't behaving according to the rules for a top-placed Soviet defector. But so long as this is proved right, and so far we've got no reason to dispute it, that's all that matters."

"According to Sasanov, this is just surface stuff," Grant said. "He hasn't even started on motives and methods yet; in-depth studies are going to take months, in conjunction with our own experts and the Americans. What shall I tell Kidson?"

"Tell him to get everything out of him. And not to worry about the authenticity, that's our problem. Just keep Sasanov talking and talking. I'll drop down in a week and see you all. But I've got to take this to the top. I think she'll be rather pleased with the department, don't you, Humphrey?"

Grant twitched his mouth into a tight smile. "I think so, Chief."

9

"**Y**our German's pretty good," Peter Harrington said. "Where on earth did you learn a Bavarian accent?"

They were strolling up the Kurfürstendamm, part of a slow-moving crowd of shoppers and sightseers.

"I spent six months in Munich," Davina said. "Being finished, or rather finished off. I loathed it."

"Why? Munich's a lovely place—the people are quite jolly, too."

"Not in the school I went to," she retorted. "It was dreadfully snobbish, with Baroness this and Countess the other, and the few English girls were the worst. We met selected young men from nice families, and trailed round the art galleries and museums, and looked at the ruins left by Allied bombing. It was all right if you were pretty and extrovert. I wasn't. I just learned German, that's all. My parents were far more disappointed that I wasn't a social success; they didn't seem to notice that I was almost bilingual in six months."

"I get the feeling," Peter said, "that you've quite a bit of resentment against your family. You weren't the favorite, I take it?"

She laughed. "Favorite? God—that's a joke. My brother was killed in a plane crash—he was training for the Fleet Air Arm; and that left my beautiful sister, Charlotte, and ugly old me. No, I certainly wasn't the favorite child."

"Aren't they proud of you now?" he asked her. They were walking the wide central thoroughfare; he stopped to look in one of the elegant shops.

171

There was a window display of very expensive handbags, and silk scarves.

"They don't know anything about my job," she answered. "That's nice, that maroon bag with the scarf—it must be Hermes, they do the most gorgeous designs. I bet it costs a fortune."

"What do they think you do, then?" Harrington asked. They began to walk on.

"They think I'm personal assistant to the Chief," she said. "He and my father have known each other for years. My mother tries to be tactful and asks how I'm getting on, rather like talking to someone about school—'How's the work going,' you know the sort of thing—and then drops hints about career women ending up lonely old maids. She means well, but I find it embarrassing."

"I don't know," he said thoughtfully. "You're a damned attractive woman. I've told you so before, and I mean it. Especially in the last year, you take a lot of trouble with yourself. Don't you want to get married? You could pick and choose, you know."

She smiled; an ironic smile followed by an impatient shake of the head. "I had one try," she said. "I got myself a nice suitable man, and he ran off with my sister and married her instead."

"Charming," Peter Harrington said. "She must be a real blossom."

"Oh, don't make any mistake," Davina said. "If you met her you'd be bowled over, just like everyone else. There's never been a man who didn't fall head over heels as soon as he saw her . . . except one."

She quickened the pace. Harrington looked at her; there was a slight curve on her mouth, almost a smile.

"And who was that?"

She gave him a mischievous sideways glance. "Ivan the Terrible," she said. "He preferred me. Let's go in and have a cold drink; I'm thirsty."

"There's a café there." Harrington steered her toward it. "Just tell me, how in hell did Ivan ever meet your sister?"

"Because I took him home for the weekend," she said lightly. "They thought he was a Pole, from the embassy. It was quite an interesting experiment. It doesn't matter telling you about it now. I got permission from the Chief, and we spent the weekend at home. That's when I went to bed with him for the first time. And there was my sister waiting for him to knock on her door. It was quite funny, looking back. . . ."

They sat at a table on the pavement. A waitress came over for their order.

"Two beers, please." Harrington offered Davina a cigarette. "You know I feel rather jealous?"

"Don't be silly," Davina said gently. "You don't feel anything of the sort. You can't help chatting me up, Peter, just to keep in practice. Not that I mind; but don't expect me to take any notice, will you?"

"That's up to you," he said.

The cunning bastard, he thought to himself. He knew how to get his hooks into her. "He preferred me." No wonder she'd fallen in love with him. But he said nothing; they drank the cold beer and watched the crowds pass by on that lovely summer day in late June. There was a distinctive atmosphere about West Berlin: there was gaiety and life, and exhilaration that was infectious. And through the heart of the city ran the obscene Wall, with its watchtowers and barbed wire and the armed Vopos patrolling, their machine pistols ready. And behind that wall there lived the luckless members of the German Democratic Republic. They were due to cross into the East the following morning. Harrington had booked seats on the morning bus that went through Checkpoint Charlie; their papers were ready for inspection, and they had an elderly aunt of Helga Jaeger's living in the Eastern Zone and anxious to see them. The aunt, duly provided by the Chief's East German network, would be waiting on the other side of the checkpoint when they disembarked. Davina had seen a photograph of her, dressed in the clothes she would be wearing. She had memorized it at the language center.

On the way back to their hotel, Harrington stopped at the bag shop.

"Let's pop inside and ask how much that is," he suggested.

She started to refuse, but he had gone in and she had to follow. He was looking at the maroon leather bag and scarf she had admired.

"Peter," she whispered urgently. "Don't be silly—I can't take a thing like that with me into the East. It's obviously made here!"

"It's a two-way traffic," he said. "You could have bought it on a visit to the West. Anyway, you like it, and I want to give you a present. So be a good girl and shut up!" He paid, and Davina winced at the price.

"Don't wrap up the scarf," he told the salesgirl. "My wife will wear it."

"You're crazy," she said when they were outside. "But it's lovely. Thank you very much—it was a sweet thing to do."

"Just a token of my esteem." He grinned. "Those colors suit you. Come on, we're going to celebrate our last night of freedom with a bloody good dinner and a bottle of wine. I might even join you in a glass."

"I think you might," she told him. This time she took his arm and held it until they reached the door of their hotel.

They had dinner in the new Adlon Restaurant; the rich German food was accompanied by a superb Rhenish wine. Peter Harrington kept up a continuous line of jokes and nonsense. Neither of them had spoken a word of English since they arrived in Berlin. He kept his promise and only sampled the wine; she felt quite lightheaded when they came out into the warm night air, and he found a taxi to take them back to the hotel. They had a double room with twin beds. There had been no awkwardness the previous nights; Davina was too keyed up to notice who went to the bathroom first to change, or to respond when Harrington tried a feeble joke about living the part.

That night was different; the wine had gone to her head, she felt relaxed and affectionate toward him. The expensive bag was on the chest of drawers, the Hermes scarf neatly folded. It was generous of him to buy her a present like that. She wasn't used to being given things. She undressed first, brushing her teeth with extra care, and making a silly face at herself in the bathroom mirror.

"Good evening, Frau Jaeger. That's a new white mustache you're wearing." She began to giggle.

He was in his robe when she came out. "What were you laughing about?"

"Oh, nothing. Just something ridiculous. That wine has gone right to my head. I'm going to have a hangover tomorrow morning."

"Never mind," he said. "It'll help you to look like an East German."

He pulled the bedclothes down for her. "Get in, then. Kiss good night?"

When he tried to open her mouth she pushed him away. "No, Peter. I'm sorry."

He didn't argue or persist. He let her go at once. "Pity," he said gently. "Pity that Russian got there first. I'm getting rather fond of you, you know. Sleep well."

He switched out the light. She felt herself drifting into sleep. Her dreams were fragmented, trouble-filled. She woke, heart beating too fast, gripped by anxiety from a nightmare she couldn't remember. East Berlin. Then Russia. The days spent with Peter Harrington had been a flight from reality, pretending to be tourists, treating themselves, like truants sneaking a day out of school. The new day was very real indeed, and, lying awake in the darkness, with two more hours before daybreak, Davina Graham began to be afraid.

Jeremy Spencer-Barr was in the bugproofed room outside the head of chancery's office. Elizabeth Cole's superior officer was with him.

"We've arranged a new rendezvous for the Daughter's contact," he said. "It's the biggest bookshop in Moscow, on Red Square. He goes there once a fortnight to collect the books he's ordered. His next trip is on Thursday. He's been following this line independently of meeting Lizzie Cole. It doesn't do to start new habits around here. You go to the same bookshop at three o'clock sharp on Thursday and order a copy of *Crime and Punishment* in the English translation. Say you want to translate it back into Russian. Your contact will be by the counter and he'll recognize you when he hears the book mentioned. They don't have a copy in stock, because we've checked. He will suggest you apply to the university for a loan of one of their copies. That tells you who he is. He'll wander off and you'll start looking through the shelves. When you're both out of sight, he'll make his report. All clear?"

"Perfectly clear, thank you," Jeremy said. "How do I get to Red Square? Public transport?"

"No, you walk," was the answer. "Start taking walks round the city, starting today. Visit the Kremlin Museum. It's worth seeing anyway. Wander round to Red Square and sightsee—Lenin's tomb, the Tsar Bell, St. Basil's Church. You've got a secretary, take her with you. Let her show you round. You'll be watched, naturally, so pretend to be interested, even if you're not."

Spencer-Barr looked surprised. "I'm looking forward to it," he said. "I think Moscow's a fascinating place." He seemed unaware of the condescension in his tone. The older man gave him a sharp look.

"Then why don't you go into Lenin's tomb," he said. "It'll only take four hours in the queue." He saw the young man smile, as if he'd said something amusing. He formed an instant dislike of him.

"I don't think I need to go that far," Jeremy said. "I'll go to the bookshop on Thursday; three o'clock by the foreign-translations section. Do I know what this contact looks like?"

"I've never seen him," was the answer. "But he's our only contact with the Daughter. He's a university lecturer, a young don in our parlance. Member of a group of dissidents, an offshoot of the Helsinki group monitoring human-rights violations. All those poor devils are either dead or locked away. These people are anonymous; they don't speak out because there's no shred of tolerance for them and they'd just be arrested. So they work underground, collaborating with the Western embassies, principally ours and the Americans', supplying information about arrests and acts of illegal oppression. Sometimes more than that. You can appreciate that their actions place them in more danger even than people like Scherensky and Belezky. If they're caught, they'll be accused of spying. And that means the firing squad."

"Well, they are spying, aren't they?" Spencer-Barr said. "Passing information to us and the Americans. What exactly is this man's relationship to the Daughter? Is she sympathetic to the dissident movement?"

"Sympathetic to her mother, who's in the Lubyanka. And scared stiff she'll end up there herself. That was Lizzie's last report from Daniel. That's his code name, as you know. In the Lion's Den; in more ways then one. All our dissident informants have the code names of the Prophets. This one seemed particularly apt when we chose it. That's the name he'll use to you."

"Thank you very much," Jeremy said formally. "I've got all that firmly fixed. I'll start my tour of the city straight away. Does my secretary have any idea that I'm more than Michael Barker's replacement?"

"None at all. So play it dead serious with her. She's quite a nice girl, so it shouldn't be too much of a bore."

Jeremy Spencer-Barr gave him a direct look from his humorless blue eyes. "Nothing about my work will ever be a bore to me," he said.

The older man had been in the Intelligence Service since his army days. He had developed a natural cynicism about enthusiastic youths. He also had a shrewd instinct for the rare species of man who crops up in the secret world at odd intervals. He committed his thoughts to tape, when he was alone. These in turn would be typed and filed for dispatch to London. Ambitious, sharp, overconfident. He gave his opinion of the new recruit. And then he added the last words, which his Chief and Humphrey Grant would understand: "Would undertake any assignment." That meant that the polished young gentleman was the type who could be told to kill and wouldn't hesitate. He switched off the tape and took it back to his desk and locked it away.

Jeremy Spencer-Barr set off for his tour of Moscow with an excited embassy secretary who thought him terribly good-looking and felt guiltily pleased about Michael Barker's heart attack.

"Oh, it's bliss to be home," Charley said. She stretched her arms above her head and turned her beautiful face up to the warm afternoon sunshine. Her father and mother smiled happily at each other. She was a delightful companion to them, always cheerful and full of amusing anecdotes about her life in London. Just to look at her lifted their spirits. She was one of those rare women who always looked glamourous; she was as lovely without makeup, in shirt and slacks, as she was when dressed for a party.

"The garden is looking marvelous," she said to her mother. "There's always such a lovely smell round this terrace."

"That's the Lilium regale," Mrs. Graham said. "They don't last very long, but they have a heavenly scent. Be careful of the sun, darling, it gets very hot here. You don't want to burn."

"I don't want to get freckly," Charley answered. "That's the pest of red hair, you get covered in freckles like a brown egg. Don't worry, I put on some cream first. I should go back to London with a lovely light tan. Not that I feel like going back."

"Why don't you stay, then?" Captain Graham suggested. "You could spend a few days relaxing here. It'd do you good Charley. I think you lead too hectic a life up in London on your own."

"It hasn't been that hectic," she admitted. "I've been going out a lot, but there's nobody interesting around." She opened her eyes and sat up. "In fact, the one man who takes me out regularly spends a lot of the time asking me questions about Davina."

"Really?" Her father was surprised. "Who is he—and why should he take you out to ask about her?"

"That's what's been bothering me," Charley said. "He's called Jeremy Spencer-Barr. He works in the Defence Ministry and he says he's met Davina once or twice. I didn't take any notice at first, I thought it was a bit boring, but he kept on. Every time we went out. You remember that Pole she brought down—well, he was asking questions about him too."

"What sort of questions?" her mother asked.

"About their relationship," Charley answered. "I was rather silly to mention it in the first place, in fact I played it up a bit. Actually it was the first time I met him, at the cocktail party after I left here that weekend. Then he took me out to dinner, and he asked a lot of questions about Davy, and the Pole. I got rather fed up with it. I thought at the time, Lord, what's so interesting about them? Then he said something that worried me afterward. He said, "She got a job I wanted. If they'd known she was having an affair she wouldn't have got it. That sort of thing doesn't go down well." I was quite worried in case he was going to get her into trouble because of something I'd said. I didn't expect to hear from him again, because he was going to America; I didn't like him very much actually. Then he rang up out of the blue and said his plans had changed.

"Next time I saw him," Charley went on, "he started the questions again. Just slipped in here and there. Had I seen Davy lately? Hadn't she mentioned the Pole before bringing him that weekend? Couldn't I remember his name or what he did at the embassy? It seemed so odd; I suppose I noticed it because he wasn't the least interested in me. I felt he was taking me out so he could find out about Davina and this man."

Her father frowned. "It certainly sounds like it," he admitted. "What was this job he talked about? I don't understand that at all. What is his position? After all, Davina's a personal assistant; he can't have wanted that!"

Charley paused; both parents were looking at her anxiously.

"There's something else," she said. "Probably ridiculous."

"What was it, Charley?" her mother prompted. "Tell us."

"Oh, you probably don't even remember. There was a Russian who disappeared over here last year. They found his body by Beach Head. A couple of months ago or more."

"I remember," her mother said suddenly. "It was on the news and there was a lot of fuss in the papers."

"There was a photograph," Charley said. "A blown-up thing, very grainy, taken of this Russian when he arrived at Heathrow. Did you see it, mother?"

Mrs. Graham shook her head. "I don't think so; I don't remember it."

"I expect you'll think I'm absolutely mad, but I thought it looked like Davy's Pole."

"Good God," Captain Graham exclaimed. "I remember that picture, and I remember thinking the same thing. What a coincidence."

His wife got up. "I keep the old newspapers," she said quietly. "I'll see if I can find it." She went inside the house.

"It's nonsense, of course," Captain Graham said after a pause, "but we might as well look together if your mother can find it. Here she is. Any luck, Betty?"

"Yes, it's *The Times*, May ninth."

She spread the paper out on the garden table. The three of them looked at it.

"That's the picture I saw," he said.

Charley stared down at it.

"It's a better reproduction than the one in my paper. It does look like him, doesn't it?"

Captain Graham nodded; he was reading the caption and the news story.

"I think it's turned cold," his wife said. "Let's go inside. Bring that with you, dear. I'll make some tea."

In the quiet drawing room, golden in the late sunshine, Charley perched on the arm of her father's chair. She slipped her arm around him.

"When did you last hear from Davy?"

"Not since that weekend. She wrote a nice letter to your mother. Nothing since. But that's not unusual. She leads her own life. In fact, we hadn't been in touch for months till she suddenly rang up and invited herself down for the weekend. Betty hasn't heard from her since the thank-you letter, or she'd have told me. I don't understand this at all, Charley. Especially this fellow Spencer-whatever-it-is. I don't understand this business about her getting a job, and why he wants to know about some Pole she brings down for the weekend. Look, darling, don't worry about it. You haven't done her any harm, I'm sure of that."

"I just hope not," she said slowly. "I hurt her badly enough once. It would be pretty awful if I did it again. I know her career means a lot to her. And thanks to me, Daddy, it's all she's got."

"You're not to talk like that," he protested. "Davina's had plenty of chances. You never meant to hurt anyone."

"That's quite true," she said. "It never occurred to me Davina wouldn't find anyone else. I just took Richard off her, that's all. I didn't seem able to help it. And I never wanted to marry him, either. You're right, darling, it was a long time ago, but I don't want to be the cause of any trouble to her now. And I don't like Jeremy. He's good-looking, he's charming in a way, very intelligent, and just not nice. That's all."

They sat together in silence for a while.

"Daddy—you don't think it's possible . . ."

"What, Charley?"

"It *couldn't* have been that other man, could it? The Russian. Seeing it just now, I was sure they were the same. She couldn't be mixed up in something, could she?"

Her mother came in with a tray. She answered the question before her husband had time. Her handsome face was grave.

"There's one way to make sure," she said. "Your father must go up and see James White. And he must tell him about this friend of yours, Charley, and his questions. So far as we know, Davina's a perfectly ordinary personal secretary and that man she brought here was a perfectly ordinary Polish diplomat. But we have got to make sure, that's all. Charley, pour out the tea, will you?"

"Yes, Mother."

She got up and took charge of the tea tray. Betty Graham settled in her chair opposite her husband's. She seldom took the initiative; her husband had been the head of the house and the family, and she had contentedly deferred to him throughout their married life. But when she did assert herself the effect upon him and her children was very positive. She addressed herself to Charley again.

"James has been a friend for many years," she said. "Your father and I have always understood that he has a confidential job in the Ministry, although naturally we've never mentioned it. So far as we know, Davina is his secretary, and recently promoted to his personal assistant. If she's got involved with anything beyond that, then I shall want to hear James's explanation. But until we do, Charley dear, you must promise to say nothing to anyone about her, the man she brought down here, or even this person Jeremy. I've been studying that picture, too. The more I look at it, the more it reminds me of her Polish friend. But the story said the body had been in the sea for several months. It was discovered only a few weeks after Davina and he had been to stay. So it couldn't have been the same person.

"Thank you, darling." She took the cup of tea from Charley. "But it's better to clear the matter up. I shall telephone Davina this evening; I should have done it ages ago, it's very remiss of me to neglect her. And you can ring James in Kent, dear."

Captain Graham saw the firm but gentle smile and knew that there was no point in arguing. "That's a good idea. Now Charley and I are going to play backgammon. I'll get the board set up."

There was silence after that, except for the rattle of the dice, and a muttered damn, half laughing, from the captain as his daughter won the first game. Mrs. Graham watched them tolerantly as she sewed. Needlework and gardening were her two passions, and she embroidered exquisitely. She was glad to see them together; she noticed how beautiful her daughter was in profile, and how young still, pushing the shining red hair away with one hand and teasing her father for being a bad loser. And she thought, as she often did in private, that there was something sad about her favorite child, so gifted with all the feminine graces, so envied by her own sex. Sad because the deeper values of fidelity and unselfishness had eluded her; she believed that love was all that mattered, without understanding that it meant to give as much as to receive.

Her thoughts turned to her other child, the self-contained, resentful elder daughter, resolutely plain and on the shelf, a reproach to her parents and her sister. Undemonstrative as a child, she had been difficult to love. She had been a silent, brooding adolescent who made adults uncomfortable. She had grown into the sensible daughter, nicknamed Davy, until such time as the boy was born; but still the nickname stuck. It was inconceivable to connect Davina with something secretive. Ridiculous to imagine that there was any connection between her and the death of a Russian trade delegate. Or the vague mystery of James White's true function in the Ministry. She didn't try to dismiss the fear that had begun to grow while she listened to Charley and looked at the photograph of a man who had been alive and in her house when he was said to have died months before. She didn't dismiss anything, because the last time she had felt this sense of darkening premonition was just before they received the news of their son's death.

"You'll be glad to hear that our operative in Moscow is in position and Miss Graham and her companion are now in East Berlin."

The Brigadier had taken Sasanov into the conference room ahead of the others. They had lunched together with Grant, and the conversation stayed on the most superficial level. They talked about the weather, the Brigadier's game of golf over the weekend; Sasanov listened to an explanation of the game without hiding his boredom. He ate in silence, his expression stony, resisting efforts to draw him out in the game of social niceties the two Englishmen were playing. When he was alone with the Russian, James White made his announcement immediately. Sasanov's head came up and he tensed; he reminded the Brigadier of a big, powerful animal that had scented danger.

"What about my daughter? And my wife?"

"Your daughter is well, and is continuing her studies at university," the Brigadier said. "There is no further news of your wife. We're still trying to make contact."

"They will send Fedya to the Gulag," Sasanov said.

He began to pace up and down.

"She won't live long in those conditions. My wife is a townswoman. They'll kill her slowly, with hard labor and too little food. And the cold."

He faced James White.

"You don't know what that word means in this little country. It's a cold that freezes the brain, that wakes you in the night in agony. It is a form of torture that never stops. Hunger and weakness and always that bitter cold eating into the body like a hungry animal. My wife will die," he said.

"We will get her exchanged," James White said. "First, we want to bring your daughter over. And that seems very hopeful."

Sasanov swung on him. "You have no one to exchange for my wife!" he shouted. "You haven't an agent of enough importance. The ones you have in prison here are all expendable. We wouldn't offer anything to have them back!"

"Why don't we sit down," James White said. "We have a few minutes in hand before the session starts. Calm yourself, Colonel. I've been thinking hard about this question of exchange and your wife. You're right, of course. We haven't got a Lonsdale or a Kroger. And the Americans certainly won't give us one of their bargaining counters to help release her. We've been insisting on keeping you to ourselves, you know. That was part of our bargain: you stay here."

"But you are sharing my information," Sasanov protested.

"Yes, sharing, but there's no cooperation in debriefing you. The Americans don't like that. But I keep my word, Colonel."

Sasanov hunched forward, his head lowered; the animal simile recurred to James White.

"Vina is out there, too," Sasanov said. "And there is one of our agents in place here."

"What makes you think that?" The question was asked almost casually.

"Because I'm not a fool," Sasanov snarled at him. "I know how my own organization works; I've known there was a KGB penetration since the fire at Halldale. And you haven't found them, have you?"

"Not yet," the Brigadier admitted. "But we will."

"How?" Sasanov demanded. "Months of investigating, taking statements, cross-examining the suspects, letting them go again, waiting for absolute proof—I know your methods, Brigadier, and they won't do for this! By the time you are ready to charge the spy he'll have made his escape, like Philby and the others. That's why you must let me look for him."

He took a cigarette out of the box on the table and then put it back in disgust.

"I can't smoke those things. Vina always got me Russian cigarettes."

"Kidson should have done the same," the Brigadier said. "How do you mean, look for him?" He didn't sound very interested. He swung his foot in its highly polished leather shoe and gazed at it for a moment or two before looking at Sasanov.

"Show me what you've got," the Russian said. "Let me analyze it. I haven't got time to waste, Brigadier. That agent could mean my wife's release. Think of the danger to Vina and the others! Let me work with your investigators and find him."

"I'm afraid we can't interrupt the debriefing," White said. "I couldn't justify it."

"I can interrupt it," Sasanov said flatly. "I can stop talking!"

"If you do," White answered pleasantly, "I shall cancel the rescue operation and recall my people from Russia. Never try to blackmail me, Colonel. It makes me very obstinate."

"You don't have to interrupt the sessions with Grant and his experts," Sasanov countered. "Just let me have the information your investigators have got on file. I can go through it myself, alone. It is to your advantage as much as mine. I want my wife released; you have a team in Russia and a Soviet agent loose. I will know better than anyone how to look for him."

The Brigadier examined his shoe again.

After a pause he said, "Very well. We'd be glad of your assistance. So long as you maintain your present level of information with Grant and his people. And here they are. Good afternoon, gentlemen. Shall we take our places?"

He glanced at the half-dozen men and smiled in his genial way, as if he were about to chair a routine board meeting in a company that was making a satisfactory profit. He saw Kidson go up to Sasanov and say something which made the Russian nod in agreement.

They disposed themselves around the big mahogany table: Grant, the supreme professional coordinator; Kidson the psychologist; a Soviet foreign-affairs expert called Franks; Holmes from the Department of Trade; Longman from the Ministry of Defence, with his assistant; and finally the representative of the Foreign Office, Arthur Warburton, a former Moscow diplomat with a long record of service within the Eastern bloc. There was a stenotyper who recorded every word spoken. Grant cleared his throat in his pedantic way and tapped a pencil on the table top, exactly like a schoolmaster calling his class to attention. The Brigadier could see quite clearly how his brilliant assistant annoyed his colleagues.

"We can recap on yesterday's session," he said. "By reference to the transcripts. Everyone has one? Good. Study them, and then perhaps Longman would like to begin."

White watched Sasanov. He didn't consult the papers in front of him. They had been translated into Russian to make it easier for him to read and digest them at speed. He was closed to the room and everyone in it, if his expression was an indication. The rather square face was set, the eyes hidden by half-lowered lids, the jaw clenched. He wanted to root out the KGB operative. It had occurred to White from the start that he hadn't once suggested that the man they were looking for was a home-bred traitor. He heard Longman from the Ministry of Defence open the session. He was a brisk man in his middle forties, a naval captain seconded to the highly secret section of the Ministry that operated with SIS.

"If the internal coups you disclosed to us yesterday are successful inside the UAE countries on the Gulf, that will open the Strait of Hormuz to Soviet naval domination," he said.

Sasanov answered slowly in his very good English. Davina Graham had achieved that, apart from anything else. "The coups are timed to start within six weeks of each other," he said. "Beginning with the palace revolution in Dubai. After the ruler's assassination, power will be seized by the Minister."

The Brigadier had read the transcripts the night before. The plan outlined by the Russian was simple, yet terribly cunning in its conception. The ruler of Dubai was a stern but beloved autocrat, a devout Moslem who lived a comparatively spartan life in comparison with his sons and his principal advisers. His death would be the result of traveling by helicopter with one of his younger sons, a Prince Mohammed, who liked to pilot his father. The Prince was known to be as wild as a hawk, restless and power-seeking, secretly resentful of his older brothers. The plan to sabotage the helicopter would allow the Minister to accuse the elder sons of bringing about their father's and brother's deaths, to arrest them and take power himself. He would have the support of the Army, which regarded itself as bound in loyalty to Prince Mohammed. Western observers would see no peril in the Minister's assumption of power; he had never been suspected of Soviet leanings. In fact, his liking for luxury and Western ways was known to be catered to by Britain and the United States.

The death of the Sheik of Kuwait would be caused by poison, administered by a woman in his harem. The woman was a plant, provided by the PLO. She had been chosen for her remarkable beauty and skill as a dancer; she had already pleased the Sheik and was taken with him when he traveled. His heir was already under the domination of a favorite with Soviet connections. The Sultan of Oman would be brought down by an internal revolution; the military dictatorship would be fronted by extremist Muslims. The fall of Saudi Arabia would happen automatically from within. The preparations for a rising against the King and the royal family had been in train for the past four years. It would begin with a second assault upon the Grand Mosque in Mecca. By the time the United States and the West had interpreted what was happening, the whole bloc to the Persian Gulf and the Strait of Hormuz would be invested with Soviet sympathizers, and the seas open to the Red Fleet.

"The result of this," Sasanov went on, "will be a military confrontation with the United States."

"In other words, a war," Captain Longman interposed.

"A confrontation is not expected to develop into a war at that stage," the Russian answered. "Our experts believe that fighting between the forces of the United States and ours will be avoided. With a consequent loss of face for America. But that is going too far ahead. The subjugation by subversive violence of the oil kingdoms of the Gulf—that is what we have to study first."

Kidson was making notes with his pencil; they appeared to be notes but were actually line drawings: odd shapes connected here and there with sharp angular lines. Occasionally he glanced up and watched Sasanov, who was on his feet, addressing the men seated around the table. In repose Sasanov was a dour man, with a sense of humor that was quick and unexpected. But here, surrounded by men of his own stamp, he projected considerable power. He spoke with fluency, answered and parried questions with authority. The drawings on Kidson's pad grew blacker as he underlined some of them.

The session was interrupted for cups of tea and dry army-issue biscuits, as Grant called them. Kidson and White left the room separately, ostensibly to go to the lavatory. They met in the washroom.

"I see what you mean," the Brigadier said. "He is certainly fluent. Every name, every date, is to hand. It is extraordinary."

"And he's dripping with sweat," Kidson remarked slowly. "Did you notice that? He's tearing himself inside out, and I don't know why." He went to the basin and rinsed his hands.

"We'll know soon enough," the Brigadier said. "He's asked to join the hunt for the Mole. It'll be very interesting to see if he finds him. He wants to get his wife released, he says. And he makes constant references to Miss Graham. Perhaps that's where the conflict lies—bear that in mind; he'll find our traitor for us."

"And if he doesn't?" Kidson asked him.

The Brigadier turned the doorknob. "We could lose those poor devils we sent to Russia," he said.

The village of Zhukova is on a bluff overlooking the Moscow River. Irina Sasanova had asked Volkov if she might go for a walk that afternoon while he had work to do. He had assured her she could go where she liked; he recommended a particular spot outside the village settlement, where he said she would have a fine view of the Central Russian Plain. It was very hot, but a delightful breeze blew in from the river; it cooled her as she walked. It was not the route she and her parents used to take when they walked their dog on summer weekends. Sasanov liked the beaches bounding the slow-moving river; Irina couldn't have borne to retrace their steps. Instead she paused on the high point, with the village to her left; and behind, the modern yellow-brick villas and traditional pine and clapboard houses looking so tranquil enclosed in their neat gardens and screens of pines. Moscow was only twenty miles away, but it was easy to imagine oneself in the heart of the countryside. She sat down, pulling at strands of grass, weaving them between her fingers until they broke. Before her the Central Plain undulated into the distance, suggesting an infinity of rolling land. The warm breeze stirred her hair; below her the sand beaches glittered in the sunshine, with figures dotted on them. Bathing and fishing were forbidden for the ordinary Russian citizens who crossed Ouspenskaya Bridge and trekked to the public beaches, because the river supplied the capital with its water. But on these, the beaches where the privileged owners of Party dachas picnicked and sunbathed, fishing was allowed by special license, and swimming was permitted. In the larch and birch forests surrounding Zhukova village and its complexes of dachas, there were the remains of trenches dug in the last war for the final defense of Moscow against the German armies. They had never been used; the invaders had been held and driven back and then, like the French in 1812, annihilated in the ice and snow.

It was the third weekend she had spent with Antonyii Volkov since the night she became his lover. As a reward, he had promised to let her see her mother.

She hadn't cried since that first night, and only then when he was fast asleep and she could weep into her pillows. She drove back to Moscow in his official car. She went to classes at the university as usual, and when she came back to her apartment the old *dezhurnaya* was waiting for her by the lift, cringing and asking if there was anything the Comrade Sasanova wanted. She had already slipped in to tidy the apartment for her. Irina walked past her without answering. Volkov's protection was having very early results. The next was the restoration of her right to shop at No. 2 Granovsky Street and to buy clothes on the third floor of Gum, reserved for the Party elite. She had dinner with Volkov during the week, and the car was waiting for her after the final class at the university at the weekend. She had no communication with Poliakov until he took the sociology class the following week. Sitting on the hill, she clasped her knees and closed her eyes; she rocked herself slightly, like a child or a very old woman. It was Sunday, and the next evening Volkov had arranged for her to visit her mother. A single tear slipped down her cheek; she brushed it off and got up. It was time to go back to the dacha. He was taking her to the Bear again, and afterward he would want to come back to Zhukova and make love.

"Mother," Irina entreated, "Don't cry—please don't cry."

She held Fedya Sasanova in her arms, and she could feel how thin she had become. They had brought Fedya up to an interview room, and then, to the surprise of both women, they had been left alone. Fedya clung to her daughter and sobbed. And as she embraced her, she whispered, "Don't say anything; they're listening in. Have you any news of your father? Just tell me, quickly."

Irina kissed her, "Don't be upset," she said loudly. "Try to control yourself." And then in a whisper, "I'm waiting; I'll have news soon."

Fedya was wearing a plain clean overall; she had been allowed a brush and comb and a small mirror. Her food rations had improved suddenly. Nobody had questioned her again, but she had been told to copy out a letter that horrified her. And copy it again and again, with variations. This happened in the middle of the night, without any explanation. She gazed at her daughter through the brimming tears, and tried to smile.

"You look well," she said. "Are you studying hard? You mustn't worry about me, I'm being well looked after. We can sit down here."

There were two upright chairs, which Irina pulled close facing each other. She sat opposite her mother and reached out to take her hands in hers.

"I'm working hard," she said. "Oh, Mother, I don't want to reproach you, but why did you tell lies about my father? Don't you realize what you did? You knew he wasn't well? Why didn't you alert his superiors?"

The hands holding Fedya's were squeezing hard in warning.

Anguish of mind had sharpened her wits. She hung her head and muttered. "I know. I know I did wrong. Try to forgive me, Irina. I deserve to be punished for it. I just hope the authorities will be merciful. But you must forgive me—you must. Now that your father is dead . . ." She gave way to a flood of tears.

I mustn't cry, Irina reminded herself. I mustn't betray myself. She knows what I'm doing, she understands I don't mean a word.

Aloud she said, "He'd be alive if you hadn't failed him. But what's done is done now. Listen, Mother, Comrade Volkov let me see you. He says you'll be given a chance to rehabilitate yourself. You've got to work hard and obey the rules, and you won't be away for very long. Will you promise me to do that?"

Fedya signaled to her daughter to get up. They had been allotted ten minutes and the time was nearly up. She embraced her again, and whispered in her ear, "If you get a message—if I say 'your little mother' don't believe it. It will be a lie. I'll never come home, my darling. It doesn't matter. Go to the West. Go to your father. . . . Tell him I love him."

The door opened and the guard came into the room. He put his hand on Fedya's arm. "Time is up," he said. He took her away, and she glanced over her shoulder at Irina and gave a wan smile.

"Goodbye," she said clearly, "little daughter." It was the old-fashioned Russian endearment from parent to child.

Irina was escorted out of the building. Volkov's Volga car slid to the side entrance. The driver opened the rear door for her. She asked to go home to her apartment. On the journey back he glanced into the rearview mirror, as instructed, but she wasn't crying. She appeared quite calm, he reported later. The *dezhurnaya* crept up to listen outside the apartment door once she had gone inside, but she heard nothing until the girl switched on the radio to a program of popular music.

That evening, without warning, Antonyii Volkov called on her. He sat down in the small living room and accepted a glass of vodka. She was pale and puffy-eyed. She had kept her tears until she was alone, as he expected shc would. IIis opinion of her courage had been right. She was a brave and resolute creature, although naive. He listened while she described her meeting with her mother, and when she thanked him he only nodded. He accepted a second vodka. Then he told her he was sorry to bring her bad news. The head of the Committee for State Security had been reviewing Fedya Sasanova's case. In spite of all Volkov's efforts on her behalf, they had refused to be lenient. She was being shipped to the Kolyma labor camps the next day. The complex at Kolyma were the worst of all the penal colonies, deep in the Arctic Circle at the eastern end of Siberia. No one sent there had ever returned. He set his glass down on the little table by his chair, folded his hands and watched her, waiting.

"Do you have an English translation of *Crime and Punishment?*"

The girl assistant at the foreign-books counter shook her head.

"No," she said brusquely. "We don't have that in English."

"Would it be possible to order one?" Jeremy Spencer-Barr inquired.

The assistant shook her head. She seemed to enjoy frustrating him. "I couldn't say," she said, and turned her back on him.

Spencer-Barr felt a touch on his arm. A young man was beside him.

"Excuse me, but I heard you asking for *Crime and Punishment* in English."

"Yes, I did," Jeremy said. "Apparently there isn't one, and nobody can help. I want to improve my Russian by retranslating it."

"Well, you could try the library at the university," the man suggested. "If your purpose is study, they might lend a copy."

"Thank you very much," Jeremy said. "That's most kind. I'll go along there."

He walked away; the Russian lingered, asking for books which he had ordered.

"They're not in," the girl snapped. She had heard him offer to help to the foreigner and she was sullen.

"I sent for them a month ago," Poliakov protested. "I need them for my students. Why can't you ever get anything quickly?"

"Because we don't print them, Comrade," she sneered. "We only sell books. If you want to complain, write to the printers."

She picked up a sheaf of bills and marched away from the counter.

Poliakov made his way to the shelves at the back of the shop. He stopped beside Spencer-Barr, who was reading a book of Russian verse.

"My name is Daniel," he said.

Spencer-Barr didn't look up from the book. "What news of the Daughter?"

Poliakov took a book from the same shelf and opened it.

"Worrying news," he said. "I won't have an opportunity to see her before next Thursday. Rumors have been going around the university."

"What kind of rumors?" Jeremy asked, turning a page.

"Rumors that she's under some Party boss's protection," Poliakov murmured. "An official car has picked her up every weekend. I checked on it myself. It belongs to Antonyii Volkov. KGB."

Spencer-Barr closed the book of poetry and slotted it back into the shelf. "Meaning she's working for them? It wouldn't be made public if she were."

"That's what I tell myself," Poliakov said. "Volkov was her father's superior. She could make a deal to help her mother."

"It'll be interesting to see if she mentions him on Thursday," Jeremy said. "If she doesn't, we'll have to do something about her. Otherwise you and all your people will be arrested. We can't have that." He ran a finger over the row of books and pulled out another one.

"Leave a bus ticket in this book of poetry to let me know you've seen her. I'll meet you here at three o'clock on Friday."

Poliakov nodded. "We'd better go now. You leave first."

"Good luck," Jeremy said. He replaced the book and walked away.

10

"**O**h, my dear, my dear, how happy I am!"

The gray-haired woman embraced Davina, and then kissed Peter Harrington, enthusing over them loudly. She wiped her eyes and said, "Forgive me—it's so long since I've seen Helga. She's so like my sister. . . ."

They walked away, one on each side of her, their arms linked, watched by the sullen Vopo border police. They caught a bus to the Oktoberstrasse, a residential district built since the war. The gray buildings housed apartments, their façades grim and uniform; each building had a caretaker who was in the pay of the State Security Police, the merciless SSD who held the population of the city in total subjection.

The woman introduced them to the man on duty in the hall below her apartment.

"My niece and her husband," she said, "Herr Jaeger and his wife, Helga—they've come all the way from Hamburg to visit me! Isn't that wonderful?"

She hurried them to the lift, and they went up to the fifth floor. She opened the green-painted door, and they went into the apartment. It was one room, with a kitchen and a shower. Three people did in fact seem like a crowd.

"I've done what I can," she said, "but you're not encouraged to decorate too much."

She stripped off her coat, and she seemed taller and younger. The

191

fussiness of manner had disappeared. She held out her hand and shook theirs in turn.

"Sit down," she said. "I'll bring some coffee. And don't worry; this place is quite clean. I have it checked regularly by a friend. He works in an electronics company."

She had a bold smile; it made her look quite handsome. She was the widow of a trade-union official who had been killed at Auschwitz by the Nazis after a life spent struggling for socialism and freedom for his fellow workers. Frieda was her code name; she had been part of the Communist underground that operated through the war inside Germany. She had never been caught, and her cover was so skillful that when the Gestapo seized her husband she was considered too unimportant to warrant more than a brief, brutal questioning. She came out with a broken nose and three cracked ribs; but she was free and able to continue her work. The Russian liberation of her country had seemed to Frieda and to thousands of other left-wing Germans the justification for all they had suffered. In the smoldering ruins of Berlin they waited for the Red Army to deliver them. The deliverance was such that Frieda nearly lost her mind. An orgy of looting, rapine, summary executions and sheer savagery erupted in the city and engulfed every German citizen, regardless of age or sex or political creed. Frieda managed to reach the Soviet command post in her district, hiding in the ruins and avoiding the groups of drunken soldiers who were breaking down doors and dragging people out.

The Russian commander was quite sober. She was brought in and pushed to her knees in front of him. She began to shout and protest at what was happening; she told him who she was and the name of her husband, and of the Party membership which had cost him his life.

She was never clear about the details of what happened next; she had a memory of the Soviet commander taking her to the door and shouting in Russian. She was taken to the guardroom, where a dozen grinning men stripped and raped her, jeering and calling her comrade. She was found that night lying in the street outside the post, semiconscious and naked, bleeding from internal injuries. Two old men carried her to shelter in a cellar, and a little group of terrified people cared for her. There was a period in the hospital, and then discharge. Where there had been chaos, now she found order. The streets were being cleared, supplies organized; the people cowered under a domination as iron-hard as the Nazi terror. This was East Germany under its Communist liberators; it became the German Democratic Republic under the newly formed government of Ulbricht. Frieda got a job in one of the new factories that were being built; she worked in the kitchens. She never mentioned her Party membership and she had a set of papers belonging to someone else, who had died during the first three months of Russian occupation. She had a new name, a new identity. Her mental and physical health recovered slowly, and with it the spirit that had survived life in Nazi Germany, and found the will to fight again. By the end of 1973 she had enrolled as a British agent, providing cover for infiltrators and refugees.

The bogus Dieter and Helga Jaeger were two names to her; she knew as little of their real purpose in Berlin as they knew about her true identity. Suffering had not dimmed the quick intelligence, or the humor; she assumed her garrulous elderly skin and just as easily threw it off and laughed at herself.

"I call her my *Doppelgänger,*" she explained. "Fussy Frieda. That dirty spy downstairs doesn't have to sneak after me; I drive him mad telling him all about my day in the factory and what I bought for dinner, and how I've got a niece coming to visit me—he almost hides when he sees me coming! I'm more worried about the couple who live down the hall. He's a driver in the Ministry of Agriculture, she works in the Charité Hospital, but they have good clothes, a color television set. You don't get luxuries like that from being an honest worker. I think he works for the SSD. That's why I'll slip you two out before they get back. Is everything clear?"

She addressed herself to Peter Harrington. As soon as they had crossed into East Berlin, Davina noticed how he changed. The middle-aged Englishman, with his rakish air and schoolboy humor, had disappeared as if he had suddenly stepped into a hole at her side and vanished. Peter Harrington had become Dieter Jaeger. He not only dressed like an East German, he walked like one, with a serious expression on his face, a brisk way of speaking and a tendency to push in front of her. The change was fascinating to her; she watched him while he and Frieda examined the two sets of papers with their new identities. He was a true professional; watchful, keen and very wary. He passed one set of papers to her.

"Give Frieda your West German passport and visa," he said. "As soon as we get out of here, you're Gertrude Fleischer, and I'm your husband Heinz."

Davina took the East German passport and opened it. Her own face stared at her. It was quite a shock till she remembered they had taken several sets of passport photographs at the house in Langham Place. Gertrude Fleischer, aged thirty-three, married, height five feet six inches, hair color brown, eyes gray, distinguishing marks none; home address, 331 Hoffburg, Karl Marx Platz, East Berlin 6. Occupation, secretary. She shut the narrow blue booklet; there was an envelope addressed to her, with an official postmark. She took the enclosure out. It was a visa, stamped by the Soviet Embassy, granting entry to the Black Sea resort of Livadia. She put the document and the passport into her handbag.

Frieda stood up. "I'll walk you both to the bus; we'll board together and I'll get off three stops down. You continue till you get to the Air Terminal Building. From there you'll be taken by bus to the airport. Your flight leaves at nine o'clock."

"What about the people who are taking over our West German passports?" Davina asked.

"Don't worry about them," the woman said. "Even if they were caught, they know nothing about you. I'm the only one who does. If I don't get the signal that they've reached the West by this evening, I shall disappear for a few weeks until it's safe or we know what's happened. But don't worry. We've done this run dozens of times and it's always worked. Let's go now."

She followed them out into the narrow corridor, and she was Fussy Frieda again, chattering and bustling into the lift and out past the caretaker. She paused, hanging on to Davina's arm.

"We've had such a lovely visit," she said. "And now they're taking me to the Brümmerhaus for coffee and cakes—such good chocolate cake they have there. . . ."

Her voice faded as they walked away down the street. There was a small line at the bus-stop sign; before they joined it, Frieda whispered, "Good luck," and then she separated from them.

It was very warm, and the men wore open-necked shirts, the women dowdy cotton dresses. Nobody spoke. When the blue-and-white bus came to a halt, they all filed on board and took their places. Frieda found a place in the front; she didn't look at Harrington and Davina. She got off three stops later, and the last they saw of her was a bent figure hurrying along the road with her head down as if she were walking against a wind. Schönefeld airport was a well-designed, compact terminal, a status symbol for the East Germans, and constructed with imagination and a kind of stark elegance. It contrasted with the general air of drab functionalism that characterized the rebuilt city. Harrington looked at his watch; like Davina's clothes and accessories, everything was German-made.

"Our next rendezvous is in the self-service cafeteria on the first floor of External Flights Terminal Two," he said. "We've got a bit of time in hand; I'd like something to eat, wouldn't you?"

Davina shook her head. "I'm not hungry," she said. "There's such a dreadful atmosphere in this place. Why do we have to go to the cafeteria? Are we meeting someone else?"

"Not exactly." For a second the old impudent grin appeared. "We came into East Berlin on a day pass; we're going to the Crimea for a holiday. We need luggage, my dear Gertrude. Christ, what a name to give you—I'll never remember it. Helga wasn't too bad."

"I kept thinking of Helga the Hyena," she said, and she giggled nervously. "I don't dare to laugh over here—it might be considered a crime. Everyone looks so dour and miserable."

"Life in the workers' paradise is no joke," he said. "I just wish some of our cozy intellectual fellow travelers could be sent here for a year without an exit permit. They might see corrupt old democracy in a new light. Here we are."

The cafeteria was at the top of an escalator. It was full of people lining up at the self-service counters. Harrington took a tray; he chose a liverwurst sandwich, apple torte and two cups of coffee. He paused after he had paid at the checkout; it was a tiny hesitation while he got his bearings. Then, as Davina followed, he headed toward a table three in from the center aisle. There was a man sitting there reading the *Ostdeutsches Gazette*. Peter set down the tray and slid in beside the man, who lowered his newspaper a few inches and glowered at being disturbed. Davina took her coffee; she sipped it in silence while he ate.

Announcements came over the loudspeakers. Flights were called to Warsaw, Cracow, Bucharest. Harrington finished the apple torte and pushed his plate away.

"That was good," he said. "I'm looking forward to this holiday, Gertrude. But you mustn't let me eat too much."

She pulled herself together and said quickly, "No, of course not. You don't want to put on weight again. I've got to be careful, too."

"They say the Russian food is very rich." He leaned toward her. "It's the bathing and the beaches I like. And doing nothing for a while."

"We're very lucky," she said. "A holiday like this really sets you up for the winter. What time is our flight?"

"Soon," he answered. "It'll be called soon."

"Excuse me." The man sitting next to him folded his paper and got up. Harrington left his seat and stood aside to let him pass.

The man pushed his way out. Harrington sat down again.

"What a pig," Davina said. "Did you see him glaring at you while we were talking about the holiday? When do we get the luggage?"

"It's under the table," he said softly. "He left it for us. There's the flight being called now."

She listened to the metallic voice: "Aeroflot Flight 4270 to Moscow is boarding at Gate No. Five. Passengers will proceed to Gate No. Five as soon as they have checked their luggage." From Moscow they would catch the shuttle to Simferopol in the Crimea.

Harrington stretched under the table; he hauled out one suitcase and then a smaller one. Both had name tags tied to the handles. Herr Heinz Fleischer, Frau Gertrude Fleischer.

"You take the small one," he told her. "This is an egalitarian society— women carry their own bags."

They went down the moving stairs and across the wide expanse of the ground floor with its check-ins and ticket offices.

Harrington slowed as they neared the Aeroflot check-in.

"I'm scared," Davina whispered to him.

"Don't worry, the nasty bit is getting through to the plane. We'll be all right. Stick close to me and say nothing."

There was a long walk to Gate No. 5. She had to hurry to keep up with him, and it made her breathless by the time they arrived and joined the line of passengers waiting to go through to the departure area. Two uniformed officials examined the passports and visas; they took a long time, reading the documents and referring back to the passports. The second man fixed each traveler with a cold, aggressive stare. Davina felt her legs trembling; the sense of breathlessness increased. Oh God, she said to herself, they'll know there's something wrong just by looking at me . . . if they see my hands shaking.

"Gertrude," Harrington snapped at her over his shoulder, "get your passport and visa ready. Come on, it will be our turn next. Here, give them to me."

She stood a little behind him, wondering if the panic inside her was visible on her face. Harrington was like a rock; brusque with her, subservient to the officials—it was a performance to admire for subtlety. A petty bureaucrat, assistant manager in the local Vehicle Licensing Office in a suburb of the city. He bullied his wife and toadied to the authorities. His passport and visa were examined; it seemed to Davina that the officials spent longer over their papers than on those who had gone in front of them.

She was beckoned forward, and there was no Peter Harrington to hide behind. The official studied her passport, glanced up at her, turned back to the visa and to the passport again.

"Frau Fleischer?"

"Yes," she said. Her throat was so dry that her voice sounded harsh. The official didn't speak; he stared at her. She didn't know that this charade was part of the system of keeping the citizen in a state of apprehension even though he was doing something perfectly legal. The passport and the documents were stamped and handed back to her. Harrington took them immediately and stuffed them into his pocket.

"Come on," he said impatiently; and they were through. All that remained was the personal search. Hand luggage was sped through an X-ray machine. Davina saw her expensive maroon leather bag vanish into the X ray, and reappear on the other side. Nobody else had such a smart piece of personal luggage as that distinctive bag. It stood out among the plastic purses and shabby carryalls; even the briefcases carried by traveling businessmen were of inferior quality. I should never have brought that, she thought suddenly; it stands out a mile.

"Through here," someone directed her, and she walked through the metal-detector screen, and a uniformed woman security guard gave her a body search. Harrington was in front of her, waiting. She joined him, and he dropped down into a seat.

"Good girl," he murmured. "You were great. Here's your bag."

She took the handbag from him and placed it under her chair.

"I've never been so frightened in my life," she said. "When they started looking at the papers I shook like a leaf."

"That's just part of the technique," he said. "I should have warned you. They like people to be scared. I must say Langham Place does a nice bit of forging."

"I saw people looking at my bag," she said. "I shouldn't have brought it. Nobody else had anything from the West."

"Stop worrying," he whispered. "You're just imagining it. People bring in luxuries when they cross over."

"Can't I leave it behind? There's nothing in it but makeup and paper tissues—"

"Now, that *would* draw attention to us, wouldn't it?" he said. "No woman in her right mind forgets a hundred-and-twenty-quid bag. Stop fussing, will you?" He sounded genuinely impatient.

"I'm sorry," Davina said. "I'm just nervous, that's all."

Fifteen minutes later they were aboard the Ilyushin jetliner, buckled into their seatbelts, embarked on a twelve-hour flight and an overnight stop at three in the morning.

The big plane began to taxi out into position at the edge of the runway. Peter Harrington gripped her hand.

"Relax, now," he said gently. "We're on our way."

The jet took power and began to speed along the black path outlined by brilliant landing lights; it left the ground with a thrust of the engines and began a smooth climb into the darkness. Davina looked out the window at the twinkling lights of the city as they grew smaller and finally vanished.

Russia . . . the Russia Sasanov had talked about with a poet's love, speaking of mankind's need to identify with his native land. They were going to the Crimea; he had once described to her the incredible carpet of spring flowers there, stretching into infinity; the glittering waters of the Black Sea lapping the miles of beaches; the pine forests, the subtropical climate and wonderful plant life. The place where he had spent his honeymoon—with Fedya. " . . . If I could show you Russia," he had said to her, "you would understand. One day, maybe you will go there. Then you'll think of me."

She freed her hand from Harrington's and turned her head to look out the little window at the blackness outside. When drinks were being ordered, he spoke to her twice before she heard him.

Poliakov gazed at Irina Sasanova over his clasped hands. They were drinking tea, and he was leaning toward her, his elbows on the table.

He had overheard remarks among the students; some were intended to be heard. Keeping her back after class was causing rumors. She was either a favorite or they were beginning a relationship between teacher and pupil which was forbidden at the university. He had left a note in her book asking her to meet him at a café near the big bookshop on Red Square. He thought she looked thinner and pale, with deep shadows under her eyes. She was wearing a pretty cotton dress with a flowered print, and elegant high-heeled sandals. Such clothes were reserved for the elite who had access to the third floor of Gum. She hadn't worn anything new like that since her father disappeared. He tried hard to be detached, to smother his fear that she had decided to betray him. The KGB car had called for her several times; once someone had glimpsed Volkov sitting in the rear as the door was opened and she got in beside him.

"If she doesn't mention him, we'll have to do something about her." He remembered the cold-eyed Englishman's words as he looked at Irina.

She put her teacup down and said, "Why are you staring at me? Is there anything the matter?"

He said the first thing that came to mind, and it happened to be true. "I was thinking how pretty you are," he said. "But you don't look well."

Her face flooded with color; it was pale one moment and bright pink the next.

"I'm glad," she said quietly. She picked up her empty cup and put it down again. "I'm glad you think I'm pretty. But you're right, I don't feel very well."

He filled her cup. She's going to tell me, he said to himself. If she were a liar and a betrayer, she wouldn't blush like that—or look at me in that way.

"What is the matter, then?" he asked.

There were no tears in her eyes; there was a dreadful vacancy in them, as if there was nothing left to suffer.

"They've sent my mother to the Kolyma camps."

He reached out and clasped her hand. "Oh, my poor Irina—that's terrible news!"

"She'll never come back," she said. "It's the worst place on earth. Nobody ever comes back."

"How do you know this?"

She was holding fast to his hand. "Antonyii Volkov told me. I've been sleeping with him; I thought it might help her."

Poliakov was an emotional man. Irina saw the look on his face, and her heart jumped and fluttered like a bird in her breast. Many times when she was in bed with Volkov she tried to imagine that it was Poliakov holding her. But the fantasy didn't last, because the young tutor would never have hurt her, and Volkov liked to inflict pain.

"Do you despise me, Comrade?"

"No," he said violently. "No. You did it for your mother. There's no shame in that. *He* is the shame—the scum of the earth!"

"He let me see my mother," she went on. "She was not too bad, a little thin, but otherwise they hadn't hurt her. I really thought she might be allowed home after a short sentence. But she knew. . . . She whispered to me, 'I'll never come back.' That's what she said. But I didn't believe her. Volkov had hinted he could get her off after a few months in a correction center. Then he came around that night and told me she was going to Kolyma the next day. I tell you something: he enjoyed it. I cried, I lost my head and got down on the floor to kneel and beg for her, and he was enjoying seeing me suffer. He wanted to go to bed with me when I was like that. And afterward, when he'd had a sleep, he told me to make coffee and something to eat. I did it, Comrade Poliakov. I was like a dog that's been beaten. I gave him the food and wondered why I didn't take the bread knife and stab him in the back."

"Thank God you didn't," the tutor said. "Thank God."

"Then he started talking about my father," Irina went on. "How he had been so sick before he went to England. And he was watching me all the time. Then he said, 'You know, I don't believe he's dead after all.' I didn't say anything. I was too dulled, too hurt, to respond to it. He said it again. 'I think he's in the West. Now, if you could persuade him to come home, then I can promise you your mother would be released immediately.' He knows I'm in communication with my father," she said slowly, "and he was offering me a bargain. Get him back and your mother goes free. *He* had her sent to Kolyma."

The tutor bent his head and gave a low groan of despair.

"Then we're all lost," he said. "He's just waiting to arrest me, and then the others. How does he know? Did you tell him? Did you?" His tone was fierce.

She looked at him steadily. "No," she said. "I didn't tell him anything. He knows my father is alive and hiding in the West. He knows we've had word from him, but that's all. My mother hasn't told him anything because of me. But the way he said it, 'If you could persuade him to come home'—somebody has told him."

"What did you say?" Poliakov was not convinced; he was very white and his hand trembled. He muttered to himself, My God, they could be waiting outside for us now.

The girl was calmer than he was. "I said I'd do it," she told him. "I asked him to tell me what to do, how to get a message to him. He just smiled and didn't answer. I asked again, because I thought he wanted me to beg. Then he said, 'You'll get the opportunity. I'll tell you when it comes.' Then he went out of the apartment and left me. . . . What am I to do? I'm frightened to meet you again; he'll have me watched."

"Yes, he will," the tutor said. "And the other students have been gossiping—first about me and now about the car that comes for you. There is too much talk, Irina. . . . Listen: I'll leave a note in your essay book in two days' time, after the lecture. That will tell you where to find me."

"Have you got news from my father?"

She looked so anxious and pathetic that he only just prevented himself from telling her about the new contact in the British Embassy. But in all societies ruled by tyranny, the first casualty among its people is trust. He shook his head.

"Nothing," he said. "But we'll hear something soon. Be patient." He squeezed her hand again. "Be very careful."

"I will," she said. "Volkov won't do anything to me. He's going to use me to destroy my father. I'm safe for the moment anyway. But you be careful, won't you, Comrade?"

He nodded. "I'll leave first," he said. "There's a back entrance through the washroom. I'll slip out there. Can you pay the bill?"

"He gives me money," she said flatly. "I can pay."

He nodded to her again, and hurried away from the table to the toilets at the rear. The back door opened out onto a narrow street. He paused in the doorway, looking up and down, but there was nobody in sight. He walked away from the place as fast as he could.

Volkov knew. . . . How much did he know? If he knew about Sasanov's message to his family, then he must know the channel that transmitted it. Poliakov broke into a cold sweat of fear again. Why hadn't he acted? Why was he playing his cruel game with Irina and her mother, unless it was genuine and he really did intend to blackmail the defector into returning? Poliakov shook his head as he hurried on, his lips moving in frantic arguments with himself. It was too difficult, too complex, for him to see the truth. He was an intellectual, a liberal. Only the mind of a spy could unravel the sinister motives of another spy. He went into the bookshop on Red Square and left a bus ticket in the volume of Russian poetry, the signal for the meeting with Spencer-Barr the following day.

Sasanov was alone; Kidson had provided cigarettes and vodka and the snack meal he had wanted instead of dinner. Then he left the Russian with the photocopy files sent down from London. Sasanov had read them through once, to get an impression of the contents. Now, with a halo of cigarette smoke hanging in the air overhead, he was reading page by page and making notes.

There was Davina Graham's personal file. He read that, and occasionally he frowned. It didn't bring her to life. It was a collection of facts that suggested a cold spinster, uninterested in men because of an early disappointment, a desexed woman with a man's intellect. Words like "reliable," "meticulous," occurred regularly in her first-year notes; she became ingenious, inspired, and finally "a potentially brilliant operator on home ground." That was last year, before she was put in charge of him. "Most unlikely to become involved with the subject." And, reading that, Sasanov smiled. Then the investigations began after the Halldale fire. Her friendship with Peter Harrington was analyzed; the dates, places and times of their few meetings were recorded, their own statements cross-checked. Harrington's name was accompanied by a coding for his own file. That was there, too. There was her account of their stop at the motel, which had saved both their lives. The cross-check showed that she had omitted hiring the room for sex purposes. Her weekly reports to the Brigadier had not been included. Sasanov understood their reluctance to let him read about himself. Even his interview at the Garrick Club had been abstracted.

From the moment Halldale was attacked, Davina had been under close surveillance by her own people. Every telephone call was monitored; there had been bugs hidden in the little flat. The tapes were not included, but they were referred to when their relationship and her concealment of it was discussed. Suspicion had centered on her at one time: investigators hurried back to check her past at the university; even the faithless fiancé was scrutinized for pro-Soviet leanings.

Sasanov muttered impatiently as he read. What a waste of time. All they were investigating was a woman in love. To his surprise the last interviews with Grant and the Brigadier had been included. He did not know that they had edited out the signing of the official undertaking and the earlier references to it. He read her spirited defense of his interests and her reproaches to the Brigadier when he reneged on his promise to let Sasanov go. He paused, seeing her in imagination. He knew exactly how she would look, and the tone of her voice. She had a resolute courage. He knew it well. The details of her role in Russia followed immediately afterward. His frown grew deeper. Once he exclaimed out loud. He closed the file and dropped it on the ground. His face was grim.

He began the long, thick dossier on Peter Harrington, which went back for nearly twenty years. There were a dozen such dossiers to be read: the personal file of every member of the security staff at Halldale, the investigators' reports on the fire itself, the Sussex police investigation of the accident to the van driver; the nurse who had mentioned a devoted grandson who used to take her out and suddenly stopped visiting about the time of the fire. It would take days to read through everything in detail and to sift through the evidence and the conclusions in his search for a clue . . . a clue to the Soviet agent who had discovered that he was hiding in the nursing home. Sasanov lit a cigarette. The fire was a typical Moscow operation. The man who attacked the van driver on his way to Halldale Manor had been on a motorcycle. That much the injured man had told the police before he died. Tracks were found by the road, and marks in the ditch indicated that the machine had been hidden there. The tracks were clear on the direction back toward London, and then lost on the main road. No trace of the killer had been found. Police information didn't point to an underworld contract; the nature of the bomb ruled out ordinary criminal activity. Only the Center people had access to that kind of weapon. So the Brigadier's men were hunting for one man while the Scotland Yard Special Branch was searching for another. Sasanov opened the file on Peter Arthur Harrington, aged forty-eight, and began to read it very carefully.

On the floor below him, Kidson and Grant were having their own private conference. They had just spoken to the Brigadier on the telephone. Neither looked very pleased.

"Why couldn't the Americans have waited?" Kidson asked. "What's the point of coming down here right in the middle of it? It could easily throw him off balance; do they realize that?"

"They wouldn't care," Grant said. "We've let them know there's top-grade information coming, and they bloody well won't be satisfied with what we choose to give them. They're insisting on hearing it for themselves."

"I suppose we couldn't keep it quiet," Kidson grumbled.

"Not after the Chief saw the Prime Minister," Grant said. "She insisted on telling the Americans, and naturally they want one of the Cousins to sit in. Serves us right for electing a woman. They've no real judgment."

He pursed his thin lips in disapproval. Kidson hid his smile. Poor old Robespierre. If he had his way the world would be populated only by men.

"I think we'd better warn him," he said, indicating Sasanov above. "I'll drop a hint tomorrow. I wonder if he'll find anything we missed. He's keen enough—wouldn't have dinner, just wanted to spend the evening working through our files."

"It's a good opportunity for him to throw suspicion on one of our own people, isn't it?" Grant muttered. "I'm beginning to have doubts about him, Kidson. He's blowing Soviet foreign policy for the next ten years, but that's not enough. He wants to expose a top Russian agent at the same time. And I don't believe that business about the wife for a moment. If she's gone to the Arctic Circle, she'll be dead long before we could negotiate any exchange with the Russians. He knows that as well as we do. But the Brigadier is playing along with him. He's even tried to convince me that he believes Sasanov's motives are entirely genuine."

"I'm beginning to think they are," Kidson answered. "I've said from the start, he's in a state of high tension. It's not the usual way, but then he's broken all the rules so far. He's not as cold-hearted as you might expect, in spite of what he's been. We know through the dissidents that he did try to help Belezky. We also know that he's a very affectionate husband and father. And he cares more about Davina Graham than you think. She seems to have had quite an effect on him. We know she made a fool of herself, and she's not the impressionable type."

"She's a frustrated career girl," Grant snapped. "All Sasanov did was drop his trousers and she thinks it's love. If I'd been in the office at the time, I'd never have advised the Chief to send him off with a woman."

"Then he mightn't have come round at all," Kidson pointed out.

"What matters is, he has. He's given us everything; more than we expected, and at twice the usual rate. He may know it'll be too late to save his wife, but he needs to try, to hope. And he's worried sick about Davina Graham. I don't find his eagerness to dig up our Mole as suspect as you do."

Grant stood up. "Time to go in to dinner," he said. "I wonder whom he'll pick out."

Kidson held the door open for him and they walked out into the corridor toward the private dining room.

"God knows," he said. A burst of laughter drifted through from the big room where the officers in training had their meals. "But it gives me a very uncomfortable feeling."

Spencer-Barr paid regular visits to the bookshop, and the surly assistant had become more friendly. He bought a lot of books and spent time wandering around the shelves. He was establishing a habit. He knew the significance of the bus ticket, and he bought the book of poetry. The following afternoon at three o'clock he was back at the counter, asking if he could change it for something else. The assistant gave him a credit slip and he moved away to the bookshelves at the back. Poliakov arrived five minutes later. They placed themselves in a corner where the shelves angled, with a view of anyone approaching. Spencer-Barr listened while the tutor explained what had happened to Irina.

"We're all in terrible danger," he concluded. "Volkov is using the Mother as bait to get the Father to return. The Daughter says he knows there's been communication between them. But he doesn't know the details. That makes no sense to me."

"I'm afraid it makes some rather nasty sense to *me*," Spencer-Barr said. "If he had information from his own end, it would naturally include you, because you're the link between the Daughter and the Father. If he doesn't know about you, it's because he's getting information from the West, and the informant there doesn't know the details."

"Oh, my God," Poliakov groaned. "I don't understand this—someone in the West is giving information about us to the KGB? Can that be true?"

"It looks like it," the Englishman said. "Unless, of course, he's more interested in getting the Father to come back, and then he'll pull you and your friends in when he's ready."

He saw the Russian turn white, and said brutally, "That's probably the case. The main point is he knows the Daughter can get word to the Father. That's going to complicate our plan, because he's going to hang on to her till he's ready to put her in action. And you're quite sure she's not working for him and stringing you along at the same time?" Poliakov said, "I'm certain. I believed her. She isn't betraying us." He cleared his throat a little and looked embarrassed.

"I think she's in love with me," he said.

"Then you'd better play on it," Jeremy said. "Sleep with her if you can. In the meantime I'm going to refer this back to London. I think we'll have to speed up our operation and get the Daughter out ahead of schedule. I should get an answer in the next two days." He pulled out a textbook on collective farming. "This is the mailbox. I'll leave a message when I've heard from London. He pushed the book back onto the shelf. "I shouldn't think anyone would want to read that rubbish," he said. "Considering you have to buy your grain from the capitalist West. Meet me the next day—at the Science Exhibition. Same time as today. I'll go first."

He walked away, leaving Poliakov to waste a few minutes before he left the shop. The young man was still pale, and sweat shone on his forehead; he wiped his face and tried to still his nerves. He hated the arrogant foreigner, so safe behind his diplomatic immunity, so openly contemptuous of him for being afraid. And he hated him for degrading Irina Sasanova. "Sleep with her if you can." He called Spencer-Barr a crude name under his breath. Then with an effort he composed himself, wiped his damp face once again, and walked out into public view. There were a few people in the section; two were occupying the assistant, who didn't look up or see him. A man came up to him suddenly, and when the man barred his way Poliakov thought for a second that he was going to have a heart attack. But the man only asked where the French textbooks were situated. The tutor said he didn't know, and hurried on to the street door. It was some time before he stopped shaking and feeling out of breath.

When Spencer-Barr returned to the embassy he went to the code room in the basement of the main building on Naberezhnaia Monsa Toreza. The principal coding officer was the only person beside the head of chancery and the regular intelligence officer in the trade department who knew what Jeremy's real function was. He sat down and composed a long Telex to the Brigadier in London, which the coding officer put into code and transmitted. Then he went back upstairs to his desk. There was a reception at the Indian Embassy that evening; he was looking forward to it. He enjoyed the social side of embassy life, because it provided scraps of gossip and information which could be useful one day. He was already popular with the senior diplomats and their wives. He was always charming, attentive to the women and deferential to the men. And he usually positioned himself near the Russians. Nobody had any idea that he was fluent in the language.

The Tsarist Summer Palace at Livadia had been turned into a health center specializing in cardiology. The magnificent Great Livadia Palace was the venue for the Yalta Conference, and had been opened as a museum devoted to the conference and an art gallery for contemporary Soviet painters and sculptors.

It was Davina's suggestion that they should go and see it. Harrington agreed, but without enthusiasm.

"I'm not mad on sightseeing," he said. "And one museum devoted to the cultural achievements of the great Soviet Socialist Revolution should do me for a lifetime. But we'll go if you'd like to see it."

"The architecture is marvelous," she said. "And we don't have to spend much time inside. I really want to see the gardens."

The façade of the palace was breathtakingly beautiful, snow white in the hot sunshine, framed in magnificent pine trees and spectacular gardens. They went into the Yalta Conference museum and wandered around the exhibits; neither felt any enthusiasm for the art gallery.

"Well, at least we've seen where the West lost the war after beating the Germans," Davina said. "I wonder how many millions died or became slaves as a result of the decisions made here."

Harrington said, "There's no such thing as a fair treaty any more than there's a just war. Come on, let's go outside—you said you wanted to see the gardens."

"So I do," she retorted. "I find this place oppressive; everywhere you turn you're having their opinions forced on you. All those superlatives—the Great Patriotic War, the Glorious Revolutionary Struggle . . . And I thought all the palaces were stripped and torn down in the Revolution."

"Some of them were," Harrington agreed. "But the summer palaces escaped the mobs. They like to show Livadia because they can point out how the royals lived in opulence while the people starved. It makes good propaganda. They've got all the jewels and the Fabergé treasures in the Kremlin. One thing I'd like to see is good old Catherine the Great's little pornographic room. But they don't show that to the public."

"Come on," she said. "Let's wander round. The gardens are gorgeous, aren't they? Look at that avenue of palms, and that staircase leading onto the terrace. Did you read the book *Nicholas and Alexandra?*"

"I thought you were thinking of it," he said. "Brings them to life, walking round here and seeing where they lived. She was mad about mauve, wasn't she—symptom of a depressive personality."

"I wonder whether the Tsar would've survived if he'd married someone else," she said. "You can't help feeling sorry for her, but she really ruined him."

Harrington took her arm, and they began to walk up the marble staircase to the upper terrace.

"History is determined by trends; personalities have far less impact than we think. Nicholas was a weakling, and Alexandra was a strong-willed neurotic. They were perfect for the time and the trend, as it happened, but they weren't responsible for it, and the Revolution was part of the worldwide upheaval of the time. Nothing could have prevented it."

"You sound like Karl Marx," Davina said.

"Or Henry Ford," Peter retorted. " 'History is bunk.' That's what he said. And Marx said pretty much the same. History *is* bunk the way we're taught it, because the personalities feature far too much. The Romanovs are a good example. We learn all about the Tsar and Rasputin, when the real reason for the Revolution was an irresistible economic and sociological change."

She stopped and stared at him in mock surprise. "Good Lord, don't tell me I've found something you take seriously? You're quite a student of dialectics. No wonder you get visas for a holiday in the Crimea!"

He grinned at her. "Now, Gertrude, let me remind you of something else Henry Ford said, about his customers and the Model T: 'They can have any color they like so long as it's black.' I wonder whether it was humor or just pure cynicism. But is proves my point. People are the sands on the shore; history is the wave that moves them, not the other way about. Now, that's a fine view over the sea, isn't it? Just think of that family taking their tea out here and looking at that, never thinking for one second in their lives that they'd all be dead in a basement room before the decade was over."

"Don't," she shuddered. "What a horrible thought."

"No more horrible than the poor devils freezing to death in Siberia while the Tsar was sunning himself out here," he said. "The point is, the Tsar's gone but there are still people in the Gulag. So nothing very much has changed in some people's condition. Maybe they're just born unlucky."

"You're very morbid," she accused him. "I've never seen you like this. Ever since we got here you've been drawing parallels about how rotten human nature is, and how nothing changes no matter what we do. What's the matter with you?"

He walked on down the terrace; groups of holidaymakers were climbing up the stairs and clustering around the marble balustrade, looking out to the breathtaking view over the Black Sea. Children called to each other and tried to climb up. Harrington paused in a quiet place; behind them the tall windows which opened out to the terrace flashed fire in the hot sun. There was a rich scent of roses from the beds below them.

"What is it?" she said again. "Are you worried about something?"

He nodded, looking out to sea. "I don't like Russia," he said. "I get the feeling something's going to go wrong. I know it isn't; it's just the country. It broods over you. Don't you find that? It's so bloody enormous."

"I think it's beautiful," she answered quietly. "I'd like to see so much more of it. I think this is a paradise—the climate, the scenery, the plant life. I don't feel anything sinister about it at all."

He looked at her. "No, I suppose not," he said. "But you didn't find anything sinister about Sasanov either. Maybe Russia would suit you. Let's go back to the hotel and see if there's been any message for us."

"All right, but it's too early. We won't hear anything till next week."

"I wish they'd hurry up," Peter Harrington said. "I'll be really glad to get out of here."

They walked out of the grounds and back along the beach road to the Intourist hotel where they were staying. Neither of them spoke on the way.

Kidson was absent for the morning meeting. Grant made his apologies, and the session with Sasanov began. That morning he concentrated upon Soviet plans to turn the Saudi-Arabian King off his throne and to neutralize the rest of the family, except for a distant cousin with sufficient royal blood to put himself forward as a candidate. The attack on the Grand Mosque was to be carried out by specially trained guerrillas composed of Shi-ite Moslems, Saudis, who would front for the fanatics of the Fedayeen and the Palestinians, all Moscow-trained and armed with the latest weapons, including small-caliber rockets. The murder of Sheik Yamani was to take place just before the uprising. Under the guise of a Moslem rebellion, the royal family would be taken and killed, and the puppet Prince put on the throne. The Prince had long been suborned by Russian promises of power in return for his support. His father had been a prince of the blood royal, but his mother was a Jordanian Hashemite; her son was plagued by tribal as well as family jealousy, seeing himself passed over in the king's favor for others of no higher rank. He was, as Sasanov described him, a weak, vindictive man, paranoid in his suspicions, obsessed with a false sense of grievance. His hatred of the pro-Western Yamani had been a factor in making him a Russian sympathizer.

Arthur Warburton from the Foreign Office was completely absorbed; the Soviet expert Franks took his eyes off the Russian only in order to make quick notes. The stenotyper's hands flew over the keyboard, and the big room was silent except for the deep voice of Sasanov. He was sweating as he talked, and at invervals he pulled at the open neck of his shirt as if it were buttoned and restricting him. He had power and authority, and he had captured them all—the hardened diplomats and experts, the steely Longman from Defence. Only Grant remained aloof, clinically detached, observing and making silent conclusions. He wondered what would happen when Kidson came back.

Kidson returned in midafternoon. He had driven down from London, and he was hot after the journey. He went into Grant's room first.

"The Chief says I've got to tell Sasanov exactly what Spencer-Barr sent in the Telex. He says that Sasanov'will know how to interpret it better than we will. Set a thief to catch a thief. That's his view. I'm not looking forward to it. How did the morning session go?"

"Like all the others," Grant answered. "A mass of details, names, times, motives, etc. Political dynamite—you should have seen Warburton's face. You go and see Sasanov and break the news. I canceled the afternoon session anyway, so there's no need to hurry. I'll be here if you want me."

It seemed to be at least five minutes before Sasanov spoke. Kidson had lit his pipe and was sitting on the sofa opposite him. He had given him the Telex and said briefly, "This came last night. We hate to do this to you, Ivan, but we've no chance of acting successfully without your help. Please read it."

Sasanov was normally healthy-looking; he had tanned from walking in the bright sunshine. Now his face turned a dull gray; the eyes seemed to sink into his head, and the cheeks drew in; he looked suddenly old. He put the decoded Telex down. The change to anger was gradual as Kidson watched him while he fiddled with his pipe and matches. He had never seen naked fury alter a man's whole facial appearance. It shocked him.

"Antonyii Volkov—and my daughter. He has my daughter and he's raping her."

"It doesn't say—" Kidson began, but suddenly Sasanov bellowed at him.

"I know what Volkov likes! I know what he does to Irina!"

He leaped from his chair and beat his clenched fists against his forehead. It was a primeval gesture of rage and agony.

"I will kill him," he shouted. "I will go back and I will tear the head off his body for this—with these two hands!"

"Steady yourself," Kidson said quietly. "You can't do that. You can only get at Volkov through us."

He didn't think Sasanov had heard him. He had lapsed into Russian, and some of it was difficult to understand because he was stumbling over the words. "Fedya, Fedya . . ." He recognized the constant reference to Sasanov's wife. He knocked out his pipe and got up. He put his arm around the Russian's shoulder.

"Steady," he said again. "Calm yourself. We've got to save your daughter. You are the one person who can help us now. Sit down and I'll get us both a drink."

Sasanov pushed him aside, but then he dropped into his chair and picked up the Telex again. Kidson handed him a glass of brandy. He drank it straight down. He looked up at the Englishman.

"Kolyma is death," he said in English. "Volkov knows I will understand that. No more brandy, I have to think. I have to put myself into his mind and see what he is thinking."

He got up and moved around the room, from the door to the window; pacing, pausing suddenly, and beginning his restless walking again. Kidson had a very small brandy himself.

"We must go back to the beginning," Sasanov said. "To my relationship with Belezky. My friendship with him was known; I made no secret of it. I tried to help him when he was arrested, but always by advising him to plead guilty and hope for mercy. That was known, too. But he was Volkov's prey, and Volkov wanted him destroyed. So he sent him to the psychiatric hospital and they killed him. His wife went to the Gulag. The others were arrested and punished in the same way. Volkov had broken the inner circle of Soviet dissent. He is an ambitious man; he loves cruelty and he loves power. His eyes are fixed upon the highest job of all, the Director of State Security. He wants to become the head of the KGB and take his place in the Politburo. His ambition is well known, and the present Director is not a young man; he must retire next year. But the job has to be earned. Only a man of exceptional qualities can hope for the appointment. So Volkov needs to prove himself. First he has established that I defected and am being hidden in England. The attack on your safe house at Halldale proves that. But it failed and he knows that too. Then he finds an excuse to arrest my wife. Why? Not because she told the lie that was expected of her—she identified the body as mine, and the Soviet government gave it an official burial. Her arrest is part of Volkov's plan to bring me back to Russia. So he is sleeping with Irina. He *knows* how I will react to that. Everything he is doing is aimed at me, don't you see that?"

"What makes him think we'd let you go?" Kidson asked.

Sasanov hesitated. "I think he is planning an exchange," he said slowly. "Something to make you send me back. And he is able to do this because he has an agent here—the same agent who planned the firebomb attack, the agent who knows Irina can get word to me about what is happening to her. That agent will have told him we are planning to take Irina out of Russia. How much he has told Volkov depends upon who he is. And where he is." He looked at Kidson. "That's why I must find him. Otherwise Volkov will win."

"Do you remember Davina Graham's sister?" Kidson asked him.

"Yes," Sasanov frowned. "I remember her. Why?"

"Because she may have just come up with something," Kidson said. "Her father went to see the Chief; he was worried about Davina. The sister had been home and told him someone was asking her questions about Davina, and about you. Or rather the Polish diplomat you were supposed to be. The Chief thinks it would be a good idea if you saw Mrs. Ransom and questioned her yourself, since you've taken on to find the Mole. Have you made any progress with those files?"

"I've got some questions," Sasanov said. "New questions; the files don't have an answer. When can I see the sister? Why not tonight? There isn't any time to be slow and British," he said roughly. "My daughter and three of your agents are in Russia—sitting in Volkov's hand, like mice in a trap."

"I'll call London," Kidson said. "I can drive up with you. She can't come here."

The flat in Portman Place was on the first floor. Charley opened the door to Kidson, and for a moment she didn't recognize Sasanov because he was wearing a hat. When he stepped into the hall and took it off, she gasped out loud.

"Oh, good Lord—it's you!"

"Good evening," he said.

Kidson took her gently by the arm. "I'm sorry I didn't warn you your sister's friend was coming with me," he said gently. "I'll explain everything."

Charley was going out to dinner; the call from Brigadier White's office had been friendly but firm. Her father had been to see him, and he too was rather worried about Davina. He hadn't said in what respect. He was sure she'd be able to answer a few questions if he sent someone around after six-thirty. So nice to talk to her—it was ages since they'd met; she must lunch with him one day if she was free. . . . The call ended, and she had hardly said anything but yes, of course. She had got dressed early, and decided that really there was nothing to be nervous about, and it might be amusing to meet someone from the Ministry of Defence. Floating black chiffon and her ex-husband's present of a pearl-and-diamond choker gave her an Edwardian look. Kidson gazed at her with admiration.

She offered the two men drinks, moving gracefully between them and the serving cart, and settled herself on the sofa with a provocative smile at Kidson. She was determined not to show that she was nervous. The Pole looked grim and rather ill-humored, as if her attempts to be polite were wasting time. And, oh, he did look so like the photograph of that dead Russian.

"Mrs. Ransom," Kidson started off. "Would you tell us about this friend of yours who kept asking questions about your sister? Mr. Spencer-Barr, wasn't it?"

She nodded. "Yes, I thought it was very odd. I told my father about it." She turned toward Sasanov as he spoke to her.

"Tell me when you first met this man," he said. "Try to remember everything he said and you said. Can you do that?"

"I think so," she said. "I've got a very good memory. It was the same evening I left Marchwood, that weekend when you were there."

Sasanov listened. After a time he asked her questions.

"Why did you think he was interested in your sister and me?"

"I didn't know," she said. "It seemed so funny at first. I kept feeling he didn't really like me or want to take me out. That's what made me notice it, I suppose. Every time he asked some question, either about Davy or else you and Davy."

"What sort of question? What did he ask about her?"

"Had I seen her lately; was she still in the Defence Ministry. . . . He mentioned that she'd been given a job in preference to him. He seemed very annoyed about it. He tied this in with you and tried to find out if you and she were having an affair. I said I didn't know. I thought he might try to get Davy into trouble."

"And what did he ask about me?" Sasanov said.

"Had I met you again. I said no. I told him I hardly ever saw my sister.

I even told him why—because of my first marriage; she probably told you about that."

Kidson saw the dislike on his face when he nodded and said, "Yes, she told me. What did you think he was trying to find out from you?"

Charley hesitated.

Sasanov prompted her. "About where Vina was, if she wasn't in the Defence? Did he want to know if were living in the same place? Did he ever try to find out an address—anything like that?"

"No." She shook her head. The light gleamed in the piled-up silky red hair. "He just asked general things; I felt he was trying to establish something he could use against her. He said she wasn't supposed to have a relationship with a man in this job she'd been given." She turned to Kidson. "That's what really worried me. I felt he might hurt Davy's career in some way."

Sasanov said casually, "You told him I was a Pole, didn't you, the first time you met?"

He saw a little color creep into her face.

"Yes," she said. "Yes, actually I think that was what made him interested. I couldn't give him any details because I didn't know any, except that your name was Pavel."

"And he seemed happy to accept that?" Sasanov asked. "You were happy to accept it, weren't you?"

"Of course." She looked startled. "Why shouldn't I be?"

"No reason at all," he said.

He signaled to Kidson, who stood up.

"Thank you, Mrs. Ransom; it's very kind of you to see us, and you've been very helpful. I hope we haven't kept you late for your dinner party."

She gave him her hand, and her angelic smile. "Not at all. I hope I've been useful."

Then she took him completely by surprise. She glanced at Sasanov. "Pavel, would you mind if I spoke to Mr. Kidson alone for a moment?"

"No, I'll wait in the hall." Sasanov went out.

Charley let go of Kidson's hand, and the smile disappeared. "He *is* Russian, isn't he? The one who was supposed to be found drowned—I thought I recognized him from the newspapers. What is Davina mixed up in?"

Kidson didn't know it, but there was a strong look of her mother in the set of Charley's lovely jaw.

"Mrs. Ransom," he said quietly, "I can't answer either of those questions. I'm sorry."

"Davina and I haven't ever been close friends," she said. "But she *is* my sister. And I hurt her very badly once. She's not just a secretary, is she? She's doing something dangerous, I can feel it. Where is she, Mr. Kidson? I have a right to know."

Kidson made a quick decision. Charlotte Ransom was not a fool or she wouldn't have seen through Spencer-Barr. Or recognized Sasanov. The one thing she must do was keep silent now.

"She's in Russia," he said. He saw her turn ghost-white. "One word of this, one whisper about Pavel or your sister, and she could be in very great danger indeed. I know we can rely on you, Mrs. Ransom. Not a word. Not even to your family."

"I promise you," she said. Her eyes filled suddenly with tears.

Kidson had a wish to take her in his arms and comfort her that really shocked him.

"I couldn't bear it if anything happened to her," she said. The tears were blinked back and the stubborn look returned. "Don't worry; nobody will hear anything from me. Will you let me know when she comes back?"

"I will," Kidson said, and he meant it. "Goodbye. And thank you."

He joined Sasanov in the hall, and they let themselves out. They went down in the lift, Sasanov pulling the hat down to shade his face. They crossed the thickly carpeted foyer, passed the doorman in his cubicle, and slipped into the back of the waiting car.

As it sped up through the park toward Marylebone, Kidson said to Sasanov, "It doesn't look good for Spencer-Barr, does it?"

"What does your Chief think?" the Russian asked him.

"He was shaken rigid," came the answer.

"And what do you think?" Sasanov continued.

"I'd rather not commit myself till I have heard Spencer-Barr's explanation," he said after a pause. "There must be an explanation."

"I'm sure there is," Sasanov said. "But he isn't here to give it. He's in Russia, heading a rescue mission for my daughter. Can't this driver go any faster?"

"Not till we're on the motorway. We'll be back in just over an hour."

"I want to get back to those files," Sasanov muttered. "There's something I missed. The answer to one of my questions. No, wait a minute. Where is that place, Jules's Bar?"

Kidson stared at him.

"In Jermyn Street. Why?"

"Tell the man to go there," Sasanov said. "Now!"

11

Spencer-Barr got an answer from London by late afternoon. He was called into the decoding room, where the principal coding officer gave him the unscrambled message: "Your communication received and being given urgent attention. Date for Daughter's rendezvous advanced to 25th. Departure the same day. Contact Daniel and advise. Final arrangements to follow."

Jeremy gave the message back; it was marked with the prefix MSD—meaning most secret, destroy. It went into the shredder.

"Thanks," he said to the clerk, and walked out. He went upstairs to his own small office and sent the secretary out for a cup of tea. He sat rather still when he was alone; then he picked up a pencil and began to tap it. The tapping went on until the girl came back with the tea. She had provided some cookies as well. She thought Spencer-Barr terribly attractive, and she paid him little attentions to find favor. He hadn't asked her out since his first sightseeing tour of Moscow, and she was disappointed.

He smiled at her. "Biscuits? That's very kind of you, Jane. What's my social engagement this evening?"

She looked up his desk diary. "We've got a reception here," she said. "And there's a supper and a recital at the French Embassy. You're down for both."

"Very hard on the liver, this sort of life," he said. She giggled appreciatively.

He had received a long letter from his girl friend, Mary, in London.

215

He hadn't answered yet, and felt guilty. The letter was like Mary: sensible, affectionate and undemanding. She mentioned that she was inquiring about an Intourist trip to Moscow in the autumn, as she would like to see him. She thought his appointment would last the usual two years. He looked at the secretary and thought of Mary. He did miss her. If he managed this affair successfully, he might still get to New York—or even Washington. Washington would suit him better. . . .

The twenty-fifth was only eight days away. London had certainly accelerated after his message. But there were no details yet. That was a bloody bore, he thought. They must have everything worked out to the last minute on an operation like this. Harrington and Davina Graham would be waiting at Livadia. The Daughter had to get a pass to leave Moscow. It was cutting it a bit fine. It was just as well he'd got the message before the reception tonight. He left his office early and went to his apartment in the embassy compound to shower and change.

Poliakov had found the bus ticket in the book; the following day he met Spencer-Barr at the place agreed for an emergency rendezvous, the Science Exhibition on Stalingrad Avenue. It was a big, sprawling modern building with a series of small courts separating the different sections. Poliakov hurried to the atomic-energy complex at lunchtime. He found Spencer-Barr gazing at a mockup of molecules and the related atoms. It looked like a very complicated toy, all colored balls and oblongs and delicate structures. Spencer-Barr didn't turn his head.

"The Daughter's to go to Livadia by the twenty-fifth and be ready to leave on the same day. No other details are available at the moment, but she must get a pass to Livadia. Contact her and impress on her she's got to be *in situ* by that date. Meet me in the bookshop in two days and I'll have further news for you."

Poliakov stared at their reflections in the glass case protecting the exhibit.

"That's seven days," he muttered. "What happens if she can't get there in time?"

"She won't get away," Spencer-Barr said flatly. "She's got to get the pass. What progress have you made with her?"

The tutor reddened. "I haven't seen her," he said shortly. "I'll tell her tomorrow."

He turned and walked away. Jeremy watched him in the glass until he left the room. Then he spent the next hour wandering around the exhibition. Science had been one of his best subjects.

The postcard was in their pigeonhole in the entrance hall of the hotel.

Davina saw it and pulled Harrington's arm. He said quickly, "I've seen it. We'll just get the key and take it casually."

The key to their room and the postcard were handed to them by the woman receptionist. She was less surly than the rest of the hotel staff; she spoke good German and offered to arrange a coach tour, or an organized boat trip around the coast. Peter said they preferred to spend the time on the beach or wandering around the permitted areas of the resort.

They had come in from swimming. Russians did not encourage scant bikinis, and walking around in minishorts or bra tops was forbidden. There was an old-fashioned air about the beaches, with bathing huts and seats along the promenades; it reminded Davina of childhood visits to Brighton and Hove. Harrington looked brown and fit; she was inclined to burn unless she was careful; he had teased her because she was pink and freckled, and her hair had turned redder in the sunshine.

He glanced at the postcard and then handed it to her.

"From your Aunt Frieda," he said.

Davina saw the receptionist watching them while she pretended to sort some keys; she had certainly read the postcard. Davina turned it over and read the meaningless message written in *Schrift*: "Hope you are having wonderful holiday. Trudi getting married on the 25th. We're all busy preparing for the wedding. Do send a postcard. Love from everyone, Frieda."

They went up the stairs to their room on the second floor. It had a pleasant view over the seafront. Harrington held out his hand for the card. She gave it to him. He sat on the bed and took a pocket diary out of his jacket. He opened it at the calendar page and began to write on the postcard above the lines of writing. It took him only five minutes, and then he gave it back to her. The decoded message read: "The Daughter will reach you on the 25th. You depart the same day. Further instructions will follow."

She nodded and he took it back; he lit the corner with his lighter and held it till it flamed and curled up. It burned out in the ashtray, and Harrington washed the mess down the basin, scrubbing the burn marks off the ashtray. Then he washed the basin itself and ran the taps for some time to clear the pipe.

"The twenty-fifth," he said. "That's a Saturday. Good day for a wedding. It's about time Trudi settled down."

"I'm sorry we won't be there," Davina said. "But it can't be helped. Do you feel like eating yet?"

"I think a beer first," he said. "Hurry up if you want to change, and we'll go out."

They spent as much time as possible out of the hotel and away from
their room. It was unlikely to be wired, but Harrington said every
Intourist hotel was monitored and all the staff were police spies who
reported on everything said and done by foreigners. Even the Iron Curtain tourists were subjected to the same rigorous scrutiny as visitors from
the West, and they were not encouraged to make friends with the Russian
holidaymakers. Russians didn't welcome attempts to talk to them, since
they were frightened of being seen with foreigners. Fear was as effective a
screen as barbed wire. The Intourist visitor saw what he was meant to
see, and had no contact with ordinary Russians. Otherwise he could enjoy
himself. They sat down in an open-air café and bar, Harrington choosing
a table which was on the perimeter and not too close to others. There they
could talk.

"She'll be here on the twenty-fifth. That's seven days from now. How
am I going to sleep in that bloody awful lumpy bed with you for another
seven nights and not give way to my ravening desire?" He grinned at
Davina. "Freckle-nose," he said, "why don't you dye your hair red? It'd
look rather smashing."

"Why don't you shut up and be serious for a minute," she retorted.
"Seven days. And how are we going to get her out?"

"We won't know till the next bulletin," Harrington said. "I'm damned
if I can see how we're going to get her away the same day. Still, that's not
our worry. Our job is to be here and take charge of her when she comes.
And get the hell out as fast as we can. . . . Feeling nervous?"

"Yes," Davina admitted. "I feel permanently nervous."

"You don't show it," Harrington remarked. "You're not a girl who
frightens easily. I'd say you'd never been really scared of anything in your
life."

"Well, you'd be wrong," she retorted. "I'm actually terrified of small
spaces. You didn't know I was neurotic, did you, Peter?"

He shook his head. "Claustrophobia's pretty common, but you don't
mind narrow lifts or planes, so it can't be that bad. What do you mean by
small spaces?"

"Walk-in cupboards, ladies' loos, anywhere small and low-ceilinged
where you could get locked in. I shut myself in my mother's wardrobe
when I was about seven; I was mad about high-heeled shoes and I used to
go and try hers on and walk about in them—looking just like Minnie
Mouse. She had a rack of evening shoes in the bottom of her wardrobe
and I was in there one day when I heard her coming. I wasn't supposed to
go into her room, so I hid. She saw the door ajar and shut it. Then she
went out and I was locked in the dark and couldn't get out. I don't know

how long it was before someone heard me screaming. I went quite crazy with fear. I don't even remember being let out or anything. They had to get the doctor and I was told afterwards he had to put me right out, I was in such a state. It took ages before I'd even go into her room afterwards or open my own clothes cupboard."

"How very nasty," he said. "Poor you. You look a bit green even talking about it." He leaned over and patted her hand. "Are you really nervous about this business or just saying it to make me feel manly and protective?" He flashed the engaging grin at her.

"It's a funny kind of nervousness," Davina said. "A sort of scared expectation—you feel your stomach's full of butterflies. Is it always like this, or is it just the first time?"

"It's always like the first time," he said, "because each job is an original. I'm always scared all the time, every time. In a way I wouldn't enjoy it if I wasn't."

"But you're not enjoying this," she said.

"Maybe I'm getting a bit past this level of risk," Harrington said. "I enjoyed New York, because it was a game where you made up your own rules. I had my two contacts and I was looking forward to running them. But this is bullet-in-the-back-of-the-neck stuff. I'm not too keen on that. Sorry." He checked himself. "That was a stupid thing to say to you. Forget it."

"It doesn't matter," Davina said quietly. "I know what to expect if anything goes wrong. It just feels odd, to be cut off like this. We know now the date the girl is coming. And that we're supposed to leave the same day. But that's all. We don't know how or where—it's a sort of vacuum. I find that very nerveracking. I can cope with things so long as I know what they are."

"That's because you're not a pro," he said. "Pros don't want to know the details. Then if they get caught, they can't tell them. I must say, you've been very good. The only trouble is, you're too pretty for an East German lady. Even with your pink nose." He smiled at her and patted her knee under the table.

"That's better," he said. "You haven't smiled much in the last few days. I wonder how Ivan the Terrible is getting on with the boys back home. Spilling his heart out, do you think?"

"I hope so," Davina answered. "And I believe he will. He keeps his promises."

"You gave him a pretty good incentive," Harrington said gently. "You put yourself up as the collateral."

"I keep thinking about his poor wife," she said slowly. "It's hard to believe people could be so vile—to punish her for something he did. A perfectly innocent woman."

"It's to punish him," Harrington said. "Tell me something: what happens when you get home?"

"Nothing happens," Davina answered him. "There's no reason for me to see him again. And I promised I wouldn't try."

"Supposing he wants to see you," he persisted.

"I don't think he will." She gazed past Harrington toward the blue sealine. "He knows there isn't any future for us. I came into his life and he came into mine; it was always temporary. The one thing that matters is that it ends well. I'll never regret a moment of it; I want him to feel the same. And then I can go back to work and get on with real life." She gave him a little quick smile. "You don't believe me, do you?"

He lit a cigarette and handed it to her. "Not a word," he said. "But we won't argue about it. Ten more days and then the fun begins. Whatever the fun is. Come on, the food looks dismal here. Let's see if we can get into that fish restaurant the old bag recommended. Intourist two-star, Comrade."

He paid for his drink and they left the café; he took Davina's arm as they walked down the long promenade together. In their old-fashioned summer clothes, he in baggy gray trousers and open-necked shirt, she in a cotton dress and sandals, they looked as if they too belonged to a dead age of twenty years ago, moving through a world inhabited by ghosts.

Volkov patted the seat beside him; he spent one or two evenings a week with Irina in her apartment. Every weekend was spent at his dacha. He had taken her to the Bolshoi and to a restaurant afterward. He didn't seem to mind that their relationship was becoming public knowledge. She felt as if he were enjoying the gossip, flaunting his mastery over the daughter of Ivan Sasanov.

"Sit here, beside me," he said. She did as he suggested, and he took her hand and stroked it.

"Why do you want to go to Livadia? It's such a long way. Are you trying to get away from me, *dushinka*?" He always called her "darling" when he was going to frighten her.

"No, of course I'm not," Irina said. "It's just that I'm tired; the university closes for the summer next Tuesday. I'd like a vacation in the sun." She said almost boldly, "I thought you could get me a pass."

"I could," he agreed. "I can do most things for you. But I want to know why you need this vacation so quickly. Are you studying so hard? Don't tell me I'm exhausting you; a lot of loving is good for girls."

"I'm working hard," she admitted. "I think it's worrying about my mother that's made me feel so run down. It's been a very hard year for me, Antonyii."

"You do look a bit pale," he said. "Maybe the sun would do you good. Will you feel better if I tell you your mother hasn't reached Kolyma yet?"

She swung around to him and seized his hand.

"Oh, Antonyii! You mean you've—they've changed their minds? Where is she?"

"In a stopover camp, about four hundred versts from here. I managed to delay her final journey—by telling the head of our Service you had agreed to help us, to help us get your father back. You understood that, didn't you? You must persuade him to come back to Russia."

She thanked God he hadn't a hand fondling her breast, as he often did when they were sitting like this. Otherwise he would have felt the leap of terror her heart gave. She hung her head, hiding the fear in her eyes. Her voice was low and tremulous.

"I've been thinking about it, every night and day. But how? How do I do it?"

"By going to join him," he said gently. "By going to the Crimea as your friends have arranged."

He didn't look at her; he lit a cigarette and took his time, drawing on it, puffing out smoke, snapping the lighter shut. He didn't need to watch her; he heard the intake of breath that turned into a gasp, felt her spring up and leave the sofa. When he looked up she was standing close to the window.

"What's the matter?" he asked her lightly. "Didn't you think I knew all about it? About your tutor at the university? I've known every move you've made, every thought in your mind. I know the lies you've told me. But I haven't done anything about them. I have tried to help your mother, and I saved you from being arrested a long time ago. Don't think it was because you slept with me. I can have any girl I want."

Irina turned and slipped the catch on the window. It swung open.

"If you jump out," Volkov said, "I'll have Poliakov in the Lubyanka in an hour. Instead of holding your mother in a labor camp, I'll have her brought back, too, and questioned—questioned very hard, like your tutor friend, and *his* friends."

He didn't move from the sofa; he swung one leg over the other and moved his foot to and fro. Irina Sasanova closed the window. She latched it. Then she turned around to face him.

"What do you want me to do?" she said.

"I want you to take your vacation in the Crimea," Volkov answered. "I'll get you the pass to travel. I want you to go on meeting your contact Poliakov. I want you to do exactly what British Intelligence tells you. And at the same time, you will do what I tell you."

After a pause he added, "Come here."

She came and he drew her down beside him. He slid his hand inside her blouse.

"Ah," he said. "How your heart is beating! Is it just fear? Or is it hatred too? It doesn't matter. I'm the only friend you've got. You'll come to love me in the end. . . ."

Irina found another message in her essay when she collected it with the other students. It was taped to the center page. "Meet me at the near end of the Ouspenskaya Bridge tonight at nine." She flushed the scraps of paper down the toilet and telephoned Volkov from the public booths in the university central hall. That evening she took a bus to the Ouspenskaya Bridge, and at nine o'clock on the warm summer's evening she met Alexei Poliakov. He took her arm, and they began to walk slowly across the bridge that spanned the wide yellow waters of the Moscow River. Couples were walking along the public beach; Russian children are allowed to stay up as late as their parents, and groups were paddling in the water, running races ahead, their laughter and calls light as birdsong in the evening.

Irina had taken off her sandals; she trod the soft sand in her bare feet, the shoes swinging from her left hand. They looked like young lovers strolling on the beach. He found a secluded place, a spot half hidden by a clump of bushes growing out of a dune of sandy soil. They sat down together, and he put his arm around her. Irina closed her eyes and leaned against him. His body was warm, his hold on her gentle. I love him, her thoughts whispered; I love him, I can't do it. She straightened herself, and gently disengaged from him. At the sight of his face, grave and concerned, the tears overflowed, and the next second she was in his arms, and they were kissing frantically, clumsily in their need for each other. . . . And then she told him. They lay huddled together behind the shelter of the bushes while the sky grew black above them, the stars came out, and there was no one left on the beach.

"He knows everything," she whispered. "About you, and the Crimea, about my father. And he wants me to do everything, to pretend to you and the people helping me, while he watches and manipulates. I'm to get my father to come back to Russia. That's all he tells me. Go to the Crimea, do what the British Intelligence tells you, and I'll tell you what to do next. And he's holding my mother as a hostage. If I don't do what he wants, she'll go to Kolyma. And you'll be arrested. He said, 'your tutor friend, and his friends . . .' " She shivered, and Poliakov held her closer.

"What am I to do? If my father comes back because of me, Volkov will arrest him—and he won't leave you alone when I've done what he wants. And there's my mother—oh, God, sometimes I feel like killing myself!"

"Don't," the young man begged her, "don't ever say that."

"I promise you," Irina went on, "I stood by the window in our flat and I was going to jump. He knew it; he just said if I did that he'd have you in the Lubyanka and bring my mother back for questioning. He meant he'd torture you both."

Poliakov stroked her hair and soothed her. His pale face and dark hair made him look ghostly in the fitful moonlight. He murmured loving words to her and held her against his heart. He was a gentle man by nature, in some ways timid, a creature of the spirit and the mind who abhorred violence. He raised Irina's face to his and kissed her.

"Get the permit from him," he said. "Go to Livadia, and these people will get you away from Russia. That's all you must do. Don't think about anything else."

"I'm not going to leave you behind," she whispered. "I'll ask him for two passes. We can go together. If he says no, then I won't go, either," she said fiercely. "He wants my father back! If I can be brave enough, just once, I'll get you away, too. No, don't argue with me." She put her hand to his mouth. She was stronger than he was, braver by nature. He loved her all the more for her courage. His desire rose at the touch of her fingertips on his mouth. He didn't want to argue with her; he wanted to love her, and carry the memory. He drew her down to him, and under the dark sky they made love, with the moon as a witness when it slipped out of the clouds.

Two passes. . . . Antonyii Volkov knew how to watch other people without seeming to do so. He found Irina Sasanova more and more interesting as a subject. His attitude to her had been that of master to puppet; he had no liking for women outside sex, and if he met one who was clever and ambitious he resented it. He blocked the promotion of women in his own service; their role was to be manipulated by men. Irina seemed ordinary enough: intelligent, but easy to reduce to frightened obedience when the skin of modern feminism was stripped away. But she surprised him.

She surprised him by her resilience; just when he thought her completely cowed, she found reserves of courage, and came back at him. . . . Two passes.

He didn't say anything for some minutes. They were sitting at his favorite table in the Bear Restaurant, and she was looking prettier than he had ever seen her.

"Why two passes? Who is going with you?" He asked the question at last.

"My tutor," Irina said. *My lover—my lover who showed me what love meant.* She drank some of her wine, and wished she could have tossed it into Volkov's face. She wouldn't have thought it possible to hate Volkov more. But it seemed that hate grew in proportion to her love.

"Have you been told to ask for him?" Volkov said gently. He smiled while he waited for the answer. It was tempting to say yes; she nearly did so. But since he knew so much, he might know this was a lie. The truth was safer.

"No," she said. "I'm asking for myself. I want him to come with me."

"Why?" he said again.

"Because I don't want him to be arrested," Irina said. She drank more wine, and he knew she was nervous. But still brave. Courage was in her eyes. She loves this poor little intellectual, he thought, and was angry for a moment.

"Why should I arrest him? He can't do any harm. I know all about him anyway." He gave a little shrug of contempt.

"You won't leave him free to work against you," Irina said. "And as he's not very important, I would like you to let him leave Russia. Please, Antonyii. I am doing exactly what you want. Let Alexei Poliakov go to Livadia with me."

"And supposing I say no," he countered.

She put the glass down and sat back. She hid her hands under the table and gripped them together to steady them. "I love him," she said. "I love him as much as my mother. I won't go without him."

Volkov signaled the waiter. "Bring us coffee," he said. "And some Polish brandy."

"I won't go," she said again. "I mean it."

"Very well." Volkov spooned sugar into his coffee. "Very well, if this little fellow means so much to you—he can go, too. Your father must come home, Irina. That is what matters. He mustn't be used against Russia by her enemies. You can convince him that he won't be punished, that we understand about his illness and what made him behave like a criminal lunatic. He will be treated and rehabilitated into Soviet society. And your mother will be with him. You will be a family again. I expect you will leave your friend Poliakov in the West when you return."

"I may stay with him," she said. "But you won't care, so long as my father comes back."

"I shall be sorry to lose you, Irina," Volkov said gently. "I hate to see Soviet citizens lose their rights and live in exile. But you can choose when the time comes. And I have something for you; you can show it to your father."

She recognized her mother's writing. She took the envelope, and he said, "No, don't open it here. Read it later." She put the letter away in her bag.

"Two passes to travel to the Crimea and stay at Livadia," Volkov said. "For two weeks vacation, arriving on the twenty-fifth. I'll send them around to you tomorrow, my dear. And now, if you'll finish your coffee, we'll go back to Moscow."

They drove back in silence. He didn't touch her or even hold her hand. She heard him hum a little popular tune as he glanced out the window.

The car stopped at her apartment; he leaned forward and opened the door for her.

"I won't come in tonight," he said. "I hope you're not too disappointed. You'll need money for your trip. I'll send that with the passes. Don't forget to read your letter. Good night, *dushinka*."

She stood for a moment on the pavement as the car drove off. Then she used the entrance key; the old *dezhurnaya* was replaced by a man who guarded the building during the night. He noted everyone who came in and out and reported anything unusual to the police. Irina went past him, up in the lift and unlocked her apartment door. It was past one in the morning. She went into the kitchen and poured a glass of milk. And she sat at the big table, where her family used to gather in the evenings with their friends drinking tea and laughing, talking, eating—arguing sometimes. With the letter in her hand, she felt the memories almost materialize out of the air, until the kitchen was thronged with ghosts. Her father, the hero figure of her childhood, the good companion of her adult life. And her mother, so warm and steadfast, an old-fashioned woman to whom the family was a treasure and not a burden. Irina had grown up with love; and there had been a different kind of love in that kitchen, the love between good friends. Jacob Belezky, dark eyes burning behind his glasses; his brave wife, who supported all the dangerous things he said. They were all there crowding around her for a moment, and then as suddenly they disappeared, and she was alone in the kitchen, seated at the empty table, with her mother's letter waiting to be opened.

The ink had run, as if tears had fallen on the writing. The letter was a sheet of paper with a torn edge; there was no heading, only the date—a week earlier. It rambled, and the handwriting was irregular and untidy, as if the person writing were very old. It spoke of her sufferings without describing them. That agony would be inflicted by the reader's imagination. It begged for help, for relief. It reminded the daughter and the husband of their responsibility, of their ability to save her. Fear and anguish ran into each other, making some sentences difficult to read. It was a dreadful, abject piece of moral blackmail, and Irina Sasanov knew that her mother would never have written it freely.

She didn't cry; she folded it and put it back in its envelope, and finished her milk. That would bring her father back; Volkov had known exactly how to blend the ingredients in that letter. But he didn't know the meaning of that signature—"your wife and little mother." ". . . If I say 'little mother' don't believe it. It will be a lie," Fedya had warned her in that last interview, seeing what might lie ahead.

"I would like to kill him," Irina murmured to herself. "I would like to ask him to come here, and stab him while he's sleeping. I'd like to give him poison, so that he could die in agony." She washed up the glass, switched out the light and went into her parent's room. She paused, looking at the bed. Volkov had defiled it. He had abused her and humiliated her where her mother and father had made love. She closed the door and went to her own room.

In five days she would be in the Crimea, and Alexei Poliakov would be with her—five days. At last she fell asleep.

It was six in the morning, and the sun was up; the birds' bright chorus had quieted as the dawn became full day. It was possible to pull the curtains back and switch off the lights. The conference room was fogged with cigarette smoke, the men sitting in a group at one end of the table looked haggard and stale. Sasanov had a heap of papers in front of him and an ashtray full of half-smoked cigarettes. There was a tray with empty coffee cups and a tepid pot, pushed to one side. Grant and the Brigadier and Kidson flanked the Russian.

"There is your Mole," Sasanov said.

"And we have sent him into Russia." James White spoke slowly, coldly. He turned to look at Grant.

"This is your failure," he said. "He was never properly investigated."

Grant's sallow skin flushed. "His background was impeccable," he said. "I only did what seemed reasonable. We had *no* indication that he was suspect."

"You had every reason," Sasanov barked at him. "The signs were all there—you didn't look! What are you going to do, Brigadier, to save Vina and my daughter?"

There was a moment's silence; then Kidson interposed quietly, "If your theory is right, your daughter will be arrested as she tries to leave and the bona-fide British agent will be held as hostage against your extradition. Volkov will then have a full hand of cards to play against us and a strong lever to force you to go back voluntarily. According to your reading of the situation he will be certainly promoted to the top job when Keremov retires in December."

"And our traitor will come back and burrow underground again," the Brigadier said. "Except that we've flushed him out. I would like to get him back and invite him down here for a country weekend." He looked hard at Sasanov. "How will Volkov arrange the finale?"

"How? I'm not sure, but he will gather them all into his net in the Crimea. He is a man who likes to play with people."

"How many are likely to be taken into his confidence?" Grant asked. "Does he work in close cooperation with his superiors? How much does he confide in his subordinates?" He was watching Sasanov closely.

The Russian frowned.

"He works as secretly as he dares," he said. "In that way he can take risks, and cover them if he fails. He hates sharing information, because he has to share the credit." He paused. "His subordinates will know nothing; they act on his orders. His plan will be kept secret from everyone."

"Including the Mole?" Kidson asked.

Sasanov nodded. "The Mole will get instructions. That's all." Again there was silence.

He raised his head and looked at the Brigadier. "Why did you let Vina go to Russia?"

James White gazed blandly back at him. "She asked to go. She insisted on it. She said it was the only way you would believe we were genuinely trying to get your daughter out."

"That isn't why you sent her," Sasanov said. "You had another reason."

"Not exactly a reason," James White admitted. "Just a very vague idea at the back of my mind. Which has proved right, as it turns out. You see, she was the one way we could send Harrington out without arousing suspicion. She was trying to help him, to get him back into active service again. It seemed to fit in rather well."

They were all staring at the Brigadier. He yawned. "Could we get some hot coffee, Kidson? Keep us all awake a bit longer?"

Kidson got up from the table, took the tray and went out.

"It's very interesting," the Brigadier went on, "because the pattern was rather obvious. You didn't see it. Colonel Sasanov recognized it; I just had a funny feeling. Harrington has been a member of the Firm since the fifties. A good chap, with a very good record. But never spectacular; just a reliable man who could turn his hand to a spot of real trouble if he had to. And then he begins to drink and slack in New York, and the two contacts he goes on about are one East German plant, obvious to anybody, and a Rumanian with very little to offer us. So he gets himself talked about and then recalled. At just the right moment. When you are in England, and the Russians can't find out anything about you. And he meets Davina, by accident on purpose; he's heard the gossip that she's your 'minder,' but that doesn't help him unless he can find out where you're being hidden. She can't be followed, because she's under our surveillance whenever she goes out. And she won't tell him anything. All those transcripts of interviews with her prove that. He can't bug the car, because the car is regularly serviced and checked. So he sets up the very simple and very clever meeting that ends in Jules's Bar, with the telephone call he knew she'd have to make. To Halldale Manor."

"And sticks a monitor on the dial," Grant murmured. "That was ingenious. It gave him the telephone number she'd called. So a Center assassin is activated to identify Davina and make certain. The firebomb follows."

"It had to be the telephone," Sasanov said. "I read and read the evidence, and I knew there was something. I know the type of monitor. It leaves a little adhesive behind it, because it won't magnetize on plastic. The telephone in that bar was plastic. Otherwise we wouldn't have found any evidence at all."

He rested his head in his hands for a moment.

"Volkov thought they had killed me in the fire," he said. "But he wasn't sure. He had my wife arrested and my daughter watched. They would find the connection between your embassy and the lecturer, and when it went on he guessed I was alive. So he seduced my daughter, hoping the news would get back to me. Then Harrington heard from

Davina again, and Volkov knew for certain I had escaped. Everything you briefed Harrington on was sent back to Volkov. The plan for Irina's escape, the appointment of that other man Spencer-Barr. Volkov knew it all. And now Harrington is in Livadia with Vina, waiting to betray them as soon as Irina arrives. How much of the plan for their escape does he know?"

"Nothing," Grant said. "They are being told by stages; it's safer. That's our only consolation at this point. You realize that apart from your daughter and Miss Graham, Volkov will be able to force confessions from the lecturer and his associates? Our whole network among the activists for human rights will be exposed and eliminated—not to mention Frieda and her people in East Berlin. This will be a major intelligence disaster for the West, and a tremendous boost for Volkov's chances of getting the top KGB post. We've got to take immediate action."

"Volkov will hold Vina and my daughter," Sasanov said. "As well as my wife. He will offer to release them and return Vina in exchange for me. He knows me well; he knows I love my wife and how I will feel about what he's done to my daughter. And he will soon discover how much Vina means to me. You must agree, Brigadier. You must send me back. I'll give you everything I can, but if you fail, and they are taken, you must promise that Vina will be exchanged for me."

White considered him for a moment, and then at last he nodded. "Very well; I promise. I may have trouble with our Home Secretary, but if he believes it's voluntary . . . The moment your wife and daughter are released and Miss Graham is handed over, you will be escorted to the other side. On one condition."

"What is that?" Sasanov asked.

"That you carry a cyanide capsule and kill yourself the minute they lay hands on you. Have some more coffee?"

"Thank you," Sasanov said. "That won't be difficult. Without my family and Vina, I don't want to be alive."

"I think our questions about Sasanov have just been answered," the Brigadier said. He and Grant were sitting in Kidson's room; they had bathed and eaten breakfast. Grant looked greener than usual after the night without sleep, but James White was pink-cheeked and refreshed. His energy amazed Kidson, who had never seen him tire.

"The tension, the debriefing that he turned into a tour-de-force," the Brigadier went on. "All signs of inner conflict, just as you said, John. But not because he was playing a part. He was telling us everything he could

think of because he was in love with Miss Graham. And she was some
kind of hostage to fate, with his daughter. The more he betrayed his
country and his old loyalties, the safer he felt they would be. Curious,
isn't it?"

"Curious how a sophisticated man of his intelligence could react like a
primitive," Grant remarked. "It just proves how deeply superstitious the
Russian character is."

"Not just the Russians," Kidson said. "Propitiating the gods is common to all human beings. The pagan comes out in different ways in
different people."

"I can't quite see it in myself," Grant retorted. "Or in you."

James White said, "And who'd have thought Davina Graham could
have such an effect on a man? I never imagined Sasanov cared a damn
about her. Do you understand it, John?"

"No, I never thought she was attractive," Kidson said. "But then I
never really knew her, did I? None of us did. But the fact is, *there* is a
man who doesn't want to live without her. Obviously, Chief, we'll have to
change our plans regarding the escape route. Thanks to Harrington every
move we've made is known. The KGB are just waiting to scoop up Irina
Sasanova and Davina Graham. How Harrington plays it remains to be
seen. The point at issue is this: if anything happens to those two women,
Sasanov is going to give himself up and commit suicide. Which leaves us
with the most important political situation since the Berlin Wall went up:
Soviet plans for oil dominance in the Gulf and ultimately a nuclear strike
against the United States. And nobody to monitor and interpret for us
from the inside. We've got to have Sasanov going every step of the way
with us. And that means we've got to make sure of at least one of those
women getting back here. What do you suggest, Grant? This is really
your department."

"I suggest," Grant said slowly, "that we halve the risk. We don't proceed with the original plan for escape via the Crimea. We get the Daughter out via Poland, for instance, and then through East Germany. We've
an excellent network in East Berlin itself. That'll have to be disbanded
immediately afterward. In the meantime we allow Miss Graham and
Harrington to think the original scheme is going ahead. They wait in
Livadia, and Volkov waits for the girl to arrive there and for Harrington
to make his move. By which time she should be on her way to the West.
The embassy can fix her up with the necessary papers, and they won't be
looking for her because she's expected to take the other route."

"And how do you think Volkov will react when she doesn't turn up in Livadia?" the Brigadier asked.

Grant pursed his thin lips. "That depends on whether he decides to arrest Miss Graham and blow Harrington's cover by doing so. Personally I don't think he'll do that. Once Sasanov's got his daughter, holding Miss Graham isn't going to count for all that much. But one has to take that chance. What do you think, Chief?"

"I think we should do as you say: halve the risk. Make sure of one, anyway. Go ahead with the new arrangements, Humphrey, will you? And you reassure Sasanov, John. We've got an afternoon session, and our Langley cousin will be breathing down our necks fairly soon."

White paused and said, "I suppose we'll have to tell them we've got a leak? It'll cause a terrible fuss about our security again, but we dare not withhold the truth in case everything blows up in our faces and we have to lose Sasanov. We don't have to tell them it's a home-bred traitor. Besides, we've got a little bone to pick with them ourselves when their man comes over tomorrow night. Grant, send a Telex through to Langley, will you?"

"How brave is she?"

Poliakov didn't hesitate. "I think she's very brave. Only a brave girl would have asked for a pass for me. And got one from Volkov."

"Good enough," Spencer-Barr said. "You're sure she'll go through with this?"

"I think she would be glad to," the tutor said. He drew himself up slightly. "But it won't be necessary. I've made my own plans for Volkov." He placed a hand on his pocket. Spencer-Barr's surprise only made him look supercilious. "You've made plans? What are you talking about— and what's in that pocket?"

"A knife," Poliakov said. "I am not going to Livadia; I am going to Volkov's office this afternoon and I will kill him. Then Irina will be able to get away. She has her pass; she can take the plane tonight. After I've killed him, I will stab myself."

"I see," Jeremy said. "You've got it all planned. A grand heroic gesture?"

Poliakov reddened at the mockery. "You can sneer if you like. But I shall do it."

"I'm sure you would," Spencer-Barr said. "Except that you'd be searched before you got within a mile of Volkov's office, and nobody sees him alone. He has a bodyguard with him. It was a brave idea, but I assure you, this kind of thing is better left to the professionals. You give this to Irina and tell her to get Volkov around just before she leaves. She must tell him it's very urgent, make any excuse, but get him to the apartment. And he must be out of there before an hour at the latest after he's taken the stuff."

He passed a twist of paper to Alexei.

"Put that in your wallet," he said. "And for God's sake be careful. It's tasteless and colorless; it dissolves in about two seconds. And it takes effect about an hour later. The symptoms make it look like heart failure."

Alexei put the paper twist in his wallet. "I understand," he said.

"Now, you've got the rest of the plan clear, haven't you?" Spencer-Barr sounded impatient. "There's a shuttle to Simferopol at seven this evening. You meet Irina at the airport and you fly out. You can spend the night there and get the morning bus to Livadia. When you're in Livadia you contact Heinz Fleischer at the Livadia Castle Intourist Hotel. You go there in the morning as soon as you arrive. He is there with a woman, they're supposed to be East Germans, but he speaks Russian. They're expecting Irina, so she'd better make the call. She must use the name Trudi. Is that all clear?"

"Perfectly," Alexei said. "I remember everything. And when we make contact with these two people, I give your message."

"That's right," Jeremy said grimly. "Tell them the departure plans and what I've told you. You can trust them. I can't do more to help you than that—there isn't time. Your one chance is to get away over the weekend before the KGB start collating Volkov's information. They'll be busy covering up his death for the first twenty-four hours. They don't like people to know the KGB is mortal. Especially at his rank. You've got a good chance," he said harshly, "but not if you bungle anything!"

"We won't bungle it," Poliakov said. "I know what we have to do and we'll do it."

"Right," Jeremy said briskly. "Be at the airport and ready to go. After that it's up to you. Good luck."

They didn't shake hands, although they were the only people in the science room of the Science Exhibition. Poliakov watched the Englishman walk down the long hall, his steps echoing on the marble floor, and turn out of the exit. He had a purposeful walk and a swinging, athletic step. Alexei thought how much he hated him. He made the tutor feel inadequate just by looking at him. He, Poliakov, was not strong enough or clever enough to know how to kill Irina's tormentor. He was to sneak to the airport and wait for her like a little dog. He could be trusted only with messages. That was one part of his instructions he was going to ignore. He left the building a few minutes later.

The American observer from the CIA at Langley arrived at Heathrow and was driven straight to Hampshire. Humphrey Grant was waiting to meet him. He entertained him at dinner with the rest of the team debriefing Sasanov, and afterward took him aside in private. The American was a quiet-spoken Southerner in his midfifties; he had worked under Bush but had been retired during the purge of the early seventies. He had been brought back when the effects of a demoralized intelligence service, hampered by legislation, resulted in the debacle in Iran.

"I'm looking forward to sitting in tomorrow," he said.

"We start at nine-thirty," Grant said. "You've got a detailed report to refer to, haven't you? How has your service analyzed the information so far?"

"We think it's primary information," came the answer. "We're treating it at Presidential level. I'm glad to have the opportunity to absorb it at first hand. We are naturally very concerned about this leak." There was a hint of rebuke which Grant had been expecting. He was ready for it.

He said frostily, "Besides Ivan Sasanov, there's another matter my Chief wanted me to discuss with you—before you sit in on tomorrow's session."

"My pleasure," the CIA official said courteously. He was on guard like a fencer, his charming manners the foil on the rapier.

Grant assumed his infuriating schoolmaster attitude, head poked a little forward, hands clasped behind his back. "I would like to discuss one of our operatives with you," he said. "In strictest confidence, of course. He spent some time in the United States. A Mr. Jeremy Spencer-Barr. Does the name mean anything to you?"

Antonyii Volkov smiled at Irina when she opened the door. He saw her expression alter as his driver stepped forward to come into the apartment with him.

"You don't mind Yuri, do you?" he inquired.

He went past her into the little living room. Irina hurried after him; the big bodyguard loomed behind her.

"We're in the kitchen," she murmured to Volkov. "I've got the samovar nice and hot for some tea."

He went on smiling at her. "Thank you," he said. "And where is your little tutor—in the kitchen, too?"

"Yes," she said. "Yes, he's there. Waiting for you."

Volkov took off his cap, and the driver stepped forward and took it from him.

"Before we sit down at the table together," Volkov said pleasantly, "I want you to tell me something. Yuri—go into the kitchen. I shall come in a minute. Now, Irina, why this urgent message? Why did you want to see me today so badly?" He caught her chin between his fingers and raised her face; the fingers pinched tighter and tighter until she winced.

"Because he doesn't believe you'll let him go," she said. "He won't come with me unless you tell him to."

"What a stupid young idiot," Volkov said mildly. "Any man in his right mind would want to go to Livadia with you. And then to England. Because, you *are* going to England. Did you read your mother's letter?"

He saw the hatred glimmer in her eyes, like sheet lightning before the first thunderclap.

"Yes, I read it."

"And how do you think your father will feel when he reads it?"

"He'll come home," she said. "He'll come home to get her released."

"And you'll be able to convince him that it's a genuine letter, won't you—after all, you've seen your mother in prison, haven't you? He'll know that everything she has written is the truth. And of course you'll do your best to persuade him."

He was waiting for an answer. Courage blazed up in Irina Sasanova.

"I won't have to; my father won't let my mother suffer on his account. He'll come back because he'll want to kill you!"

To her amazement Volkov burst out laughing. "You're a real little firebrand—what a pity I have to lose you! Come along, I want to see this poor rabbit of a tutor; you'll eat him alive, my dear. What you need is a strong man like myself."

She saw the desire in his eyes and cursed herself for showing spirit. Resistance from her aroused him more now than when she was cowed and frightened. He mustn't stay, Alexei had warned. He must leave the apartment within an hour after he had drunk the tea. She turned away from him and hurried to the door.

"You won't say that when you meet him," she challenged.

Poliakov got up when they came in. The samovar stood in the middle of the kitchen table. There were a bottle of vodka, salt, lemon, sweet cakes to be eaten with the tea, and dishes of pickles to neutralize the vodka.

The driver lurked in a corner, arms at his sides, staring inward toward them. For a moment Volkov and the tutor faced each other. Volkov calmly examined him.

"You are just a boy," he said. "No wonder my Irina wants to protect you. Let's sit down, shall we?"

Poliakov pulled out a seat and managed to knock over a glass. He apologized, and wiped the sweat from his pale face with his shirt sleeve.

Volkov watched him with a slight smile; he pointed to a place next to him and said to Irina, "You come beside me."

"What would you like?" she asked him. "Tea or vodka?"

"You have prepared a feast for me," he remarked. "I think I will have a cigarette first. But you help yourselves."

Irina poured tea for herself and handed a cup to Poliakov. She didn't dare to look at him.

"I understand that you're hesitating about going to Livadia," Volkov said to Alexei. "After all the trouble Irina took to get you a pass," he chided. "Why don't you want to go with her? Aren't you being very ungracious?"

Alexei sipped his hot tea and coughed, turning red as it burned his mouth. It was a moment or two before he could answer.

"Excuse me, Comrade General, I burned myself. No, please, don't think I don't want to go to Livadia; it's a wonderful change to have a vacation and to get a pass to go with Irina. I don't know how to thank you." He was running the words together in his nervousness.

"Then why am I here?" Volkov inquired. "I was told you were afraid to go. Afraid I'd go back on my promise to let you take a little trip together. Isn't that so?"

"Yes," Poliakov admitted. "Yes, I was worried about it. Irina tried to convince me, but I couldn't believe . . ." He hesitated.

"Go on," Volkov prompted. "Nothing annoys me except when I'm told lies. Tell the truth, my boy. Always tell me the truth."

"I thought you'd have me arrested," the tutor mumbled. "I didn't see why you should let me go."

Irina had poured a glass of tea for Volkov; a slice of lemon floated in it. It came to rest in front of him, and Volkov glanced sideways at her. The tea was clear as the glass containing it. The powder had dissolved instantly.

"The cakes are good," she said. "I made them."

"They look good," Volkov remarked. "Did you know they tried to poison Rasputin with cakes? They put enough cyanide in them to kill ten men. He ate them all and nothing happened. Why don't you have a cake, my dear?"

"I will," she said.

Volkov put the glass down without drinking anything. He stubbed out his cigarette and pushed back his chair.

"I'll answer your question," he said to Alexei. "I will let you go with Irina because she is doing something for me. You are her reward—if that's what she wants." He turned to her and said, "Now we will excuse ourselves. We shall say our goodbyes in private." He caught her by the arm and pulled her to her feet.

"Antonyii," she began, "Antonyii, please—"

"I left my office early to be with you," he said. "I'm not going to waste my time."

He was asleep when Poliakov stabbed him. Irina pressed both hands to her mouth to stifle the scream that would have awakened him, and the tutor plunged the knife into his back, pulled it out and drove it in a second time. Volkov gurgled into the pillow; his body heaved and twitched as his punctured heart flooded and stopped.

Irina rolled away from him as blood began to run down his naked back onto the sheets. She stood naked and trembling all over, whimpering with shock. The tutor came to her and gathered her in his arms. He was shaking.

"Get dressed," he said. "Hurry, my darling, and get dressed."

"The guard," she cried out. "What about the guard?"

Poliakov said quietly, "I gave him the tea. He's unconscious. He'll be dead soon. As dead as that pig. Did he hurt you?"

The tears welled up and spilled down her face. She cried in his arms for a moment.

"No," she said. "No. . . . Oh, Alexei, Alexei, how could you do it? I never thought you could do such a thing. Oh, God, what are we to do now?"

"Leave here," he said. He bent and dragged a red soaked sheet over Volkov's body. "Don't look at that," he said. "Put your clothes on and get your suitcase. Hurry."

When she came into the kitchen, she gasped. Poliakov was dressed in the driver's uniform. The coat hung big upon his narrow frame.

"I've got my own things on underneath," he said. "We'll take his car. We'll drive to the bus terminal and leave it somewhere. Then we'll catch the flight to Simferopol. You look faint—are you all right?"

"I'm all right," Irina said. She saw the driver's legs sticking out behind the kitchen table, and looked quickly away.

"They won't be found for a day or two," she said. "It's Friday. He went to his dacha on Fridays."

"We'll be out of Russia before they look for him here," Poliakov said. "I'll lock this door and the bedroom. Come on, let's go now!"

The old *dezhurnaya* peered at the lift as it came to rest on the ground floor. She settled back in her seat when she saw the KGB uniform and the girl who was the KGB General's mistress. It didn't do to seem curious about her now; she was too well established. The old woman showed how tactful she was by closing her eyes and pretending to be asleep. Forty-five minutes later Volkov's car was driven down a side street at the back of a warehouse. There Poliakov stripped off the uniform and the heavy boots and hid them under the seat. He took Irina by the arm and carried her suitcase. They walked to the bus depot and boarded the bus to Vnukovo airport. An hour and a half later, their passes and documents stamped, they climbed up the stairway to the Tupolev jet making the scheduled twice-daily flight to the Crimea.

Jeremy Spencer-Barr had got two seats for the evening performance of the Bolshoi Ballet that Friday. The program was Prokofiev's *Romeo and Juliet*, danced by the prima ballerina, Maya Plisetskaya. Jeremy had invited his secretary to go with him, and he was back in his embassy apartment in the compound by Kutuzovsky Prospekt, getting changed for the evening, when his doorbell rang. He scowled, wondering who had decided to drop in without being invited. He hated casual callers. He pulled on his jacket and opened his front door. The senior intelligence officer and the head of chancery were standing there.

"Good evening," Jeremy said. "Do come in." He wasn't the type to be caught off balance. He looked politely but inquiringly at each of them.

"I'm afraid I'm going to the theater in about fifteen minutes," he said. "What can I do for you?"

"We want to have a talk to you," the senior intelligence officer said.

"I've got tickets for the Bolshoi," Jeremy said. "I'm taking my secretary. If we're not in our seats when the curtain goes up, we won't get in till the interval." He looked annoyed.

"Sit down, Spencer-Barr," the head of chancery said.

"We had a top-priority Telex from your Chief in London. You're suspended from all embassy duties."

He couldn't hide the shock; for once his composure deserted him; his mouth opened and he gaped at them. "Suspended? What on earth do you mean?"

"We mean," the intelligence officer said grimly, "that you're off the case. When did you have your last contact with Daniel?"

Jeremy hesitated. It's gone wrong, he though in panic; they messed it up. "Yesterday," he said. "I gave him the message as instructed."

"You gave him something else, didn't you?" The head of chancery was leaving his subordinate to ask the questions. He merely listened, watching Spencer-Barr with a chill dislike.

"You didn't pass London's message on to Daniel, did you? I'd ring up your secretary and tell her you've got a sudden temperature. Summer flu—she'll believe you. I'm afraid you won't be going to the ballet tonight."

Jeremy looked from one to the other. "Very well," he said. "I'll phone. Can I ask one question first?"

"Depends what it is," his interrogator said.

"Has anything happened to Antonyii Volkov?"

"Not that we would know." The answer was curt. "If Daniel did what you told him, it'll be kept very quiet indeed. Make the call."

Spencer-Barr dialed through to the girl's number. He made his excuses and hung up before she could do more than say how sorry she was he was ill. Then he turned back to the two embassy men.

"I'll get you a drink. What would you like, sir?" he asked the head of chancery.

"Scotch and water."

"I'll have the same," the intelligence officer volunteered.

Jeremy poured the drinks and handed one to each of them. His manner was cool, even supercilious. He sat down and crossed one leg over the other.

"Well, gentlemen," he said. "What is it you want to know?"

This time it was the head of chancery who spoke.

"How long have you been working for the CIA?"

The submarine attached to the NATO naval base had sailed down through the Bosporus to the coastal port of Midye. On the night of the twenty-fourth the craft submerged and left her moorings for the open sea. Her captain maintained a steady course at middepth; among the normal complement were three SAS commandos, specially trained in underwater combat; the officer in charge was a first-class yachtsman, and the submarine carried a very special piece of equipment. This consisted of a fiberglass hull that could be assembled in sections to a span of twenty feet, complete with collapsible masthead and a small gasoline-driven outboard motor. There were six inflatable life jackets and an inflatable raft for emergencies. The commandos were equipped with small arms. The captain was a former Polaris commander who had been assigned to Turkey after his tour of duty in the Atlantic was over. He had sealed orders which were broken only after they had submerged. He read them in his cabin. They gave him a specific destination and a time to reach it, surface, disgorge his special cargo and go below to wait. The orders stated that the commandos were to return exactly on schedule; the submarine was to take them on board and return to base immediately. The young commando captain had his orders; the last part tallied exactly with those issued to the commander of the submarine. His mission was to pick up three passengers in the port of Sevastopol and return with them to the rendezvous point. If they had not appeared within a waiting time of fifteen minutes, he was to raise anchor and move off.

12

Davina looked at her watch; it had a luminous dial, and the date showed as the twenty-fifth. The time was 4 A.M. It was the time Sasanov used to wake when they were in the Shepherds Bush flat and his spirits were at their lowest. Often she felt his disquiet even in her sleep and stirred beside him, waking in sympathy. She thought of him more during the silent hours before dawn, when Peter Harrington snored on his own side of the bed and she huddled away from him. He had made no more attempts to sleep with her since they left West Berlin. He joked and flirted as usual, but he was tense and the falsity showed. He had become very nervous as the twenty-fifth approached. He often drank a lot at dinner now and fell quickly asleep.

She stretched, crossing her arms behind her head, and thought of Sasanov with her body as much as her mind. She longed for him in those sleepless hours, remembering the power of his lovemaking, the need for her which made up in passion what it lacked in subtlety. She would never want a subtle, premeditated lovemaking; Sasanov had spoiled her for anything but his own brand of bold desire. She wanted him so badly that she couldn't rest and the man beside her was an irritant. Then common sense rebuked her for permitting sensual fantasies that would never materialize again. She wouldn't see Sasanov when she returned to England. It was over. The goodbye said in that squalid safe flat had been their real farewell to each other. Then the temptation whispered that perhaps

241

when he met his daughter he would want to thank her, see her just once more.

And he'd said something in Russian to her and murmured, "I'll say that to you in English when you come back." But whatever it was, she wouldn't hear it from him. There had to be a break, and she had promised herself and the Chief that she would make it. There was no future for her with Sasanov. He would make his life with his daughter and wait in hope for his wife's release. Better to have loved and lost than never to have loved at all. The cliché came to mind to torment her. She had never loved before she met him. The realization sobered her; love for him was more than the ache in her body for his body, far more than the feeling she had had for the man she'd been ready to marry. She hadn't loved Richard in any way as she loved Ivan Sasanov, and had loved him for months before they became lovers. She'd concealed it from herself, hiding behind her professionalism, her indifference to men after that one brutal disappointment. Only when she took him home to Marchwood, and saw her sister setting out to charm—then the pretense fell away and she suffered the worst pangs of jealousy. And because she loved him she was lying awake in an Intourist hotel on a highly dangerous mission in the middle of Russia. She hadn't maneuvered herself into this to convince Sasanov that her department was genuine. She hadn't placed herself at risk to back up his interrogators and round off her role for the Brigadier. She hadn't really given a damn about any of that. She had gone to Russia because she couldn't bear to see Sasanov suffering on account of his family. She had gone because she wanted him to be happy, and because his happiness was more precious to her than her own. And this was what love meant. What *he* had meant when he dismissed her sister with the simple statement "But all she would do with a man is take. I needed a woman who could give."

Davina eased herself up on the pillow. She thought suddenly, I don't hate Charley anymore. I can forgive Charley because she took something away that wasn't worth having. She left me free to find the real man. Poor Charley. With all her beauty and success, I don't think she's ever felt what I feel now—or ever will. I feel quite sorry for her.

Davina slid over the edge of the bed and onto the floor. She wanted a cigarette and to be alone, away from the sound of Harrington's breathing. Above all she didn't want him to wake and intrude. She found her robe and slipped into it. The night was very warm. She groped on the dressing table and found the cigarettes and Harrington's lighter. Then she opened the window very quietly and stepped out onto the narrow balcony. There was a three-quarter moon, and the view across to the shore and the sea was black and silver; there were little regiments of waves advancing to the beach, crested with white foam. She could hear the soft hiss as they drew the sand and pebbles with them. A few lights glimmered from the street lights immediately below. There was no sound but the gentle fall of the waves, and the moonlight fell on the black surface of the sea in a bright silver swathe that vanished on the horizon. She lit the cigarette and leaned against the window. Once when she was a child, the family had been on vacation in Cornwall and they had all gone for a swim in the darkness. She had swum out on a swathe of moonlight and imagined how easy it would be to swim forever in the silver sea. She remembered her father coming alongside and telling her sharply to go back, she had swum out too far for safety.

And then Davina saw the ship; it had crept around a headland and appeared on the dark sea glittering with tiny lights. She watched it moving very slowly, seeming to be almost stationary, until it reached the moonlit sea lane, and its lights were challenged. It was not a big ship and not very far out. It was gliding onward, making for the port. It must be one of the cruise ships run by Intourist, returning from a trip around the coast.

"Davina? Is that you?"

She turned, and the light in the bedroom flashed on. Harrington was sitting up in the bed. He looked tousled and bleary-eyed.

"What the hell are you doing out there?"

"I couldn't sleep," she said. She came into the room and rubbed the cigarette out in the tin ashtray. "I didn't want to wake you, so I went onto the balcony. It's a gorgeous night. I was watching a ship come in."

"Oh?" He got up, pulling his pajamas into place. "Let's have a look." He went to the balcony and stepped out.

"It's a cruise ship," he said. He came back inside and pulled the curtains back. He fumbled for the cigarettes and snapped his lighter irritably till it flamed. He glanced across at her, puffing on the cigarette.

"You know what I think?" Davina shook her head. "I think that's our escape route."

"The ship?"

"Yes; I just had a feeling, seeing it come like that—right on time." He went back to the window and stared out.

"They'd never get her out overland," he said quietly; it was almost as if he were talking to himself. "Even with all the documentation. There wouldn't be time before the alarm went off. It must be the sea."

He turned back to Davina. "Across the sea to Turkey and then by air to England. Courtesy of NATO. That must be it. Why haven't they told us the route?" He turned back to the window, pulling on the cigarette until the tip glowed crimson. "Why didn't I think of that before?"

"Does it matter?" Davina asked him. "You seem worried by the idea. If you're right, surely it's safer than trying to get her out overland?"

She watched him, frowning; his body was stiff with tension, angled against the window frame, and the tiny beacon of cigarette end was trembling in an unsteady hand. "They'd never get her out overland." . . . Her mind was trained to pick up nuances; eight months of living with Sasanov had honed her instincts razor-sharp. Surely, *we'd* never get her out. But he'd said "they" as if he were talking about the opposition. She had a quickening of alarm. It was only a slip of the tongue; not to be taken seriously. He'd started to drink in the last few days; that worrried her more. It showed that the strain was telling on him. And he had to be sober and alert for what was coming. If he was right and their escape was planned by sea.

She went to the window and joined him. There was no sign of the ship; the port itself was invisible from their balcony. To her surprise he dropped his arm around her shoulders and pulled her close to him.

"I'm getting old for this sort of thing," he said. "You're a brave girl, Davy; you wouldn't care to give an old yellowbelly a bit of home comfort, would you?"

Davina pulled his arm away. "No," she said. "I wouldn't. Don't start that again, Peter."

"Why not?" he demanded. "I'm not that bloody unattractive, am I? I've slept in the same bed with you for ten days, and I've been a very good boy. You can't deny that."

"I'm not denying it," she said quietly. "But I'm not in love with you, and I'm not going to bed with you. So why don't we just get some sleep?"

He threw his cigarette through the open window; the butt end made a tiny bright arc as it fell.

"Would you believe me," he said slowly, "if I said I was in love with you? Would that make any difference?" His hair was on end; in the garish electric light he looked tired and dispirited. He paused by the dressing table and picked the warm butt of her cigarette out of the ashtray. He looked at it and dropped it on the floor.

Davina came over to him; she hooked her hand through his arm. "You're not in love with me," she said gently. "I'm just here, that's all.

We've only got another twenty-four hours to go. Let's hope you're right, and that ship is going to get us away. Why don't you go back to sleep for a couple of hours? It's nearly five now."

"What about you?" he asked.

"I'm going to go out for a walk," she answered.

"You don't have to," he mumbled. "I'll behave myself—promise."

On an impulse of pity, she kissed him lightly on the cheek.

"I know that," she said. "I won't sleep now anyway, and the fresh air will be nice. I'll see you at breakfast." She gathered her clothes, hesitated for a moment and then said, "I'll change in the bathroom. You turn off the light and go to sleep." She let herself out of the room.

Harrington didn't get back into the bed. His heart was jumping and he found it difficult to breathe. He switched off the bedside light and stationed himself by the balcony. He could see down to the street below. Her figure came into view, turning right to walk along the road that led to the seashore. She didn't look up at the hotel. He stayed still, watching her until the bend in the road hid her. He stepped back into the room, tripped over the little ledge, and swore. He was still unsteady on his feet. He switched the light on and went to the table. His lighter and cigarettes lay there, with a crumpled ten-ruble note and a few loose coins. And his wallet was beside them. The butt in the ashtray was warm; that meant she had taken a cigarette, used his lighter. What else had she touched while he was asleep? It was the German-made wallet that had been given him by the department. It didn't have a secret compartment as his own did. He kept it in his back pocket, buttoned in securely, during the day and hid it in his drawer at night under his clothes. But not last night. Last night he had got drunk and forgotten his routine. He had fallen into bed and snored like a hog while the wallet lay on the table for anyone to find. If she had turned curious, or suspicious . . . He tried to still his trembling hands as he opened it and fumbled with the inner compartment.

It was still there. Relief changed to panic, and because he was so frightened he became drunkenly furious with Davina. She might have seen it. She might have discovered what he really was. That kiss would be the touch of Judas, just to quiet him. He called her a bitch out loud while the alcohol set his nerves into frantic jangle and played havoc with his reasoning. He'd asked her to sleep with him because he was lonely and not sober, because he needed warmth and comfort in the guise of sex. She wouldn't have him. Either because she didn't want him or because she had been spying, prying. . . . He held the wallet in sweating hands. One side of him liked her, found her attractive, had bought her a wildly expensive present in a sentimental moment when he could forget what he was going to do to her at the end.

And then the idea came to him, and the sheer cunning delighted him. It seemed a piece of brilliant ingenuity. And irony too. It would serve her right for rejecting him. Serve her right for being on the other side. He found nail scissors and a needle already threaded in her little sewing kit in her drawer. The threaded needle was a bonus; he couldn't have got the bloody thing into focus to do it himself. He spent five minutes with the scissors and another five with the needle, concentrating fiercely. Then he put everything back in her drawer. He went along the corridor to the bathroom and washed his head and face in cold water to sober himself up.

It was almost five-thirty when he came down in his shirt and trousers and stockinged feet to the foyer of the hotel below. The desk where the telephone was kept was in semidarkness, although it was dawn outside. Harrington switched on the light and picked up the receiver. The ring was transmitted to the receptionist's room on the ground floor; she woke at once and aroused her husband. They came across the hall together, converging in menace on the man sitting in her seat with the telephone in his hand. The husband rushed toward him.

"What are you doing? Put that down—how dare you sneak in here!"

Harrington said a few rapid words to him in Russian. The man turned to his wife; she clutched his arm in fright. For a moment they both stared at him. Then they stammered apologies and hurried back to their room. The operator answered.

"Moscow," Harrington said. Then he gave the number.

The operator recognized the first three digits of the special code. She connected him at once.

All telephone calls prefixed by the digits 669 were transmitted immediately to the KGB offices on Dzerzinsky Street. The night-duty operators on the switchboard put the calls through to the duty officer in each section; Harrington's call at five in the morning went to Volkov's Internal Security section, and was relayed by the duty officer onto tape. By eight-thirty on Saturday morning, Volkov's principal deputy was in the office and the tape was played over for him. The message was coded. The first two words indicated it was top priority and the second that it was intended for Antonyii Volkov. The deputy was the young officer Tatischev who had accompanied his chief to the mortuary when Fedya Sasanova identified the body sent from Britain. He could not decode the message without Volkov's special key, which was kept locked up in Volkov's private office security box. This box could be opened only by two keys used in unison; one was in the office and the other was kept by Volkov himself. Tatischev put through a call to his superior's dacha. He was used to the secretive way in which the Comrade General worked; he had served him for seven years and had learned not to ask questions. There was nothing he could do about the message from Livadia, in spite of its top-priority urgent prefix, except trace Antonyii Volkov. By twenty minutes to nine, he learned from the caretaker that the Comrade General had not come down to Zhukova as usual on Friday night.

He might arrive that morning. Tatischev put a call through to his apartment. It rang for some time; Volkov's driver, Yuri, did duty as orderly and servant. He should have answered the telephone. Tatischev swore to himself. No answer from the apartment. That probably meant that they were already on their way to Zhukova. He booked a second call into the dacha in an hour's time, and settled down to some desk work.

In the hostel in Yalta, Irina and Alexei slept in each other's arms; she had been silent on the flight, numbed with the shock of what had happened. Every time she closed her eyes she saw Volkov's body and the spreading bloodstains on the bed. Poliakov seemed to know instinctively how to comfort her. He held her hand firmly, ordered vodka from the hostess, and whispered to her to bear up. They were going on a holiday; she must appear cheerful. You never knew who might be on the plane and watching. She had always been the stronger in moments of crisis; now he was in command. The one and only act of violence in his life had given him stature. He had found the courage to save the situation when everything went wrong; killing Volkov had paid for Irina's misery and thrown the Englishman's contempt back in his face. He was a man in the real sense; a brave man who had taken decisions and saved them both. He felt exhilarated and bold. And Irina was content to be protected. Content to be loved by him and to face the future with him. They had spent a passionate night and promised each other a lifetime of love. She had no dreams; it seemed when she woke that there had never been a Volkov, only the new, confident Alexei Poliakov, who had turned out to be a hero.

They caught the first bus to Livadia. It was a glorious hot morning; the sun hung in a brilliant sky, round and glistening like a golden coin; the lush plants and palm trees made them feel as if they had left Russia for some tropical paradise. They walked away from the terminal hand in hand, with their suitcases, and passersby winked at them, thinking they must be on their honeymoon.

Davina had walked for a long time, long enough to see the dawn flush on the horizon and the splendor of the sunrise. There was not another human being on the beaches or the streets. She could have been the only person in the world. She had always liked solitude; sometimes she wondered whether it was because she had no choice. She had been a lonely child, always wandering off by herself. Until she met Sasanov she had never lived in close proximity to anyone. Night and day, weeks turning into months, getting closer and closer to him, and incredibly she had never once been bored. She walked along the silvery beaches by the edge of the sea and felt as if there was a mysterious communication between them, fostered by the country he loved so much. He would never see Russia again, but the loneliness of the exile would be bearable with his daughter beside him and the hope of his wife's exchange. Hope was the lubricant of life. She had to hope that they would escape, that Harrington's hunch about the ship was right and she had seen their rescuer sailing across the silver moon path on the sea that morning.

What would her own life be, when she got back? She couldn't run away from the reality of loving Ivan Sasanov. It had to be faced, and, once it was accepted, she would come to terms. Loneliness again; a special kind, as if a hole had been punched through and her heart had fallen out; the hunger that kept her awake at night. They were the price for what she was doing, and that price had been agreed before she went. "You must understand that you can never see him again." James White, with his quiet ultimatum; the steely face of Grant. "You've made a fool of yourself and it can't go on." And her own acceptance: "I know that. I know it's finished as far as we're concerned. All I ask is that you'll let me go out and bring his daughter back." The bargain had been struck and there was no going back.

She had signed the document. She had her work; not a major career, her affair with Sasanov had finished that. But enough to interest her and give her independence. And she had the memory of those eight months and the moment when he turned to her in the garden in Marchwood and said, "I don't want your sister." She didn't mean to cry; the salt breeze dried the tears, and her cheeks felt stiff. She'd slept badly and her nerves were tightening in anticipation of the day. Even Harrington was tense, drinking heavily.

He had changed since they left England. Not just when he was playing the part of Heinz Fleischer and doing it superbly. But when they were alone, the easy banter had a hollow ring to it; temper lurked under the surface. He had seemed upset by the cruise ship, as if in some way its appearance had cheated him. "They'd never get her out over-land." . . . She stopped suddenly, while a wave sneaked up and ran over her feet. *They*—it was such an odd word to use about himself and her. There was a prick in her mind, like a tiny thorn embedded under the skin. She dismissed it and went on walking till it was time to go back to the hotel and meet him for breakfast.

As she turned to go through the door, a young man stepped aside to let her go first. He had a girl with him; she had blond hair and was attractive in a simple way. They both carried suitcases. "Thank you," Davina said in Russian. She had picked up a few basic words. He nodded to her and smiled. She went through ahead of them; Irina and Alexei Poliakov fol-lowed. They went to the reception desk.

"Excuse me," the young man said to the woman at the desk.

She looked up and said sharply, "This hotel is not for Russians. You ought to know that."

"I do," he said quickly. "But we are looking for a Herr Fleischer— please, it's important. Is he here now?"

She remembered the phone call and the sharp exchange from the East German. Even though any contact with Western tourists was forbidden, and discouraged even among Eastern-bloc Communists, she dared not turn the couple away.

"Yes," she said hurriedly. "He's here. His wife just came in; she's gone through to the restaurant. Table nine."

Irina nudged him. "We'll go through," she said. "If that's all right."

"Perfectly all right," the woman said sullenly. She turned away from them.

Peter Harrington came down the stairs as they walked into the dining room. They came to the table where Davina was sitting.

"Frau Fleischer?" Alexei Poliakov said softly.

Harrington saw them and stopped in midstride. He was staring at the girl. The blond daughter of Ivan Sasanov. With an unscheduled man. The pause was only for a second. He reached the table just as Davina was taking the girl by the hand.

"We weren't expecting you," Peter Harrington said. "I don't know how this will affect our plans."

He didn't see Irina Sasanova stiffen angrily. He was talking to Polia-kov as they walked along the beach. They had drunk coffee and made conversation in the dining room of the hotel. Harrington had suggested a walk in the open air where they could speak freely.

Alexei Poliakov couldn't help turning red. "I'm sorry," he said. "I was told I could come with Irina."

"I wasn't leaving without him," she said.

She spoke poor German out of courtesy to Davina. Harrington rattled on in Russian. He looked tense and irritable; the arrival of the young man seemed to have disturbed him out of all proportion.

"We are still waiting for the final details of our escape plan," he said. "I hope they confirm your story. Otherwise, I'm afraid you'll have to stay behind!"

Irina put her hand on Davina's arm, to slow her down. They dropped behind the two men. She had felt immediate sympathy with the older woman from the moment they came face to face in the hotel. Harrington's open hostility to Alexei had put her on her guard at once.

"Is he in charge of the escape?" she murmured to Davina.

"Yes, he is," Davina answered.

"Why is he so suspicious of Alexei? Of course the British know he is going with us! Why is this man making so much trouble about it?"

"Probably because he wasn't told," Davina said. "And I think he's rather on edge till we're safely on our way. Don't take any notice; it'll be all right. I just wish we had the final instructions."

Irina slowed her steps to increase the gap between them and the two in front.

"We have them," she said quietly.

Davina stopped. "You do? But why didn't you say so?"

"Alexei was going to," she said. "But this man is being so hostile with him. I can tell you, can't I? Do you understand me? My German isn't very good—"

"I can understand perfectly," Davina said quickly. "Don't worry about mistakes. Just tell me what we've got to do."

"We take tickets for the *Alexander Nevsky* cruise this afternoon," Iri-na said in a low voice. "It goes around the coast and stops at Sevastopol this evening. There is a dinner and a dance on board for the passengers. We have to slip away and get to the marina where the sailboats are; a sailboat with the Polish flag flying, and three men on board, will be anchored just outside. They will send a boat to take us on board. I have to wave a colored handkerchief at them as the signal."

"Oh God," Davina said, "it sounds desperately chancy. What happens if they're not there or we're late? Why couldn't we go to Sevastopol by road?"

"Because we don't have passes," Irina explained. "You can't travel freely in Russia. You have to get permission to leave the resort. The cruise ship is the only way."

"Well, we'll just have to get it right," Davina said. She looked at the girl and said gently, "You're very like your father."

"You know him?"

"Yes," Davina said. "I know him. . . . Any news of your mother? He's been so anxious for you both."

Irina hung her head. "I have a letter from her," she said. "She was made to write it. I don't know whether to give it to him or not."

"Think about it when you get there," Davina said.

Harrington turned around, frowning. "Come on, catch up. What are you dawdling about for?"

Irina caught hold of Davina's arm. "There's something else," she whispered quickly. "We have to warn you that the KGB have an informer. They know why we're here. They know my father sent for me."

Davina felt as if the ground had dropped away under her feet. She turned to the Russian girl in horror, every vestige of color draining away till she was sickly gray under the tan.

"What? You mean they *know*?"

"Yes," Irina whispered. "The man at the embassy told Alexei to warn you. They don't know who it is; but he can't have told them about the cruise ship because only Alexei and I and the embassy man know we're going that way."

Davina made herself walk on; Harrington was slowing down to let them catch up with him.

. . . Spencer-Barr was the man at the embassy. Spencer-Barr, whom Peter Harrington had never trusted. And he had warned about a spy, a spy keeping the KGB posted on the whole plan. She felt as if she might be physically sick.

"He's dead," Irina whispered. She gave Davina a triumphant look. "Alexei killed him."

"Killed whom?" Davina stared at her. "Who's dead?"

"Volkov," the girl answered. "General Volkov of the KGB. He was my father's boss. He had my mother arrested and he made me sleep with him. He is letting me escape so I can persuade my father to come back and give himself up in exchange for my mother. Alexei stabbed him. He was so brave," she said, and her face glowed. "I never thought he could do such a thing. He poisoned the bodyguard too. That man is not going to leave him behind," she added fiercely.

Davina said, "Oh God, what a dreadful thing—did you see it? Did you see him do it?"

"I was in bed with Volkov," the girl said. "Alexei came into the bedroom and stabbed him. He was very sadistic; he liked to hurt people. He always hurt me when we went to bed. They won't be found for a day or two: he always went to his dacha at the weekends. He'll be missed on Monday, and by then we'll be away."

Davina disengaged her arm. "I've got to talk to him." She nodded toward Peter Harrington. "You go and wander around with Alexei; there's a café near the Livadia Palace—it has a green canopy and tables outside. Meet us there in half an hour. Peter! Wait a minute, will you?"

She reached the two men, and Irina spoke rapidly to Poliakov in Russian. They turned and walked away. Harrington swung around to Davina.

"What's all this about? Why did you send them off on their own? They're not supposed to go out of our sight! What are you playing at? What was that girl saying to you, back there where I couldn't hear?"

It was as if she were face to face with a stranger. He loomed over her, his face contorted with anger.

"I don't know what those bloody fools in London are playing at," he said furiously. "They saddle us with this boy friend of hers, just on Spencer-Barr's authority; how do we know he's genuine? He could be a bloody plant, for all we know—and they use him to pass the details of our exit! Why not communicate direct with us?"

"He's told you, then," Davina said slowly.

"Yes," Harrington sounded impatient. "We catch the cruise ship, go to Sevastopol and then get ourselves in place for a pickup by yacht. Exactly as I said this morning. We're going out by sea. There'll be a sub waiting to take us on board. Personally I think it's a bloody chancy operation. Too much margin for error. What was she saying to you?"

"Much the same," Davina answered. "Her German's very bad."

They began to walk slowly onward. It was becoming very hot, and the sands shimmered like diamond dust under their feet. The beach was filling up with sunbathers. Children played on the fringe of the sea, and a group of young men were playing ball, laughing and falling about in the water.

She walked on beside him, and he said casually, "They shouldn't have gone off alone. We should keep them in sight till we get on that ship."

"And that was all?" She asked the question without looking at him. "Just the plans for getting away from here?"

"What else?" he countered. "I just hope he's got it right. We'd better make our way to that café. I don't want to lose them."

"We won't lose them," she said. "They'll be there."

He slipped his hand through her arm. "Sorry I shouted," he said. "I just don't like surprises when the operation is as tight as this one."

"That's all right," Davina murmured. They walked on slowly.

"Well—" he sounded as if he were making an effort to be cheerful—"we'll be on our way by this evening. I wonder how many yachts we'll find flying the Polish flag."

"You don't think we're going to get away, do you?" Davina asked suddenly. He doesn't want to frighten me, she said to herself. That's why he's not telling me about the KGB informer; of course that's the reason.

"The one thing that worries me is Poliakov," he said. "Why should we believe he's genuine? All we've got is his word for it. And Spencer-Barr, poking his nose in. I never trusted that little bastard."

"I know," Davina said. "You said so before. Tell me, truthfully, Peter—do you suspect him of working for the Russians? Is that what you think?"

"He could be," he muttered. "And so could that boy. Sent along to keep an eye on us and give the signal when we're nicely compromised, boarding that Polish yacht."

She didn't answer; she walked with her head down, wanting to pull her arm away from him.

"That's terrifying," she said slowly. "Is that what can happen?"

"That's how they'll do it," he answered grimly. "Set a trap and catch us red-handed escaping. I don't want to frighten you, but it's better to face facts."

"Yes," she said. "It is. I'm glad you told me. What time is it?"

He looked at his watch. "Twelve-ten," he said. "Time to meet them."

She managed to free herself from him; he had quickened his pace and she was able to glance sideways at him. Peter Harrington, the colleague of fifteen years, the cheery, rather pathetic figure who wandered around the office corridors and propped up the bar in the local pub. A funny man, rather like a naughty boy surprised by middle age; always good for a laugh and able to enlist sympathy at the same time. Likable and trustworthy; even his halfhearted attempts to sleep with her were endearing. He hadn't withheld the truth because he didn't want to frighten her. He had frightened her with a lie instead.

She felt herself begin to shake; panic threatened her as it had never done in her life, so that she wanted to turn and run, blindly. But there was nowhere to run to; only the golden beach and the sunshine and the crowds of Russians and tourists enjoying themselves. And Peter Harrington striding on beside her. He was trying to throw suspicion on the young man; on Spencer-Barr, who had sent the warning. He didn't know that Poliakov had killed the KGB General; he was lying about him to Davina to discredit anything he said or did. He was lying about everything. She saw them sitting at a table in the café, shaded by the green canopy. They were close together, holding hands.

"You stick close to her," Harrington said suddenly. "I want to take him off and have a private talk before we get on that ship together. After lunch; okay?"

"What time does the cruise ship leave?" Davina asked him. She had to clear her throat before she could speak naturally.

"Five o'clock," he said. "I think we should go back to the hotel for lunch. I'll book the tickets for the cruise."

"All right," Davina said. She came to the table where Alexei and Irina were sitting. She pulled out a chair and sat down very quickly because her legs were weak. She managed to smile at them both and say to Irina in German, "Have you had a nice walk?"

"Yes," she replied. "It's so beautiful here. My mother and father used to come for vacations."

Then Peter Harrington leaned close to her and said, his voice full of concern, "Tell me—what news of your mother?"

Davina sat back, guessing at the conversation; seeing Irina's eyes swim with tears. In the middle of it, Irina turned to Davina and explained in German, "We talk of my mother. I have this letter from her."

Davina saw Harrington take the letter and slip it into his jacket pocket. He explained in a whisper, "Safer for me to carry it. If anything goes wrong, it mustn't be found on her." She saw him reach out and squeeze the girl's hand.

Poliakov was listening to them and nodding. He gazed at the girl with adoration. He had killed the loathsome Volkov; he looked like a poet. At his whisper Irina wiped her wet eyes and made herself smile. Though Davina didn't understand their words, there was a tenderness between them that moved her profoundly. And the sincerity of Irina Sasanova and Alexei Poliakov pointed up the falsity of the man sitting opposite them. The false kindness, the false sympathy; she was watching a performance as calculated as the assumption of his East German identity. He had taken off one mask and donned another; she felt sick as she watched him. The KGB had an informer; everything they planned was known, except the means of their escape. And now Harrington knew the plan; Harrington had the compromising letter from Sasanov's wife; Harrington was going to buy the tickets for the cruise ship. Harrington, who had made the tiny slip of saying "they" when he talked about his own operation. Harrington who had lied to her, whose nerve was fraying while they waited because he had no information to pass on. He was hostile to the young man because he had reckoned on dealing with two women both of whom trusted him completely. And he was going to take the tutor away, to have a private talk. Predictably, he wouldn't come back, and they would have to board the ship without him. She shivered; cold sweat broke out on her body, and the panic threatened her again.

"You all right?" He was bending toward her, kind, fond old Peter Harrington; his hand came to rest on her arm. "You look a bit seedy."

She managed to smile at him, a tight little smile that hurt her dry lips. "Just nerves," she said. "I'll be glad when we're on our way."

"We all will," he said. "Let's go back to the hotel and eat there. No point in drifting around till five o'clock. You'll feel better after lunch," he said to Davina.

They got the bus back to the hotel. In the foyer she excused herself.

"I couldn't face food," she said. "I'll go and lie down for a bit. I'll feel better if I sleep." She saw them move into the dining room and took the lift up to the room on the second floor.

She washed her face in ice-cold water, changed out of her clammy dress. She sat on the edge of the bed and lit a cigarette. Her hand was steadier.

She had to think it out, carefully and coolly, marshaling every fact. This was the way she had been taught to think, to analyze. Her reactions outside had been hysterical because suspicions came at her like shrapnel, flying in at tangents, striking in different directions at once. If that slip of the tongue was right, Harrington was speaking from the other side when he said "they." Accusing Spencer-Barr of treason while he suppressed the Russian's warning about the real danger only confirmed her first view. She closed her eyes, concentrating. How circumstantial was their meeting, all those months ago in the office in London? How deliberate the playing upon her sympathy, the joking questions about Ivan Sasanov? How convenient had been his recall from New York after a publicized lapse into drinking too much? There was a dreadful pattern emerging even as she remembered their meetings, some by chance, others arranged by him. He had become seedy, unreliable, after twenty years of active service and good reputation. He had got himself recalled after Sasanov's defection. And he had latched onto her because he knew she was the Russian's minder.

Those were the facts and the circumstantial evidence; they damned him even without the instinctive knowledge of his deception. That had come to her so strongly that morning that she had almost lost control of herself. She had seen him as a liar as much as heard him. Seen him play-acting with the two young Russians, pretending to be sympathetic, hiding his hostility to Poliakov after his lapse when the young man took him by surprise. His solicitude for her was false, too; he was poised like an animal, ready for anything to happen. The suspicion had become certainty; he was the enemy, had always been the enemy. He was the Mole who had sent the firebomb assassin to Halldale Manor. Sasanov had warned her that such a man existed—a traitor within the service. Worst of all, she had involved him in the escape plan, and, unsuspecting, the Brigadier had agreed that he should go. She put out the cigarette and began to search his clothes and belongings. Her crash course at the so-called language school had included where to look for bugs, microfilm and weapons masquerading as tubes of toothpaste, brushes, pens and pencils, suitcases, shoes with hollow heels. She worked very quickly and found nothing. She stood in the middle of the room and looked around her. He had no weapon of any kind; not even a tiny signal transmitter, such as could be fitted into a lighter and had a range of over a hundred miles. Was it possible she was mistaken—that her suspicions were hysterical? And then, lying on the chest of drawers, she saw the expensive Hermes leather bag he had bought for her in West Berlin.

Major Tatischev didn't know what to do. General Volkov had not gone to his dacha, and there was no reply from his Moscow apartment. He had not notified his secretary or Tatischev of a change of plan. The top-priority message was locked away, unanswered. By noon, Tatischev decided to go around to the apartment himself. He took a man skilled in lock-picking with him. A few minutes inside the place assured him that his chief had not spent the night there; more puzzling, his razor and toothbrush were still in the bathroom, and his robe hung behind the door.

The valet Yuri's things were still in his room. He returned to his office feeling very uneasy. The General's car was not in the garage; he had left his office early the previous afternoon and not phoned in since. Tatischev sent for his secretary, and fortunately the young man was found at home spending a long day in bed with his girl friend. He came to the office soon after one-thirty, looking very apprehensive. He's afraid, Tatischev thought; so am I. We all live in fear of making a mistake. He stared at the secretary, whose adam's apple went up and down in his throat as he tried to swallow.

"You say the Comrade General left early in the afternoon?"

"Yes, Major. About three o'clock."

"He didn't say where he was going? No, I see. Did he indicate that he would come back or go to the country? . . . You don't think he said anything. Hmm. He had no appointment for that afternoon; he just left the office?"

The secretary swallowed hard again. The nervous tick was beginning to madden Tatischev.

"I think he had a telephone call," the young man said nervously. He never dared discuss his superior's private life with anyone, not even the girl he lived with. He wouldn't have said a word about the call except that the major was becoming suspicious of his answers.

"What call?" Tatischev shouted at him. "You idiot! Why didn't you say so before? Who telephoned him?"

"I don't like to say," the secretary stammered. "It was private. The General wouldn't want me to discuss—"

"The General is missing!" Tatischev yelled at him. "I'll take the responsibility. Who phoned him?"

"A girl," the secretary said. "He gave me a number to call if he was there and needed in an emergency. I never had to use it."

While Tatischev was ringing the number and the telephone shrilled unanswered in Irina's apartment, the address was traced. At about the same time the civil police had summoned up enough courage to take action about the car with a KGB license plate which was blocking a side street near the Somoyonov airport. Their call to the transport section in the Dzerzinsky Street complex did not get channeled through to Tatischev in time. He was standing outside the front door of Irina Sasanova's apartment, bullying the old caretaker because she was fumbling with the master key.

He knew as soon as he stepped inside that the place was not empty. There was a heavy silence that he recognized; he had seen many men die and many dead men. He had brought two security guards with him. He heard one of them shout from the kitchen as he himself broke open the bedroom door and saw the outline of a body covered by a blood-soaked sheet. General Antonyii Volkov's uniform was neatly folded on a chair, with his boots standing like sentries underneath it. An hour later, when the security guards had cordoned off the building and the street, and the two bodies were spirited away through the service entrance at the back, Tatischev went through the pockets of the General's jacket and found the key that opened the special box to the decoder.

"You sit out in the gardens," Harrington said to Irina. "I'll go up and see if she's all right."

"She did look very pale," Poliakov remarked. "I hope she's not sick with anything."

"Just travel sickness," Harrington quipped automatically. Neither of them laughed. Dour buggers, he murmured to himself as he left them. Russians had no sense of the ridiculous. Not that he felt exactly humorous himself.

Out of sight, his expression became grim; he made his way to the reception desk and walked around it to the inside. He spoke quickly and very softly to the receptionist, who immediately showed him into the inner office where the private telephone was kept, and went out closing the door. Harrington sat down and picked up the receiver. There had been no message for him. It was nearly nine hours since he had sent his message to Volkov. He had not expected a reply direct to the hotel before late morning. He reminded himself that it was a weekend and Volkov would certainly be out of the city. It would take a little time to reach him. His intuition that early morning as he watched the cruise ship coming into harbor would have alerted his Moscow chief to the possibility of an escape by sea. Some precautions would have already been taken. . . . But he should have been contacted, his message acknowledged.

He was frowning and the frown became a scowl as he dialed the code number and delivered a second message. The diary he had used as a key for British Intelligence communication had a double function. The message he spoke into the Moscow recorder was given the double prefix of most urgent, top priority. Decoded, it gave full details of the plan to get Irina and her companion out of Russia by means of slipping the cruise ship at Sevastopol and being taken off by a yacht flying Polish colors. Security services in Sevastopol were to be alerted, and the two women and the male Russian were to be arrested as they attempted to go ashore. He himself must be allowed to escape and keep the rendezvous. He requested urgent and immediate confirmation that the message had been received and the plan put into operation. He gave his code name and ended with the call sign. He pushed open the door, nodded briefly to the scared woman behind the reception desk. He had no intention of going upstairs to Davina; he had decided during lunch that his idea of taking Poliakov aside and handing him over to the local militia, or else killing him, was a solution born of panic.

The unexpected had unnerved him; he had seen a Spencer-Barr agent in the young man, with his convenient cover story of being Irina Sasanova's friend. His reaction had been bad; he admitted that. The nerves were ragged, unsettled by his resumption of alcohol, but only in the short term. He had been falling asleep drunk and waking with the shakes, his heart thudding against his chest wall like a battering ram. That was how he had awakened at dawn that morning, to find the bed empty and Davina standing out on the balcony in her nightdress, watching the cruise ship. And his wallet lying on the table.

He had been terrified and angry, still drunk as he joined her in the moonlight, and the finely tuned intelligence had acted independently of the vodka in his brain and said, That's how they'll get her out—by sea, on a ship like that one; probably *on* that ship. The same intelligence had made use of the Hermes bag. Thank God for his sharp instinct. If you could thank God for a thing like that. Thank God for the lovesickness afflicting the two young Russians; that couldn't be manufactured or taught at Moscow Center; not even where men learned the language of counterfeit emotions, just as they did at Langley in Virginia and Langham Place in London. Alexei Poliakov was no British agent sent by the loathed Spencer-Barr. He was exactly what he said he was: the girl's lover, running away to the West with her. Harrington had only to see them together to know it was the truth.

He didn't have to worry about Poliakov. Volkov's Crimean henchmen would deal with him—as *he* had promised to deal with the KGB informer when the young man whispered Jeremy's warning. "Don't worry," he had said—the tough professional straight out of a second-rate spy film— "I'll know what to do about him." And the poor fool had believed him and offered his idiotic help. "Please, call on me. I'm braver than I look—I could kill a man." And Harrington had pressed his thin shoulder and said, "Of course, you could."

He paused in the lobby. Upstairs was Davina, his excuse for gaining time to make the call. Her nerves were giving out; no criticism of her, he said to himself. She was brave enough, and cool. Old, hardened pros like himself got sick when the eleventh hour approached. Love was her motive, too. Like the girl and the youth with his poet's face.

He didn't want to think about Davina. He needed to be alone, to sit for a few stolen minutes in the golden Russian sunshine, surrounded by the beauty of the garden. Russians knew how to make houses and gardens beautiful; they knew how to take a pleasure resort like Yalta with its reputation for healing the sick rich of the old order, and turn it into a paradise for ordinary Russians. A place where the humble worker could afford the benefits of a health spa; where families could take their vacations and gape at the splendors of dead men's palaces, now turned into museums or converted to sanatoria for their use. Provided they got the official passes entitling them to go there, and the permits to travel. No society was perfect, Harrington reminded himself. It didn't matter, being cynical. He couldn't help himself. He had to have a private joke at the expense of everything, sacred as well as profane. He found a garden chair under a tree and moved it into the sunshine. He sat with his eyes closed, face upturned to the sun.

Fifteen years of work with James White's service; five years of treason. It had happened so gradually, while he was stationed in West Germany. The contact was light as feather down at first, a mere whisper from the enemy. His motives were honest to start with: he inclined his ear to the whisper, intending to pass its message back to London. And then he had delayed. The contact was a West German, a journalist he had known and liked for many years. The theme was corruption; everyone had his hand out and was taking something for himself. The Cold War was over, but the departments kept the intelligence war going to keep themselves in jobs; the men at the top were setting themselves up for retirement with numbered accounts in Switzerland, while the field workers plugged on and were pensioned off with sixpence at the end.

Money was to be made. It was time Harrington thought about himself and his own future. He remembered it, sunning himself in the hotel garden. He very seldom examined his motives or allowed himself to think back to the days when he was straight. The suggesion had been cleverly timed. He had no prospect of real promotion; his work was stale and his bank account tended to show up in red. He was bored and afflicted with the restlessness of middle age, when the hair starts coming away on the comb and sex is once a week. He dabbled, very carefully at first, allowing himself to be firmly propositioned. The money was disproportionate to the effort. He took it, and the slope to serious treachery was only a gentle incline. They didn't need to blackmail him; Harrington was honest enough to dismiss that as an excuse. He had begun to enjoy being a double. His Swiss account grew, and his skill was being really tested; feelings of inferiority and resentments buried over the years began to exact vengeance on his colleagues.

He made crude jokes about Humphrey Grant in public and presented himself as a buffoon, well past his best. He took the UN job and set up a front with the Rumanian and the East German while he passed to the latter highly confidential information about Anglo-American intelligence within the United Nations countries. He was told to get drunk and seem to slip, to get himself recalled to London. He had found drinking all too easy; the habit had taken hold before he realized that it was an issue separate to following instructions. He had waited for weeks to bump into Davina Graham. And everything she did helped his pursuit of Ivan Sasanov for the KGB. Taking him with her was the final irony, the *humeur noire* that appealed to his sense of a malevolent fate manipulating men. It was a shame it had to be Davina. He opened his eyes and rubbed them; for a moment his vision swam black and gold after the sunlight.

He blinked at his watch; it was three-forty-five. One hour and a quarter before the cruise ship sailed. No message had come from Moscow. No acknowledgment of his two messages. He shrugged off fear; if they made a foul-up from their end it wasn't his fault. It wouldn't be his fault if he had to go to the captain of the ship and show him his authority to stop Davina and the others from going ashore. And he'd need that authority at sea. The captain wouldn't unquestioningly accept his word as had the receptionist and her husband in the hotel. He got up and went inside; he paused at the desk and looked inquiringly at the woman. She shook her head. Nothing. He called Antonyii Volkov a crude obscenity. And then he saw Davina coming in from the garden with Irina and Alexei Poliakov.

Tatischev was in his office with the decoded first message on the desk when the second call from the Crimea was decoded and put in front of him. The first had alarmed him enough; the urgency and openness of the second, demanding the arrest of three people, all referred to by code names, was impossible to implement without breaking into Volkov's safe and reading his files. He dared not take the responsibility. He put an urgent call through to Volkov's superior, the Director of State Security, in his magnificent dacha in the Usovo complex reserved for the members of the Politburo: General Igor Kaledin, who would not now appoint Antonyii Volkov as his successor as head of the KGB.

It was some time before Kaledin returned the Moscow call. He had been taking his ease on the reserved beach, dozing like a tortoise in the sun, when he was told there was a very urgent call from Volkov's assistant Major Tatischev. The major chewed a cigarette until the tobacco stung his mouth and he spat the pieces into the ashtray. He was frantically watching the time as he waited. Kaledin was old; he couldn't hurry back to the dacha. It was over half an hour before Tatischev was able to speak to him. He blurted out his account of the discovery of Volkov's body in Irina Sasanova's apartment. Yes, yes, he stuttered, the security police were already searching for her. A full report was being got ready and would be sent by dispatch rider to him at Usovo. But the two messages from Livadia were marked top priority, and already the time limit had elapsed; he didn't know whether to carry out the orders requested, and he had no knowledge of the agent signing himself Danton.

On his end of the line Igor Kaledin hesitated. He knew who Danton was: the Mole working in SIS Personnel in London, the Mole activated to find and pinpoint Sasanov for assassination. According to Volkov he had succeeded and the traitor had died in the fire at Halldale Manor. Danton was on the cruise ship. And he would have the last-resort weapon issued to all officers of the KGB. He hesitated, but only for a moment. Power shrouded him like an invisible mantle, a power so immense that only the occupant of Lenin's chair in the Politburo could countermand his orders. The messages referred to the Daughter, a male companion and a British agent who would be on the cruise ship *Alexander Nevsky*, bound for an evening stop at Sevastopol. Without access to Volkov's private records, there was no way of knowing who they were.

"You say the cruise ship has left Yalta? Yes; radio an order to the ship's captain. Tell him to act immediately when requested by a member of the State Security Service who is a passenger on the ship. And no one is to be allowed to leave the ship at Sevastopol until the officer makes himself known. Open General Volkov's private safe and have his files ready for inspection. I am coming back to deal with this myself. One more thing . . ." He let a pause develop, while Tatischev sweated blood for fear he had done something wrong. "One more thing, Major. Take all necessary action to maintain security over General Volkov's murder. Remove all witnesses. There must be no scandal. When Irina Sasanova is

found, have her brought to the office so that I can question her myself."

He hung up, and Tatischev slammed down the receiver. He grabbed
the bunch of keys on their silver key ring, the keys which he had seen
Volkov use and which never left his possession. Each was numbered. He
rushed through to the General's private office where his safe was kept.

"What am I going to do?" Davina whispered the question to herself.
"How am I going to stop him?"

The bedroom was stifling hot, the afternoon temperature was climbing
into the eighties, and she had been walking up and down as if she were in
a cage. For a moment when she was in despair, she thought of Sasanov,
waiting in England, trusting and hoping, and forced herself to be calm, to
try to think ahead.

There was no need to put the evidence together, to justify by careful
reasoning her suspicion that Peter Harrington was a traitor. The final
proof was in her hand.

She had been so angry that she shook as if she had a fever; she threw
the thing she had discovered hidden in the lining of her bag onto the floor,
where it glowed red in a patch of sunlight.

Then she stopped and picked it up, and put it into the pocket of her
dress. "A gun," she said to herself. "If only I had a gun." But there was
no gun, and she wouldn't have known how to use it if there were one. The
sense of helplessness was so frustrating that her eyes filled with tears and
she dashed them angrily away. She called herself a fool, a fool wasting
time imagining how she could outface a man trained to kill or cripple
with one blow.

Cunning, not false heroics: that was the only way to get Irina Sasanova
and the boy to safety. She recognized that, and accepted that it could be
done only if she remained behind. She looked at herself in the mirror; the
face seemed strange to her, hollow-cheeked, the tanned skin taut, great
shadows around her eyes. She hadn't prayed since her childhood, but she
did so then, in a whisper. "Dear God, give me the courage. Don't let me
think about it. Just make me brave."

Then she opened the door and went out and downstairs to look for the
girl and the boy.

They took a bus to the port; she sat with Irina, while Harrington and
Poliakov found seats in front. Harrington was in a talkative mood; he
kept up a flow of Russian to the young man. She hoped he didn't notice

how quiet and uneasy Poliakov seemed. Beside her, Irina stared out the
window; her bright prettiness had gone since Davina had found her in the
garden. She looked sallow and she bit her lower lip with nerves. God,
Davina pleaded, don't let him notice anything . . . don't let him suspect. . . .

They got off at the port, and Peter Harrington took her arm.

"There's the *Alexander Nevsky,*" he said. "Nice ship, isn't she? The
two of them seem very glum—he hardly said a word."

"Not surprising," Davina said. "You never drew breath. They're just
terribly nervous, that's all. I nearly passed out myself at lunchtime."

"I know," he said. "But you mustn't worry. Everything's going to go
smoothly. I feel very confident."

"You didn't this morning," she reminded him. Keep talking to him, act
normally, whatever happens. "You were paranoid about the wretched
young man," she went on. "You frightened the life out of me talking
about Spencer-Barr working for the other side—no wonder I went at the
knees! What's made you so optimistic all of a sudden?"

"Don't be cross," he murmured, bending toward her. She caught a
waft of alcohol on his breath—people were wrong when they said vodka
didn't smell. "I just got worried, that's all. I've got nerves, too, you know.
He's all right, I realized that after a bit. I just don't like the unexpected in
this business. And I'm sure that little creep isn't what he's supposed to be.
I'm going to have a good dig round when we get back."

"Yes," Davina said slowly, "I should do that."

Igor Kaledin sat leaning forward, his elbows on Volkov's desk, bifocal
glasses on the humpy bridge of his nose. He was a heavy pipe smoker and
there was a bank of blue smoke above his head. He had finished reading
the file on Sasanov that Volkov had written up himself and kept locked
away. It was open at the last page of entries. Antonyii Volkov was known
to be secretive, greedy for exclusive credit, but not even Kaledin had
appreciated how he operated until he read the papers. Everything had
been run off the copier by Volkov himself; all tapes of calls, interviews
and messages were kept in duplicate in his private safe and placed on
general file only when the project was successful. And not all of them
were, as Kaledin discovered, skimming through other files whose code
names he recognized. Any evidence damaging to Volkov had been destroyed. Only what damaged others was included in his official reports.
Kaledin refilled his pipe and lit it, puffing the strong-smelling tobacco

smoke; the back of his leathery neck was a dull red, and the red of mounting anger glowed in his little eyes behind the glasses.

The defection of Ivan Sasanov had been a major political disaster to the Politburo; its propaganda value to the West had not been fully exploited by British Intelligence, who had obliged the Russians with a faked-up corpse. And Kaledin knew that Sasanov would need a period of negotiating with his hosts before he decided to tell them what he knew. And what he knew was of such vital importance that the Mole, Danton, had been recalled from New York and set to work in the SIS headquarters to try to find him. The fire bomb at Halldale Manor seemed to have succeeded; this was the point in the file where Kaledin's blood pressure started to rise in proportion to his anger. Volkov had not believed it, but he had kept this opinion to himself. And he had concealed Danton's confirmation of that opinion. He had told no one that he knew Sasanov had survived. The enormity of what he had done and what he had risked showed the immensity of his ambition. And that ambition was stated in his own neat handwriting, in the notations which were a kind of personal journal, never intended for anyone to read and gloat over but Volkov himself.

He was aiming for Kaledin's crown. To bring the Soviet Union's most damaging defector in twenty years back to Russia would prove his worth and Igor Kaledin's incompetence. And for this he had arrested Fedya Sasanova. An act which had it come to light would have proved conclusively that her husband was alive and working with the West. But the arrest had been kept a secret, as secret as the detailed and repellent account of his seduction of the daughter. Kaledin had not the slightest objection to any form of pressure, mental or physical, being applied for a political end. The hideous cruelty practiced on dissidents in the special psychiatric hospitals had his full approval, but he operated on two levels in respect of his officers' conduct. Political expediency justified any aberration; abuse of power to satisfy degrading personal tastes brought the whole organization into disrepute. It mocked the symbolism of the shield that was the badge of the KGB, the defender of the State against its enemies outside and within. The old man growled with rage at what he read. To frighten and blackmail the daughter, to hold the mother hostage—these were recognized gambits in the game Volkov was playing. But to pander to his base instincts, as part of that game, affronted Kaledin's puritan instincts. He detested degeneracy; he persecuted homosexuals on principle; he favored the death penalty for rape.

And so the plan progressed, each phase developing as Kaledin read

Danton's reports and details of the denouement planned at Sevastopol. Irina Sasanova, and the university tutor Poliakov, and a British woman agent masquerading as an East German tourist would be seized as they were about to embark on a yacht in the port falsely carrying Polish colors. Danton was to be allowed to escape and reach the yacht, returning to England to continue his work. The next and final phase in Volkov's plan was to negotiate with the SIS and the British government for the return of Sasanov in exchange for the freedom of his wife and daughter and the repatriation of the British woman agent. Danton had it on the best authority, that of the woman agent herself, that Sasanov was prepared to come back to Russia and submit to punishment to save his family.

It was all as neat as a jigsaw puzzle; all the complicated pieces fitted and merged to form the picture Antonyii Volkov wanted. An outstanding Soviet intelligence coup, masterminded and executed by his subordinate without Kaledin's knowledge. But the vital piece in his picture was being bundled into a grave within the confines of the KGB hospital at Kuntsevo. The head was missing from the hero figure in the completed puzzle. Volkov had foreseen every eventuality except the one which had overtaken him in Irina Sasanova's bed. Kaledin shut the file. He looked at his watch and calculated. The cruise ship was on its way. The captain had received his radio message. Nothing could happen while he made up his mind what course to take.

13

Sasanov noticed that the American observer did not appear again after the first day's session. The courteous Southerner had been introduced to him briefly, and had sat down at the table between Kidson and the naval captain from the Ministry of Defence. He made notes; Sasanov knew the recordings of the sessions would be copied on tape and given to him for dispatch to Washington. He didn't ask questions; after only one morning and afternoon he was absent from the debriefing and didn't appear in the dining room. The next morning Sasanov asked Kidson where he was. Kidson looked very tired; he was his calm and pleasant self, but there were signs of strain.

"He was called back suddenly," he told the Russian. "Some internal crisis or other. We're sending them the tapes and they're happy with that for the moment."

Sasanov frowned.

"That is strange," he said. "They made so much of having their man here in person. Why didn't someone come out to replace him?"

"No doubt someone will," Kidson parried. "It doesn't worry me if they're not here in the flesh. I find them a difficult mixture. That chap, for instance. Old-World charm and Southern-gentleman approach to everything, and underneath it I'd say he was totally unscrupulous. I never liked their strong-arm tactics."

"Maybe not," Sasanov said. "But we respected them. More than your service. You don't like killing enemy agents and you'd rather let your own

traitors escape to Russia than put them on trial. We have never understood you. I don't understand you, either."

"You understand us better than you make out," Kidson said. "You'd
give yourself up to save your family and Davina Graham. You threw
your life and your career away because of what was done to your friend. I
can't imagine our colleague from Langley doing either." There was bitterness in his voice.

He said to Sasanov, "We're due to start in ten minutes. You go down to
the conference room and I'll join you."

When Sasanov had gone he went to the window and opened it. The
warm summer air fanned his face; his head throbbed with the painful
migraine that plagued him when he was under stress. He knew the CIA
would not be sending another representative to Hampshire. They would
get the tapes and that was all.

The Brigadier's disclosure that there was a leak to the KGB had
prompted them to activate their agent Spencer-Barr ahead of White's
revised plan.

Their reaction had produced an overkill response—literally, because
Spencer-Barr had arranged the murder of Volkov so that the escape from
Sevastopol could take place. The instructions sent to him to change the
escape route had cited Volkov's lone-wolf method of operating. This had
given the CIA man in Moscow the idea of stalling a KGB arrest by
murdering the man who was to give the order. Spencer-Barr had ignored
his instructions from London and obeyed Washington instead. Without
knowing that the source of the leak and the real danger to Irina Sasanova
was waiting for her in Livadia, he had transmitted the original British
plan for the escape by sea, and delivered everything into the hands of
Peter Harrington. And there was nothing London could do to stop it.
Even Spencer-Barr's confession that he had included a warning of KGB
penetration would be passed to the Soviet agent in person. He and Grant
had combined with the security chief in the Moscow embassy; from
Spencer-Barr's admissions and the evasive answers of the Southern gentleman from Langley, details of the disaster had been pieced together.

There was no means of warning Davina Graham and the two young
Russians that they were joined up with a KGB agent; no time to obtain a
pass to the Crimea and send someone out. It was already July 25 and the
cruise ship *Alexander Nevsky* would be docked in the port and waiting to
take on its passengers. The NATO submarine would have set out from
Turkey and be on its way to the rendezvous point in the Black Sea.

The machinery had been started on its complicated program; he and his Chief and Grant could only sit helplessly in the English countryside while Harrington drew the net around his victims. Kidson was not a man of fierce emotions; he was opposed to extremes in any form; he prided himself on not hating anyone. But he hated Peter Harrington enough to kill him. Not just for the failure his Service would suffer; that was the least of his reasons for wanting a fellow human dead. But for the waste of Sasanov, whom he had grown to respect and like, and for the two young people fleeing tyranny. And for the woman who had amazed them all by showing her capacity for loving and inspiring love. All of them would be destroyed in their different ways, their sacrifices wasted. He closed his eyes, the migraine making him feel nauseated. He had spent all night with Grant searching for a way to warn Davina Graham. A call from Moscow to her personally would alert Harrington at once; all calls were monitored, especially those to foreigners, and there were no agents within a hundred-mile radius of the resort. She was as effectively isolated from the outside world as if she were marooned at sea. They had driven themselves to despair during the night, and found no solution. It was vital to keep Sasanov in ignorance that their plans had gone wrong. He had been puzzled by the disappearance of the American observer; the gentleman had been flown home with the Brigadier's personal protest to the Director in Washington, and there would be no replacement at this stage. And ahead, thought Kidson, feeling his aching forehead, was the task he dreaded most, and no one else but he could do it. Telling Sasanov that they had lost them all.

The NATO submarine surfaced at 5 A.M. that Saturday; its scanners reported clear skies above. Within two hours the hull sections of the yacht had been assembled, the mast fixed into place and the small but powerful motor secured astern. The SAS captain and his crew were in shorts and sweat-shirts; they looked very bronzed and fit. Automatic weapons and grenades were stowed away in the bottom of the boat in a wicker picnic basket. They launched her from the side of the sub; the sea was calm, but a fresh breeze was blowing south-southwest.

The young captain's name was Fergus Mackie; he was twenty-seven and his last tour of duty had been undercover in the bandit territory of Armagh on the Ulster border. He grinned briefly at the sub's commander.

"Thank you, sir, all ready to set off. We'll rendezvous with you at twenty-two hundred hours. If anything goes wrong we'll send the pre-arranged signal; otherwise give us an hour's grace."

"Fine." The naval commander saluted him. "We'll be waiting for you. Good luck."

Mackie turned to his crew. "Cast off," he said. "Start motor and get out of here before she submerges."

The yacht swung to starboard and skimmed some hundred yards away from the long dark body of the submarine.

"Stop the motor," Mackie said. "Hoist sails. There she goes!"

The submarine slid under the surface, and her wake spread fanwise from where she had been. The yacht bobbed up and down on it. Mackie's lance corporal was another Scot, Bob Ferrie, a small, terrierlike man. He said to his officer, "Makes ye feel like a child abandoned by its mother, sir, seein' her go like that."

"How would you know?" Mackie grinned at him. "You never had a mother. Come on, let's get her set on course. From now on we sail; we've got plenty of time and the wind's just right."

"Lovely day for a sail, sir," the third of his men called out.

"Certainly is," was the reply. "Let's make the most of it. Run up the Polish flag."

The *Alexander Nevsky* was one of the smaller ships of the Moldiva Line; she carried a crew of eighty and accommodated up to two hundred passengers. She plied the coast route around the Black Sea ports, from Tibesk in the north around to Yalta, and from there she stopped at the picturesque seaside resorts of Bukim, Talinin, Sevastopol. She was a well-equipped vessel, with cheerful décor and pleasant bars; there were an organizer for deck games and the inevitable Intourist guides for the excursions ashore. The trip around to Sevastopol included a dance and dinner for those passengers who planned to visit Sevastopol in the morning tour. The ship stayed overnight and returned to Yalta the following day.

Peter Harrington went to the bar on the sundeck; he ordered a Stolichnaya vodka—the lethal Russian ninety proof—and a dish of pickled cucumbers and onions.

"Have some," he suggested to Davina and the young couple. "Wonderful stuff—nearly blows your head off! It was Stalin's secret weapon at the Yalta Conference." He lowered his voice. "He got that old idiot Roosevelt drunk on this and he got Poland and half Germany given to him on a plate." He put his head back and laughed.

"Please," Poliakov whispered to him, "don't talk like that." He gave a nervous glance around them; nobody was sitting near, but the barman was looking at them.

Harrington patted his knee. "Don't worry, my friend. Nobody can hear me. Sure you won't have some?"

Poliakov shook his head. "I think we'll go on deck," he said. He took Irina's arm and led her firmly away toward the door.

"He doesn't approve of me," Harrington remarked. "Have a sip," he said to Davina.

She didn't want to take the glass, but he insisted. She barely touched the vodka. Using the glass after him disgusted her.

"Don't you think you should be careful?" she said. "That's practically pure alcohol."

"I'm only going to have one," he said. "Just to send the butterflies in my stomach to sleep. What's happened to yours, Davy? You look like the village schoolmistress, all prim and pursed up. It doesn't suit you."

"Getting drunk doesn't suit you either," she retorted. "I'm going on deck, too."

"Wait a minute." He reached out and caught her arm. "What's the matter with you? You've been snapping my head off every minute. I'm not going to get drunk! What sort of bloody fool do you think I am?" he whispered angrily.

Davina pulled herself free of him. "I don't know," she said. "What sort of a bloody fool *are* you? You tell *me*?"

She turned and walked away. She had to get away from him; everything he did maddened and disgusted her, and it was showing. While he sat playing the fool, acting out his threadbare part for their benefit, she had longed to strike the glass of vodka out of his hand.

He wasn't going to get drunk; he was just fortifying himself for the moment when he betrayed them. She stood by the ship's rail, looking down at the blue water crested with white foam as it rushed away from the sides.

She took in a deep breath to steady herself. The sun was gloriously hot, and the clean sea breeze whipped at her hair. She mustn't do this; she mustn't show her feelings or he might suspect something. She had to go back to the bar and find him and stay at his side until they docked at Sevastopol. First she needed a final word with Irina.

"You know what you've got to do?"

Irina nodded. "Yes. We'll do it. But we're worried about leaving you."

"You mustn't think about it," Davina said. "I'll come after you. But you must use what I gave you only if the worst happens. You understand that?"

"Yes," Irina said.

"I want you to do something else, a favor," Davina said quietly. "If I don't get to the yacht, when you see your father would you give him a message from me?"

"Of course," the girl said. She looked unhappy. "I don't like to do this—nor does Alexei. . . ."

"Just tell your father I send him my love."

Irina Sasanova looked up sharply. "I send him my love." *Ich habe ihm meine Liebe geschickt*: the words had only their literal meaning in German; they were not used in any other context. And she saw the truth in the other woman's eyes, and the film of tears that made them brighter.

Her love . . . Suddenly she understood the deeper meaning of the risk that this woman was taking to make sure that she and Alexei got away. She laid her hand on Davina's and said gently, "I will tell him . . . but you will escape, too."

"If I don't see you again," Davina murmured, "good luck. Say goodbye to your friend for me. And whatever you do, don't hesitate and don't look back for me."

Then she turned and walked quickly away from them. With the back of her hand she wiped the tears that had slipped onto her cheeks, and squared her shoulders. She made her way back to the bar and to the table where Peter Harrington was sitting. He looked up and smiled at her. She smiled down at him.

"Had a breath of fresh air?" he asked. "Not feeling so cross with me?"

"I'm sorry," she said. "I just get upset when you drink too much. Get me a glass of wine, will you? Then we might do a tour of the ship."

He looked genuinely pleased; she marveled at his ability to deceive. He hurried to the bar and came back with a glass of chilled white Crimean wine. He reached out and took her hand. She did nothing when he squeezed it.

"You know something? I hate getting on the wrong side of you. You're a funny girl, Davy; I'm not surprised Ivan the Terrible fell for you. You may not realize it, but you've done a lot for me. You've made me feel I'm worth something still. That's why it's so important to me that we bring this off. I want to shine for you; you know that?"

"You want to get away with a whole skin and so do I," she retorted, forcing herself to sound friendly. "And those poor kids outside."

"Where are they, by the way?" He asked it very casually.

"I saw them outside on deck," she said. "Wandering round holding hands."

"Love's young dream," he said. "She's not bad-looking; bit on the heavy side for me. I like them slim. If she had your figure, she'd be quite something. Tell me, is she anything like Ivan?"

"Not to look at," Davina said. "Just an expression sometimes."

"And are you really never going to see him again?"

"I told you. No. I signed an undertaking."

"I bet that was Grant's idea," he said sourly. "Miserable fairy, that's what he is. If you never see Ivan again, then you might possibly consider me as a second best. . . . You don't think I'm serious, do you?"

"No," she said pleasantly, hating him and trying not to wrench her hand away. "If I said yes, you'd run for your life. But I'm not going to, so don't worry. Why don't we go and explore the ship?"

"Good idea. Why don't you leave your bag with the barman instead of carrying it round? Here, I'll take it." Harrington heaved himself up. She wondered whether he had drunk a second glass of vodka while she was out on deck. He didn't seem quite steady. She let him take the Hermes handbag and give it to the man behind the bar. Then they went out on deck.

The yacht was in sight of Sevastopol harbor; there had been a good steady wind and they had made faster time than expected. Mackie dropped anchor and furled the sail. He and his men unpacked food and drink and lay sunbathing and picnicking in good view of watchers from the shore. The boat bobbed on a steady swell, whipped by the wind. Mackie looked at his watch, and after twenty minutes Bob Ferrie reported a passenger ship to starboard, heading for the harbor. Mackie crouched in the scuppers and trained binoculars on her.

"It's the cruise ship," he said. "Right on time. Pull up anchor and make sail; we'll tack about till she's docked. Then we make for the port."

14

The captain of the *Alexander Nevsky* had received his radio instructions just before they docked. No passengers were to be allowed ashore; he was to follow any orders given by an accredited KGB officer who was among the passengers. He sent a message back acknowledging receipt of the signal, and gave his first officer orders to keep everyone on board. Passengers joining the ship at Sevastopol were to be admitted, but no one was to leave. The first officer went on deck to supervise the lowering of the gangway and to post a petty officer and two seamen, one of them armed, at the top.

Harrington and Davina were standing on the upper deck; they watched the ship ease into position and dock. She had hooked her arm through his and was unaware of how tightly she was holding on. He stepped away from the rail. He smiled, and the tone of his voice was very casual.

"We'll be off any minute now," he said. "They're getting the gangway into position."

The loudspeaker announcement brayed out just as he finished speaking. She felt him go rigid.

"What is it? What are they saying?"

"Ssh, wait—I can't hear . . ." And then he said, "Oh Christ," and she saw the mask of apprehension cover his second's exposure of relief.

"What's the matter?" she whispered. "What is it?"

"They've stopped passengers from going ashore," he said. "Oh Christ, that's really done it. We'd better get the other two and stick together. Listen, I'll go and see what I can find out. It may be just till the people joining the ship have come aboard. We could still make the harbor in time. Go and find them; I'll go to the bridge and see what the score is."

Davina watched him hurry away. Not to the bridge but to the bar and to the handbag left there for safekeeping. Irina and Alexei were waiting around the bulkhead out of sight. She ran to find them. The gangway was fixed in position. The two seamen and the petty officer were grouped at the top, and a chain spanned the opening.

She called to Irina, "Now quickly! Tell him for God's sake not to seem hesitant. Hurry!" Then she went back to the rail, gripping it with hands that trembled. She hardly dared to watch what happened when Alexei Poliakov and Irina Sasanova went to the head of the gangway.

Harrington rushed up to the barman.

"The lady's handbag," he demanded.

The man shook his head. He resented the foreigner's tone. "It's not here," he said sourly.

Harrington stared at him. "What do you mean? I left it with you before we went on deck!"

"She came back for it," the barman said. "I gave it to her."

Harrington started to swear at him and then stopped. Steady, he told himself. Steady. Volkov got your message; they've closed the ship; they can't get away. They'll be arrested any minute. But you need that handbag, just in case. And then he paused again, remembering that he hadn't seen Davina carrying it since she left the bar.

He turned back to the surly young Russian.

"Are you quite sure you gave it to the right woman? The one sitting here with me?"

"Quite sure," came the answer. "A German woman; she was the one drinking in here with you, Comrade; I gave her back her bag."

"When?" Harrington demanded.

"About half an hour ago." The barman turned his back on Harrington and began replacing bottles on the shelf above. Harrington swung around; he hurried outside and toward the bridge. A seaman on duty barred his way. He snapped at him in Russian.

"I must see the captain. Official business."

"I am sorry. No one is allowed onto the bridge."

Harrington took a deep breath and said, "I am an officer of the KGB."

The seaman stiffened. "I can't let you pass without your authority, Comrade."

Harrington didn't waste time arguing. He said, "You'll regret obstructing me," and turned away. He found Davina leaning on the rail where he had left her.

Alexei Poliakov had marched straight up to the petty officer standing by the top of the gangway. His expression was grim, and there was an arrogance in his approach that put the petty officer on his guard. Irina was at his heels. He spoke to the man in a low, sharp voice.

"Open the gangway! KGB."

The officer glanced down at the palm opened in front of him and saw the red identity card flick open and shut faster than an eye could blink. He came to attention and saluted. He snapped at the seaman on the left, and they immediately unhooked the chain.

Alexei caught Irina by the arm and they reached the quay. The petty officer didn't watch them; the chain was replaced and he kept his eyes inward on the ship. No one in his senses queried the holder of the red card, with its shield and crossed swords on the front. At least no one of his rank. And you didn't peer after them either. You did what you were told and you minded your own business. The holder of the KGB card was the one Soviet citizen to whom the rules never applied.

"Where are Irina and Alexei?" Harrington asked her.

Davina turned around from the rail. "I couldn't find them," she said.

He looked shocked and strange for a moment. "What do you mean? Where's your bag?"

"I don't know," she said again. "Why?"

The effort he made to keep calm was so great that it showed in the deep breath he took, the deliberate unclenching of his hands.

"I went to get it from the bar, and he said you'd already collected it. Where is it?"

She shrugged; she felt extraordinarily brave, reckless. They had got away. She'd seen them disappearing into the crowds on the dock. The handbag, with its ripped-out lining, was floating somewhere out at sea.

"I must have left it behind when I went to the ladies' loo," she said. "I thought you were going to the bridge, to find out what had happened. What's all the fuss about my bag?"

"No fuss," he said slowly. "I couldn't get on the bridge. Listen, there's something very important in your bag. I must get it. I put it there for safekeeping."

I'm sure you did, she taunted him inwardly. And you'll never guess who used it just now to get off the ship.

"I'll go and look for it," she said. "Why don't you go and look for Irina and Alexei? I won't be long; meet me back here."

She dawdled on her way to the toilets; she didn't bother to go inside. She gave herself ten minutes and then went back. He was not at the ship's rail. She found a deck chair and sat down; she had cigarettes and matches in the pocket of her dress—the pocket where she had hidden his KGB card before she gave it to Alexei. She lit a cigarette and leaned back, closing her eyes. The exhilaration drained out of her, leaving a cold little flutter of fear in its place. Something had certainly happened; some move had been made against them when the passengers were not allowed to leave. There was nothing more she could do but wait . . . wait for the inevitable. There was no hope of getting to the yacht without Harrington, even if the embargo was not connected with them and was lifted in time. And it wouldn't be. Tourists were being allowed to come aboard; there were a lot of them and the process was slow. By now Irina and Poliakov must have reached the yacht marina on foot. It was already too late for her. She sat in the deck chair as the last of those embarking came on board, and the sun began to set.

There was a chill in the air and she shivered. In the restaurant on the second deck the orchestra began to tune up. The dancing would begin quite soon. She got up and went to the rail again; she looked at her watch. The yacht should be well on its way out to sea by now—unless Harrington had got to the captain and they had been intercepted. She closed her eyes and prayed again, very simply, Dear God. Don't let it happen. Let them get away. And when she saw Peter Harrington coming toward her, she knew by the sag of his shoulders and the hesitation in his step that the prayer had long been answered.

"There!" Alexei dragged Irina to a stop. "There they are—look!"

There were many yachts moored in the marina; most of them were large motor-cruisers; a few were small, privately owned. East European flags abounded, flying the hammer and sickle alongside out of courtesy to the host port. Rumanian, East German, Hungarian and Polish. There were three Polish vessels: a big oceangoing motor cruiser; a smaller type with two women enjoying the last of the sunshine; and a small, sleek, single-masted yacht, with three men on board. The Polish flag fluttered in a brisk little breeze blowing in from the sea.

"It must be they," Alexei insisted. "Women wouldn't be on board and that's a very big boat next to them. It's that little yacht—I'm sure!"

They moved closer to the edge of the long jetty; Irina pulled off the bright-yellow handkerchief she wore on her head. One of the men on the little yacht was watching the marina, and seemed to be watching them. She shook the little scarf out and waved it in her right hand. Instantly the man in the yacht waved back.

"It is they," she whispered to Alexei. "It is . . ."

Mackie was waving at them, grinning; it was a recognition of friends so far as the spectators were concerned.

Irina was amazed to hear a voice from the boat shout in Polish, "Hey, there! We thought you weren't coming—jump into the dinghy."

They lowered the little rubber dinghy; one man pulled on the mooring rope to bring himself and the dinghy alongside the jetty. He held out a hand to Irina Sasanova. He had a brown face and bright-brown eyes, white teeth showing in a broad smile.

"Hold tight and step in," he said in Polish.

She caught the hand; the grip was like an iron band, the muscles of his arm swelled under her full weight as he helped to swing her into the dinghy. She swayed and almost lost her balance till he lowered her onto one side of it. He reached out for Alexei Poliakov and helped him down. Then he began to haul on the rope to bring them alongside the yacht. Hands helped them climb aboard; nobody spoke, but to her surprise Mackie put his arms around her and kissed her on both cheeks. The man in the dinghy was pulling himself back to the jetty. He tied up the dinghy and leaped ashore. The yacht was moored to a bollard; he pulled the rope loop free and threw it into the water. Then he jumped down into the dinghy, cast off and paddled the few yards to the yacht. It was done so quickly and with so little effort that people on the jetty didn't have time to offer help. He swung himself up and into the yacht; the dinghy was hoisted aboard and made fast at the stern.

Irina and Alexei were given glasses; there was a brief touching of them, as if they were drinking a toast, and then Mackie nodded to Bob Ferrie and mouthed the words "Start engine. Raise anchor." The throbbing sound drowned their whispers. They were asked, in Polish, "Where are the others?" and Irina answered, "They didn't get away. One of them was a traitor. The other one stayed behind to help us. Don't wait; she said you must hurry as fast as you can."

She hid her face against Poliakov and began to cry silently as the anchor was pulled aboard and the yacht swung its sharp prow out to sea. From the moment she had waved her handkerchief until they cut the engine and hoisted sail as they left the harbor, fewer than fifteen minutes had passed. It seemed to her and to Alexei as long as every moment of their lives. Only the crew appeared cheerful and relaxed; they were laughing and making remarks to each other in what she guessed was English. The one who spoke Polish brought out sweaters for his companions and one each for them.

"It will get cold," he said. "We've got about two hours' sailing ahead of us. Let's hope the wind holds. Do you want anything to eat?"

"No, thank you," Alexei said. He pulled Irina closer to him. "Where are we going?"

The man asked a question of the big crewman who had embraced Irina. Mackie nodded. "You can tell them. No harm in them knowing."

"We're going to a pickup point just outside Bulkina, near the promotory. It will be dark by then and we'll find our sub waiting for us. We'll be in Midina by tomorrow morning. Sit tight, now, we're getting a really good wind." He grinned down at the girl and the young man. They looked drawn and exhausted and the girl was still wiping her eyes. "Don't worry," he said. "Everything's going to be fine."

"What did she say about the others?" Mackie asked him.

"Said one of them was working for the Russians. The other stayed behind and let them get away. She said 'she,' so it must be a woman. Bloody brave, sir. I wouldn't fancy being caught by that lot."

"Nor would I," Mackie said. "So let's keep her running, in case they send something nice and fast in pursuit. The sooner we get inside that sub the better!"

Darkness came upon them quite suddenly; two powerful lights beamed out from the yacht's prow; they were flying before a strong wind, the spray shooting up on either side of them. Irina huddled inside Alexei's arm.

"I can't believe it," she whispered. "I can't believe we're going to get away . . . I keep thinking of her, Alexei. If only I could pray to something for her. They'll shoot her, won't they?"

"No," he whispered, comforting her. "No, they won't do that. I believe in God, Irina. I've been a Christian for a long time. I have been praying for her ever since we left. Shut your eyes, my darling, and try to sleep."

After a while he sensed that she had indeed drifted away. Banks of clouds covered the moon; when the wind blew them apart, the moon shone briefly on them, and he could see how wan and exhausted she looked. He couldn't sleep himself; the little ship was cutting throught the seas, but she was pitching and he was feeling sick. As they came in sight of the promontory, guided by the slow flashing of its yellow lighthouse beam, the wind dropped. The yacht was in total darkness, its headlights extinguished while they were out at sea. Mackie had the motor started, and they began to move across the steady water, making a wide sweep around the promotory; then the engines cut out, and they used what little wind there was to track to and fro within the same area. Mackie checked the time; they were only twenty minutes behind schedule. The waiting sub would pick them up on her scanner, and surface. Irina had wakened; she sat beside Poliakov in the stern. The crew were silent, maneuvering the little yacht.

They didn't see her surface; the clouds were dense, the blackness was impenetrable. They heard the rush and gurgle of the seas as they parted, and a hooded light winked in signal. Ferrie uncovered his signal lamp and rapidly acknowledged. The yacht began to move toward the light, and the shape of the submarine became apparent, with men moving on her deck. More lights came on, carefully hooded and dimmed against reflection, guiding the yacht close up. The sea was calm and it was possible to launch the dinghy and lower Irina into it, followed by Alexei, who was dizzy with seasickness. The Polish-speaking crewman paddled to the sub's black sides, threw up a rope, which was caught, and caught in turn a flexible ladder.

He heaved the Russian girl up with his shoulder under her buttocks, until she was clinging to the ladder, inching her way within reach of the seaman above, who grabbed her wrists and pulled her up. Poliakov was more athletic. The spray slapping against the submarine soaked them to the skin. Men shepherded them to the conning tower and down the open hatch into the belly of the ship. The dinghy went back to the yacht; the wicker basket containing the arms and grenades was loaded in, secured on a rope and hauled aboard the sub. Mackie gave the order to scuttle; Bob Ferrie opened the sea cocks, then both men dived overboard and swam to the parent submarine. They climbed the ladder, joining the Polish-speaking corporal, who was deflating the dinghy

"Chuck that back in." The naval commander came up to them. "Let's get below and under way."

The dinghy was heaved back into the sea, air hissing from its open tubes. The yacht was settling down by the stern. The SAS commandos didn't wait to see her go. They scrambled up to the conning tower and down the hatch. Five minutes later the submarine slid gently below the surface. Inside it, watched by Irina and Alexei Poliakov, the commander shook Fergus Mackie and his men by the hand. The two young Russians were each given cups of very strong sweet tea laced with brandy. They looked at each other, and at the men who had rescued them, and began to laugh and cry at the same time.

"They are not on the ship. We have searched everywhere, and there's no place they could be hiding."

Harrington faced the captain; the captain looked uneasy. He was in a weak position, made weaker still by his delay in seeing what he now knew to be a very senior KGB officer. Radio confirmation of his claim had come in from Moscow, and while the dancers jigged and shuffled under the fairy lights on deck his men had searched the ship from stem to stern, looking in the smallest possible spaces where a person could hide, and had found no sign of the missing girl and the young man. The petty officer on duty at the gangway stood stiffly in front of them and swore he had not allowed any passengers to disembark. The two seamen said the same. They were dismissed, and outside the captain's cabin the petty officer spoke low and briefly to them.

"Good lads. We didn't let any passengers through. The KGB aren't passengers. We know nothing and we say nothing, and we can't get into trouble. Remember, we'll lose our seaman's cards if anything gets out. Back to your posts!"

He wiped his sweating face with his sleeve and hurried away. Loss of his card meant that he would be unable to serve on any ship again. He could be sent to anyplace in the interior as a punishment, and put to any work. His men would suffer the same. Nobody was going to say anything when the KGB was involved, at least until the KGB asked the questions. He was not just being careful, he was being loyal. He went down to the mess deck and swallowed a vodka; it made him sweat even more, but it steadied his nerves.

In the cabin Harrington turned angrily on the captain.

"If they're not on board," he said, "then they've somehow got ashore. And you've let two dangerous criminals wanted by the Security Police escape from your ship. I wouldn't like to be in your place, Captain, when we get back to Yalta!"

"They could possibly have jumped overboard," the captain suggested. "But they would have been seen if we were near the harbor. Perhaps they did it at sea." He looked hopeful. "If they did, they would have drowned. The currents here are very strong outside the coastline."

"That's what you hope," Harrington snapped. He turned away in fury. They wouldn't have committed suicide by trying to swim ashore when they had no reason to think they would be detained on the ship like everybody else. If they jumped after the announcement prohibiting disembarkation, they would certainly have been seen. The ship was already docked; it was an impossible alternative. They must have got past the goons on the gangway; there was no other explanation. He lit a cigarette, his hand visibly unsteady. They had gone. That was the only fact. And because Davina Graham's bag had been stolen when she left it behind in the toilet, he had wasted all this time in making the captain check his credentials with Moscow. The lack of his red card had prevented him from having Davina and the other two arrested as soon as the ship docked. As soon as it became obvious that, apart from the one precaution, Volkov hadn't arranged anything to secure them, he had been frantic; and while he argued with the sailor at the bridge and searched for Davina's bag with his vital authority hidden in it, Irina Sasanova and her lover had slipped ashore. By what means nobody could tell, but they had vanished. Volkov had lost one of his major bargaining counters, but at least there was one left. He turned back to the captain.

"I want to speak to Moscow, ship to shore," he said. "And there's a woman on board I want arrested. She was concerned with these criminals. At least we won't lose her!" He threw Davina's passport on the table.

"Bring her in and have the Intourist man interpret for you. She doesn't speak Russian. I'll tell him what to ask her. And get that phone link through as soon as possible! I want a person-to-person call with Comrade General Antonyii Volkov, Department of Internal Security."

While Harrington waited, he gave a short sharp briefing on how Davina Graham was to be interrogated. And he remembered her telling him that she had always been terrified of enclosed spaces.

As soon as she saw the seamen coming toward her, Davina knew she was going to be arrested. She waited for them; they seemed to be moving in slow motion, like characters in a film running at half speed.

Her heart gave a series of rapid beats, as if it were lurching in her chest. The dread that overcame her was like paralysis; she didn't shake or move; she sat motionless and watched them coming nearer and finally stopping in front of her. She didn't understand the Russian words, but there was no mistake about the hands pulling her to her feet and closing in on either side of her, propelling her toward the companionway.

They took her to a cabin, and there were two men inside. One wore the uniform of a ship's captain and the second was the Intourist guide responsible for passengers. The guide spoke in German.

"Your passport and visa—where are they?" The tone was harsh, the faces around her coldly hostile.

"My husband has them." The speech had been rehearsed often enough. She knew it was all lies and useless, but there was nothing else to say.

"Your name, and details."

She said, "Gertrude Fleischer; my husband is Heinz Fleischer. We are citizens of the German Democratic Republic, on holiday at Livadia. What is wrong? Why have you brought me down here?" And then because it seemed the obvious thing to say, "Where is my husband?"

"Under arrest," the Intourist interpreter snapped. "Why do you not keep your passport and documents with you? Why do you say your husband has them? Why don't you carry them in your own handbag?"

The handbag. That's what they were after. The bag she had told Harrington must have been stolen because it wasn't in the toilet. It had vanished, like Sasanov's daughter and the tutor.

He swung away from her without a word of explanation. She stayed where she was, and then the seamen came. She wet her lips quickly with her tongue; they felt cracked and dry. She had been warned not to do that if she was questioned, it was a sign that the suspect was lying. But she wet her lips and answered.

"It's a good thing I didn't keep them in my bag. My bag was stolen this evening when I left it in the ladies' toilet."

"And you didn't report it?" the guide sneered at her. "You didn't report a theft immediately? Did you lose money? Why are telling lies, Frau Fleischer? Don't you realize you could be in serious trouble?"

He paused, and she felt the captain staring hard at her. Now she was beginning to shake; she knew she was looking frightened because there was a brief exchange of satisfied looks between the two men. And where was Harrington? Spying on them from the next-door cabin—waiting for her nerve to give way?

The questions were only a form of provocation. They knew who she was and why she was on board the ship. Harrington had told them. They would go on threatening her and accusing her of lying until she gave them all the satisfaction of breaking down.

I'll see you damned, she murmured to herself. I'm Gertrude Fleischer until that bastard comes face to face with me and says I'm not. And she squared her jaw and said in her most obstinate voice, "I am not lying. Why don't you send for my husband? He has my passport and all my papers."

Fear can take the form of reckless boldness. Her legs trembled under her, and her heart was flying around like a loose bird, hammering to get out; she folded her arms over it, as if to keep it close, and stared back at her interrogator. She didn't know it, but she looked very like her father as he stood on the bridge of his cruiser in the last war and set course for the enemy.

The Intourist guide spoke briefly to the captain. He nodded. When the man turned back to her there was open menace in his expression. He advanced a step toward her; he stabbed his forefinger at her, almost touching her face.

"If you won't cooperate with me, and the ship's captain," he said very loudly, "then you will be handed over to the Security Police when we reach Yalta. We are returning there immediately. You will be locked up till we dock and they come to take you away."

The place where she spent the next three hours was an old locker; it had no ventilation apart from the crack under the door, and no light. She felt around the walls with her hands and started taking long deep breaths to stop herself from panicking and screaming. There's no such thing as claustrophobia. It's just a cupboard. They're trying to frighten you into admitting that you're not Getrude Fleischer, and the minute you do that they'll really have you. They'll break you in pieces to find out how Irina and the boy escaped. And they haven't caught them, don't you realize that—otherwise they wouldn't need to do this to you. They'd have you all in together and gloat. So steady yourself. Look, there's a light shining under the door. Sit on the floor and get close to it. That's it, crouch down so you can see the light. You'll forget it's dark and so small in here because you can imagine the corridor outside. You'll hear someone pass in a minute. . . .

All right, then, cry, curse, talk to yourself. Do what you like, but stop thinking about the space. Breathe deeply, make your heart stop racing; it *can't* if you take deep breaths. Remember, that's what women are taught in natural childbirth, and they are able to relax and stay calm. Think about Sasanov—no, don't think about him or you'll start thinking about his wife and what's going to happen to you. . . . If you hold your breath long enough you can make yourself faint. Dear God, why don't I just pass out. There, someone's walking past you, you can hear them. Maybe they've come to let you out. . . .

When they did let her out, she blinked, her eyes stung by the light. She walked quite steadily along the passage in the bright artificial light, and in through the door into the cabin. And then she saw it wasn't a cabin but a closet, low-ceilinged and tiny. As the door slammed and the light went out, she heard herself scream before she buckled at the knees and fainted.

Igor Kaledin sipped his glass of hot tea. They had brought the samovar to Volkov's office, with cheese and savories, and a bottle of Polish brandy. The blinds were drawn and a clear light fell over his shoulder onto the papers piled in front of him. The rest of the office was in soothing semi-darkness. He had spent the whole day there, hunched over the records of Antonyii Volkov's seven years of tenure, piecing together the plan he had devised to give him Kaledin's post in the Politburo. The fact that he was dead didn't deflect the old man's anger; the fact that his death had caused a chain of circumstances due entirely to his treasonable secrecy was what enraged Kaledin. There had been no chain of command, no fail-safe for an emergency, such as his murder in a girl's flat. Danton's message had gone unanswered until it was too late to do anything effective about it. And by the time Kaledin had unraveled the identities of the people it referred to, the ship itself had docked, and, as the latest report handed in by Major Tatischev confirmed, two of the fugitives had got away and made their rendezvous. People had seen them in the marina, boarding the yacht with the Polish colors at its masthead. Just as Harrington's frenzied conversation on the ship-to-shore telephone had explained to Tatischev. The yacht had put to sea, and though they sent search planes to look for it, it was like hunting a pea in a featherbed. They would never be found, and doubtless the submarine that took them on board was well on her way to Turkish waters.

Far from bringing Sasanov back, Volkov's only accomplishment was to comfort him in his exile, by sending him his daughter. There was, of course, the Englishwoman; she was under arrest on the *Alexander Nevsky*. Harrington had assured the major that she was valuable, very valuable. Kaledin had listened with irritation to Tatischev's reports on the traitor's attempts to retrieve the situation. She would be valuable as an exchange, in due course, but not for Sasanov. Volkov's analysis stressed his devotion to his daughter and his wife. The woman was his lover, Harrington insisted. Kaledin shrugged the information aside. Men didn't give themselves up to save a woman they'd known for a few months. Sasanov had not made any move when his wife was arrested. The British wouldn't let him; they had obviously held out this rescue attempt as the bait to keep him on their side. The higher his hopes, the greater the reaction when they were disappointed. If Volkov had succeeded and the daughter joined the wife in the Gulag while the British agent answered questions in the Lubyanka, then Sasanov might have proved useless to his British hosts, and a deal could have been arranged. A man's commitment to his own safety, even to the ideals which had made him defect, wouldn't have stood up to that test. Especially not a man of sensitivity, like Sasanov, with his conscience rubbed raw by the death of Jacob Belezky. He had been a brilliant officer, but always hampered by his capacity for human feelings when those feelings were out of place.

Volkov had contrived a masterpiece of intelligence work, aided by Danton the Mole. His superior sat and drank his tea and pondered on how to make use of it. Major Tatischev waited in the shadows, perched on an angular modern chair. He didn't dare to interrupt or even to clear his throat while the second most powerful man in Soviet Russia sat in the swathe of light from the lamp behind the desk, drinking tea and brandy, looking like an aged tortoise gently falling asleep. Tatischev sneaked one hand over to his wrist and pushed the sleeve back. It was past midnight.

"Major?"

He jumped to his feet. "Yes, Comrade Director General."

"You will take a plane to Simferopol," Kaledin said. "You will go to the *Alexander Nevsky* and bring Danton and the Englishwoman back. Take them to the Lubyanka. Hold them there till I come. Send the woman to be interrogated."

The message came through from Turkey late on Sunday morning. It reached Grant just as he was going down to lunch in Hampshire. It came by special courier from the office in London, where the duty decoding officer had phoned for a dispatch rider as soon as he read it.

Grant read the message. It was a long one and it told him that at least part of the escape had been successful. Irina Sasanova and the university tutor were safe in Turkey and would be flown to London that evening.

Davina Graham had not got away; Peter Harrington was a Russian spy and an officer of the KGB. His identity card was in the young couple's possession. Grant folded the message and slipped it into his pocket. He was already five minutes late for lunch and he was meticulous about time. They hadn't tried to carry on with the debriefing since Friday. Sasanov was showing signs of great tension and anxiety; his concentration had suffered, and it was a waste of time. Kidson played chess with him and parried his demands for news. But they couldn't be fended off much longer. He knew they would soon hear of the success or failure of the operation.

Grant was sorry about Davina Graham. His regrets were quite impersonal; he had lost an agent and a colleague, and he felt the blow. His imagination did not dwell on what was happening to her. Instead it concerned itself with Peter Harrington, safe in Russia with his masters, joining the elite little band of Foreign Office traitors living in Moscow, awarded with dachas and special privileges for betraying their own country. Grant would have liked very much to resuscitate the old wartime assassination department. But Harrington would never suffer for what he had done.

Grant opened his door and hurried down to the dining room. He apologized to his colleagues for being late. As they left the room he stopped Sasanov.

"Come with me," he said. "We've had news." The Russian grabbed his arm; Grant was very thin, and the grip hurt him. He winced. "Upstairs," he said. "We can't discuss it here."

It was quite impossible, Grant explained later over the telephone. They couldn't deal with him. The Brigadier would have to come down and talk to him himself. James White apologized to his wife for disrupting their weekend, and set out for Hampshire.

It was not going to be easy; if Kidson and Grant between them hadn't been able to cope with Sasanov, then he had to take the responsibility. He frowned as he drove. "Frantic," was the word Grant had used, and it wasn't one of his usual adjectives. His daughter's escape hadn't pacified Sasanov. He was ranting and raving about what had happened to Davina Graham. Her loss was certainly a dreadful price to pay; he dreaded the visit to his old friend Captain Graham to tell him that his daughter was in Russian hands. He dreaded it, but as soon as he had settled Sasanov as well as possible he had to face that duty and go down to Marchwood.

He arrived at the Hampshire mansion in the late afternoon. He was calm and composed as always, but there were lines on his face which hadn't been visible before the weekend.

"Get her back," Ivan Sasanov said, "or you'll get nothing more from me."

"Don't you think we're going to try?" the Brigadier countered.

"I don't know!" the Russian said. "You sent her out because you wanted to dig up your Mole. You risked her life for your own purposes, nothing to do with my daughter, and she sacrificed herself to save Irina. So you give me Irina like a birthday present and think it's enough. It isn't," he said violently. He stood facing White; he glared down at him with eyes sunk deep in his head; his face was gray. "I will not speak another word to your experts until you get her back."

"You're asking the impossible," James White said. "And you know it. The only exchange they'll make for her is you. And that can't happen. We made a bargain. If the plan failed you could go back. It didn't. Our job was to get your daughter here and we've done it. What happened to one of our agents was only incidental to the deal we made."

"Not to me," Sasanov shouted at him. "Not to me! You think I will leave Vina in Volkov's hands? They have the two people I love—my wife and Vina! You call this operation a success? It's not a success for me." He turned away and dropped into a chair; he sank his head in his hands.

James White waited for a moment, then he said quietly, "Wait till your daughter gets here. We only know the bare facts. She'll be able to tell us exactly what happened. Then we can try and work something out. Will you try to be calm till she comes?"

He didn't like emotional displays. The tears running down Sasanov's face embarrassed him deeply. He coughed and looked around for Kidson. He was skilled at dealing with this kind of thing.

Kidson came to the rescue. He said, "This won't be much of a welcome for your daughter after all she's been through. You should think of her."

"I do," Sasanov muttered. "I'm glad she's safe. But she'll understand. Russians have hearts, Brigadier, not like you English."

James White glanced across at Kidson and shrugged. "You've made arrangements to bring them here direct from Heathrow, haven't you, John?"

"Yes." Kidson nodded. "The plane is due in about an hour. If they land on time we should have them up here this evening."

"I'll stay," the Brigadier said. "There's nothing more to be done or talked about, till we know the position exactly. I'll leave you, Colonel Sasanov. We'll talk again when you've seen your daughter."

Kidson came with him to the door and slipped outside.

"What the devil are we going to do?" James White whispered to him.

"I don't know," Kidson answered. "I'm afraid we're in for a very difficult time."

They gave Davina enough sedative to blanket the hysteria; she was able to walk to the plane with Harrington's assistance, followed by Tatischev and two KGB officers in civilian clothes. She was so disoriented that she accepted Harrington's help; she felt weightless, suspended; she knew she was walking, but her feet didn't feel in contact with the ground.

The flight was short, and somebody gave her something to drink that made her fall asleep. Harrington moved his seat as soon as she lost consciousness. He felt queasy and uncomfortable, but he consoled himself with the thought that it would all be done by drugs from now on. He calmed his nerves with a large vodka and tried to doze until they landed at Moscow. He stayed in his seat beside Tatischev while Davina was strapped into a wheelchair, covered in blankets and taken off the plane first. When he came down onto the tarmac there was no sign of her.

He turned to the major and said brightly, "Moscow at last! I've dreamed of this for years." The major's expression was stony; looking at him for approval, Harrington felt a spasm of alarm. The eyes were hostile, there was no welcoming smile on the tight mouth. He tried again. "I've always wanted to meet Kim Philby." The sky above them was bright blue with a battalion of fleece-white clouds advancing slowly toward the sun. Harrington looked up and wondered why he felt so cold.

"The car is waiting for us," Tatischev said. "Come."

They crossed the tarmac, and outside the airport building they entered a big black Volga. One of the KGB officers sat on the other side of Harrington. Tatischev took a cigarette and lit it; he stared out the window.

Harrington locked his hands to steady them. He felt his lips quivering as he asked the question. "Where are we going?"

Tatishev didn't turn around. "We are going to the Lubyanka. General Kaledin will see you there."

When Harrington began to shout and swear, the man beside him held a revolver to his side. Nothing was said, and he fell quiet.

* * *

When she opened her eyes the bright light in the ceiling seared as if she was staring into the sun. She closed them quickly, and a voice said in English, "You are awake, then. Would you like some tea?"

She didn't want to sit up, she wanted to slide back into the peace of her drugged sleep, but strong arms were pulling her upright, and then she was slapped sharply on the cheeks until she had to open her eyes because they were full of tears.

"Some tea?" the voice said again, and at last she focused on the speaker. She was quite young, very neat in her gray uniform, with brown hair braided around her head. She reminded Davina of a games mistress at her school, but then of course it couldn't be she; she wasn't at school, she was—where? She asked the question.

"You are in Russia," the interrogator said. Her English was easy to understand, as she had very little accent. Davina didn't want to drink the tea, but it was put into her hands and she sipped it. She discovered that she was very thirsty. Her head had begun to ache so badly that she felt sick. She wanted an aspirin and to lie down and go to sleep again. The woman had said she was in Russia. It seemed an odd place to be. What was her games mistress doing there? Miss Handley. Jill Handley, that was her name.

"Why are we in Russia, Miss Handley? Could I have some aspirins, I've got a terrible headache?"

The interrogator looked across at the man who had slapped Davina awake. "They've overdosed," she said in Russian. "It's impossible to get through to her till she comes out of this. She thinks I'm someone she knows." She scowled at her assistant. "How am I supposed to work when those idiots in Yalta send her back like this? I shall put in a report about it. Give her some painkillers and let her sleep through till the afternoon. I'll get Dr. Ivliev to give her a stimulant and shake her out of it. I'll come back at five o'clock." She got up and walked out of the cell.

"The bastards," Harrington muttered to himself, "after all I've done."

He had smoked through his last packet of cigarettes. The fact that he was waiting in one of the private offices had restored some of his courage. A cell would have demoralized him completely. After the initial shock of going into the Lubyanka building, he pulled himself together, his brain sharpened by fear. He wasn't to blame, but that wouldn't stop an old tyrant like Kaledin from blaming him just the same. Taking him to the Lubyanka instead of the KBG offices next door was a bad sign, not the way to welcome a retiring Soviet agent who had come to claim his reward after years of useful service. He alternated between terror and truculence, and either his bloody watch had stopped or the time was passing like a snail with a broken leg.

Kaledin was coming to interview him in person. He comforted himself with calling the head of the KGB every obscene name he could think of, and then rehearsed his excuses and reproaches all over again. Kaledin was a legend, a tyrant with human idiosyncracies, unlike the monster Beria and the chilling Shelepin. Harrington wondered what was happening to Davina; what the hell were they wringing out of her down in the interrogation center? He no longer felt distaste, least of all pity, for what she might be suffering. His only concern was whether she might be persuaded to cast doubts on him. Drugs took time, of course. You had to disorient the brain before you could manipulate the personality into saying whatever was suggested. Maybe they didn't want to waste time. Maybe they wanted answers quickly. In which case the little hors d'oeuvres in the ship's locker would seem like a party game compared to what they were doing to her at that moment.

He looked at his watch again; it was past five o'clock. He had been waiting for seven hours. There was a guard on the door outside. He went and sat down again, and depression washed over him; no cigarettes and no drink, nothing to calm the fears his imagination loosed on him. He sagged forward in the chair and held his head between his shaking hands.

In another room Major Tatischev watched him on closed-circuit TV. He turned to his assistant. "Telephone the Comrade General; suggest that he come in an hour. The subject will be ready for him then."

"I apologize, Comrade Lieutenant," Tatischev said. "The sedatives were given by the doctor on board the *Alexander Nevsky*. I had no control over the dosage. You say she'll be ready to answer questions soon?"

"She's ready now," Davina's interrogator answered. "I want some indication of how much time I have, Major. I dislike hurrying my work."

"I know," Tatischev said soothingly. She was a formidable officer, one of the most successful and ambitious; so clever that not even Volkov's antifeminism had been able to prevent her promotion. Kaledin had placed Davina Graham in her hands; she was quick to complain and report other people's mistakes. He didn't want to antagonize her. "I know how dedicated you are," he said. "But I can't answer that question until the Comrade General has decided. I suggest that you begin the preliminary examination and I will send word down as soon as I know what the Comrade General wants done. He did say he wanted everything from her."

"That could take three months," the lieutenant snapped. "Or until tomorrow morning, depending upon the technique I employ. It's most unsatisfactory, Major, but I will do my best. I will start with questions and answers and see what her attitude is. If it is uncooperative, I'll send up for the General's orders."

She saluted him and marched out. Tatischev sighed. A nice figure. Not pretty, but pleasant-looking. The braided hair would hang past her waist if it were loose. But she was not a woman. Whatever inhabited the body, it wasn't female.

"You're feeling better now?"

Davina nodded. "Yes." Her voice sounded hoarse and strained; there was a continuous tremor running through her body, which she could not control. She had been wakened and given an injection, and the sleepy confusion cleared very quickly.

"You know where you are?" the woman sitting beside her asked.

"I think I am in prison."

"You are in the Lubyanka in Moscow," the cool voice went on. "I expect you have heard of it." She saw the Englishwoman stiffen and the pupils in her eyes dilate with shock.

The reply was a whisper. "Yes, I've heard of it."

"You've heard a lot of Western lies about torture and drugs and brainwashing," the lieutenant said.

Davina raised her head and looked at her. "I have been tortured," she said slowly. "Before I got here."

"That was a mistake," the interrogator dismissed it. Her victim was showing signs of spirit; she prided herself on being impersonal, but she actually resented courage in another woman. "There is no need for unpleasantness; all we ask is cooperation. You have come to Russia as an enemy. You are the aggressor, not we. We have a right to ask you questions. You will be treated with every consideration and fairness if you answer truthfully."

Davina leaned back. *This isn't a nightmare. . . . I'm not imagining it or dreaming . . . it's real. I've been arrested and I'm in the prison where Fedya Sasanova was kept, where all the other brave people have been brutalized and destroyed. If I think of Ivan it'll help me . . .* She had closed her her eyes for a few seconds, a brief prayer for courage mingled with her invocation of the man she loved.

"Why did you come to Russia?" the voice was hatefully monotonous. There was a silence, and the lieutenant said, "We know why. We know everything, so you are just being stupid. Your friend Mr. Harrington has told us everything. He hasn't protected you. Or the two traitors who escaped."

Her friend Peter Harrington—their *friend, the double agent who was an officer of the KGB. Remember the card. Remember that's how Irina and Alexei got away. . . . God, keep my brain clear—don't let me say anything, don't let me answer anything she asks. . . .*

"If you know," Davina said wearily, "then why are you asking me?"

To her surprise the woman smiled. "Because we want you to admit your guilt in this disgraceful attack upon Soviet sovereignty," she said. "Don't you understand how much in the wrong you are? Don't you realize you have committed a crime in a country which has never done anything against you? I want you to see this. I want you to see that you and Mr. Harrington are criminals and deserve to be punished. Only when you admit this to yourself can Soviet justice be satisfied. And perhaps consider being merciful."

Harrington again. They didn't want her to know he was a traitor—or were they trying to find out if she did know? It was too difficult to see the traps behind the cliché phrases culled from some Kafka nightmare. *Say nothing, answer nothing . . . don't think forward, just hold on for now. . . .*

"You were sent to Russia as an enemy agent." The interrogator's tone had changed. It became harsh. "Who briefed you? Who gave you your orders? Whom did you meet in Russia?" The questions were snapping at her. Without time for an answer. The lieutenant got up suddenly, stood looking down at Davina, and shook her head. "Harrington isn't being obstinate," she said, almost sadly. "There's no point to what you're doing. He's being reasonable; he knows he has to cooperate in the end. Just as you will. He is making things easy for himself. I'm a Soviet officer, but I'm a woman. I feel sorry for you; I shouldn't, but I do. Men are all the same: they always save themselves at our expense. I'm going to leave you for ten minutes. Would you like a cigarette?"

"No, thank you," Davina said.

"I want you to think while I'm gone," the woman said quietly. "Think about what happened to you on the ship. I won't let that happen to you again. But you've got to cooperate with me. Otherwise I can't help you."

She turned and let herself out of the cell. The door closed and the automatic lock clicked like a pistol shot.

Davina sat up slowly and swung her legs to the floor. She stood by the edge of the shelf bed, supporting herself against it with both hands. She felt sick and off balance; the continuous nervous tremor had become a shaking fit. The cell was cold and there was an acrid antiseptic smell. She saw the bucket in the corner, and turned away, clutching at the bed for support. She was too weak to move about, her body had lost its coordination through massive nervous shock, followed by sedatives and stimulants. She sank back, huddled on the edge of the bed, cradling herself with her trembling arms. *I won't say anything, I won't even think of anything. I'll make my mind a blank and above all I won't think about what she just said, about the boat. . . . I'll think about Ivan when he sees Irina . . . he'll be so happy . . . I'll think about that. . . .*

"You ruined the operation," General Kaledin said slowly. Major Tatischev translated.

Harrington's face turned red; he was putting up more of a fight than the major had expected. "I won't accept that, General. I carried out my part without a hitch. I sent the warning to Moscow in plenty of time. Nothing happened. I sent another message. Nothing happened. The breakdown in communications was not my fault." He turned away and lit a cigarette. He cupped his hand around the lighter. His hands were shaking and he didn't care. Just as he feared, they were throwing the blame on him. Fear and despair had undermined his courage; he had begun his interview with Kaledin by cringing, and then suddenly got angry and started to argue. And instinctively he realized he had taken the right attitude. The old man was less contemptuous; he looked at him while he spoke through Tatischev. He was testing Harrington, punishing him for a lapse which was only one in a series of lapses. But he was not going to abandon him, and Harrington was sure of that.

"The General admits that things went wrong in Moscow," Tatischev said. "But the final mistake was yours. A mistake, he says, that would have disgraced a first-year trainee in the Leningrad Institute! He wants to know why you put your card into Davina Graham's handbag. He says he thinks you were drunk."

"I was not!" Harrington declared. "I've already explained it three bloody times. I woke at five in the morning and found her rooting round among my things. I was sleeping in the bed with her and I couldn't even hide it under my pillow! I had one more day to go and I hid it in the lining of her bag because I could make sure she had it with her and get hold of it at any moment! How the hell was I to know she'd lose it in the one place I couldn't follow? The lavatory—sombody stole it and threw it overboard. It was just the most damnable luck, that's all."

"You could have had Sasanov's daughter and the tutor arrested before they had time to escape," Kaledin said. "There is no such thing as luck. You were incompetent." He watched Harrington while the major translated. The man looked sleazy, unshaven. His hands shook. But he was defending himself with skill. And the real blame lay with the duplicity and secrecy of Antonyii Volkov. Harrington had made a serious error of judgment, and Kaledin had already decided how to make him pay for it. He had decided many things during the afternoon. He spoke directly to Peter Harrington and this time in slow, halting English.

"You will go back. To London. Finish your work."

Harrington's jaw went slack. "Go back? I was told I could retire. That's not keeping to your bargain, General—you promised me I could get out and settle here. I don't want to go back!"

"The General says it is your last chance to redeem yourself with us," the major interposed. "He admits that Volkov's heart attack caused the breakdown in our communications, but he still holds you responsible for losing your card. The situation is very serious, but we can still retrieve it. You can retrieve it."

"How?" He stared at the General and his aide, his face sullen and drained of color. Go back. Jesus Christ, he muttered to himself, that's the last thing I want.

"We can release you," Tatischev said. "Your cover is still intact; your position with SIS will be stronger than ever. Your mission here was a success."

"Like hell it was," Harrington interrupted. "I've lost an operative— they won't like that. And how am I going to get back in one piece? I'd be suspected immediately. It's too risky, I won't do it!"

"We will arrange the details," the major said coldly. "And you will carry out our orders. You have no alternative, Danton. If you refuse to complete your mission, you will never live in comfort in Moscow or enjoy the money that is due to you. You will have forfeited your right to be rewarded."

Harrington saw Kaledin's old hooded eyes considering him. No luxury flat, no private dacha. No money. Fifteen years of risk for nothing. They knew he wouldn't throw it all away.

"I give you this chance," the General said. "You take it." He spoke in Russian to the major and then advanced toward Harrington. He held out his hand. Harrington took it. There was nothing else to be done. "Goodbye," Kaledin said.

The major hurried to open the door for him. They went out together.

Peter Harrington flung his half-smoked cigarette onto the floor and stamped on it. He swore long and loudly. Half an hour later a civilian appeared with a bottle of vodka and a tray of food, caviar and smoked meats; the food was indicative of his restored status. He stifled the impulse to throw the whole lot in the man's face. He wasn't hungry, but, oh God, how he wanted a drink. He had to go back. And he had to rely on Kaledin to provide him with a story that his true Brigadier would accept.

He was picking at the food when Major Tatischev came in. The Russian noted that the level of vodka in the bottle had fallen by half. He looked at Harrington with distaste; he could see by his eyes that he was partly drunk.

"You will stay here for the time being," he said. "There is a comfortable suite used by visiting officers. That has been given to you."

"Thanks," Harrington jeered. "Sure it isn't a bloody underground cell?"

Tatischev ignored the remark. "I will see you in the morning," he said. "I will give you your instructions then. That is the last alcohol you will be allowed. Make the most of it." He turned and walked quickly out of the room. Harrington saw that the uniformed guard was still on duty outside.

The ten minutes lengthened into an hour. Davina had no watch, but she began counting up to sixty when the woman didn't come back, dividing the time into minutes to keep herself occupied. And to keep herself from thinking.

In another room just down the corridor, her interrogator was drinking tea. She looked at her watch; she nodded to the KGB sergeant and he stood up immediately. "Go and get her now," she said.

He paused by the door. "How long shall I give her?"

"Until I tell you," she said. "I'll come myself when I've finished my tea."

It took two men, helped by the sergeant, to force Davina into the tiny black space. The door was slammed and locked and the screams were sealed off by the soundproofing. The room containing the tiny torture chamber for claustrophobics was completely silent; a little seeing eye set in the door penetrated the blackness through infrared, and an observer was able to monitor the behavior of the victim shut inside. A microphone switch was beside it. The sergeant lit a cigarette. His men stood at ease, waiting. He straightened and hid the cigarette by his side when the lieutenant came in. She went to the door and peered through the seeing eye; she flicked the microphone switch down, and the room filled with piercing screams of terror.

She cut the sound off and looked at her watch. "Ten minutes more," she said, "then test again. She should be unconscious by then. Take her back to her cell. Get the doctor to check her blood pressure and heart and report to me." She glanced at the young sergeant and said, "Your hand seems to be on fire. You shouldn't smoke in here."

The guard nearest the door held it open and she went out.

Kaledin was very tired. He leaned back in the armchair in his office and dozed for a little, awake and yet asleep, his brain in neutral. He was old and subject to stress; his blood pressure was low. He opened his eyes immediately when the major came in, exactly as the little clock on his desk showed a minute to midnight.

Kaledin heaved himself out of the chair and stretched. Tatischev waited for him to speak. He went over to the desk and sat down; he took a cigarette out of the silver box, and the young officer had a lighter ready as it reached his lips. The General inhaled deeply. He was not supposed to smoke; he listened to his doctors and then did what he liked.

"We have to decide on our priorities," he said slowly. "This woman Graham knows a great deal we would like to know. In ordinary circumstances she would be a useful catch. She could tell us about Sasanov, his state of mind, his deal with SIS. But it would take time and we don't have that time."

"No, Comrade General," Tatischev agreed.

"We don't want London putting those two on display for the press. We don't want the world to know that Ivan Sasanov is a traitor who defected. Officially he is dead and buried in Russia. That is what we bargain with London about. They will believe that. They will want their agents back. We will give them back, Major, because our first priority is Ivan Sasanov. The truth is, we can survive their propaganda coup; we can survive the scandal of another senior officer defecting. But we cannot permit Sasanov to betray Soviet policy in the Middle East. Our first attempt to silence him failed. I was not in charge of it. It failed and Volkov concealed that failure. Now I will deal with the matter. There won't be a second failure."

"No." The Major nodded. "No, General, there won't."

"Send down to the interrogation center," Kaledin said. "Tell them to suspend questioning the woman. She is being sent back to London. I will see her in the morning myself. I will tell her that Harrington has bargained for their freedom and she owes her life to him. His position at home must be as strong as possible."

"I'll telephone now," the major said. He slipped out of the office to his own room.

Five minutes later he was back. "I'm afraid there has been a mistake," he said slowly.

Kaledin raised his head and looked at him.

"The lieutenant exceeded her orders. The woman has completely collapsed. I have ordered her removal to the medical floor."

Kaledin said nothing for a moment. He finished his cigarette and rubbed it out in the ashtray until the last tiny red spark was gone. The stub lay crushed and lifeless. "I trusted that girl," he said. "I promoted her and gave her responsibilities. Now she does this. She has failed me." He stood up wearily.

"I am going home to bed," he said. "Major, I leave you to deal with this. Deal with the woman Graham; she has to be patched up to go home. Otherwise Danton's credibility will be destroyed. But she must be useless to London. Useless to anyone." He paused for a moment. "I want a full report on the lieutenant's action. Now send down for my car. Good night, Major."

"Why didn't you send up for the General's instructions? Why did you take the initiative and damage the prisoner?"

She was standing in front of the desk, the morning sun making patterns on the Turkish carpet at her feet. She looked haggard, the brisk self-confidence had disappeared. She stammered trying to defend herself. "I didn't damage her, Comrade—it's a very simple technique, I've used it again and again with complete success, just let me explain—"

"I know the explanation," Tatischev interrupted. "You've already given it, and it's not an excuse for disobeying orders."

"She would have become completely dependent upon me," the woman protested. "It saves so much time—weeks and weeks of establishing personal contact with a prisoner. She wouldn't connect me with the torture—I'd be her only friend."

"It's a very old technique," the major said, "It's been used for years in various ways. You had no right to use it on this particular woman without the General's permission. You haven't answered—why did you do it?"

"Because it wasn't more than a conditioning exercise—it would have had to be done anyway. She hasn't suffered any physical damage. She's under sedation now, I've seen her—"

Tatischev cut her short. "She answered no questions," he said grimly. "You established nothing, and you reduced her to a mental wreck. I believe you acted from personal motives, Lieutenant." He watched her, surprised at how much he was enjoying himself. She had damaged the careers of several competent officers with complaints to the General. "I think the prisoner resisted you and you set out to break her as a punishment." He saw the guilt flash into her eyes and knew that the accusation was true. "I shall put this into my report to the General. You're relieved of your duty."

She hesitated; she bit her lips and started to speak. "Please, Major, don't do that. I assure, you're wrong. I acted only from a sense of duty. My work means everything to me—my career will be ruined!"

"I'm afraid it will," Tatischev said. He picked up a folder and began to read it. He heard the door close behind her. He would recommend that she be transferred to one of the women's transit camps, where her sadism wouldn't do any harm. That would finish her for good. He telephoned for Peter Harrington to be brought up.

Harrington sat down; he was shaved and tidy, but he was shaking with hangover.

"Now," the major began, "these are your instructions. You will return to duty in Lond—wait, please, till I've finished. I'll answer all questions afterward. You will discover where Sasanov is being hidden and send the information back to us. By our calculations, it will take months to debrief him in depth; he'll keep the really important information to the end. So we have time to act. We will activate a team, and this time we will eliminate him. There won't be any more mistakes. That is your assignment: find Sasanov for us. As soon as you have completed this mission, we will arrange for you to come to Moscow. A further half-million rubles will be credited to your account. That should make life very comfortable when you are living here. I think the terms are very generous."

Harrington nodded slowly. "Fair enough. The money's good, but I want a foolproof story to go back with. I don't have to tell you that if the slightest doubt attaches to me, I'll never get within a hundred miles of Sasanov."

"We have a story prepared for you," the major said. "It's simple but ingenious. General Kaledin himself worked out the details. You made a deal with us. You pointed out that neither Irina Sasanova nor Poliakov had access to secret information. But their propaganda value could be exploited to damage Soviet Intelligence, because Irina Sasanova's flight proves that her father was a defector and exposes the Soviet story of his suicide. That we are extremely anxious to avoid."

He paused, and Harrington said, "Right, so far so good."

"In view of this, we have made contact with London and a deal has been made. In exchange for their silence about the escape and Sasanov's presence in the West, we are releasing you."

Harrington had begun to frown. "Just a minute," he said. "I have classified information. You wouldn't give me back in such a hurry. They won't swallow that."

"They have swallowed it." Tatischev smiled. "They are insisting on an immediate return for that very reason. If we delay, then they will call a press conference for Poliakov and Irina Sasanova. If we needed information, we would delay, of course, and keep the negotiations running. They would expect that."

"They would," Harrington muttered, thinking of Humphrey Grant. His reputation for catching people out made him the most feared investigator in the Service. And he had never needed violence. Harrington wiped his sweating forehead. He shook his head. "You won't get round that one," he said.

The major said curtly, "You underestimate General Kaledin. He has foreseen the problem and made provision. Davina Graham has been interrogated. When she returns to London she will believe that she gave us a lot of classified information. You will support this. Her access to secrets makes her far more important than you. We got what we wanted from her, and we can afford to send you both back as they are demanding."

Harrington got up. "I don't like it," he said. "I don't want her back in England. What *did* she tell you?"

"Nothing," Tatischev said. "Due to an error of judgment by her interrogator, she is not in a fit state to question. And wouldn't be for some time. But it is more important that you get back and we silence Sasanov.

So she is going with you. She will be discredited and you will be a hero. Make sure you fill the part."

"Don't worry about that," Harrington said sourly. "I've been playing the good fellow for years. What state is she in?"

"Under drugs, very confused. It is being suggested to her that she betrayed everything to save herself. She will be convinced of this. She'll be completely useless to the Service—if she doesn't commit suicide at some point."

He saw Harrington's eyes widen for a moment and then narrow in a sneering smile. "You wouldn't by any chance be dropping that little seed into her mind at the same time, would you? You are a pretty lot."

The major got up to end the interview. "What we do," he said, "is for our country. Not for money. You will leave in forty-eight hours, when she is well enough to travel. That gives you time to perfect your story."

He went to the window and turned his back on Peter Harrington.

"You're going home, Davy." He was leaning beside her, and his breath was sour on her face.

She tried to shrink away from him, but the seat belt was tightly buckled and she couldn't move. They had placed her near the window of the plane, so she could see out, and the row of seats in front had been removed, so she had plenty of room.

"Don't cry," Harrington said. "There's a good girl. You had a rough time. You couldn't help it."

She felt so weak, crying was like breathing. She couldn't stop; it was difficult to bring her hand to her face to wipe the tears away. She let them flow and stared out the merciful window at the vast sparkling blue sky. She didn't need Peter Harrington to comfort her, to make excuses. She knew what she had done. She knew why she was on the jet flying to London from East Germany. She had betrayed everything to the KGB to save herself. Ivan, James White, her country, the people she worked with. They had given her a rough time. Peter was right. So rough that she had to keep the memory of it locked away, and thank God the drugs they had given her helped to keep it hidden. But it lurked like a beast in a cage underground, threatening to break out and spring on her. She would go mad if it did. As mad as the faint terrifying echo of someone screaming and screaming in her mind, and that someone was herself. . . . Harrington was being kind, telling her not to blame herself. Why did she hate him, when he was being kind? Her hatred of him was so intense that she shuddered when he patted her arm, and the smell of drink on his breath made her feel sick. She was so guilty, so despicable; such a coward. She should have died first. She wished he would go into the abyss of guilt and self-disgust. . . . She didn't want to ge back and face the people she had betrayed. Face Ivan Sasanov and say, "Your wife was braver—they shut me up in a dark place and I gave in and told them everything."

The beast was out; the cage door had given way, and it had indeed sprung on her. For one terrible moment the panic of memory engulfed her; her whole body convulsed with fear and she gave a shuddering cry of recollection. Immediately the German nurse traveling with them had left her seat and was bending over her with an injection ready. Davina opened her eyes and made the greatest effort of will she had ever made in her life.

"No," she said. "I don't want that. I'm all right."

When Harrington took her hand she pulled it away. "Leave me alone," she said. The beast had sprung and now it lay curled at her feet. She forced herself to look at it. Claustrophobia. That was what they had done. She was shivering and shaking, but she could whisper it to herself. You've been afraid of it ever since you were a child. How did they know that? How did they know what torture was beyond bearing for you? And the answer came from her subconscious, so raw and quivering on the surface. You told Harrington. And he told them. That's why you hate him. You hate him as much as you hate yourself. . . .

"Try to sleep," his voice murmured beside her. "And don't you worry about a thing. I'll explain it to the Chief. He'll understand."

She didn't answer him. She kept her head turned away toward the window. She was crying soundlessly again, and, sitting close to her, he could feel her body trembling. They had cracked her open and there wasn't a mark on her to show for it.

He felt safe enough himself to feel sorry for her. Pity it had to happen, but spying was a dirty profession and there weren't any Geneva Conventions to protect the people who got caught. She had been brainwashed while in deep shock; she believed herself guilty, and the burden of that guilt would incapacitate her for life. Or make life intolerable for her. He shied away from that. He leaned toward her and saw that she had fallen asleep. The shaking hands lay slack in her lap; her face was so drawn and colorless that she could have been dead.

Harrington looked at his watch; another forty minutes and they would land at Heathrow. London had been warned to send an ambulance for Davina. He had his story rehearsed until it was word-perfect, and he had already slipped into his role. Gallantly defending Davina Graham, a little chastened by the experience and the danger, not quite as cheeky as usual, but modest about his part in getting them released. He settled back in his seat, feeling full of confidence. Good old Harrington—he was coming home as the hero of the expedition.

Major Tatischev was also feeling satisfied. He had spent some time with Igor Kaledin, and emerged promoted to lieutenant colonel and attached to his personal staff. He went to work in Volkov's office; by the evening he had shredded every scrap of paper and destroyed every tape connected with Ivan Sasanov. The official record was closed after the Halldale Manor fire; there would never be any evidence that Volkov had known he was alive and had implemented a plan to get him back to Russia. Nobody would ever know that Igor Kaledin had nearly been the victim of a coup. The role played by Danton went no further than his activities in aiding the firebomb assassins. No mention was made of Irina Sasanova's flight or the disappearance of Alexei Poliakov. They would be officially recorded as working in separate cities in southeastern Russia. When he finished clearing out the office, he attended to the matter of the captain and crew of the *Alexander Nevsky*. Each man was assigned to a different ship, and the captain himself was promoted to the command of one of the big Morpasflot oceangoing liners. The next thing to be done the following morning was to settle the last detail, close off the final outlet of Volkov's secret. Fedya Sasanova, waiting in transit for the death camps at Kolyma.

"She'll be all right," Harrington said. "I'm afraid they got pretty rough with her." He shook his head. "I still can't believe we got away," he said.

Kidson said gently, "You worked a miracle to get back, Peter. We thought you'd both gone down the drain. Well done. The Chief sends his congratulations. He'll be along to sit in on the debriefing as soon as you feel up to it."

"I'm fine," Harrington said stoutly. "They didn't have much of a go at me. They reckoned poor Davina was the weak link in the chain. I just sat under guard and sweated it out. How are the lovebirds? How's Sasanov?"

Kidson beamed. "He's in great form. The reunion between him and his daughter was quite moving. He wants to thank you himself. I think we might break security long enough for that," he said.

"That's very nice, very nice indeed," Harrington said. "I'd like that."

Kidson had met them at Heathrow; Davina was taken to a separate car by a woman Harrington hadn't seen before. She had her arm around her and was talking to her very gently. She looked like a nurse. Kidson, after shaking hands and congratulating him, drove him from the airport. They were going to Hampshire, where he could rest for a few days and be debriefed.

It was a lovely day, and he settled back to enjoy the drive. His story was word-perfect; he knew exactly how to tell it, with the right mixture of self-deprecation and excuse for Davina's crackup. He would be very gallant and defend her hotly if there was the least criticism. And all the credit for their release was his; he had convinced Tatischev of the KGB that they had more to lose than gain by keeping them. His Service wouldn't rub the Russians' noses in it over Irina's escape; Poliakov would not give press interviews or discuss the plight of dissidents in the Soviet Union. Neither he nor Davina Graham was of much use to anybody and certainly didn't merit an exchange. They were only field operatives, and expendable. There were discrepancies, of course. The KGB were notoriously vindictive when thwarted. He had to make their reasons for releasing their two victims very convincing. The organized leak from the Soviet end would help. He hummed a little tune as he looked out on the green English countryside.

"I hope nobody's going to blame Davy," he said earnestly as they turned into the gates of the Ministry's training center and the big ugly building loomed at the end of the drive.

"No question of that," Kidson reassured him. "She's gone to a nursing home for a few days; our doctors will check up on her. She'll be sent on sick leave. I just hope she hasn't suffered any permanent psychological damage. But she's a steady type of girl. As you say, she'll be all right. Here we are."

The car stopped and he got out. Harrington followed him. The mock-medieval front door swung open, and Grant appeared. He came forward and held out his hand.

"Welcome back," he said. "Well done!"

Harrington winked at Kidson and followed them inside.

He was given a very good lunch, with a fine Château-Latour; Harrington felt he could indulge himself in a few drinks this once, and enthused over the wine. Even Grant's sepulchral face twisted into a brief smile as the conversation flowed among the three of them. There was a choice of port or brandy, and Kidson produced a box of cigars.

Harrington grinned. "I must say, I feel like the prodigal son! I just wish Davina had been with us."

"I'm sure you do," Kidson said. "I could arrange for some flowers to be sent to her, if you like. It might cheer her up."

"Do that, will you—thanks very much," Harrington said.

Grant looked at his watch; it looked too big on his bony wrist.

"I think the Chief will be ready for us now," he announced. "Let's go down to the conference room, shall we?"

The debriefing took nearly three hours; Harrington was quite tired at the end of it, and he felt liverish from the heavy lunch and the wine. Brigadier James White had done most of the questioning himself. He was generous in his praise for the way Harrington had turned a near-disaster into triumph. "You haven't lost your touch," he said. "You're as good as you ever were, my dear chap. I don't think we'll waste you in Personnel again!" There was a general laugh.

"Thank you, Chief," Harrington said. "Now I've answered all the questions, I'd like to ask one."

James White nodded. "Of course."

Harrington put on a puzzled half-smile. "I didn't see the youngsters leave the ship," he said. "I heard the announcement that no one was going to be allowed ashore and I thought, just as I told you, Christ, that's done it! I rushed off to find them, but they weren't there. How did they get past the guards on the gangway?"

James White slipped a hand into his pocket; he gazed at Peter Harrington with a quiet smile. Suddenly there wasn't a sound in the room. He took his hand out of his pocket and laid the red identity card, with its shield and crossed-swords insignia, on the table.

"They used this," he said. "It seems to belong to you."

"Sit down, Comrade Sasanova," Lieutenant Colonel Tatischev said. "I hope the journey wasn't too tiring for you?"

Fedya Sasanova gazed up at him. She showed no expression; she held her hands folded in her lap, and waited. The journey had not been tiring. She had been taken by train and given a sleeping compartment. She was guarded by a woman officer of the KGB who wouldn't tell her where she was going, but was otherwise friendly and considerate. Fedya had learned not to question when things went right. She had spent long sickening weeks of anticipation in the transit camp, waiting every day for the move to the white horror of Kolyma, until her ability to suffer through anticipation became dulled into a hopeless resignation. She saw others come and go, and when she was called out from her hut and told to get ready for a journey she bowed her head and whispered goodbye to the few still waiting, and believed that the journey would be her last.

Now she was in the KGB's headquarters on Dzerzinsky Street, and the young man was the one who had accompanied Volkov to the mortuary. He was being very friendly, and this frightened her. Fear began to well up inside her; the unnatural calm of despair was deserting her in the face of this friendliness. The comfortable chair, the courteous inquiries, the pleasant smile. Her heart leaped like a fish on the end of a line.

"How is my daughter?"

"Very well," Tatischev said. "You don't have to worry about her. You must wonder why we've brought you here. Well, I'll tell you why."

He brought his own chair close to her. "I have been told to apologize to you, Comrade Sasanova, for a terrible miscarriage of justice. The highest authority, General Kaledin himself, has ordered your release. The service is not afraid to admit when it's in the wrong. You should never have been arrested. If Comrade Volkov were still alive, he would be facing the courts for what he did."

She looked horribly thin, and her skin was the gray-white common to prisoners. He felt genuinely indignant for her.

Her mouth went slack. She stared at him. "He's dead? Antonyii Volkov?"

Tatischev nodded. "A heart attack. When the authorities examined the records, his criminal action became known. You were imprisoned on a false charge—a charge invented by Antonyii Volkov. You identified your husband's body, didn't you?"

"Yes," she whispered.

He nodded again. "And you were right to do so; your husband is dead, and that was his body that was buried. You only told the truth, and for this you have been unjustly punished. Will you accept the apologies of the service? General Kaledin will see that you receive the pension awarded to a general's widow. The rank will be posthumously conferred on your husband. A new apartment has been allotted to you; all your privileges are restored, Comrade Sasanova. From now on, you are under the special protection of the KGB."

She couldn't find any words; she stared at him and her mouth turned down and began to quiver. He didn't want her to cry; she was shocked and weak, and when she realized how generously she'd been treated her tears would turn into smiles of gratitude.

"Where is Irina? Why do I have to change the apartment? Did Volkov do anything to her?"

"No," Tatischev said firmly. "Your daughter is alive and very well. But you won't be able to communicate with her. She can't get in touch with you. You must take this on trust, Comrade. You must trust the service from now on, and rely on it without question. Do you understand that?"

"Yes," Fedya said at last. "I understand. And she is happy?"

It cost Tatischev a real effort to answer without bitterness. "I think so. That's all I can tell you. You must be content with that."

She didn't say anything for some moments. She was released; Volkov was dead, and the authorities wanted Sasanov to be dead, too. She would be rewarded for the lie instead of punished, because official policy had changed. Irina had vanished. But she was well, and there was something angry in Tatischev's eyes when he said that he thought she was happy. It was just possible, like a gleam of dazzling sunlight behind a storm cloud, that Irina had got to the West. She would believe that, and one day she might find out if it was true.

She said, "I'm very grateful, Colonel. I'm very honored to be under your protection. I bear no ill-will for what happened to me."

He gave her a warm smile and squeezed her hand. "I have a personal contribution to make to you, Comrade," he said kindly. "You have a pass to spend two weeks in the sanatorium at Alupka. Treatment and rest will restore your health. The arrangements will include a flight to the Crimea and back. I hope you enjoy it."

He came down to the front of the offices with her, supporting her with a hand under her arm. An official car was waiting and took her to the select apartment complex in the suburbs of Moscow reserved for the Party elite.

She felt well enough to buy summer clothes by the end of the week. She boarded the flight to Simferopol and was met by another official car, then driven to the splendid resort of Alupka and the sanatorium reserved for high Party officials and their families. She carried a little ikon of Saint Nicholas the miracle worker, given to her by a fellow prisoner in the transit camp. It was crude and the paint was worn away in places, where the devout had held it in their hands when they prayed. Fedya kept it hidden, and slept with it under her pillow. The woman who gave it to her had gone to Kolyma. She had been a practicing Christian.

"I'm glad to see you looking so well," the Brigadier said.

"I've had a long leave," Davina answered.

He smiled his pleasant smile. "You've earned it, my dear. I gather you won't have any more problems. Our doctor was very pleased at the way you pulled out of it."

"I know," she said. "But I wouldn't have, except for one thing. I knew Harrington was the traitor. When he got me to remember that, the whole thing started to make sense. I could believe what he told me then; I could believe Humphrey when he came to see me. He was very good in his odd way. He actually took hold of my hand when he was assuring me I hadn't given anything away, that it was all a trick." She smiled at the memory, the Brigadier was glad to see it. She was still a little too pale and grave for his liking. "He let go pretty quickly," she added. They both laughed.

"Funny chap, Humphrey," he said. "Doesn't like human contact. I've seen him go to the most extraordinary lengths to avoid shaking hands. Now—Marchwood must have been lovely at this time of year. How's your mother's garden?"

"Full of flowers, as usual," she said. "She believes it's because she talks to them. I've never been able to grow even a potted plant."

"She's a wonderful person," he remarked. "She knows how to manage your father; I had a lot of stick from him about what happened to you. He was threatening to sue the Ministry and go to his MP and God knows what else! She calmed him down, though. I don't suppose you knew about all the fuss."

"I didn't," she admitted. "I'd no idea my father would take it like that. He's never been overfond of me."

"That's a sad thing to say," James White remarked. "And not true either. He doesn't show his feelings; you're rather alike in that way. But he cares very much for you, and I ought to know it. I'm afraid our friendship will never be the same. He won't forgive me for sending you out."

"That's not fair," Davina said quietly "I wanted to go. I'll try and explain it to him. I just didn't talk about it to either of them. My mother never asked a question. She just gathered me up and spoiled me to death for the whole two months. I felt like a little girl who's had measles." She laughed. "Perhaps I should have talked about it, but I didn't want to worry her. I didn't think she'd understand and she'd just get fussed and frightened. Same thing with my father. He was very kind, too; I shouldn't have said that about not being fond of me. He really did his best. Breakfast tray in my room, lots of red wine because my mother'd said to him I looked anemic. The funny thing was, Sir James, my sister Charley was the only person who asked me what happened and made me tell her. I didn't want to, but she went on and on. She's the most persistent girl I've

ever known. And she always gets her own way. So I told her. I told her
every damned thing. And do you know what she did?"

"No," he prompted. "What did she do?"

"Burst into tears," Davina said. "Threw her arms round me and cried
like a cloudburst. I ended up having to comfort *her*. Anyway, I'm back
now, and getting very bored. When are you going to let me come back to
work?"

"That's what I wanted to discuss with you," James White said. "I
thought a quiet lunch was a good way of doing it. You do look well, but
you also look depressed. Are you?"

She stiffened. "Not in the least. Please, we've had the psychiatric stuff.
I hope I'm not going to be dogged by this sort of thing."

"Not at all," he answered. "But if you're not depressed, why are your
eyes full of tears? Use your handkerchief, Davina, and don't be silly.
You're not the only person in the world who isn't happy."

"I know that," she said. "Believe me I'm so angry with myself, I hate
self-pity. It's just that I need something to do, to take my mind off
things."

"That's exactly what Sasanov says." He said it quite casually. He saw
her face flood with color. "He's complaining about being bored, restless.
His daughter and that chap Poliakov got married, you know. I think he
misses them."

"Yes," She opened her bag and fiddled with her cigarettes and lighter.
"I expect he does. . . . And there's no news of his wife, I suppose? That
really haunts me—now I know what they can do to people."

"Well, there is news actually," he continued. "Would you mind too
much waiting till we have coffee before you smoke? Thank you—they are
a little old-fashioned in the club dining room. Yes, there is news, as I was
saying. She was released from prison, and apparently she's being treated
very well. It took some time to filter through to us, but very generous
amends seem to have been made. She's on what's called the KGB special
list. That means she's under their protection and woe betide anyone who
even gives her a parking ticket. There's no question of her leaving, of
course. We'll try and let her know her daugher's safe and happy by the
same little route that brought us news of her. So you needn't worry about
her anymore. We were able to set Sasanov's mind at rest."

"I'm very glad," Davina said. "Sir James, you haven't answered my
question. When can I come back to work?"

"You can't," he said. "Unless you tear this up."

He slid the envelope toward her, and her hand trembled as she opened it. "Under Section 4, sub-section 21, I, Davina Claire Graham do solemnly undertake never to see or communicate or cause communication to be made . . . " She said to him in a breaking voice, "What do you mean? For God's sake, what do you mean, tear it up?"

"I mean that you can't have your old job back unless we get rid of that piece of paper. You do want to come back and look after Sasanov, don't you? At least I hope you do. The man's impossible without you. Here's our coffee. You can smoke now if you like. That's a nice smile, my dear. I think I'll have a cigar."

"He's upstairs," Humpgrey Grant said. "The Chief said we weren't to tell him. He wants it to be a surprise." His expression conveyed his distaste for the Brigadier's little charade.

Davina walked through the vaulted Victorian great hall of the officers' training school. A young man in battle fatigues glanced at her as she crossed his path. The ugly mahogany staircase rose up in front of them, flanked by profusely carved heraldic lions, with the all-too-recent coats of arms painted and gilded on shields between their forepaws. Grant thought she looked strange; he couldn't have called any woman attractive. Her hair was longer and loose, she seemed much younger; there was a girlish expectancy about her that he thought positively unbecoming in a woman of mature age.

"Upstairs," he repeated. "I'll lead the way."

The room was at the end of a wide corridor. Grant opened the door and stood back. Davina stepped past him and into the room. Sasanov was reading; he didn't look up.

He said, "If it's you, Kidson, I don't want to play chess. Leave me alone."

"I can't play chess," Davina said.

Grant told John Kidson about it afterward. He needed a drink, he said, to get the taste of all that awful sentimental rubbish out of his mouth. "They literally *rushed* at each other," he exclaimed. "He jumped out of the chair and ran at her with his arms wide open, and she threw herself into his embrace, and then thank Heaven I shut the door. I could hear their voices laughing and talking all down the corridor. I gather they want dinner upstairs, and champagne! I hope the Chief knows what he's doing." He pursed his thin lips. "She seemed such a proper type of woman," he said. "You'd never believe she could behave like that."

John Kidson didn't answer; he only smiled.